A KISS BEFORE YOU GO

"Perhaps I shall marry while you are gone," she said teasingly. "And move away."

"You can't," he said. "The only way you can marry is with my permission."

"What if you never return?"

He had not considered that. It was something he thought about before every voyage, but this time it was different. He feared leaving this precious girl and never returning.

Spellbound, Honey watched his face change, watched the blue of his eyes fade to smoke, his head dip toward hers. He pulled her against him, savoring the gentle swell of her hips against his thigh, the soft lift of her breasts against his chest. Her heart thumped against his ribs as his mouth melted into hers. The slender wrist he still held pulsed rapidly against his fingers, while his free hand stole around the small of her back, holding her close.

A faint sigh purred from her throat. His kiss shook her to the very depths of her soul.

COLLEEN CAMPBELL

CASTAWAY HEART

ZEBRA BOOKS
KENSINGTON PUBLISHING CORP.

FOR GLENN,
FOR AMANDA,
FOR MY MOTHER.
THANKS FOR THE SUPPORT,
THE PATIENCE,
AND THE SHOVE.

ZEBRA BOOKS

are published by

Kensington Publishing Corp.
475 Park Avenue South
New York, NY 10016

First printing: May, 1991

Printed in the United States of America

Prologue

Somewhere in the South Atlantic; 1690

The six-year-old girl clung to the lifeless body of her mother. Her reddened eyes resumed a look of desperate fear as the door of the hold opened and she was hauled out. It was dark. The deck pitched below her feet, and the stiff cold wind brought fresh tears to her eyes.

"This voyage is over for you, dearie!" The man who spoke to her was ugly and dirty and his laugh was harsh.

"No! No! I want my mama!" she cried, trying to wrench herself away from the iron grip. Another man brought her mother's limp body forward.

"No, Mama! Mama!" she shrieked, clawing at the form as the sailor mercilessly heaved her mother's body overboard.

"No! Mama!" The child was scooped up from behind.

"You and yer ma got all eternity together, lass," he said, hurling the tiny form over the rail into the blackness below.

She heard her own shriek and clawed at the air,

knowing she couldn't swim, knowing only that the black depths of the sea lay below her. But she never struck water; she smashed into something hard and wet and sank from the pain as if she were drowning.

"Mama?" she sighed, before slipping into the blackness of her own mind.

"There's no savin' yer ma, child," the man's voice whispered. "But maybe there be some hope for you, Honey."

Chapter One

An Island in the South Atlantic; 1700

The ship hovered in that shimmering hazy void somewhere between the sea and the retreating thunderhead to the west. The storms had ended several hours before, and the blazing sun rose over the eastern horizon into a clear blue sky. Though the seas pounded the western shore of this tiny island daily, today, in the aftermath of the storms, the surf growled its way in and hissed its way out, moving with the tides. It was life in endless sound, endless motion.

From her perch on the high side of the island, a young woman watched in awe as the majestic sails lost their shimmery, not-quite-real waver and the wooden vessel pitched into full view.

This was not the first such ship she had seen, but somehow she felt it was the most proud. It sailed right out from under that still-flashing, rumbling cloud in the west through the freshly washed trades. Usually after storms as violent as those of the last weeks, ships would not be seen for many days. Like the crabs, they would hide until all the noise and wind were gone. And there were other ships that would hover in that in-between space for a short while, then just fade away. The ship was moving like the ones that sailed right by her without stopping; it would disappear eventually to where the sun set. She smiled. She liked to see those ships that sailed the full length of the ocean. They made her feel less alone.

Her stomach rumbled loudly. The ship was quickly forgotten, replaced by the thought of food.

She climbed down the bluff to the sea-drenched rocks at the edge of a tidal pool, just behind the boulder that made up the foot of the cliff. As Barley Boe had done when he was still here, she would go every morning to look out over the sea before going to the rocks that held her breakfast. A time-softened version of his craggy face flitted through her mind. Barley Boe was her only memory since waking up here on this island. His words and brief teaching of survival were her life. Beyond him, beyond the island, there was only the dim throb of a headache coupled with the blackest of nights.

The image faded. Her gaze concentrated on the sandy bottom of the pool as a fat crab marched along. With deliberate slowness she slid her hand into the calm water, her fingers extended and ready. Moving with agonizing care, she delved deeper and deeper still before pulling the creature from its salty home.

With fascination she watched the crab's frantic movements. Its bulging eyes rolled out of control and its claws snapped furiously. Just then her stomach growled loudly and the pain of hunger assailed her again. Without a second thought she picked up a rock and brought it down, crushing the crab's head. She used the stone again to crack the shell in order to find the meat inside.

Images of this morning's ship wove through her mind. It would still be too far away to see clearly, but there had been something about it . . . there *was* something . . . Filling her fist with meat, she stood, carefully moving over the rocks and past the boulder that sheltered her little tidal pools. Yes, it was still there, and drawing nearer. She tossed the length of hair from her face before returning to her place beside the pool.

"Daddy!" she cried, her eyes suddenly wide. She jumped to her feet, but the stabbing pain that ripped through her head caused her to slump to the ground. The thoughts were lost, but the pulse that raced through her veins continued to accelerate as the ship drew nearer.

Captain Christopher Ames stood on the uppermost deck of the *Wing Master*. He stood tall, his legs parted to brace himself against the dip and roll of the waves. The wind played a constant tug-o-war with his billowing shirt. With a long glass pressed to his eye, he scanned the vast watery horizon until he spotted the lump barely visible in the distance. Never had he failed to recognize land for what it was.

Dropping the glass to his side, he leaned on the rail, waiting for the wind and the tides to bring him closer to the island. Or was it a mainland, a continent? He couldn't tell from this distance, but he knew it was dry land, a bearing by which to map his course.

It was perhaps a half hour before he raised the cold brass ring back to his eye again. In the center of the black circle he could now see the island, lush with greenery and highlighted by a willowy figure standing on the bluff watching his sails.

The state of her undress stole his thoughts. Shreds of fabric covered her bosom, a long shred of leather, tied at her hips like a skirt, was slit from hip to ankle on one side. It fluttered in the wind, exposing exotic golden brown skin the same shade as his own. Long blond hair, softly blowing on the breeze, streamed down her back. The details of her face blurred in the distance, but the curves of her youthful body were clear.

"Mr. Price!" Christopher's voice bellowed over the rustle of the flapping canvas.

"Aye, sir," Jared Price said as he seemingly appeared from nowhere.

"I thought you said that the closest parcel of land be that one with no water."

"Aye, sir." Jared shrank slightly as the glass was thrust at him.

"Then what, pray, do you call that? A mirage?"

Jared placed the glass to his eye just as the woman turned from the sea and ran inland. The smaller man gasped, jerking the glass from his eye as if to confirm the sighting with his naked eye.

"That be no mirage, Cap'n. Charts could be wrong, but don't see how we coulda mislined by the sunrise. Course, the best reading comes from the stars. 'Tain't no explanation for the other."

"No, there isn't, is there?" The captain scanned the shore one last time, snapping the long glass shut. The ship dipped forward, slapping into another swell. Spindrift rained from the bow.

"Send Mr. Grey to my cabin at once, and ready a longboat. Set course for that island." The captain turned from the rail to squint at the aging Jared Price, the best navigator he'd ever had and possibly the only person, besides himself, who could get a bearing on where they truly were in order to navigate their course home.

"Aye, aye, Cap'n," the older man said as he disappeared down the gangway.

Left alone, Christopher looked down to the decks below. The sight of his men filled him with pride. They were tired, thirsty, and lonesome for their homes and families—a dozen men who had waged a good battle against the forces of nature and won. They sat idle now against the battered crates and ropes that littered the main deck.

They were three days out of Charleston with a load of tobacco when the first of five storms hit them. They handled that. Less than six hours after the first storm ended, the second struck, and Chris was forced to turn south to keep from capsizing. Then, without warning, the third hit. Before they had time to recover, the fourth battered the sea and their ship for three full days. The last storm had been the strongest of the five. It lasted as long as the fourth, making this day's sunrise the first they had seen in more than a week.

From the captain on down to the lowest swabby, they were all exhausted. He had ordered them to rest until he could figure out where they were. Charting a course back to England was a task Christopher had thought would be easy, but it seemed now that the chartmaker had palmed him a set of long outdated charts. He'd have to rely on the stars. The island before him—assuming he was where he thought he was—was charted as bone dry, but the foliage he now saw was clearly more than two years old . . .

The captain hurried down the companionway to his cabin in the rear of the ship, one deck above the hold, two above the waterline. His cabin, the largest aboard, monopolized the wide panes of glass along the rear of the ship, giving him a panoramic view of his beloved sea. The wider-than-usual bed built into the wall was covered in a deep blue velvet spread—his one indulgence, now wet and stained with salt water. The rest of the cabin was plain, with its cupboard, desk, and table fixed to the decking.

"Whew! You'll have to burn six ton of oil to dry out this mess, Chris." Geoffrey Grey passed through the door, his booted feet splashing in the puddles as he walked.

"At very least," Chris said as he pulled a tin bottle and two cups from the drawer of his cabinet. He handed a cup to the first mate and poured them both a drink.

"Select six with best cap and ball. We're taking a party to shore," he stated.

"Yes, I heard. You suspect a trap?"

The captain recorked the bottle. "It's not often you find an island mischarted without good reason. Could be a pirates' den. That woman was blond." He said the last almost to himself.

"Could be castaway," Geoffrey said before swallowing his drink.

"Maybe." Chris refilled their cups before returning the bottle to the drawer. "Whatever it is, it's damned curious. The island is charted as bone dry."

Geoffrey fell silent, watching his lifelong friend and companion lay out his two finest pistols. He was as accustomed to his captain's gruff on-deck persona as he was to his drawing room manner, which was indeed a sight to behold. A man as tall and full-shouldered as his captain, dressed in formal breeches and hose, could charm petticoats from the ladies, young and old alike. And how they adored his handsome face and rakish wit, vying for his attentions in their own flittery ways. Once Chris told a girl that his favorite color was sea blue, and at the next ball no other color gown was present, except of course for Ariel Blackmoore's.

"And if it is a pirates' trap?" Geoff snapped back from his thoughts.

"We would see the ship in the bay if it were, or some sign along the beach. If there is no ship, there will be no pirates. Get a man in the nest, though." Chris tossed the scotch into his mouth, swallowed fast, then turned back to his pistols. "If it is a castaway then we have a holiday well deserved, and we will have saved some poor soul from a life alone."

"That was some poor soul I heard about," Geoff mumbled.

The captain's eyes flicked up to his first mate as he jammed a pistol into his leather belt; his lawn shirt billowed briefly before settling over the pistol grip.

"Yes, as well as the rest of her." Chris smiled for the first time as he tied his overlong hair into a tail at the nape of his neck. "Ready?" he asked, securing the knot.

"Aye, Cap'n, ready as ever." Geoff followed the captain from the cabin along the companionway to the short flight of stairs at midship. They crossed a narrow planked bridge aft and mounted steps to the platform reserved for the captain and his navigational crew members on the rear quarter.

Jared Price had the wheel, but he stood on a box to reach it. Chris chuckled at the picture Jared made, his rapidly shrinking body atop a battered crate as his muscles, still strong, held the wheel firmly from the rocky bluffs that threaten to smash them. His course held them just to the edge of the stiff undercurrents as he skirted the island.

"Bit strong here, Cap'n," Jared grunted as he struggled against the current. The cordlike tendons popped out on his arms.

"I'll take her." Geoff jumped toward the older man and took the wheel from behind.

"Yer not going in there?" Jared hawked at his captain. "That's suicide, if'n ya do get around them rocks . . . What about pirates? Ya know . . ." He shook a warning finger at the island as he stuttered over the fears he couldn't quite put into words.

"Well, what did you think we were going to do when I told you to set course?" Chris said, watching Jared and wishing the old man had not aged so much on this last trip. Jared's days at sea were almost at an end. Chris hated to lose him, even if the old man's sea sense had dulled.

"I thought you had a mind to sail around it . . . That's all yer should do, water or no! We kin last another day without!" His voice trembled as he spoke.

Chris shook his head, tossing a glance at his first mate. He remembered the days when Jared would have taken on the whole lot of 'em singlehandedly if it meant even one drop of fresh water for his crew.

"Your point is well taken. Perhaps a landing party should investigate first?" One brow rose over a bright blue eye as the captain asked his question.

"Aye, six with best shot, while the rest wait a safe distance out," Jared nodded, his near-toothless mouth compressed in an expression of finality.

"Good advice, my friend. Give the order to police this deck," the captain agreed, his concern switching from the aged Jared to the crew. He hated to put them back to work so soon, but kindhearted gestures wouldn't save them if they rounded that island to find the entire Tortuga Armada waiting for them.

Jared wasn't the only one on board who was wary of the small island. A hum had started on the main decks as the crew alternately worked and looked toward the nearing landfall. Who did the captain think would fight this battle?

They had already saved themselves from an angry sea, but even with the weapons available, who had strength enough left to fight again? Chris saw their glances and was sure he knew what they thought; nevertheless, he gave the signal that sent three men into the ropes. Two separate waves of canvas lost their billow. Three more men scrambled to furl the wilted sheets. They must know that this valiant approach would never have been made had the need for water not been so dire. There was irony in that, he thought, as the frigate slipped dangerously close to the outcropping of rocks. During the storms that had battered them for five solid days their supply of fresh water had become tainted with the sea. And what was a storm, after all, but fresh water? Yes, there was irony in that.

Silence engulfed the crew as the island loomed up beside them and the ship dipped low to starboard. The crewmen lined the rail, their breaths trapped in their lungs as they waited to be tossed into the reef.

Another signal sent the next row of sail to the decks. The ship slowed to less than half its speed—not enough to save them should the currents suddenly change to run them aground, and certainly too slow to outrun whatever might lie in the cove. But the ship righted itself and pulled back from the rocks that threatened destruction, skimming to the right side of the island. All eyes watched as the island seemed to slide slowly past the ship. Bit by tiny bit the cove came into view. A collective sigh broke the tension as the cove proved to be empty. But three sets of footprints dotted the storm-wracked beach.

Chapter Two

"Lower the boat, Mr. Grey." Chris watched as Geoff shot out his orders and the sailors moved to obey. The wide rope netting was slipped over its anchors before being tossed overboard to hang at the side of the ship. The first of the six chosen for duty scurried over the side to hold the longboat steady as it was lowered by winch. No sooner had the boat touched water than the other five men filled it, leaving a place at the bow for the captain and a place aft for the first mate.

"Should this prove a trap, old man, you get these young salts out of here. No stopping for the likes of us."

Jared nodded, but Chris knew Jared too well. He'd stay and fight for his captain as surely as it would mean his own death.

Less than twenty minutes later the longboat scraped the beach.

"You three search the left side of the beach, you three . . ." Geoffrey started.

". . . straight up the middle. If there's water, it will be there, where the greatest concentration of foliage grows," Chris finished for him. He decided that he and Geoff would handle the other matter themselves.

The winds tossed Geoff's hair as he examined the sets of footprints set close together on the sand. The sizes appeared to be the same.

"Well," he looked to his captain. "Lead." Geoff teased the man who had just undermined his own orders to the search party. The captain clearly had plans in mind. Geoff was convinced that the prints were made by one and the same person, or that the other person was at least no larger. There was little doubt that Chris had come to the same conclusion.

Chris drew a deep breath. "Smell it? Fresh water, that way." He pointed toward the center of the island. "Those three won't be gone long; we'll go this way." Chris stumbled to the right, his sea legs compensating for the dip that wasn't there. In the back of his mind he heard his father's voice: "Too much time spent on too rough a sea can make a man lose his taste for solid ground," the man had said with a wink. *"And* your woman. Take care, boy, for no bounty can be worth the loss of a good wife." It was one of the few things he remembered. And like the other wise bits of information his father had given him, this one was as true as the dip and roll he expected to feel as his boots melted into the not-quite-solid ground.

They followed the ribbon of beach, each savoring the smell of fresh water and baked sand coupled with the tang of the sea. It might have been months since Chris had seen home, but this was a paradise he could live with. His gaze followed the bright white sand as he walked toward the bluff.

Exotic birds watched from their perches in the high palms. Fruits of several varieties hung from other trees. The bluff to the west worked as a natural windbreak, keeping the inner island relatively calm.

The trees had suffered little damage here, while the outer edge looked ravaged. Plenty of sun, lots of shade, and the birds for company. He wondered if rescue for a castaway might not be a mixed blessing. But then, he realized, not all people felt as he did about civilization.

He glanced up and there she was, crouched beside a tide pool, her body tense as she slowly extended her hand into the pool. She sat unmoving, her long hair falling a little to the side. By the expression on her face, he guessed her to be young, but her body was that of a woman. In one fluid movement she pulled her hand from the water with a fat red crab caught just behind the pinchers. At the same moment her lashes lifted, bringing her gaze to face them. Large, forest green eyes met vivid blue in a fleeting moment of recognition. In the next second she was on her feet, a gasp ripped from her throat, her eyes darting wildly for escape, the crab thrashing wildly at her bare feet.

"No!" Chris leaped forward, his hands reaching out to stop her. "We won't hurt you!" His words were loud and harsh, and the girl shrank back against the boulder that blocked her escape.

"Chris, you're frightening her." Geoff stepped up even with his friend, his hand pressing Chris's down. "Gently." Geoff moved in front, stepping onto the rocky formation that separated them from her. She was trembling now, her eyes wide more with curiosity than with fear. Still, her chest heaved as her heart pounded hard against her ribs.

"You speak?" he asked softly, taking a small step toward her. He could see her rapid pulse in the vein at her throat. "You speak?" he said again in Spanish, then in French.

"Don't be afraid, sweetheart . . . we won't hurt you." Geoff took another step toward her, his hands extended in front of him, palms up. "There now, you understand, don't you, honey?"

Her eyes stayed on his fingers as he moved closer, but her head jerked up at the sound of the words. Her fingers moved to her forehead. She brushed a spot, then glanced to her fingertips. There was no hurt there. No blood. Her hand dropped back to her side.

"That's right, honey, we won't hurt you." Gratified that he found something she related to, Geoff chanced walking right up to her. "There, you see, it's going to be fine." He reached for her hand and placed it carefully in his own. A smile lifted the corners of his mouth until his eyes dropped down to her clothes, little of them that there were. There was no mistaking the paper-thin fabric, its bleached out silk patterns almost lost.

"Come on, now." He smiled again, snapping his gaze back to her face. "This man back here is big and tough and loud, but he won't hurt you." Geoff pointed to Chris, then smiled back at the girl. "He's got one of those hearts that doesn't like to show itself very much."

She brought her free hand up, her fingers curved softly as she watched his mouth. Her own lips parted and moved, but no sound came out.

"What's your name?" he asked in his softest voice. Her eyes met his and her brows drew together in frustration.

"Ho, Cap'n—!" Leftkin called from behind Christopher. His jaw dropped as he spotted the first mate and the girl. "An' I thought the ol' cotter was daft," he mumbled.

"Aye," his companion answered, his gaze locked on the young woman's.

"What is it?" Chris turned to look at the pair, who stood gaping at the half-naked woman.

"We found a little cavelike spot near a fresh water spring, and these." Leftkin held out a pair of small girls' slippers wrapped in a piece of yellow calico. Chris took the parcel.

"Mine!" The girl jerked herself out of Geoff's hold. In seven bounds she snatched the bundle from the stranger's hands, but in her haste the contents flew from her hands and scattered over the shore.

"Oh! Oh!" she gasped, throwing herself to the ground after her possessions. Tears flooded the wide eyes, which were no longer afraid but angry.

Chris dropped quickly beside her, scooping up and handing her a slipper, amazed at her single-word outcry.

This was not the language barrier he had expected. But then, neither was the girl herself, displaying the body of a woman and the temperament of a child. He closed his eyes for a moment as he contemplated the situation. How long had she been here alone? His mind reflected briefly both on the charts that had misrepresented this island and the size of the small slipper. It was obvious that she had outgrown the slipper some years ago.

Geoff moved from the rocks to watch the exchange. He was shocked speechless as he helped the girl to her feet. He moved a quick hand to her forehead, and his fingers brushed the soft warm flesh until he encountered what he suspected, a gash well healed with time and the small lump that marked a once cracked skull. He glanced down to find her looking up at him; mistrust cloaked the dark green eyes. Then he scanned the contents of the parcel. A small silver comb of elaborate design and an earbob of some sort of blue stones; a man's ring bearing a lion's head, and some abalone shell fragments. Geoff nodded in response to Chris's curious look. A knock on the head that severe meant one of two things: she had been struck permanently stupid or else she'd forgotten who she was and where she'd come from. Sometimes memory returned; other times it did not.

"Ho, Cap'n," another voice called from behind.

"Wait for me at the landing!" Chris snapped back. His face was angry as he shouted the words.

His sudden explosion made her jump, and her eyes grew wide as she leaned into Geoff, who rolled his eyes heavenward without looking away from Chris.

He realized too late that he had scared her again. "Oh, Christ!" he muttered. "You take care of her, I'll take care of that!" Her jerked his head toward the woman then back toward the beach and stomped off after the four he had just sent away.

Geoff smiled after his captain as he watched him march along the beach behind his crew. It would seem that for the first time a problem had arisen that Chris did not know how to handle.

"Will you show me your treasures?" Geoff calmly smiled at her.

The girl watched Chris until he was out of sight before she turned back to the man beside her.

"Blue diamonds," she whispered as she held out an earbob of sapphires intermingled with smaller diamonds.

"Lovely," Geoff said. "Why didn't you speak earlier when I asked you?"

The girl's head tipped sideways, her green eyes following his lips as he spoke. Her brows knit together in confusion.

Geoff moved his fingers carefully to her mouth, then to his own. "Speak?" he said. She only looked more confused. "Well then, what other treasures have you there?" He picked up the slipper. "Yours?" he asked.

Her head nodded vigorously as she snatched it up possessively.

"How old is a child that wears this size slipper?" he wondered out loud. His stomach knotted at the thought of this woman left alone all these years, understanding only the simplest words and expressions.

"Come on," Geoff smiled and reached for her hand. "Let's find Chris and Sanders. That old salt has had a brood of kids, and I think he'll have the best notion of what to do with the likes of you." His smile broadened at the thought . . .

Chapter Three

As morning turned to afternoon, the captain of the *Wing Master* watched his crew hauling water barrels ashore to fill.

He turned in the crow's nest, a glass to his eyes, searching the sea for unexpected company.

He had still not completely discounted this find as a pirate's trick—possibly a trick that had fouled with the storms. A pirate ship could have sunk in the gale, and the woman, being of clever nature, could be playing the role of castaway. It was difficult for him to believe that a child had survived the sea and life alone on an island, to come of age with little but fruit and seafood to live on. It struck him, though, that she had indeed intended to eat the creature raw, and had in fact done so before by the looks of the shell fragments on the stone beside her.

To worsen his mood, he found himself attracted to her warm, tanned flesh, left exposed to the sun by her skimpy costume. There was something indecent about lusting after a woman whose mind could be only that of a child. It was fine that he had a way with the ladies that made them eager to accommodate him, but he had never taken one who had not already been taken, or who hadn't invited him herself.

There should be something gratifying about rescuing a castaway, yet no gratification surged through him. Something was wrong here. Something about that girl bothered him and he couldn't place it. The faint flicker of recognition, that particular shade of green in her eyes, so very much like another's . . . But that couldn't be; she was dead . . . All he could do was watch and wait and be ready when disaster struck. His instinct was that there wouldn't be long to wait.

"Ho, Cap'n," a voice called from below.

"Found somethin' you ought to be seeing, sir." Chris swung around to find another seaman trotting his way. He waved to them both and scrambled down from the crow's nest.

"'Tis a skeleton, sir," the sailor explained at Chris's questioning look. "Or part of one, that is. The clothes are seaman's stripes, old as they are."

"A wash-up?" Chris asked, glaring in the direction his crewman had indicated.

"Too far in to be a wash-up, and the bones is bleached. Been baking in the sun for some time now."

"Is there enough left to bury?" the captain asked as the three men took to the nets, dropping into the waiting boat.

"Could be if'n you could get past them turtles."

Chris cocked an eye at his informant. "Since when are you afraid of a turtle?"

"These ain't just turtles, sir!"

"Good. Crack a couple of 'em; we could use the meat. Then get a hole dug and say the words."

"Aye, Cap'n."

Chris turned and glanced back toward the tidal pools just as Geoff ushered his charge to the beach.

One might think they were lovers by the way they moved across the sand, her head bent slightly toward his. Just then the woman's eyes took in the ship that rolled in the harbor. Her expression of awe was one Chris thought he might never forget. But then the awe faded and a touch of fear washed over her face. She pressed the heel of a fist to her forehead, her eyes shut tightly. Seconds later the expressions were gone. Only a childlike serenity remained, and she ignored the ship as though it were part of her everyday life.

Chris's eyes shifted to follow hers to his ship. The *Wing Master* was a beauty, a replica of the *Crystal Wing*, her sails now furled tightly into the beams. She was only two years old and worthy of any salt who dared to sail her. The storms of the last weeks would have ripped the masts from a lesser ship. His chest swelled in pride, though his pride deflated with her sudden disinterest.

Geoff appeared at his side. "I thought we should ask Sanders a few questions. He's had enough children to be able to tell us a little about this."

"After six sisters of your own and two years studying medicine you need to ask someone else's opinion?" Chris's eyes followed the girl's in the direction of the crew rolling the last barrels from the little forest. One barrel rolled away from a pair of sailors, who gaped at the half-naked savage who seemed so unaware of her effect on them.

"Christ!" Chris muttered, pulling his shirt from his breeches and stripping it off. Without warning, he dropped the shirt over her head. She jerked in surprise as he yanked it, none too gently, over her face. Furious eyes emerged from the collar, and she flushed at the sight of Chris's bared chest as the fabric billowed down around her knees.

"Yes, well, that doesn't mean I know a lot about

'em. I mean I know just enough to survive." Geoff laughed as he stepped between the two, silently showing her, in his brotherly fashion, how her arms fit in the sleeves and how to roll the cuffs back from her hands.

"You sit here," he said, pressing her to a little sand dune, then turned back to Chris.

"These treasures of hers tell a fair story. Looks like she came from a good family, Chris. These combs are silver . . ."

"Could be a pirate's waif," Chris scowled. "It could all have been stolen."

"Not these clothes. Certainly they are smaller, but calico was popular ten years ago among the wealthier families. My own sisters had closets full of them. Look at this fabric now, it has been worn at least that long."

"That doesn't mean they were not stolen for her. Rochester found a skeleton in seaman's stripes—not a wash-up, mind you. He was most likely alive a few years ago."

"So for that reason you are discounting the fact that she might have come from a good family?"

Chris's gaze strayed to the girl wearing his shirt. She had placed her nose next to the cuff and was sniffing it. He stifled a grin, forcing his eyes back to his first mate.

"Even so, they could have been on the same ship. Besides, I can't see that it would make any difference now."

Geoff peered at his captain's hard-set features and grew angry at his friend's attitude. "Perhaps we should charge her here and now with thievery and hang her at sunset."

"That is the question, Geoff. What do we do with her? Take her home to your mother, as if she hasn't enough to worry about? I don't know the first thing about children, much less those that come packaged like that! What if she's daft, Geoff, and her family intentionally set her adrift in order to hide their shame? What if they don't want her back? Do we take her back for the sport of others? And let's talk about the trip back, with a dozen men who have not seen their homes or their wives in more than three months. And what if she has no family left and ends up starving in the streets? You know of the women who are left to the streets to fend for themselves. How long do they live? How long before they end up just like . . ." He stopped and took a breath, "Don't you think it is worse punishment to be removed from this paradise for the cold shores of England?"

He spoke the last more to himself than to his friend. London was his birthplace, but the sea was his home. It was at sea that a man and his crew were one together, all pulling for the same thing. England was a greedy place, where men murdered for gain, where women and children starved in the streets or in debtors' prison, where your neighbor could be trusted only when you could see both his hands. It was no place for this beautiful child. He was almost tempted to leave her where he found her.

"For heaven's sake! Does she look daft to you?" Geoff smiled tenderly to see her so fascinated by the smell and feel of the fabric against her skin. "She's got a nasty scar just below the hairline, and she can't remember, that's all. She'll learn. She'll just be a few years behind the rest. For that matter, I know of a certain aunt that might enjoy having someone to look after . . ." Geoff smiled at his friend. "Since she has lost her boychild to the arms of the London ladies."

The captain's mouth pressed into a hard line; he

knew there was no way he could leave the girl behind, just as there was no way for him to justify the rest of his feelings right now. As close as he and his first mate had always been, there were some things he couldn't say to Geoff. The best he could hope for was to return the castaway to her family, if he could find them, just as he had been returned to what was left of his.

"We shall discuss her final destination later. She can have your cabin, and mind you, she is your responsibility," he almost growled. "And the first man that so much as touches her will answer to me and so will you! I'm going to get another shirt."

Geoff smiled as Chris stormed back toward the ship. "I knew he'd never leave you here, honey." He looked to the girl, who smiled back at him. "Hmmm. Honey. That seems to fit, doesn't it . . . ?

Honey watched as Chris left and another man appeared. Unaccustomed to so much activity after spending most of her life alone, she found it best just to watch. Sailors of all shapes and sizes moved around the beach hauling big round barrels. Others found sticks of driftwood and moved them into a pile in the center of the beach. And others still retrieved buckets and pots. A long black stick with a hook on it had been pushed into the sand near the pile of driftwood. All so foreign, yet somehow familiar.

"Now that she's back with her own, if she's all there, maybe what's missin' will come back. I've seen 'em where they got so scared they turned stupid for a time. Only one never come back. Saw his ma knifed in the street, and to this day he ain't said a word." Sanders's crude voice drifted down to where she sat as she reinvestigated the shirt she wore. Gathering the fabric in her hands she pressed the shirt into her face to breathe the fragrance of it. Not a pleasant odor, but then there was a certain appeal to the warm musky scent that surrounded her.

"Ya see there, she had been taught something, else she wouldn't stay there like ya told her." Honey looked up in time to see Geoff smile; she smiled back, seeing him as a friend for the first time.

His dark hair was pulled back into a tail at the nape of his neck, like the tall man's, yet Geoff was smaller—both shorter and more lean—than the one they called captain. His face was oval and softer, and his voice didn't have that deep, soul-shaking quality that left her heart thumping, nor were his eyes as deep and vibrant an ocean blue. More than that though, Geoff was instantly likable. He didn't make her feel as if she had just fallen off a rock, which she had learned from experience made it hard to breathe. Chris was beginning to make her feel that way, scaring the breath out of her most of the time.

"Thanks, Sanders. Stay close, though, I may need you later." Geoff laughed as the older man turned to make his way over to the fire.

"All right, you." Geoff turned back to her, "It's time for your first lesson. Sky," he said, pointing to the sky.

Her head tipped back to look up at the cloudless blue sky. *Sky*. The word caressed her brain: *I knew that*, she thought. "Sky," she repeated, a little thickly.

"That's what I thought! You've left your working parts out in the rain too long. They don't work well after they get all rusty," he chuckled.

"Sand," he said, scooping up a handful and pouring it into her fingers. It was warm and silky to the touch. She had rolled in it often, had sat on it to watch the sun go down, and had even napped in it. "Sand," she smiled as the grains caressed her fingers.

Next came trees and birds and shells. Finally she pointed to the graceful three-masted frigate floating just outside the cove.

"Ship," Geoff said.

"Oh, ships." A broad smile lifted the pretty mouth, a secret light seemed to glow from her eyes.

"You watch them from the bluff, don't you?" he asked.

"Watch . . ." She nodded, then in a serious fashion she said, "Hungry."

"Yes, I suppose you are. You never had the chance to finish your breakfast, did you?" Geoff smiled at her again. "Patience, they'll be lighting the fire any time now."

No sooner had Geoff spoken than someone touched the flint to the woodpile. Slowly yellow flames began a flickering dance around the interlaced pieces of driftwood and ship's refuse. The small flames licked higher and the fire grew until it crackled and hissed. The men cheered when the cauldron was placed on its hook and swung over the dancing flames. Seamen hauling buckets laden with seafood poured their catches into the boiling pot.

"Come on, we'll move closer." Geoff pulled Honey to her feet. Wood smoke drifted her way and for the first time in years she inhaled the scent of home. "Fire." She focused on the beautiful golden flames.

"That's right," Geoff exclaimed before turning to a crewman with a question. Honey ignored the interruption and continued toward the flames, eager to hold something so beautiful in her hand. Had she done this before? The thoughts were so familiar . . .

The sight of the beach faded out and a warm room

appeared: it was dark save for the fire that danced before her eyes. It was so beautiful.

"No, Honey! No!" The woman's voice called from her memory, but as once before, she blocked out the sound, bending carefully into the hearth so as not to frighten the lovely flame away.

"No! Honey!" The voice bellowed right in her ear, almost sending her headlong into the blaze. Long, strong arms closed around her small waist from behind and she was lifted off her feet. The arms dug into her ribs, forcing her stomach into her throat and the breath from her lungs. Before her scream finished, she was thrust underwater. Her arms flailed frantically as salt burned her eyes, giving her only a blurred view of her murderer. Abruptly she was hauled up by the collar of her shirt, sputtering and choking. Gasping for breath, she fell against the man's hard frame.

"Are you crazy?" Chris shouted, more in fear than in anger. His fingers dug into the flesh of her arm as he grabbed the side of her face to look for damage.

"You're damned lucky. All you lost was a little hair," he growled, pulling her close to lift her into his arms. She could feel the strong beat of his heart through his wet shirt, but all she could see was a cold, angry face that she had seen somewhere before. It was a look that evoked her deepest, darkest dreams—dreams that stole her thoughts.

"No . . ." she sobbed, pulling away from him. She turned toward the shore, where she could see Geoff waiting, his face masked in fear and disbelief, but the water sucked her down and she met the tide face-first. It was Chris who pulled her up again; then Geoff was beside her, taking her from Chris's hold.

"Thank you, Chris," he said, a smile beginning to curve his mouth. "But you see, she thinks you've just tried to kill her."

"What?" The captain's eyes narrowed and he glared down at the terrified girl who trembled against her new friend, sobs of fear racking her body.

"She doesn't know about fire, or she doesn't remember. She didn't even know she had set her hair on fire. As far as she understands, you grabbed her for no reason and forced her into the water."

"Ooh . . . hell!" Chris snarled. "I sure hope she isn't looking for an apology!" He spit out the words then trudged toward shore. "I'm going to get a dry shirt!"

Chapter Four

Honey stood at the rail of the frigate, dressed in men's knee breeches and a fresh white shirt that covered her from shoulder to mid-thigh. The stiff winds gave the loose-fitting shirt a life of its own, alternately pulling then pressing the fabric against her firm young body. Her hair was confined in a long ponytail held by a black bow.

It had been four weeks since they had left her little island behind and she was homesick. The air was cooler than what she was accustomed to, and the color of both the sky and the sea had changed to dull, cold blues. She had changed too. The changes were more inside than out, in feeling more than learning, though Geoff worked with her every day on her speech. Often he would walk her around the ship, explaining what each piece of rope or sail or crate was for.

She found that most words came easily to her. She couldn't remember speaking this much before, but somehow she was more and more able to understand and answer questions. But her feelings were changing even more—like the way her heart pounded whenever Chris was near her. A rush of heat would assault her face and her knees would weaken a little. It must be fear, she reasoned, for Chris always seemed so angry at her. He often seemed to be yelling at her, and since they had come on board the ship she could do nothing to please him.

First it was the clothes Geoff told her she must wear. Using himself as a model, he explained how each piece was worn and how it should be fastened. She had done exactly as he had said, slipping the pants up over her hips and fastening them at the waist, but they were binding and tight and she disliked the coarse feeling of them against her skin, so she removed them, returning them to Geoff where he stood on deck. She hadn't noticed how all activity on deck abruptly halted as she padded naked across the wooden floors. Both Geoff and Chris, who had been talking together at the time, assumed the most peculiar expressions. Then Chris grabbed the shirt from her bundle and forced it over her head before yanking her below deck. She hadn't understood a word of his tirade, but his tone was clearly angry.

Geoff spent a long time with her after that, explaining that clothing was an important part of a young woman's life and trying to convince her that she would need it to keep warm once they arrived in England. Their conversation lasted nearly an hour, most of it was spent waiting patiently for Geoff to find the words to make her understand why she needed clothes. She still didn't understand, but to keep Chris from getting angry again, she kept the clothes on after that.

Then there had been the food. Cooked food was a phenomenon that she didn't recall at all. It had smelled so good that she hadn't waited for directions on how to eat it. Instead, she dug into the piping hot stew with both hands, burning her fingers severely.

Geoff had been there instantly to pour cool water over the injury and to explain the use of eating utensils. She tried using a spoon a few times, but abandoned it when she learned that hot food cooled with time. Chris was furious to find her dipping her fingers into her dish. He made it quite clear that she had damned well better master the spoon and learn how to eat in a civilized manner by the time they landed in London or else . . .

Honey matched his glare. She was tired of this man bullying her and she was tired of being afraid of him. She grasped the spoon and thrust it first into the stew, then into her mouth, chewing in exaggerated movements, her glare never wavering from his hard blue eyes as she did. Geoff stifled his mirth. It was the first time she had ever wished that Geoff had not been in the room.

The worst, though, had been the night that a tub had been pulled into Geoff's cabin and filled with steaming water.

"It's called a bath," he had explained. "Not many people in London perform this act of washing, but it has been found among those of us who do that illness is less likely to plague us. And, might I add, we are a bit more pleasant to be around."

Geoff smiled as he made a grand show of his own need for a bath. She had laughed with him until she realized that he expected her to take off her clothes and climb into the hot water.

"You did swim on the island, didn't you?"

"Yes, but that water was not hot," she said, her eyes wide in disbelief.

"Well, you can wait for it to cool if you like, but mind you, I will be able to tell if you have washed or not. Now, here is a washcloth, and soap. First you, uh . . . well, rub the soap into the washcloth, then rub it all over your . . . self. See? And don't forget your legs and your uh . . . uh . . . Well, just do everything." Geoff took up the dry cloth and rubbed it over his clothed chest to show her, then handed the cloth back to her.

She shook her head, eyeing the water with suspicion.

"Will you stay and help me?" she asked.

"Oh no, Honey . . . It isn't proper for me to see you without clothes on!"

"Why? You didn't say that before." Her head tipped to the side as she waited for an explanation.

"I think a woman should explain that to you." He shook his head, suddenly overwhelmed with all the responsibilities a parent had to deal with. He gained a new appreciation of his mother, who had managed to raise six daughters.

"You go ahead now, you'll be just fine." With that Geoff backed out the door, closing it softly as he departed. Reluctantly Honey pulled the shirt over her head, then slid the pants down her thighs to the floor and kicked them off. There was too much to understand in this new life, too many rules, and she was fast growing sick of them—the food, the spoons, clothing, and everyone who thought she should do as they decided. In a moment of fleeting anger she scooped up her clothes and flung them into the tub.

"I won't be just fine," she cried at the door, "I won't do this anymore. I want to go home!"

"Home? Where is home? You call that island we found you on home?" It was Chris who filled the door frame. He was amused, then shocked, by what he saw—the woman who stood naked in the middle of the room, the clothes that floated in the tub. In seconds he realized a mutiny was in the making.

"You spoiled brat! If it didn't please you so much

to go without clothes I'd make you go naked as punishment. Unfortunately, it isn't cold enough to do any good this time of year. As it is, though, you will bathe or suffer the punishment of the child that you are!" He stepped into the room.

"I won't!" she shouted, but she took a step back. "I'm sick of the way people treat me, especially you. It is always you who pushes me into doing what you say, and I won't do it anymore! And if your precious England is the same way, I don't want to go!"

"Well, there you are." His expression became amused again. "There is no choice in the matter, now is there? We are five weeks away from your home and only five days until we reach mine. My crew has been away from their families for months, and I think the majority will vote you out. For myself, I can think of nothing better than to turn around and place you back on the baked piece of beach you call home, especially since my aunt will probably disown me for placing such an uncivil, spoiled little brat in her home to educate and care for. Therefore, in order to protect my good standing with my only living relative, you will learn how to behave properly. That means that you will eat with a spoon and bathe in a tub, even if I have to bathe and feed you myself." Chris's smile faded and his teeth clenched as he neared the end of his speech. "Now get into that tub," he ordered.

"No!" she shot back as stubbornly.

"Last warning . . ." he growled, taking a step toward her.

Sensing her mistake, she shot around the table nailed to the floor of the cabin. But she was too late. Chris's long arm snaked out and held her tight. In one jerking motion she was off the floor, landing hard in the tub, sending sheets of water over him and the floor and the walls.

Holding her struggling form, he grabbed the washcloth and soap and started scrubbing her back and arms. When she had stopped wiggling enough to allow him to relax his hold, he soaped her hair. He finished by taking up a pail of rinse water and dumping it unceremoniously over her head.

"Oh!" she gasped, as the cold water streamed over her head and face. "You . . . you . . . !" The words sputtered from her as she pushed her wet hair from her face. Jumping to her feet, she struggled to find a word to yell at him. The lack of such knowledge sent frustration surging through her, and out of fury her hand lashed out hard against his face.

The crack echoed around the wooden cabin walls, but before it died his hand wound its way through her long blond hair and she was thrust from behind against his broad chest. Her wet body soaked the front of his already dampened shirt, and to her complete surprise, her nipples responded by jutting brazenly into his warm, hard chest. The contact with the coarse fabric excited her. A thrill other than fear drenched her, and her breath caught in her throat as she waited for what was to come next. His breath had halted too. She heard his gasp and saw the anger fade from his eyes, to be replaced by something she couldn't name. He blinked, as if trying to eradicate the emotion that assaulted him, then as quickly as he had grabbed her, he dropped her back in the tub.

He was out of the cabin only seconds before the sodden washcloth splashed against the door in his wake. To Honey's surprise, she melted into the tub and wept.

Now, only twenty-four hours later, Honey remembered Geoff's explanation about the differences between men and women. Well, some of it. The rest, she sensed, he'd left out. Like why her body surged with this new sensation, a sensation only Chris seemed to excite. And what was it about him, shirtless and swinging through the riggings to loosen a trapped rope, that brought those sensations back? He was like a hot windy day in the sand. It was on those days that a memory of haunting blue eyes always plagued her, an elusive something that beckoned but never became real. Thoughts of last night had plagued her all day, as did the memory of him on the beach on that first day, when he'd given her his shirt. As she had pressed against him in the tub last night, she had felt something long and hard, concealed by his breeches, press against her thigh. Thoughts of him made her nipples draw hard against the fabric of her shirt.

Tears blurred her vision as she looked out over the endless sea, afraid of the future she had just learned that she had. Life was no longer a day-to-day, thoughtless span of sand crabs and passing ships, of sunrises and sunsets and strange memories of haunting blue eyes.

"Hey there!" Geoff stepped up beside her. He saw her tears. "What's wrong?"

"I don't know," she said.

"I think you're just homesick." he replied, the wind ruffling his shirt.

"Yes, I want to go home. I don't want to live with Chris's aunt if she is anything like him. Can't I live with *your* aunt?"

Geoff chuckled. "Well, I suppose you could, if I had one, but I don't. I used to live with my mother and father, but since I have taken to medical school I have lived at a club in London. Next year, after I finish school, I'll marry and take over my father's holdings until he marries off my sisters. Then, if I give up the sea, I'll begin my own practice."

Honey's eyes narrowed as she turned from the rail. "Your mother and father?" she asked.

Geoff's shoulders squared. "You don't remember yours, do you?"

"No, do I have some?"

"Well, everyone does at least at one time or another." He scratched his head thoughtfully. "They are the people who teach you how to live. Your mother—and usually a governess or a nurse—helps you to learn everything you need to know in order to assume your station in life. For you, a mother would teach fine manners and sewing and . . . things girls need to know when they marry."

"What is marry?" she asked, suspicious of the word.

Geoff laughed again. "Well, how do I explain? Marriage is when a man and a woman say that they will live together forever. The woman, that's you, takes care of the house and the servants, if you are lucky enough to marry well. If not, then your duties would be to raise your children and oversee your husband's property and possessions. That makes you a wife."

"And you will be a wife too?"

"No, I am a man, and that would make me a husband. You see . . . No, I guess you don't see, but you will once you meet another woman."

"Who will I marry?" Honey scanned the deck as if looking over likely candidates.

"Well, it depends on who becomes your guardian. If it is Chris, then he will choose your husband."

"But what about his aunt?"

"Jillian has never married, therefore she has no holdings of her own. Her house and everything she has is owned by Chris. Jillian can chaperone you, oversee your schooling and such, but according to English law Chris will be your legal guardian, and his decisions over you will be final."

She felt the blood leave her face as the realization of Chris's power hit her. Chris would be allowed to do whatever he wished with her. Even in her ignorance, the thought frightened her.

"Can't I marry you?" she asked, her eyes as wide as a frightened child's. "Or couldn't you please be my guardian?"

"I'm sorry. I can't marry you because I have already given my promise to another. If my parents didn't have so many children, that might have been possible, but there are eight of us, six girls. Girls are a big responsibility, one I have only just realized. But don't worry, Chris is forever at sea and Jillian is a wonderful, loving woman. She will take very good care of you." He pushed a strand of blond hair from her face. "And my betrothed will love you. I've no doubt that you two will become great friends."

"What is a betrothed?" Honey turned her face back to the sea, certain that she wouldn't like this next explanation.

"She is the girl I will marry next year. Her name is Ariel Blackmoore. You and she are about the same age, I venture. Of course, until you regain some memory we'll simply have to guess at how old you are." He paused thoughtfully.

"There are a people wandering England called gypsies. They claim to see into the future and the pasts of people they don't even know. Perhaps one day we shall wander upon a troupe and find the truths of your past."

A smile that failed to reach her eyes lifted the corners of her mouth. But the truths of her past suddenly filled her with as much dread as her future.

Chapter Five

"Ah, spring at last!" Jillian Ames inhaled deeply as she stood at the top of her staircase. "This is the best time to clean house," she chirped to the Irish maid who followed her down the stairs. The sun had just barely begun to rise, but already one could see that it would be a fine day.

"Katie, you take the front windows; Brea, you get the crystal. I'll get to the woodwork. Then we'll continue to the south wing." The short woman walked over to the sideboard where the supplies had been set out the night before. There was nothing Jillian loved better than a sparkling house, and if it could be accomplished before breakfast, so much the better.

The only girl in the Ames family, Jillian had failed to marry, having taken a vow in her youth to marry only for love. Though it might seem that love had eluded her, that was not the case. There had been love, and the promise of a wedding—a future bright with children. All of these dreams might have come true but for a hunting accident only days before the long-awaited event. Jillian had grieved ten years for her one and only love and had never looked to another to take his place. Graciously, her parents had allowed her to stay with them. After they died, her brother George made her a gift of the ancestral home, since he and his young bride had a desire to make their home elsewhere.

After George and his wife were murdered and Christopher had disappeared, Jillian had held the property in trust in the hope that young Chris would someday be found—which, fortunately, he was. Upon his return, he too gifted his aunt with title and deed, preferring the sea and his parents' newer residence in London.

Jillian sighed as she took in the sparkling breakfast room, its large bay windows overlooking the crescent-shaped drive. Leaded glass cabinets cornered each wall, refracting the rising sun and dispersing its light in hundreds of rainbows. Framing the windows were crisp white curtains trimmed with wide bands of lace to complement the pale blue walls.

The breakfast room, entry hall, and a small sitting room made up the front of the house. Along the south wall behind the sitting room was the library. The formal dining room was directly behind the foyer; behind it, a small parlor. On the north side of the house, behind the breakfast room, were the kitchens, pantries, and storage rooms. Below this was a half cellar used to store wine. Above were the family's personal chambers and dressing rooms. Jillian's mother had always referred to the bedrooms as suites. There were nine suites in all, but rarely were more than one of them used.

Entertaining was not important to Jillian. While she sometimes attended parties, her social calendar included only the birthdays of her few closest friends.

It was this short calendar—and Christopher—that kept Jillian going; they were all she had.

Silly George, she thought, he shouldn't have challenged those highwaymen. He should have just given up the money. She was convinced that he and Regina would be alive today had he not tried to play the hero. She thought of those three agonizing years she spent wondering why Chris's body had not been found with the others, worrying about the abuse he must surely be suffering. At first it was thought that the highwaymen would demand a ransom for his return (for surely the crest on the side of the coach had identified the occupants), or, worse, that the thieves would raise the boy until he came of age and then swindle him out of the lucrative Sea Wings Enterprises, one of the first collections of merchant ships to sail the seven seas. But the passing years brought no news of him.

The clatter of hoofs brought Jillian's head up. A visitor at this hour could mean only one thing—the tide had brought her beloved nephew home at last.

"Chris!" she called, hurrying to the door that had been flung open even before she could reach for it. Her china-blue eyes sparkled as her nephew strode into the hall, a blanket-wrapped bundle in his arms.

"You're home! I've been so worried . . . What have you there?" Jillian stopped her stream of questions as a pair of small brown feet peeped out from the center of the rolled blanket.

"What is this, Chris? A girl? With no shoes? Inside a blanket?" Jillian paled, deathly afraid of scandal. "What else isn't she wearing? Why is her skin so dark?" The older woman swallowed, her blue eyes wide with speculation.

'First things first, Jilli." Chris smiled his best

smile for his aunt, then headed up the stairs two at a time. "Katie," he called over his shoulder, "we'll need a bath here." It was at that very moment that Honey's head popped out of the blanket to look over Chris's shoulder at Aunt Jillian.

As Chris turned into the first room over the landing, Honey heard the birdlike woman call out weakly, "Shaffer! Shaffer, I'll need my salts!"

Chris elbowed the door open and deposited his bundle feet-first on the floor between the bed and dressing table. The blanket slid from Honey's shoulders and she found herself standing before her own image in a silvered mirror.

"Huu!" Honey put her hand to her mouth, surprised to see another person staring back at her and moving as she moved. The strange girl that confronted her had wide, dark green eyes, yet their color paled against her dark skin. The eyes looked haunted and scared.

Chris heard her gasp and stepped up beside her. Half a smile played on his lips. "You haven't seen yourself for a while, have you?"

Honey's gaze met Chris's in the mirror. She lifted a hand toward him, then dropped her arm back to her side.

"Is that me?" she breathed in shock.

"Of course. You act as though you don't know what you look like," he scoffed, stepping away from the mirror to check the closets.

"I . . . I thought I had darker hair. And . . . I . . . guess I don't." She turned back to the mirror, her long fingers tracing the lines of her face, testing her lips and ears, and smoothing her long blond tresses.

"Darker hair?" The words startled him. He had not expected her not to know what she looked like.

But then, how could she have known? There were no mirrors on a tropical island, just as there were none on a ship, for mirrors, like women, were considered bad omens on a ship. Another facet of her predicament that he had failed to consider!

She just needs to learn what we have all been taught. Geoff's words plagued him now. He had not realized that Geoff had meant she needed to learn *everything.*

Chris opened his mouth to remind her to behave, but then thought better of it. He moved out of the room as Brea and Katie pulled up the tub.

"The kettle's on, sir." Katie dipped a quick curtsy as he passed.

"Good luck!" He saluted the pair as he breezed past them, bracing himself to meet his aunt.

Jillian was right where he expected to find her, reclining on the brocade divan in the library, smelling salts in one hand, a glass of port in the other.

"A little early for that, wouldn't you say?" he chided, knowing full well that his aunt wouldn't drink the contents of the glass. It was part of a ritual that she had grown up with.

"A savage! A dirty, heathen savage in our ancestral home! Chris, how could you!" She moaned into a perfumed handkerchief.

Chris laughed, pouring a glass of port for himself. "She is no savage, and if she is heathen, it is because she was never taught differently. She is not a savage, she is a castaway, and has been for about ten years, as near as we can figure. A storm blew the *Wing Master* into the tropics several weeks ago, and thanks to a certain chartmaker, my charts were well out of date, enough so that it was difficult to find a bearing. But as you see, we were not without success."

"You call finding that . . . that *creature* success?" Jillian's feet swung to the floor in indignation. Both the port and the small bottle of smelling salts were set on an elegantly carved table as she righted herself.

"That creature you so quaintly refer to is a woman, Jillian. A woman left to die as a child, alone on a tropical island, some ten years ago. Does it sound familiar? Did not Ida do the same for you . . . ?" He spoke quietly, forcing his aunt to see past the social standards she had grown old with and to remember her own blessings.

"Ohh . . . I'm sorry, I did not think of it that way, Chris, but imagine my shock at that face. Did you see how very dark it was? I imagined the watercolor pictures you brought back from the colonies last year. Those half-naked savages . . . the things they've done to the colonists . . ." Her voice softened as her words trailed off.

"Yes, she has lived in the sun for as many years as she has been lost, but you noticed, I'm sure, that her hair is blond, not black like an Indian's would be. And the tan will fade, I have no doubt."

"Where is her family? How long will she stay here?" Jillian asked the questions carefully, afraid that her rakish nephew might have a mind to remove the girl to his own home across town. The mere suggestion of such a thought set her head to spinning.

"That is the other problem, Jilli sweet. She has no memory of her family, only life on the island." He crossed the wide room to look over the gardens that had yet to be planted for summer.

"But . . . then . . ." The older woman smoothed the front of her morning gown and considered the drink she had left on the table.

"Then I expect that I shall become guardian to a wisp of a girl with no memory and no schooling, and hope one day that some young man might see past her lack of background and ask for her hand. Meanwhile, I plan to check with as many harbor-masters as possible. Maybe we'll find her people or learn where she came from, so that she may be returned. Mayhap there is a fortune somewhere with her family name on it."

"Oh, Chris, after ten years surely there is little chance of that." The woman's heart softened for her tenderhearted nephew who had a need to return the favor done him so many years before. "Even Jacob's ship was never reported as sunk, but what other explanation could there have been for his disappearance?"

It was a painful reminder of his father's business partner, Jacob Wingfield, another of the many tragedies that had struck more than a decade ago, beginning with the death of Jacob's wife and child. Their bodies were found stripped in a field several months after their disappearance. Despite the fact that the bodies were decayed beyond recognition, George Ames had ordered them buried in the Wingfield family graveyard. Jacob had long been at sea by then and had never returned to hear of the atrocities committed against his family.

Six months later the Ames family, returning from their country estate at the end of the summer, had themselves fallen prey to highwaymen. The entire family was left for dead, lying face-down in the mud. The highwaymen fled, but young Chris had survived and was rescued from the country roads by a peasant woman by the name of Ida, who worked at a low-class travelers' lodge. Diligently she checked and rechecked the coat of arms on every carriage that passed the lodge until one day, three years later, Jillian decided to go and close her brother's country estate and ready it for sale. At the same time she planned to call on Elizabeth Wingfield, the departed Jacob's sister, newly married to one William Humphrey. It was he who would keep the Sea Wings Enterprise going.

It was on that day, the happiest of Jillian's life, that Ida presented her with her nephew, a little worse for wear, but alive nonetheless and in full control of his faculties, with the exception of the dark memories of one terrible day.

"You do what you must, Chris; the girl will be fine with me," Jillian conceded. "I'll . . ."

An earsplitting scream filled the house. Both Brea and Katie shrieked hysterically as they shot from the room where Honey had been left.

"Oh, miss, miss," Katie sobbed, "there's a bloomin' savage in that room."

Chris heard Katie's sobs as he charged from the library, taking the stairs in leaps. He burst into Honey's room to find her cowering in a corner, tears of confusion falling from her terrified eyes.

"They attacked me! They tried to rip my clothes!" She trembled, afraid that she had again failed to do what Chris expected of her.

"Oh, Honey," Chris chuckled, "I forgot to tell you about that."

"Forgot what?" Jillian came bustling into the room to find the girl just as scared as the maids, who were huddled outside the door tying their caps extra tight so as not to be scalpable.

"I have forgotten that ladies do not dress or undress themselves. It would seem that Honey was startled by Brea's ministrations."

"Oh, dear, it looks as though we will be starting from the very beginning, won't we?" Jillian said, looking over her new charge. "Get those silly girls back in here at once and tell Katie to bring quill and ink. You, my boy, get yourself something to eat and have Cook send something up here. When you have finished, there will be a list for you to drop off on your way home, or wherever you happen to be off to this afternoon. Now go! This child and I have work to do."

Jillian looked up at her nephew's amused face. She knew he was pleased with the way she was taking charge of the situation. In truth, she was ready for something new, and if it were something to please her beloved boy, then so much the better.

Chapter Six

Honey sat before the silver mirror once more. This time her hair gleamed with freshness. Her face had been scrubbed to a rosy glow, though she wondered if the severe scrubbing she had received stemmed from Aunt Jillian's notion that her deeply tanned skin was simply filth that would wash off with a little soap.

"You're freckled beyond repair," the woman scolded. "Katie, find that stable boy and send him to the dairy for more buttermilk. Brea, have you brought the scissors?"

Jillian stood behind Honey, pulling a comb through the thigh-length strands that swept the floor behind Honey's chair. "Whatever happened to the ends here, child? They look singed."

"It was fire," Honey said as she eyed the shears Aunt Jillian was holding.

"Hmm, playing in it, were you?" The older woman looked stern, but only because she wished Honey to know right off who was in charge.

"Ah, I . . ."

"A simple 'yes, ma'am' will do." A severe eye met Honey's in the mirror.

"Yes, ma'am," Honey tested the phrase and was surprised to find it familiar to her lips. Her gaze returned to the sharp instrument Aunt Jillian was placing next to her face. A few snips and the shriveled, blackened strands floated to the floor. Quite surprisingly, the shortened ends curled ever so slightly around her face.

The process continued until almost half of Honey's hair lay on the floor, but what remained was quite pleasing to the eye. Her newly trimmed tresses now moved gracefully along the sides of her face and over her shoulders to wave prettily at the small of her back.

"It's pretty," Honey said, awed by the vision of herself in the mirror.

"Makes you look a little less savage, anyway." Jillian beamed at her handiwork.

"What is savage?" Honey turned from the dressing table to face Jillian.

"Well, it isn't very flattering, my dear, and I suppose it would do for all of us to stop saying it. It is a word that means uncivilized. Does that mean anything to you?"

"No," Honey shook her head and marveled at the slight weight and feel of her new haircut.

"No, I didn't think it would. Come over here, Honey, and sit with me on the bed. There are a great many things you have to learn, things you should have been taught as you grew up. It will be difficult for you because you must start from the very beginning. I want you to understand, too, that this is all new to me as well, but I will try as hard as you will. If you stop trying, then so must I. So have patience." Jillian smoothed the curls that framed Honey's face, then circled the younger woman's waist with her arm and gave her a little hug.

"In case you have forgotten, that was a hug," Jillian smiled.

Honey felt something inside her body swell, restricting her breath. Tears filled her eyes as she experienced her first happiness since the *Wing Master* had landed its long boats on her tiny island shores.

It was late in the afternoon before Chris's coach pulled up into his drive. Like his aunt's house, his sported its own circular road and coach house. The townhouse rage had started two years earlier and rows of them now lined the newer streets, all with alleyways behind where the servants' entrances and privies were located. Most families found, too, that it was more economical to rent livery. This was particularly true of the newer breed of gentry, those who earned their fortunes catering to those who were born with them. And of course, there were those who spent their weekends in Hyde Park—strolling, on horseback, or riding about in their carriages as was becoming the fashionable thing to do. Chris had no time for any of this. He divided his attention among his club, his aunt, his mistress, and the sea. Mostly, though, it was just the sea.

Chris took little time stabling his rig and no time at all shedding his sea-stained clothes for the tub that awaited him in his three-room suite. He leaned back and relaxed as his manservant poured another steaming bucket over his knees. Steam rose to caress his face and mingle with the smoke from the cheroot clamped between his teeth.

It might be many weeks before he was to go back to

sea. In addition to the repair work contracted on the *Wing Master*, the cargo holds still reeked of rotted tobacco. Most of the load had been jettisoned over the side after the second storm, and the small mounds of the cargo left behind had grown moldy and rotten in the tropical heat. The stench had sent practically every man on board to sleeping on the deck.

Then there was Honey. The slightest thought of her called up visions in his mind, visions of forest green eyes, so reminiscent of the eyes of the girl he should have married, set in an oval face kissed by the sun. She had a healthy, glowing, lively look that went against all fashion. He smiled, recalling the lighthearted laugh that rose from her throat whenever Geoff regaled her with a childhood story.

To save himself from the temptation of her body, Chris had locked her into his first mate's cabin. Only then could he force himself to forget that she existed. But she had begun to wither there, like a rose left too long in the shade, and his humanity overrode his reason. Opening that door had proved to be his undoing.

In his selfish male way, he had saved face by becoming harsh and demanding of her, unwilling to understand her complete ignorance. Time and time again, Geoff had tried to tell him that she only needed to learn.

It tore at him to hear her weep every night for her tropical home, to know that she feared him, feared being his ward. If only she knew! She had good reason to fear him, but not for the reasons she thought. It was his own urges that made him such a risk to her. It was the way his body responded too readily to her . . .

It must have been a longing for a past that was

gone forever that made his foolish body rebel against his better judgment. Even his manhood grew as he envisioned her on the sand beside him. She was so inviting, so warm and lovable . . .

"Damn it all to hell!" he shouted, jerking the cheroot from his teeth. "Rinse! And make it cold!"

Chapter Seven

Honey opened her eyes. The sun streamed through the wide windows brightening the yellow room. She smiled and stretched like a cat. For a moment she knew who and where she was, but then she blinked and all recognition was gone. She sighed as the sense of being lost surged through her.

"Mornin', miss." Katie tossed her curls with a quick nod. "Here's chocolate and a roll for ya, less'en you be plannin' to take a spot o' breakfast with Miss Jillian."

"What is a spot o' breakfast?" Honey imitated her Irish accent, surprised to find the redheaded maid already in her room.

"In your country, 'tis a wee bit," Katie giggled. "But don't be repeating my words or the mistress will really give ya what for . . ."

"Why is that?" Honey stretched, then rubbed her eyes. The covers dropped around her waist as she slid up in bed, exposing her bare bosom.

"Holy saints be praised, where's your night-gown?" The maid's eyes fairly popped from her face, and she began a search for the missing gown.

"I couldn't sleep in that thing. It tangled up my

legs and I got too hot. What is this?" Honey picked up a delicate cup from the breakfast tray to sniff the steam.

"Chocolate, miss. You drink it for breakfast." Katie found the discarded flannel gown in a heap on the floor beside the bed. "You better get that nightgown on before the mistress catches you."

"Will she mind if I don't wear it?" Honey took a sip from the cup. Finding the sweet brew flavorful, she finished the rest in one swallow. "Can I have more of this?"

"One's the usual. More and you'll find yourself fitting into Miss Jillian's nightdresses better." Katie laughed at her own good wit, wit that was unfortunately lost on Honey. "Well, I fathom she will get a bit testy if you don't put the gown on."

"It's the silliest thing!" Honey ripped a small piece of roll and popped it into her mouth.

"Well, what did you wear before this?" Katie asked.

"*My* clothes, I guess."

"Don't you know?"

"Well, they were my clothes but they were nothing like what you wear." Honey's gaze flicked over the heavily clothed maid, taking in her white cap, the large white kerchief that covered her shoulders, and the black skirt that was tucked up to reveal the plain underskirt beneath.

"I'll bet that accounts for your skin bein' all funny colored."

"What's wrong with my skin?" Honey demanded, meeting the maid's mischievous eye. She dropped the roll back to the tray.

"'Tain't natural, that's all. And not a whit in fashion. Why, just to take you out in public they'll have to use a keg o' powder on yer face alone."

Honey sank back among the pillows. She had no idea what a whit of fashion or a keg of powder was. But she understood too well from the comments already made that she was, as Chris had indicated, less than acceptable.

Proof of that understanding poured in all morning. Katie began the procession with three white boxes, followed by Brea with six small pink ones, then Katie reappeared with still more, followed again by Brea. The packages were delivered one right after the other. It was still morning when Brea took over for Katie, following Jillian's instructions to educate Honey in the order of dress. This task pleased neither of them. The younger maid scowled as she opened the boxes, finding several shifts, petticoats, stockings and tied garters, chemises, and corsets. Honey watched as Brea laid the pieces out on the bed. Then she dragged Honey over to stand in front of her. First, she pulled a huge shirt with short sleeves over Honey's head, then the various parts were tied together, giving it shape. Brea called it a shift. Next, stockings were pulled onto each leg and tied into place with long strips of cloth. After that, Brea instructed Honey to stand at the foot of the bed and hold on to the posts while she wrapped a bone corset around her and cinched the strings of the stays for all she was worth, torturing Honey's waist. The maid paused to catch her breath, then pulled again, flattening Honey's well-formed breasts.

"Let go!" Honey cried out. "I can't breathe!"

"The mistress says to dress ya, and this is the only way I know how." The maid gave one more jerk on the laces before tying them in a floppy bow.

"Please! Get it off! It hurts! I'm already covered from head to toe," Honey pleaded, attempting to look down at her body. She was covered from shoulder to toe and cinched so tightly she could scarcely move at all. Over all this, Brea now dropped the chemise.

"This is more than I had to wear on the ship!" Honey protested again.

"Hush, now! The mistress has important company. You'll get us all in trouble if you keep up like this."

"Who? Is Chris here?" Honey's question sounded hopeful even to her own ears, and she would have cursed herself had she only known how.

"No," Brea giggled, "It is a man, though. I think she's interviewing tutors right now."

"What's that?" Honey sighed. She was growing tired of having to ask that same question, yet without the questions she would never learn how to behave in this strange new world.

"He teaches you to read and write, and such other things like that. Some of them's very handsome, others are mean." Brea made a stern face as her hands smoothed the chemise along Honey's arms, then she whipped a layered petticoat around her waist and tied it shut.

"After Katie brings your dress up and the mistress finishes this interview, she'll want to meet with you in the library."

"More clothes?" Honey's eyes widened.

"Well, a' course, can't be going about in your shift."

"This is a shift?"

Brea simply sniffed as Katie bustled into the room with an armload of deep green linen. "Just in the nick, too. The Miss is ready for ya."

Katie handed the dress to Brea, who shook out the hem and laid the neck open while Katie helped Honey step into the mass of fabric. The sleeves were full, and rows of ruffles were stitched across the breast panel. Two more rows of ruffles lined the throat and several more were layered along the hem. The stiffly starched fabric hung like an oblong bell around her legs, almost touching the floor.

With swift fingers the Irish maids had Honey buttoned up and buckled into heeled, painfully pointed shoes. Seconds later she was out the door on her way to the library, a maid at either elbow.

"Oh, don't you look lovely!" Jillian exclaimed as she met her charge at the door. "Brea, bring me a comb and ribbon, please." The older woman drew Honey into the room. "How do you feel, dear?"

"I can't breathe," Honey answered, but her gaze was already devouring the dark, oak-paneled room. Books of every size, shape, and color lined the walls between the fireplaces at either end of the chamber. On each of the outside walls were floor-to-ceiling French doors with leaded panes. The doors to the south opened to a wide stone veranda; beyond them, mounds of earth and dried weeds stood dead and ugly. The window to the west provided another view of the same sort of debris and dried bushes.

The right half of the library was set up as a study, the left half invited pleasure, sporting brightly colored volumes and even a shelf for refreshments—several crystal decanters filled with pleasing shades of brown and amber liquids. Heavy crystal glasses glittered in the mid-morming light.

Jillian smiled at the wonder she saw on Honey's face as she looked around the room.

"Oh dear, look at that waistline!" Jillian tugged at the stiff fabric. "Why, it's much too big. After today, we'll tell Brea to let up on that corset. For now, since you are already dressed, we'll have a talk about manners. Not that yours are vulgar, mind you, it's just better to do these things right from the start."

Honey smiled, glad of the reprieve from the stays.

"First, the words *yes, ma'am* should be used in acknowledgment to myself and all of my female friends, and to any female who is married and of a respected station. It won't take long for you to learn the difference. Second, *sir* is to be used when speaking to Christopher or Geoffrey—and, most importantly, to the tutor who will be engaged to teach you how to read and write. For example, if Chris offers you a chair, you reply 'Thank you, sir,' and then curtsy, like so."

The older woman dipped in a demure curtsy; her silken gown shimmered in a pool around her, then whispered as she rose. Honey tried the move when Jillian nodded for her to do so, but her gown neither shimmered nor whispered, and the movement seemed graceless compared to Jillian's.

"I am afraid that this," Jillian's arms parted palms up, as she indicated the room, "will have to do for your school room. It has been many years since a nursery has been needed in this house."

"Yes, ma'am." Honey started from her own automatic response. It sounded so right yet so foreign. Her face grew warm, then cold; maybe she did belong here after all.

"Look at that! Things are already starting to return to you. If you have been taught the basics, and I think you have, it won't be long before you are reading all by yourself. Ah, thank you, Brea." Jillian turned her warm smile to the young maid who walked briskly into the library. She handed Jillian the comb and ribbon, then whisked back out, her skullcap bobbing loosely over bright red curls.

Honey was relieved to see that Brea's curtsy also lacked the splendor Jillian's commanded and didn't feel so bad anymore. Age could have something to do with it—age and practice.

"Here, sit here," Jillian indicated the chair before the large mahogany desk.

The comb felt good as, in Aunt Jillian's tender hands, it slid easily through her hair. In seconds, half her hair was lifted and tied back from her face in a neat bow.

"There. From now on this will be how you will keep your hair. Now, do you have any questions?"

Honey shook her head. It was strange not to feel her hair brush her ears or neck. Even with the high collar of her demure dress, the newly exposed portions of her head felt naked.

"Good. Now we will start to get you ready for a tutor." Jillian placed her hands in Honey's to pull her from her chair. "Posture is our next lesson. Here, stand up, pull yourself up from the waist. That's it . . . now push your . . . this part out," Jillian patted Honey's fanny. "Hmm . . . not much of one here, is there? Well, we can pad that when the time comes. Head up. Yes, . . . yes, good. See? Wasn't that easy?" Jillian beamed, pleased with Honey's natural grace.

Honey drew her eyebrows together in a small scowl. She felt like one of those bright red birds that strutted up and down the beach of her island. Just after the stormy season they would come out of the woods, calling in the most distressing screeches. Then they'd strut up and down the beach, their breasts thrust out as if they held sole title to the sand. She recalled the day she crossed the beach to swim in the lagoon. Those birds were dancing and flapping their wings when they suddenly bucked up and flapped toward her, their wicked talons extended dangerously. She narrowly escaped injury and never again tried to cross the sand when they were there. Such selfish, arrogant creatures . . .

"Here." Jillian's voice invaded her thoughts. "Put this on your head. Try to keep it there as you walk across the room."

Jillian placed a heavy book on top of Honey's head, but the book slid from its spot and slammed to the floor. Honey jumped and her heart lurched into her throat.

"If that one doesn't suit your taste, there are several others." The deep voice came from the open door.

Honey's eyes snapped up to see the man dressed in evening clothes filling the door frame. His appreciative gaze warmed her face. That look of satisfaction was for her and no one else. But his gaze suddenly lost that spark when it met hers.

"I've brought your things. Shaffer has them." His eyes flicked to his aunt. "I thought . . ." he began, oblivious to the blush that ignited Honey's cheeks.

Honey felt a sudden pressure in her ears, and nausea twisted her stomach. "Oh! . . ." she groaned as the room began to spin. Blackness overwhelmed her as she melted to the floor, unaware of Jillian's panic-stricken voice calling her name.

"Now what?" Christopher swore as he leaped to catch the fallen girl.

"Oh dear! Shaffer, fetch my salts . . . Christopher, what do you think you're doing?" Jillian stepped back in horror as her nephew worked at Honey's back.

"Loosening these damn things." He spit out the words as his fingers nimbly plucked the hooks from her gown. In no time at all he had dislodged the laces that cinched the very breath from her body.

"What is this? As worthless a device as ever created! No woman under my protection shall wear these confounded contraptions. I want them out of this house! At the very least, out of her room." Chris half bowed to his aunt in apology for condemning her rule in her own home, but he refused to relinquish his say-so over the woman who would be his ward. "And this dress . . . what kind of thing is this to hang on a girl? Surely something has been invented to take the place of these infantile swaddlings!"

Christopher turned back to Honey. He lifted her gently from the Persian carpet and carried her past the startled butler to her own room. Jillian followed fast on his heels.

Her slender body seemed frail under the heavy gown. The ruffles along her throat jabbed at the tender skin, raising angry welts. Her vulnerability struck him in that protected place deep in his chest, a place that had lain empty for too long.

"Trust me in this, Jilli," he said more softly as he gazed at the sweet face nestled at his shoulder. "When one is accustomed to the sea and the feel of the winds, clothing is stifling. How often have you lectured me for not having dressed in waistcoat and wig?" He placed his burden carefully on the bed, then turned to the cabinet where the other gowns were hung. Flipping through the dresses, he finally pulled out a plain pink shift. Its overdress of cream gauze was gathered simply at the neck. From there, long folds fell to the floor, captured in one ruffle, embroidered with a delicate floral design. The chemiselike sleeves were caped from the shoulder to mid-elbow, where a long straight sleeve continued to the wrist. "Here, this should do to ease her into the fashion world. Order a few more of these and I'll grant you that by late autumn she will be ready for as many layers as fashion will dictate."

"How can you be so sure?" Jillian asked. "Besides,

it isn't proper for you even to know of such things!" Jillian sounded offended, but a quick look told him she was more curious over his concern than shocked at his knowledge of woman's undergarments.

"Just trust me. Establish accounts in my name for all future expenditures." He tossed the dress aside in sudden irritation and moved quickly from the room just as the girl behind him began to stir.

"Sit with her," Jillian ordered Brea as the maid entered the room. Then she turned to follow Chris, who was already out the door and several strides ahead of her.

"Where are you going, Chris? Aren't you going to help me choose the tutor?" she called from the landing as he quickly descended the stairs. When he didn't stop she lifted her skirt and followed as quickly as her manner would allow.

He heard the disappointment in her voice and knew better than to look back. "No, Aunt, I leave that foolery to you. I have other things to attend to at the moment."

"Then shall we expect you for dinner?"

"Yes, you may," Chris answered, passing through the foyer and out the door into his open carriage. Still he didn't look back.

"But, Chris . . ." Jillian reached the door just as the carriage lurched forward. Behind her Shaffer exchanged looks with Katie.

Things were certainly different in the house these days!

Chapter Eight

Honey was alone in her room. The dizziness had passed long ago, but the strange feeling of lightness had not. As she had been instructed, she rested, dressed in just her underclothes, but she couldn't seem to stay still.

The sun was high, yet the day had gone well past noon. She pulled one of the front curtains aside to look out over the empty circular drive to the oval-shaped front yard beyond. Both the drive and the lawn were lined with rocks of all shapes and sizes. On the street side of the yard a small cove of trees and bushes had been planted off-center to her left. To her right, a dark brown split-rail fence, only two rails high and four posts wide, made a pleasant divider between lawn and street. The rest of the yard was grass, still an ugly yellow-brown from winter. On either side of the entrances short evergreen hedges formed a natural fence that circled the entire estate. Beyond that was a stone street framed by a severe looking black iron fence. If there were other houses, they were hidden among the ancient oaks.

Honey dropped the heavy curtain and moved to the other window. From there she could see the dead mass of the garden that she had seen from the library earlier. Jillian's lawn joined the neighboring lawn. There was no indication of where one ended or the other began.

She didn't hear her own sigh as she looked out as far as she could see. The grays and browns of early spring in London were an ugly contrast to the rich blues and greens of that tropical island so very far away. It hadn't been so long ago that she was standing on her cliff, breathing the rich salt air, watching the ships sail by, feeling the wind caress her skin. The dry air of London smelled foul to her nose. She thirsted for the drenching beauty of her island.

Tears gathered in her eyes, sending stabbing little prickles through the bridge of her nose. What would the rest of life be like in this bone-chilling, dreary world? More lonely than life alone on an island? Even after Barley Boe had gone to sleep forever, she hadn't felt this empty. The pain that pressed heavily at her chest was the worst she ever remembered feeling. Except for once . . . but something in that part of her mind refused to give her more than a glimpse of a woman's face, and a pain so sharp she winced as it passed from her temple to her head.

Now another memory assailed her. She could almost feel Chris's arms placing her carefully on her bed. His scent lingered long after he'd gone.

It didn't make sense that she felt so giddy every time she knew he was around. It didn't make sense that she should feel sad every time she failed to meet his expectations, or that she should even want to please him. He had taken her from the only home she could remember and forced her into this dismal routine. So why did his opinion of her matter so much? The hot tears rolled down her cheeks; an indefinable feeling made her ache inside. If only she could understand a small part of it.

She sank back into an overstuffed chair. At least Jillian had understood about the clothes. Honey smiled; she hadn't imagined that even Chris would understand, but he had. So the shift remained, as did the stockings and chemise, but the whalebone device had been replaced with a kirtle-like band that laced from her hips to just below her breasts. It defined her figure without bracing it, leaving her to breathe as she was certain she was meant to. Jillian also had had the heavy gowns removed and reboxed. Only two had been left behind: one pink and one peach, made of the lightest gauze, each with satin sashes instead of snug-fitted waist hooks to hold them in shape. At Chris's urging, Jillian had promised to order more of these lightweight dresses. Why would he care about that?

Her fingertips were cool as they massaged her warm forehead. At least Jillian seemed to care for her; it helped that someone had given her a hug.

The office of the harbormaster was on the second floor of a semicircular building situated in the middle of the quay overlooking London harbor.

It was through Seth Gaft, master of the harbor, that all reports of ships, both incoming and outgoing, were channeled. The reports included records of their cargo and intended destinations, home ports, and names of their captains, owners, and shareholders—all in a vain effort to control the channels. It was Seth who had been granted authority by the royal courts to order patrols to search ships of questionable cargo, though that rarely happened anymore. Once Seth had established himself and his office, most of the illegal activities moved out of port. Not that Seth had succeeded in ridding London of all its criminal element, but now a lady could walk the wharves without risk of falling prey to those who would sell her favors to a harem in Persia, India, or worse places. Gaft had earned the respect and friendship of the captains of reputable ships and from that had gained valuable information about what took place on the high seas, though legally he had no control there. This didn't mean he was without influence. The war between the Spanish and the English had escalated. As far as the Spanish were concerned, any English ship was a pirate ship, and the only good pirate ship was a downed one.

The heaviest reports were coming from the Bahamas, and from these Chris hoped he would find his answer.

Chris rapped on the door before pushing it open, revealing a small office stuffed with overflowing bookshelves, maps and globes, telescopes, and sextants. In the very center of the mess was the harbormaster, his head bent over a book while the smoke from his pipe curled lazily around his head. Through the wide bay window behind him, Chris had a panoramic view of the harbor.

"Why, Captain Ames!" Seth stood, setting the book aside as he extended a welcoming hand. His broad smile made him look younger than his forty years. "It's good to see you, my friend. I heard reports you ran straight into those storms off the colonies last February. Glad to see you made it through."

"Aye, fought it out. Can't beat that crew of mine," Chris smiled, releasing Seth's hand and taking the only other chair in the cluttered office.

"I have a request of you this time, Seth. It could be difficult, but the future of a young woman rides on it. I need to know if anyone reported the loss of a ship far south." Chris unrolled the chart he had carried in with him and spread the map over the cluttered desk.

"Around here . . ." With his finger he circled the island tinted with dark brown ink.

"Hmm, not that I recall. How long?"

"That's the tough part. At the very least, ten years, might be twelve." Chris met Seth's gaze over the chart. He was not surprised when his friend winced.

"I've only held this chair for two years, Chris, and I only have reports for one of those. I don 't think I can get much from the sea scuttle." Seth leaned back in his wooden chair, a hand raking his thinning hair. "I can ask, though. Maybe some of the saltier ones would remember something. Who is the young woman?"

"That is what I am trying to find out," Chris said. "I would appreciate your asking around. The ship would have had English-speaking people on board, passengers probably, possibly wealthy travelers aboard their own ship. Oh, and would you mind asking a few salts to make inquiries at foreign ports? France, Spain, if anyone happens to be going that way?"

"Glad to." Seth scratched the crown of his head as he leaned back in his chair. "But mind you, that's an awfully long time to have hope for." Behind him the crescent-shaped windows gave a fine view of the *Wing Master* and her harbormates.

"Aye, that it is." Chris nodded thoughtfully, "But I've got to try. And I'd appreciate it if you forgot to mention the girl to anyone, at least for a while." He offered his hand once again to his friend. "By the way, the cargo didn't fare as well as the *Wing Master* did. Sorry, Seth, next load."

Seth smiled and nodded, but he was disappointed. Nothing topped a meal like the Virginia tobacco

Captain Ames carried back from the colonies.

Chris stepped out into the sunshine. His second stop took him to his bank, and his third to Sea Wings Enterprises. Finally he returned home, leaving just enough time to change for dinner at his aunt's.

Reluctantly, his fingers snapped open the buttons of his waistcoat, cut shorter than the knee length that was fashionable. He realized too late that his reluctance had to do with the hint of soft cologne that lingered on his coat. The scent had even tempted him to smile once or twice as he completed his day's errands. Surely it was not the Lady Jennifer Bates, with whom he had spent last night, who'd left the delicate scent on his coat. Her choice perfume was nothing like this enticing scent. When he remembered where the scent had come from the smile quickly left his lips. How could that girl plague him so? What must he do to escape those bewitching eyes? Perhaps tonight, when he would be forced to spend the evening in her company, he would at last be able to cast aside his lustful thoughts.

Ripping the coat from his broad shoulders, he flung it over the embroidered chair that had once served his father.

It was with a fresh resolve that he entered his aunt's home sometime later. He was ushered into the parlor, where Jillian had thoughtfully placed a carafe of his favorite whisky. A fire had been banked in the pit. This room had changed little since his boyhood days. The rugs were rich golds and browns, the furniture covered in heavy brocades. The large wall tapestries blended the same golds, with deep greens woven through for accent. It was clearly one of the brightest rooms in the house, situated on the southeast corner. The windows were tall and wide, made with many small panes of glass leaded together. Each bottom half, separately framed from the top half, had been mounted on hinges so as to open outward on nicer days. Small, delicately carved tables sat next to each armchair. Of the three, two faced the fireplace and one was positioned by the windows at the back of the room. A large table was supported by lions' feet, which fanned out from a central pedestal. Lamps with crystal shades lighted the room, and a woman's writing desk with matching chair was placed to the left of the door. Completing his aunt's favorite room were matching settees. Elaborate curved arms of mahogany merged with the scrolled back. The fully stuffed settees were comfortable even if they were a bit high for a lady. But despite its overpowering femininity, or perhaps because of it, Chris had always loved this room. It appeared to be sunny even on a cloudy day, and never had it failed to lighten his worst moods.

Chris's thoughts blanked as a shadow fell across his feet. He knew who had cast it even before he glanced up.

She stole his breath. Standing there, backlighted by the foyer, she appeared like an angel, her eyes cast down as she awaited his invitation to enter the room. The gown of his choosing did much to heighten her tanned complexion, enhancing the color of her eyes and the shine of her hair.

With an effort, he collected himself. "You needn't wait for an invitation." He almost whispered the words, holding her in his gaze until her lashes lifted and she looked at him.

"Thank you, sir." She answered as softly, moving

into the room with a grace more natural than one could learn in a single day.

"Sir?" Chris's brow rose as he echoed her.

She flushed as she passed him, taking a chair near the fire, facing him. He wondered how many times she had practiced this crossing.

"I have been taught basic manners," she smiled. "Miss Jillian has engaged a tutor for me and I shall meet him tomorrow."

"I see. And the dressmaker?" Chris turned to the desk to refill his goblet, diverting his attention from the way the firelight played on her face.

"Yes, and the dressmaker," she confirmed, stealing a glance at him. He was wonderfully dressed, from his buckled shoes to his matched brocade waistcoat and vest of black, embroidered with royal blue fleur-de-lis designs. His hair had somehow become a startling gray, and she tried very hard not to look at it, or at the small bag wrapped about the tail at the back. But it was a near impossible task.

"Ah, there you are." Jillian bustled into the room. Her gown of watered silk rustled as she moved to kiss her nephew's proffered cheek.

"You look splendid, young man," she beamed at his powdered head. Jillian's smile turned to pride as she gave her attention to Honey. Her gaze followed the lines of the gown right down to . . . the young woman's unshod feet. The older woman's eyes widened in silent horror as she spotted the tips of Honey's toes peeping from beneath her gown. She worked frantically to get Honey's attention, gently raising her brow so as not to alert Chris. Luck was with her. Honey instantly tucked her toes under the gown.

She flushed, hoping Chris hadn't seen the subtle movement, for she knew he'd be angry at her again.

She quelled the knot in her stomach and prayed someone would speak soon. But Chris stared into the fire while Jillian absently straightened a lampshade. In the end, Shaffer saved the moment.

"Dinner, ma'am," he said from the doorway, his face as expressionless as always.

"Thank you, Shaffer." Jillian turned to Chris. "Finish your drink, dear. There's no rush. That is, unless you have plans for the evening."

"Of a sort, yes. However, nothing that can't wait." He set his crystal goblet aside and offered his arm to his aunt, which she accepted with a formal nod. The pair preceded Honey down the short hall to the dining room.

Shaffer looked at the floor as he held a chair for Miss Honey. A smile threatened to crease his rigid lips at the sight of a bare toe peeping at him from beneath the fashionable gown. He pushed the chair to the table, and Honey thought she saw a trace of a tear coming to the corner of his eye. She grimaced, wondering if Chris had seen her feet.

Chris didn't seem to be watching as he attended his aunt's chair before seating himself.

"We'll not be formal tonight, out of consideration for our guest." Jillian glanced at Chris, then turned a smile on Honey as she shook out her napkin and laid it across her lap. Honey watched Jillian and followed her moves exactly, until her gaze lifted to find a set of dark blue eyes scrutinizing her movements. Her cheeks flushed hot and her gaze dropped back to her plate.

"That is a lovely gown, Miss Honey," Chris stated, but he wasn't looking at her gown. Shaffer moved around the table, placing steaming plates before each person, and Chris noticed the unusual red glow about his face. The butler's pursed lips were quite out of character for the usually somber man.

"Thank you, sir." Her voice sounded strangled, and it was Shaffer who drew her grateful eye as he placed a bowl before her. Steeling herself, she dipped her spoon into her broth. "But I can't be going about in my drawers then, can I?" she stated calmly. She glanced up just as her spoon touched her lips to find two sets of horrified eyes upon her. Behind her Shaffer choked, and a tray hit the floor with a resounding crash, forcing Honey upright in her chair.

"Sounds as though Katie's been lecturing again." Chris's words were stiff and his expression bland. Jillian assumed a similar calm, but her eyes twinkled.

"Have I said something?" Honey asked innocently. She set her spoon in her soup bowl and looked at Chris. The brocade chair was suddenly hard against her back.

"Nothing that shouldn't have been expected," he answered without looking at her.

"Chris!" Jillian scolded as she watched Honey wilt before her very eyes. "Don't worry about it, child. Since we are all family, it is just another lesson that you have to learn." A sincere smile lightened her expression.

Honey looked deep into her bowl, feeling the color creep into her cheeks. A wave of warmth washed over her, leaving a clammy chill in its wake. Her lip refused to stop trembling. Jillian's predinner warning 'hide your feelings, that is what is expected,' echoed through her mind.

How did one hide a quaking lip? Drink! The goblet was cool beneath her hand but her grip lacked power. The goblet slipped, crashing into the silver candlesticks.

Honey watched in horror as the sticks fell, almost in slow motion, across the white linen cloth and onto Chris's wine goblet. The goblet fell, splashing a wave of crimson into his soup and across his white silk shirt. She covered her open mouth with her hand while her eyes, like Jillian's, watched the change of expression on Chris's face: glaring irritation, then disbelief giving way to a blank expression. He looked from the stains on his dress coat to the horrified girl across the table from him. He dabbed his mouth. Laying his napkin aside, he rose, never once taking his blue eyes from her. "Next time," he said lightly, "I expect to see the shoes that match that gown."

He gave a courtly bow.

"You'll excuse me, no doubt." Then, as casually as any man just finishing his dinner, he strolled from the dining room and out of the house, leaving Jillian and Honey in wide-eyed silence.

Chapter Nine

Christopher stood at the floor-to-ceiling French doors. The full moon drenched his nude body in silver blue light.

Jennifer Bates watched him from the bed where he had taken her for the third time in two days. His mood was one she had not seen in some time. She liked it less now than the last time she'd seen it. Had it been five years since he had buried his past? Five years since the last time his mood affected their lovemaking? As if he were punishing himself. Either way, rough or gentle, Christopher's lovemaking was magnificent. He was better than any lover she had ever taken. Her black eyes swept across his moody visage, then traveled the familiar lines of his muscular arms to his tightly rippled abdomen, which reminded her of a turtle's undershell in the moonlight.

"Come back to bed. Let it be my turn to please you," she murmured seductively, smoothing the sheet that covered her richly stuffed down mattress. Her wanton body was fully exposed and as femininely magnificent as his was masculine. She nestled suggestively into the sheets.

"Very well, Chris. Just don't disturb me when you do come to bed." She didn't cover herself but struck an enticing pose and closed her eyes, knowing he'd come to her again sooner or later.

But if he heard her he ignored her, and continued to stare out over the sleeping city. Some time later Jennifer fell asleep, alone.

The moonlight illumined everything as far as she could see from her second-floor suite. The lamps that had been placed in the long black hooks just inside the Ames property had been taken down and extinguished. Still, the city seemed to have a light of its own, unlike the island, which became black after the sun went down and stayed dark until early dawn.

Honey hooked the curtain open and pulled a chair to face the window. Curling into it, she watched the moon and wondered if it was the same one that she had seen from her island. She wondered, too, if there were stars here, as at home. She had seen none so far, but then she recalled that when the moon was so bright the stars were hard to see.

But thoughts of the moon faded as, unbidden, a picture of Chris loomed in her memory, bare to the waist and swinging effortlessly through the riggings. His shoulders flexed as he moved with ease among the ropes and billowing sail . . .

Honey awoke slowly to the sound of the birds chirping from the branches of the newly budded trees. The sun had yet to burst over the horizon, but the morning already seemed bright, if cool and damp. She stretched lazily, then moved from her chair to look out over the new day. *Things look different today*, she thought. *And feel different . . .*

She pushed at the window, trying to get it open, before her fingers found the latch and twisted it down, freeing the double windows from their frames. She pushed them open and was rewarded by a burst of fresh, crisp air.

"Mornin', miss. What ya be doing over there?" Katie looked from the smoothly made bed to the displaced chair, to the windowsill where Honey sat, her nightgown hiked up over her knees.

"Don't you know they can see you from outside?" she lectured. "'Tain't proper to be sitting in plain view of the street in your nightclothes!"

"Why?"

"Because you shouldn't. No one 'cept me an' you and the mistress should be seeing you like that." The girl hustled over to the window and drew Honey back, then reached out and pulled the windows shut with a resounding slam.

"But I like them open!" Honey insisted, bringing her foot down on the carpeted floor.

"Like to catch yer death if you're not careful!" The maid wiped her hands on her apron before opening the closet door to select the only remaining dress. Placidly, Honey allowed herself to be dressed. The creamy gauze overdress gathered at the scooped front, edging her breastbone. The sleeves puffed at the shoulder then gathered at the elbow, fitted from elbow to wrist. A wide satin sash of the same peach shade wound round her waist, restricting the voluminous fabric. The haze of the light peach underdress was scarcely visible through the yards of gathered gauze.

Angelic though she might look, Honey turned away, disgusted with the maid who was bent on seeing propriety served so well.

"Honey, dear," Jillian's soft voice sounded at the door. "Join me for breakfast, will you?" She peeked through the small crack.

Honey nodded.

"Good girl," the woman smiled before closing the door again.

Breakfast, Honey found, was a wonderful feast of steaming foods. Fried ham with eggs in a sauce that was both sweet and tangy, with tea or coffee. Coffee was a drink fast becoming a favorite of the colonies, Jillian had informed her. Best of all, there were hot rolls and butter.

"A lady doesn't stuff herself, dear," Jillian scolded gently as Honey helped herself to her third plate of softly scrambled eggs.

"But it tastes so good," Honey mumbled as she crammed another roll into her mouth.

"So I see. But unfortunately, manners need to be observed. It may be all right to eat heartily in private, but publicly you must alter your appetite accordingly. That means eat at home." Jillian's smile vanished, a soft look covered her slightly wrinkled face. Then her blue eyes twinkled again. "Listen to me, will you? I've always been a lady of the court, a guardian of rules and proper manners. How can I be so soft where you are concerned?" Her small mouth curved into a loving smile. "It appears my wayward nephew and I have traded positions when it comes to you. He was never one to keep rigid schedules and stiff rules until now, while I want to treat you the way every mother does who wants to spoil her daughter. I want to look at you and see something other than that lost and desolate expression. I just know there is life somewhere behind those lovely eyes, and I want to see it." Jillian crossed the room to fold the slight girl into her motherly arms. "And at the same time, I want the whole of London to love you, as I suddenly do."

"Even after I ruined your dinner last night?" Honey drew back at Jillian's tinkling laugh.

"Especially after last night's dinner. Chris is a fine man, don't misunderstand me, but I think he has taken his duties with you so seriously that he has forgotten what it was like to be young. Perhaps because you don't look as young as you are. Perhaps because he missed that part of life himself . . ." she said more to herself than to Honey. "But let us not worry about him. I think he will be a very long time in returning. By then, the progress you'll have made will make him understand." Jillian squeezed Honey's hand. "I promise. But to keep him happy, just remember one thing. Never repeat anything Katie or Brea might say, unless of course you are asked to. They come from another country, where customs and styles are very different and young girls are allowed to speak their minds. Here, that is not encouraged. You are the mistress, they are the servants. Never should you lower yourself by repeating their words." Jillian smiled again. "Now off to your rooms. Your new teacher will be here momentarily and I want a few moments to, ah . . . advise him."

Jason Montgomery stood quietly in the library. This, his first appointment since completing his own education, was better than any he had hoped for. And to think he was offered a bonus in exchange for remaining secretive about his new pupil! A smile played on his soft lips, brightening his handsome face. What luck this was. When this contract expired he would have a credit to his name. He hadn't listened to the cautionary words the woman insisted he hear. By God, he was a teacher, a schoolmaster, a man of integrity. However new at the profession, he was not a molester of children.

"Master Montgomery, may I present Miss Honey . . . eh . . . James," Jillian stumbled over the fictitious last name, hastily conjured for obvious reasons. "Miss James, your schoolmaster, Mr. Montgomery."

"How do you do, sir?" Honey gave a short, precise curtsy.

"Miss James." His body snapped at the waist to a bow, but his gaze stayed on the young lady who stood before him. "Forgive me, madam, but I was led to believe . . ." The man quit the bow, ". . . that I was to teach the basics of writing and mathematics and so forth. This . . . this . . . is not . . ."

He dragged his eyes from the young woman to the old one. His face set in a frozen expression of ire as he realized he'd fallen victim to a trickster.

"That is correct, Mr. Montgomery. You see, a dear friend of mine is aunt to this child and sister to the girl's sickly mother. In the effort to take care of the mother I fear the child was all but forgotten; her only education ceased when she was probably six years old. No one quite remembers," Jillian explained, carefully watching the young schoolmaster. "She will require all the basics. Nothing more."

"I see." His voice was deceptively soft as he wondered who would be so cruel as to dupe him so.

"Good," Jillian smiled at her charge. "Make a list of your requirements, Mr. Montgomery, and we shall send someone for them. It is two hours before tea; you can start now if you like."

"Yes, that would be fine. Miss Honey. . . ." He indicated the chair behind the desk. "Let us begin, then, at the beginning."

"Bring the tail down a little farther," he said as Honey practiced her letters. "That's fine. Now R."

The teacher stood behind Honey's chair. A full week had passed and only now was he beginning to believe his appointment was genuine. His pupil had indeed required the basic teachings of the very young. He had stumped her too often for her to be anything other than Miss Ames had claimed. But she was certainly not the child Miss Ames had described. Any man with eyes could see how very lovely she was. And Jason was a man with eyes.

She looked up from her task and smiled, "This is right, isn't it?"

"Yes, my dear, that is correct." He allowed his gaze the pleasure of lingering on her face. "You grew up in the out-of-doors, didn't you?" he asked, trying to guess the true color of her hair. The dark roots were just beginning to show.

"Yes," she said, moving on to the S sample on her paper. Her head bent back over the paper as she pushed her quill.

Jason's eyes narrowed as he contemplated the answer to his next question. "And how has your mother fared? Does she live?"

The quill stopped long before she looked up to him. "They don't tell me, sir," she said sweetly before continuing to draw her letters.

"I see." He leaned across the desk to watch her draw the next letter. "That is fine, Honey. Let us move now to some numbers."

The paper on her desk was replaced with a clean

sheet and the session continued until two P.M. Every day at that time the young Mr. Montgomery would pack away their books and Honey was allowed one hour of free time before dinner. Afterward, Jillian would work with her on the other lessons she required. Those lessons included sewing and the art of serving tea. On weekends her instruction included walking with grace, learning the difference in fabrics and fashion, and gardening. Though Jillian had a gardener to oversee her property, she enjoyed hoeing and weeding her own rose garden. She enjoyed her garden so much that when the days of early spring began to warm she replaced her silks and satins with muslins and her wigs with wide-brimmed straw hats and began clipping back the dead branches of last year's plants to make way for this year's flowers.

After spending so much time inside the house, Honey jumped at the chance to help in the garden. After that, gardening became a ritual for the pair. It was not until the foliage began to bud that Honey realized that England was not so dreary a place after all. The grass began to turn green and the buds on the trees burst into leaves. Lilacs exploded into frothy waves of lavender and white. Honey happily rediscovered butterflies and grasshoppers, bluebirds and robins. The cool blue skies gathered as the sun warmed the land.

The temperature stayed constant, never really becoming too warm, and on nicer days Master Montgomery moved his classroom outside for the reading lessons, which lasted for most of the four hours set aside for her tutor.

Though Jillian often ignored the bare toes that wiggled under Honey's skirts, never did she allow her charge outside without benefit of a wide straw hat. Honey's tan was only beginning to fade, and Jillian wanted nothing but smooth white skin on her in time for London's winter season. With luck and some careful planning, winter season would serve as Honey's introduction to society.

Perhaps that introduction would not be needed, she thought. She peered out from Honey's window to where the teacher and pupil sat on a ground cloth, stacks of books flanking them. Jason's head bent close to Honey's as he pointed to something in the book she held.

Jillian had not failed to notice the growing affection Jason was beginning to show for his student. Why else would Jason make such a special attempt to make learning a pleasure? Honey concentrated on the passage he pointed to in the book, her delicate features registering nothing but the mildest of interest in the speaker. Perhaps she was not ready to have an interest in a young man yet, Jillian thought. That was too bad, for Jason was a near-perfect solution for Chris's ward. As members of the working class, Jason's friends and relatives would have very little interest in Honey's family lines, if there were any. A few endorsements from Chris would be enough to pull a good salary for Jason, enough to support Honey and a home and maybe a servant or two in the bargain.

With that arrangement, Honey would never be regarded as a woman of quality, but then neither could she be considered one without a past. Yet there were indications that the child had not been of low birth.

Jillian broke off her speculations and turned back to Honey's room. She again sorted through the box that Honey deemed her treasure chest. This earbob . . . She had seen one like it before, even remembered admiring it, but where? By the linkage of the stones she could see it was an heirloom. The older woman shook her head. Probably a friend had a similar set. But it bothered her that the value of this single bob was probably twice that of some of the pieces in her own fine collection, and her sets were of the best quality. She was surprised that Honey had left it in her room. Usually the girl brought it with her wherever she went, attaching it to her collar or sleeve.

Jillian smiled, slipping the bob into her pocket. Perhaps she would have it fixed so Honey could wear her prize all the time. She looked back to the box: two silver combs and a man's lion-head ring—an odd assortment for a child to end up with. A drowning child, floundering about the sea, grasping an earbob, two silver combs, and a man's ring? Why? How could it have happened? The older woman shook her head and once again tried to push Honey's mystery from her mind.

Chapter Ten

Marcus Long sat alone at his favorite table. The club he most often frequented, The Jack an' Dandy, catered more to fops than sailors. The decor was evidence of that—lacy curtains draped with crimson velvet and trimmed in gold. White linen covered even the gaming tables, and crystal mugs rather than the standard tin or pewter were used for ale. But then, Marcus conceded, he rather enjoyed being a fop when in England. Wigged in a long curling blanket of gray, mustached cavalier style, he was drowning in yards of frothy lace at throat and cuffs. He sat bolt upright in his padded chair, one buckled shoe placed slightly ahead of the other while he carefully sipped his ale. His dark eyes snaked looks here and there, as if taking attendance in the almost deserted room.

"Marcus, my friend," Chris chuckled from behind. "I almost didn't recognize you."

"It worries me not that you did," Marcus laughed, noting how completely out of place his big, hard-bodied friend looked against these frilly trappings. "Sit. How long are you in port? Or better," he wiggled his brows in jest, "when do you plan to deport?"

"Perhaps weeks. The last cargo was tossed out during a storm. Or most of it was. The rest rotted into the boards. The deck of the cargo hold might have to be replaced; the stench would kill a buzzard. That doesn't count the repairs that have been held up due to a certain partner of mine."

"Ah, Humphrey . . . yes. Met him just last season at Brentwood. Insufferable twit. Sail him in Bloodwell's path, we'll make you an independent businessman." Marcus chuckled as he pulled his glass toward his mouth. Were the club not empty, Marcus Long would never have made reference to his alter ego. I.B. Bloodwell, privateer turned pirate, was the newly appointed earl of Brentwood. However, on occasions of extreme boredom, Marcus Long disappeared and the infamous Bloodwell shared the colonial seas with the likes of Ned Teach, better known as Blackbeard. Much to the new earl's disappointment, he was able to sail much less frequently now.

Still, on other occasions the earl was inclined to dandy about London, bedding, among others, the Lady Jennifer Bates, the widow of his predecessor. This fact was not new to Christopher, nor was Marcus rogue enough to inquire of Chris's mating habits with the lady. It was enough that they knew of each other and worked to keep the relationship amicable.

Chris laughed, "Good thought, except the twit himself doesn't sail."

"Doesn't sail?" The long-faced dandy sat back in his chair squinting one eye at his friend. "Pray, why not?"

"I've had it on good authority that he has an aversion to the sea," Chris muttered, signaling the waiter.

"Sickness?" Long's jaw came close to the table as he thought of a nonsailing man running a merchant shipping company. "Gawd! I never can get this straight. How the bloody hell did a landsman get into that company?"

Chris had often wondered the same thing. "My father, George Ames, and Jacob Wingfield were best friends; they started the company—each sailing his own ships. After Jacob's disappearance and Christine and Crystal were mur . . . he married Jacob's sister. I believe they married the day of the estate reading."

"Convenient." Marcus shook back his hair.

"Yes. Well, no matter. We have made an agreement and he stands by it, so . . . But there is another matter that I must ask about. 'Tis a matter of urgency as well as one of great . . . delicacy . . . After the storms we encountered last February, we stumbled upon an island not too distant from New Province. There was a girl on this island, a lass of perhaps eighteen or so. She had been there for at least ten years."

Marcus placed an elbow on the table and rested his chin on the heel of his hand. Chris's story drew his interest.

"And you have told no one of this?"

"Only asked if anyone has had word. It is not so impossible that someone would have heard of a ship that simply vanished on its way to somewhere."

"Like Wingfield's *Crystal Wing*?" Marcus supplied.

"Like that, yes." Chris agreed, averting his eyes almost defensively. "Should someone ask, I could find the names of that crew."

"But the cargo or location of the loss? I think not. In one respect, you are right. Many in London have relatives that sailed off and never returned. I just happen to be off to the . . . er . . . wet country next week, and I shall ask about it for you." Marcus smiled. "Perhaps one of my ah . . . tenants will have known of a booty containing children's things. Perhaps a cotton grower's family or such. I say, could that young thing be the same one that I have heard about—that sits in her window every morning communing with the birds?" Marcus smiled wickedly. He had not seen her, but a neighbor had.

"Something tells me it is," Christopher grimaced, averting his eyes to scan the club for eavesdroppers.

"And for tonight, have you a plan for the theater and ahem . . . such?" Marcus continued to grin. It had been a long week since he had seen Lady Jennifer.

Chris shook his head. "Enjoy." He grinned, signaling a waiter.

As it turned out, neither of the pair paid a call on the lady that evening. In fact, by the dinner hour, each was well into his cups and another round of cards.

Jennifer turned from the windows that overlooked her driveway. Her dark indigo velvet gown whispered as she moved. Her ebony hair, coiffed to perfection, was left unpowdered to reflect the deep blue of her gown. Unpredictable lot! Both of them, she thought. Only a few hours earlier it had been reported to her that Chris had been seen at a club, entertaining Marcus Long, of all people. She frowned as she envisioned them sitting at the same table. The picture was not amusing. Perhaps they had simply been biding their time until her guests departed. But her guests had left long ago, one of them with the intention of passing by that very club.

A couple of discreet words should have been enough to get one or the other men moving in her direction . . . possibly both. She smiled at the thought as she poured a dram of sherry. Then her lips pursed tightly and she scowled into the crystal goblet. She should not have turned William away; at the very least, she would have had company for the night. His wife, having taken to their country home for the summer, left William free to dally quite often. And while his talents were somewhat less than those she would have preferred, William never failed to enlighten her with some news of Christopher's exploits and bits and pieces of his past. These candid remarks, coupled with the coy, impromptu questions she tossed Chris's way, gave her a little more insight into the details of his tragic life.

Of course, she learned that William could tell a tale or two—especially if it meant some sort of gain for his trouble—and often as not her challenge lay in distinguishing fact from fiction. There was no doubt in her mind that most of William's tales were jealous little stories meant to undermine any interest she might have in Chris. The two were practically related, and would have been had Wingfield and his family survived. It was that bloody past that made him so unreachable. Jennifer crossed the room to ease into the settee in front of the fire. One hour passed, then another before she extinguished the lamps and took to her bed, but it was another hour still before her anger let her sleep.

Chris leaned back against the curtained wall. He was drunk beyond all his expectations. Marcus lay face-down on the linen cloth on the other side of the table. Snores emanated from his mouth, his hands still curved around the glass he had earlier accused of running away from him.

Chris rolled his head to the side. They had been reminiscing about their school days, days with their fencing masters, and . . .

His smile faded, his mirth-filled eyes stared unseeing at the floor. He was mounted for a ride on that summer day in July when the rider came up the drive, his horse frothing from the long gallop.

"What is it?" His father stumbled out the front door.

"The Missus Wingfield and the young 'un is missing. Gone in the night. My Mrs. Huff went to awaken the mistress this morning to find her bed empty and the child's, too!"

"And you heard nothing? I don't believe it. Do you know what you're saying, man!" Disbelief etched his father's face.

"Mr. Ames, you know as well as me that my mistress wouldn't leave her man ever! I'm saying they've been taken in the middle of the night. The mistress hadn't taken a stitch with her. Nor the child."

George Ames headed the search that lasted well into the weeks that followed. A ship had been sent out to locate Jacob, who had set sail for Persia two weeks before and was not due to return for another four. The search had turned up nothing but the prints of two horses cutting diagonally across the green fields. The woman after whom he had been named, Christine Wingfield, and her six-year-old daughter, Crystal, who had been promised as his bride, were gone.

Chris had loved the stubborn little girl he was to have married someday. His favorite saying when she misbehaved with him had been, "You won't get away with that once we're married!" Then he would lay his arms lordishly across his chest. But the little minx would tilt her head coyly and reply, "I shall do as I please, and it may not please me to marry you, sir."

He smiled at the memory. At nine years old one might think that he would have had better things to do than to tease a wild young girl that he would have only to tame after their wedding day, some ten years in the future.

Her decayed body was found several months later in a grove of trees only a few hundred feet from their house. It was a place that had been too obvious to search. Both bodies were stripped, and there was no way to tell how they had died. Robbers perhaps, or sailors out for revenge . . . To George Ames it was obvious that the pair had been attacked in the yard and robbed, and that the robbers fled fearing someone in the house would hear them. Yet they hunted for six months and no witnesses were found. The ship *Fire Wings* had returned from Persia reporting that Jacob Wingfield and the *Crystal Wing* had never arrived, nor had he been sighted anywhere near his intended destination.

The rumors spread quickly that Jacob had deserted his family, and there was speculation that he might even have been responsible for their deaths. Chris's father never once believed the rumors. He knew Jacob better than anyone. Unfortunately, he had no proof of what tragedy might have befallen his partner and close friend. He resolved to return to London and set sail himself, to call on every port between London and Persia until some word confirmed Jacob's innocence.

George ordered the woman and child buried in the family lots and took his own grief-stricken family back to London. They had gone but halfway when they heard the order, "Stand and deliver!" The Ames coach driver had no alternative but to pull up on the reins.

George had been prepared for the highwaymen, his pistol drawn. But as he leaped at his aggressor the other door of the carriage swung open and a shot rang out. His attention was diverted to his son, tossed face-first from the coach, and to his wife, who had stood in defense of her family. Thankfully the ball that found George's head did so before he witnessed the death blow delivered to his wife. Neither did he see the giant red stain that fed the earthen road beneath his dying son. Nor would he ever know the woman who happened along to pluck his still-breathing son from the fate he would have received at the hands of scavengers.

In her thirties, Ida worked as a serving wench in a tavern in a village far from London, along the road that connected London to Chris's country home. To earn his keep, young Chris learned to clean out the stalls where peddlers stabled their horses and where folk of ill intent passed off secrets to their trade. He emptied chamber pots and swabbed the floors after the drunks had used them. At night he would retire to a stone pallet in Ida's pathetic little house and pretend not to hear the comings and goings of her many male visitors throughout the night.

He knew he should return to London and claim what was left, but he couldn't face the emptiness and the guilt that filled him for living. Meanwhile, at the faintest rumble of a passing coach, Ida would stop whatever she was doing and run to the door so she could look at the coach's coat of arms. For three years, she checked the insignia on every carriage that passed. Then one glorious day almost three years after the attack, Jillian Ames happened by. Ida had chased the coach well past the tavern before Jillian heard her frantic shouts and ordered the coach to stop.

The reunion was both happy and sad. Chris didn't want to leave Ida yet; she needed him. But no matter how Chris begged her, the woman refused to accompany them home.

"Please!" Chris had cried, clutching her hand as he tried to lead her to the coach. Ida only smiled. "Go back to yer fine world, boy; there's no place there for the likes o' me." She kissed his forehead, unaware of the money his aunt had stuffed in her shabby pocket. But someone must have seen it, for when Chris returned to Dunn three days later with trunks of clothes and a deed to a modest house near Kent, he found only a shallow grave bearing Ida's name and a tale so horrible he couldn't stand to hear it through.

He feared to love his aunt for many years after that. He was afraid that she too would be taken from him. But Jillian took her boy to the country, to an old and trusted friend, and together they managed to help Christopher through his grief and through the guilt of being the only survivor of that terrible day. As these twelve years had passed, so had the grief and much of the loneliness.

But now there was Honey. Why must her eyes be so green? Why did her mouth beg to be kissed? Worse, why was she not Crystal? He wondered again how she might have looked had she grown up, and if her stubborn childish charm would have turned to love for him. Who knew but that she might have grown to resent him. Having been betrothed since birth, she wouldn't have been allowed any male callers and social events would have been extremely limited. While he would have been free to dally as he pleased. Crystal would never have stood for that, he was sure.

She had a stubbornness much like Honey's.

Chris glanced at Marcus, who was trying to pull himself upright. "Did we have another?" he asked stupidly.

Chris's head bobbed up and down. "Two more."

"Drinks?" The pirate swayed in his chair, his long wig slightly off kilter, his brows arched high in surprise.

"Jugs," Chris supplied with a sly grin.

"Oh, I say, the lady will be quite peeved, to be sure."

"To be sure," Chris chuckled drunkenly.

"Does her good to be left alone once in a while."

"To be sure. Steward!" Chris called across the now-busy room. "A boy, room, bring us a boy . . . No, wait. A room, boy, bring us a room . . ." His eyes rolled back as he slid back against the wall; his chair slipped forward and he sank to the floor.

"Can they do that?" Marcus watched with fascination as his friend slouched to the floor. "I say, that's the first time I've ever seen that." His head swayed loose on his shoulders before it too lolled to the table in drunken slumber.

Chapter Eleven

Both sets of French doors had been flung open, allowing the rays of the morning sun indoors. Honey breathed the scents of a warm English spring. The smell of fresh earth turned by Jillian and her gardener drifted in with the breeze, making concentration on her lessons much too difficult.

"Your mind is wandering again, Miss Honey," Jason smiled as he spoke. He too had forgone his usual black cloth suit for one of light brown, carefully trimmed with satin piping. It was quite out of character for a schoolmaster.

Honey looked over at her tutor. Her gaze had indeed strayed to the back doors, where the greys of winter had turned to luscious greens. She smiled a bit sheepishly. "Does spring always cause one's mind to wander?" she asked, a smile lightening her eyes.

"Yes, I dare say," Jason laughed. "If it is that difficult a task, perhaps we shall have to forgo the lessons and engage in something more in tune with the day. We could go outside and . . ."

"Would you teach me how to dance?" she asked.

"Why ever would you want to learn that?"

She didn't miss the adoration in his eyes this time.

"Well, I . . . I don't know, but . . ." she looked down at her feet then back at Jason.

"I am teasing you. Wanting to dance on such a fine day is not so out of the ordinary. But I confess to being a little surprised that you don't already know how."

A flush covered her cheeks. "Just another one of those things." A coy smile lifted the corners of her mouth.

How many times since she learned that phrase had she used it? More than she cared to count. But it kept her from lying to a man she liked very much. Jason didn't stumble over the delicate questions she sometimes put to him about men and women, as Geoff had, and he seemed to like her, despite her coloring and temperament. He had patience for her frustrations and helped her work her way through the problems of understanding words or numbers. She somehow knew that he was teaching her far more carefully than he would any other student. Most of all, he didn't treat her like a child the way everyone else did.

"You should know by now, miss, that there is little I would deny you."

Honey flushed under the caress in his deep tenor voice and devoted gaze.

"Come," he laughed. Snapping her book shut, he led her by the hand toward the open area near the French doors.

"This is a dance from Germany, but it doesn't have a name." He turned her to face him, placing her left hand on his shoulder and his right hand at her waist. Then gripping her right hand in his left, he curled his arm into his chest so that the back of her right hand rested over his heart.

"Do you recall left from right?" he asked.

"Yes," she replied, looking down at her feet.

"Good. Take one step back with your left foot, then step to the right, then step toward me. Ready? One, two." Her left foot moved back, then she moved the same foot to the right, tripping over Jason. Jason caught his pupil and steadied her before she hit the floor. "Oh, no, I mean back with your left foot, to the right with your *right* foot." Jason paused as he peered at the floor just below the hem of her dress. "Are you wearing shoes?"

She looked guilty as she shook her head. "You won't tell, will you?"

"No," he whispered back. His eyes scanned the room as if to search for spies. "Well then, just put your feet on top of mine," he said quietly, bringing his gaze back to hers.

"What?" She looked scandalized, then giggled as she complied.

"Oh!" The word came unbidden from her throat as his feet began to move beneath her own, first back, then to the side. Then he twirled, sending her skirts flying out around them both.

Honey laughed out loud, little giggles erupted at every turn. The room spun past her as he exaggerated his steps, his eyes and his smiles never leaving her face.

"Enough," she cried as the dizzying effect began to gnaw at her empty tummy. "Please, Mr. Mont . . . Oh, Jason, please stop," she laughed. Her hair whipped around her shoulder as he came to a sudden halt. Flushed with the movement and the warmth of the breeze that wafted through the open doors, she looked up at her companion.

"I think I have it now," she laughed.

"You're sure? I *am* wearing shoes, so you'd best be prepared," he grinned devilishly.

"Yes, really," she smiled, assuming the stance once more.

"Start on your left," he instructed, "and don't watch the floor, you'll make yourself dizzier."

"Oh, I like that." She laughed at his teasing. Settling into their pose, the pair moved clumsily at first, but he was careful not to step onto her toes, and even though she failed to do the same, she managed to do very little damage.

"There, I think you're ready for the next lesson. Now we'll add the spins." He stopped the box step that they had been doing. "The first turn we do together to the left, then we break," he said, dropping her hand. "And you turn alone away from me." With a twitch of his wrist he directed her turn. "Ready?"

She nodded, feeling his hand at her waist. There was something strange about letting a man handle her so, she thought. Then Jason began to hum again and they moved to his music.

"Left turn," he sang, twirling her to the left. "Now break, come around . . . Good!" He smiled broadly as she danced under his arched arm and back into his fold, her face set so prettily determined and self-satisfied that he couldn't help laughing. Her downcast eyes flashed up and she smiled too.

"I did it perfectly, didn't I?" Her smile was warm and her eyes sparkled in merriment. It felt good to move about. It must have been all that sitting, she thought, that had made her cranky the last few weeks.

"Ready to stop?"

"Oh, no. Can you teach me another?"

"Surely. Here is one new even to France. Let me see . . . Step in and back, and bow and spin." His forefinger rubbed his chin thoughtfully. "Yes, I think I know all the steps. Put your arms up like this . . ." He took her hands, holding them over her head. "Now step back, drop this hand, right . . . Now back-to-back and take a sidestep . . . Yes, that's right," he said, dropping her hand and turning his own back to her and stepping twice to the left.

"Turn in; now drop your left hand and arch your right to meet my hand over our heads, left hands in front low. That's right. See how it makes a circle? Now, if we turn away from each other . . ." He spoke as they turned, and, true to the dance, their hands folded up and over their heads as they turned back-to-back and came to stand face-to-face.

"How'd that work?" she demanded laughingly. "I thought sure we'd be tied in knots."

"I thought so too, the first time I tried it," he said. "But it works out every time. Want to try it again?"

"Yes, I would, but . . ." The sudden shyness that overtook her appeared from nowhere. His hands were hot and damp in hers. She glanced at the open French doors, wondering where Jillian had gotten to and hoping she was still within earshot.

"Are you getting tired?" He lost his smile.

"No, I'm not tired." She wished she could pull her hands from his without being rude.

"Once more then?" he asked. "Ready and go . . ."

He hummed a tune that brought her cream-colored skirts swishing back from her stockinged feet, then turned her in to do the sidesteps. The pair moved around the room in dance. Her eyes followed her feet until he caught her arm to bring the left down to join with his and sent the right arcing up over her head. Suddenly they were face-to-face. Jason halted the dance, looking deep into those green eyes as if searching for something he had lost there. His lips were moist; his smile was gone. Her lighthearted smile vanished and she was lost in the moment as his head bent slowly toward hers. Only a whisper of air separated them as her heart thudded lightly in her chest.

"What kind of education is this?" The deep booming voice knocked the young couple off balance.

Jason snapped upright but refused to take the expected step back from the woman he had been about to kiss. Honey didn't know enough to move away. Both sets of thoroughly startled eyes came to rest on Christopher, filling the door. He was dressed for the sea.

"Is this your manner of teaching, tutor? To make love to innocents who have no knowledge of passion?"

"I beg your pardon, sir!" Jason retorted. "Should I find it to be any of your business, I would happily explain. But I owe you nothing."

Honey watched Christopher's features assume the same expression as the night he had thrown her into the bathtub.

"No, wait . . ." she pleaded, as unsure of what was taking place now as she was of what would have happened had Christopher not interrupted. "He was teaching me to dance, Christopher, that's all."

"You are defending this molester?"

"Christopher!" Jillian's shocked voice echoed through the French doors. "What is the meaning of that statement!"

"It seems, dear Aunt, that I have entered the room here in time to save your charge from receiving her first kiss."

Honey colored at Jillian's gasp.

"Mr. Montgomery!" she breathed, rushing to Honey's side. "Is this true, child?" she asked, pulling her charge away from Jason and placing a protective arm around the frightened girl.

Honey's gaze traveled from Jillian to Chris then to Jason, whose crimson face had turned toward her. "There is no need to lie to protect me, Honey," he said angrily.

"I . . . I don't . . ." She dragged her eyes from her tutor's and looked back at Jillian. "I don't know what that is." Tears gathered in the green pools of her eyes. "I don't understand why everyone is so angry."

Jason's horrified gasp was the first sound uttered.

"I cannot believe that you could misunderstand my intentions! What has all of this been about? I thought there was some trust between us." His lips curled back from his teeth as he spoke. His eyes were hard and filled with betrayal. Chris strolled further into the room.

"I have done something wrong again, haven't I?" She trembled, her wide eyes averted from Jason's angry face.

"She's not lying to you. This is as innocent a maid as you could ever hope to find. Whatever story you have been told, the truth is that she lived alone on an island from the age of six. She has been here in England only two days longer than you have known her, and while I don't discount the fact that most women are devious by nature, this one has hardly had time to grow accustomed to shoes, much less to acquire the cleverness to deceive you."

"I don't believe this!" Jason hissed. His dream of life with Honey crumbled with her lies. The pain was so great he was compelled to lash out in hatred. He needed to hurt her as she had hurt him. "Are you saving her for yourself? No decent scholar will cross this threshold when I'm through . . ."

Jason hadn't time to finish his sentence before Christopher was upon him, dragging the smaller man up by the collar.

"You smear this woman's good name and by the graces of God, I'll cut your lying tongue out myself. As her guardian, I have rights by law to keep her safe from molesters such as yerself. Now leave my presence before I have you exiled!"

Christopher threw the smaller man toward the door as Jillian placed protective arms around a startled Honey.

She watched in horror as Christopher tossed her friend across the room, unable to quell the sympathy she felt for Jason. Christopher followed Jason out the door of the library into the hall of the main house. He looked back at the women folded into each others' arms.

"You two have something to discuss, don't you?" he said before escorting the ex-tutor down the hall.

"He won't really hurt him, will he?" Honey trembled and tears finally spilled over the rims.

"Why—" Jillian gasped, "Honey, you're not in love with Jason! Are you?"

Chapter Twelve

"I don't know how you think we can do justice to this woman in only three days!" Madame DeVries stated again in distress as she remeasured Honey's waist and length. "Turn, please. Arms up." She glanced at Jillian. "You tell that nephew of yours to hire another next time!"

Jillian only managed to shake her head in empathy. In one day, less than twenty-four hours, Christopher had managed to upset not only her own household but that of the seamstress, the shoemaker, and the stablemasters.

After showing Mr. Montgomery the door, Chris had gone on in a rage. He'd ranted about Honey's education and about the story they had told Mr. Montgomery about Honey's past and some strange account of a woman sitting in her window every morning in her nightgown communing with the birds.

"That's it!" he had thundered. "I rode in here to tell you I'd be gone for a while, and what do I find? My ward falling for the molestation of a degenerate tutor! Get your things packed. I'm not leaving this country until I'm sure you two can stay out of trouble!"

"Christopher! Really!" Jillian protested, "Anyone could have proved to be untrustworthy. Had your concerns been so great you should have taken the time to engage one more to your liking!"

"You are right, Auntie, so I have remedied that! As we speak, a runner carries a message to Franklin Stockwell. He will be expecting you within the next few days. He has assured me that he is willing to arrange his summer to take on the task of educating our ward. Now I have to go reorganize the ship that was due to depart on the morning tide. Thanks to a pair of women who desperately need an honorable man beside them, I have to see to it that extra rations are stowed aboard the *Wing Master*—now that we will be departing two days behind schedule." With that Chris had breezed from the house shouting, "Whatever is not packed by four o'clock on the morrow stays behind!"

"Oh, heavens. If we're to spend the summer in the country we'll need clothes." Jillian bustled off to write the necessary notes to be delivered that afternoon, then she set Katie and Brea to closing the house and packing. Somehow she had managed to work it all out before Christopher's deadline.

"I agree, madam; Christopher's decision is completely irresponsible. But what else can we do?" Madame DeVries shook her head again, glancing at the timepiece that rested on the shelf behind the counter. "We shall have just enough time to select hats before the carriage calls." Jillian moved from the fitting room to the counter.

"For myself, one bonnet of royal blue to match my cloak, and for the young lady, I think this russet will do for outerwear. Oh and be sure the ball gown is of royal blue velvet. The rest, be certain to do as before."

"The riding habit also in the dark russet?"

"No, no, let's see. Honey, you have yet to choose one thing. What color would you like your riding habit to be?"

Honey's eyes scanned the shop filled with bolts of cloth stacked so high she could hardly see from one row to the next. Her gaze came to rest on a bolt of palm green. "This?" She smiled hopefully.

"Oh, yes, the color is lovely. This," Jillian pointed to the green, "in velvet with a matching hat."

"Very well, but in three days? I don't know . . ."

"Fine. Can you do three of the dresses and the habit in three days?" Jillian began to pull on her soft kid gloves.

"Oh, yes, Miss Ames, that should not be difficult."

"Very well, send the rest with my maids. I venture we can do without for maybe two additional days."

"You are too kind, Miss Ames."

Honey couldn't tell if Madame DeVries's words were sincere or not, and Jillian acted as if she didn't care. Sarcasm was another part of life in civilization Honey was only beginning to understand.

The front door opened and closed somewhere behind the bolts of cloth, but Christopher's footsteps sounded on a sure path to the fitting room, as if he had been there before.

"Captain Ames!" Madame DeVries gushed as he rounded the last table. "How charming of you to call upon my shop again."

"Again?" Jillian said with a raised brow, the word both accusing and acknowledging her nephew's indiscretions at the same time.

Honey had watched the proceedings quietly. She

had learned that if she stood still and stayed quiet people would forget that she was nearby. More often than not, people had a tendency to leave out details when they realized she was present. But this situation went right over her head. She wondered which words, if any, were spoken in truth and which were meant as sarcasm. As for language, Jillian's manner seemed to speak as clearly as her voice, and it contradicted every word she said.

"Madame DeVries," Christopher nodded briskly, "You have treated my ladies well, I trust?" He smiled at Jillian then allowed only the briefest glance at Honey.

"Absolutely, Christopher," Jillian said. Chris nodded to the seamstress, who hastened to assist Honey down from the fitting stand.

"Honey?" Jillian handed the younger woman's cloak to her nephew, who slipped it over Honey's shoulders before doing the same for his aunt. Jillian led the group from the salon.

Outside, Chris held the coach door for his aunt as she raised her skirts to step up into its plush compartment. He offered less than the same courtesy to Honey, acting as if her touch might scald his hands. He scarcely waited for her to be seated before pushing the door closed and latching it.

"You're not riding with us?" Jillian peered through the small window.

"No." Chris stepped back from the black coach bearing the Ames crest on the door. "I'll ride behind."

"Are you sure?" she asked, a frown playing across her face. "You really need not come at all, you know. If it is too difficult . . . What I mean is, Charles has protected me quite well ov—"

"You needn't concern yourself." He turned from

the coach to keep her from seeing his expression.

Jillian eased herself back into her seat and sighed. He had been in a rare mood of late. She pulled her fan from her handbag and snapped it open. "That boy has me worried."

"Why? What is wrong?" Honey asked as the coach lurched forward. The driver found no easy path into the continuous stream of downtown traffic, and the women suffered several lurching starts and stops as the coach moved over the rutted roads.

"It is a long story, but one perhaps you are entitled to know. Chris was just fifteen the last time he took the road from Amesly. As far as I know, he hasn't returned to the country house since the day his parents were . . . You see, Chris's parents were murdered on that road many years ago." She took a breath and arranged her gown and hat before she continued. "It was always his family's habit to winter in London and spend each summer at the country estate just beyond Cardiff. His father's partner owned the adjoining estate. Well, it was the summer Jacob Wingfield disappeared, and his wife, Christine, and child, Crystal, were found dead only weeks after that. The gossip was that Jacob had sickened of being a married man and murdered them both, fleeing the country in his ship along with the very valuable cargo meant as a peace offering between the English throne and that of Prussia. Chris's father never believed his friend capable of such a coldhearted crime. George Ames deployed ships to search, but each returned without a hint of what might have happened to Jacob's ship. He refused to believe that Jacob would kill his wife or child. In truth, Jacob was just not that kind of man. He didn't believe in beating his wife or even—well, he was one of the most faithful men I have ever met. So it's likely he never reached his destination. And just recently, though I don't know where he obtained his information, Christopher has learned that pirates had naught to do with the disappearance, nor was Jacob's ship ever sighted around the islands or wherever it is that pirates go. So George packed up his family and set off for London. He was determined to set sail himself and find out what had happened to his friend." Jillian paused. "One would think he'd been off to find a brother, as close as the pair were. But they never made it to London. Highwaymen held up the coach long before they reached London, and when George refused to give up his purse he was murdered—along with his wife and Chris, too. Except that the ball meant for the child's brain only grazed the scalp of his head.

"Nonetheless, he would have died had a young woman not happened along. Somehow she managed to drag or carry Chris back to her home and nurse him back to health. He was but twelve years old then. He was a smart boy, but the shock of losing his family nearly killed him. He had his wits but didn't want to use them. He shunned the idea of returning to London. Instead, he stayed with Ida, helping her, so he says, to make a living. She was thirty years old and never knew who her parents were. And here was Chris, the only one left of two families who were closer than blood. Well, three years passed while I waited in London for some word of his whereabouts. You see, I was informed of the killings, but when Chris's body was not among them we thought perhaps someone was holding him for ransom."

"What is ransom?" Honey asked the question carefully, wanting to understand the entire story.

"That is when you steal something . . . that belongs to someone else . . . and, oh dear!" Jillian choked on the words while sticking her head out the window. "Driver! Pull up, I have forgotten something."

"What is it, Jillian?" Chris rode up on his huge chestnut, its hooves clattering in rhythm with the carriage horses. It was a pleasant sound.

"That item," Jillian glanced back at Honey, "the one I left at Damon's."

Chris nodded, "You are lucky we are not yet too far from the city." He wheeled his horse around and galloped back toward the center of town.

"Yes, that is fortunate," Jillian agreed, pulling herself back into her seat.

"Please, Aunt Jillian, finish the story," Honey prodded, her eyes set on the older woman's face.

"Oh, yes. Ransom is when you steal something that belongs to another, then you offer to sell it back for a huge sum of money. Often children are abducted and held for ransom; sometimes racehorses or pets or family jewels."

"And was she holding him for ransom?" Honey leaned forward, one gloved hand gripping the door handle.

"No, she was waiting and watching the road for a carriage with Ames coat of arms on it. She remembered the one on George's carriage and had faith that someone would happen by or even come looking for Chris. And she was right. But it took me three years to decide that I would never find Chris again, and since the courts would grant me no more time, I had been ordered to make my decision over which property I wanted to keep. I was awarded one of the two houses belonging to my brother. The other was to be turned over to the Crown. You see, rightfully, the one I had chosen to keep had been mine all along, but the court doesn't rule favorably for a woman, particularly one that has never married, but because of personal attendance to the queen, they granted leniency."

"Then how did you find him?" Honey sounded worried, as if the end of the story would change before Jillian had repeated all of it.

"I had chosen to keep my house in town, but also I was given permission to obtain the family portraits and whatever other heirlooms I wished to keep from the country house. So I was on my way down this very road. We were just passing a small tavern when Ida came running down the road, screaming for all she was worth. Lord! I thought she was being murdered herself, so of course I stopped." Jillian's voice tightened as she spoke. She opened her satchel to retrieve a handkerchief and pressed it to her nose.

"The irony is that had I ever been married, I'd have been in my husband's coach and Ida might never have . . . Forgive me," she said as her voice broke and tears flooded her eyes. "I didn't realize it would still affect me so deeply. Love is that way . . ."

"Where is Ida now?" Honey asked the somber question, amazed at her own strong feeling for a woman she didn't know.

"She is dead." Jillian sniffed again. "And I am ever so certain her death was my fault." Jillian dabbed at her eyes. "I was so grateful to her. We tried to persuade her to come back to London with us, and Chris offered her a partnership in a London tavern. He begged and pleaded, but Ida knew, as I did, that she would never be accepted into any society other than the one she already lived in. There was no place in our world for her, so I gave her all the money I had with me—it was a substantial amount—and then I don't know what happened. I sent a courier to her with another offer, a gift of a small farm, large enough for her to live comfortably for the rest of her life. But my courier returned to tell me that Ida was dead." Jillian watched the countryside pass by her window as she paused. "I just know she was killed over that money I gave her. I didn't think to be more careful about who saw the bundle . . ." Jillian paused to dab at her eyes again. She suddenly looked tired and frail. "Chris must have known, but he never spoke of it. And I didn't ask because I didn't want him to know about the farm."

"I don't think you could have been more careful, Aunt Jillian." Honey moved over to sit beside Jillian. "Truly, it is something that I have learned from you, just as I have had to learn in which order to put on my shift. You cannot know what you might be doing wrong unless someone who does know tells you so." Honey's arms wrapped themselves round her adopted aunt. "I think what you did was lovely. I think Ida would not blame you for trying to help her make her life better. I know, for as happy as I thought I was on the island, I am happier now with you."

The old woman looked into the eyes of the youth beside her and pulled her adopted niece close. "God has blessed me," she sighed, and she added, to herself, *with two wonderful children.*

Chapter Thirteen

Chris cantered across the field and forced his way through a thicket. He was grateful for the chance to ride alone. It was becoming increasingly difficult to ignore Honey. The more she learned, the more her eyes lost that empty look. But at the same time, her innocence blossomed.

The image of her, flushed from dancing and staring so sweetly into Jason Montgomery's eyes, assaulted him. Her day dress had just come to swirl about her legs when he had walked into the room. At first he was angry because she had not been wearing shoes. But then he had seen that searching look . . . She truly hadn't guessed at what would have happened had he not walked in. Should she look at him like that but once . . . he would be the molester, not the defender. There was a part of him that wanted to be just that. But he was her guardian, and the title said it all.

Even so, he admitted to himself, she stirred in him all the questions he had thought were quieted in his heart. Did Jacob kill his own family? Did he plot to kill his partners? If he had not, why had he not returned to claim *Sea Wings* in the three years that

Chris had been lost? Nor had he petitioned the Crown for his holdings, which were passed less than eight months later to Jacob's sister, Elizabeth, and her new husband, William Humphrey, who perchance happened to marry on the very day the court made its decision. Chris hadn't even known that Jacob had a sister, but once he met her, though, there could be no doubt that they were of the same family. Elizabeth resembled her brother closely; she was more a handsome woman than a beautiful one. She was not pretty until one got to know her, and her manner, which like her brother's, was warm and friendly.

As a child, Chris had called him Uncle Jake, and the three of them—Jake, Chris, and his father—spent nearly all of their time together at the shipyard inspecting ships, at the shipyard offices planning new ships, at one another's homes sipping brandy and talking ships, but best of all, together on the sea.

Christine Wingfield and Regina Ames often took their sewing and conversations to the parlor to let the men talk of their beloved craft, for they were happy to be friends themselves. The only disappointment was Christine's inability to carry a child through pregnancy. She conceived often, but just as often suffered miscarriages.

Chris only vaguely remembered those first months when Christine had gone through her last pregnancy. His mother, Regina, had moved into the Wingfield house and ordered all men out. Seeking to divert Jacob's nerves, George had taken his friend and Chris on a trip to the Orient. Chris smiled as he recalled Uncle Jake's look of panic at the thought of leaving his wife to suffer through her pregnancy alone. His father had laughed. "Come now, Jake, you've done what you need to do. Leave the rest to the women; believe me, you won't be missing anything.

They'll bring you a fine heir, or maybe a bride for our boy here, a spirited daughter to hold this boy on a straight course." George gave a hearty laugh at the disgust on his son's face. But Uncle Jake had soon joined in the humor, and the three of them spent four months sailing the Indian Ocean, arriving home two weeks before the birth of Crystal, his betrothed—the one who died just weeks after her sixth birthday. It was for her, not just for Honey, that Chris was setting sail again. This time not as a merchant but as a man needing to close the book on his past. He meant to accomplish two things: find out what happened to Jacob Wingfield and the *Crystal Wing*, and give a name to the woman who was a constant reminder of what he had lost.

A sudden chill washed over him, pulling him back from his thoughts. His horse had stopped and he wondered how long they had been standing in the small, vaguely familiar clearing. Glancing about for his bearings, his eyes discovered the sign carved by his own hand—a weathered piece of wood cut as a headstone sticking crookedly out of a grassy mound. It said simply, "Ida, may your rest be more peaceful than your life."

Chapter Fourteen

It was almost dark before Honey saw Christopher's horse gallop up behind the carriage. He was a commanding figure, riding tall in the saddle and strangely comforting to watch.

"He is back," she announced, looking out the window directly behind Jillian's head.

"Oh, good. I was beginning to worry," Jillian said as the carriage bumped along the pitted road.

"Do you think he stopped in that town?" she asked, trying to sound unconcerned. Why his stopping in that town should bother her, she hadn't a clue. Some emotions were still too new to figure out. But the picture of him standing over a dead woman's grave and wishing she were still alive made her stomach churn. Everyone he'd ever loved was dead now, except Jillian. His predicament was not that much different from her own, except that she had only one person to remember. The image of Barley Boe loomed in her mind. He had been there at first, and she never questioned his presence. An old sailor and a delicate child dressed in silks. He had taught her where the tide pools were, how to get the fruit from the trees when she was hungry, and what fruits helped her at certain times.

He had called her Honey.

They had been on the island perhaps a month before he had to go away, telling her not to follow him. He was firm when he told her to practice everything he'd taught her.

But Honey had been too young to understand. She'd cried as she tried to follow him, but finally he'd spanked her. And now the pain surged through her just as it had that day on the island.

She hadn't understood when she found him dead, decayed, and half buried by his own hand on the side of the island where the big turtles came to bake in the sun and make baby turtles. He had told her from the start she must never go there because the turtles were bigger than she was, and one never knew what a turtle might eat. She hadn't understood why until just that moment. He had told her that because he had not wanted her to see him die. Although it was *his* ring in her treasure chest, his real parting gift to her had been her life. Without that short time together, without those few lessons, Honey knew that she would have died of starvation. He had taught her how to survive.

"What are you dreaming about, child?" Jillian's voice interrupted her thoughts.

"I was just thinking about the island, about Barley Boe. He took care of me there."

"What?" Jillian started. "I thought you were alone on the island."

"I was when Christopher found me, but when I was little Barley Boe was there. He taught me how to hunt for the crabs and how to get food from the trees. He dug the water hole and taught me which grasses were sweet enough to eat."

"Does Chris know this?" Jillian leaned forward in her chair.

Honey shrugged. "I don't know."

"Well, where did this Barley Boe come from?"

"I don't know that, either. All I know is I woke up one morning and we were on the island. Every time I try to think beyond that my head hurts awfully."

"That is a nasty scar you have there. I thought when the time was right we would cut your hair to cover it. No one will see it then."

Honey smiled and nodded, not really caring if any one saw her scar or not.

"What happened to Barley Boe?" Jillian dug in her bag for a crochet hook and thread.

"He died, I guess," Honey smoothed her skirt and adjusted her small cape as she nestled closer into the corner. Fatigue was beginning to take hold.

"You can not guess such a thing, my dear. Either he died or he left the island. Which was it?"

"He went away from me, to the part of the island where the turtles come. He told me not to follow him, but I did, many days later. He could not see me or hear me, and he didn't move at all. And he looked all funny and bumpy, sort of . . ."

"He died—you are right. Tell me no more," Jillian wrinkled her nose in distaste. "And you saw no one after that?"

"No, only the ships flying back and forth across the sea."

"You speak as if you were Crystal herself! That child . . . what a match she would have made for Chris! Often she would say that Chris had best mind himself or she'd leave *him* for the sea."

Honey started at the sudden pain at her temple and unconsciously massaged her scar. She wanted to laugh, knowing that Chris often said "Women are a curse to a seagoing vessel!" Something told her it was indeed a tragedy that that little girl died before her time.

"Yes, the jolting is beginning to jar my bones, too." Jillian glanced at Honey. "Open that door there and tell the driver to pull up for dinner and a rest."

Honey opened the door and repeated what she had been told. The rush of wind through the small door smelled of horse and road dust, and suddenly she experienced the distinct feeling that she had done this before.

Chris pulled his horse up beside the carriage as it rumbled up the drive to Amesly.

Though it was well past midnight, the manor was blazing with light from attic to cellar. The oaks and pines along the drive had grown over the years. The oaks now umbrellaed over the drive and the pines stood as shadowy sentinels behind.

Hastings, the butler, waited outside the open door for his master . . . a master he had not seen in twelve years. Chris saluted the older man before he slipped from the saddle to open the door for the ladies. Jillian had awakened as the carriage came to a stop, and now she emerged with all the grace she could muster. Honey's eyes, however, refused much more than a weak flutter as she was carried from the carriage by her guardian.

"Are we there, Mother?" she murmured as Chris mounted the stairs to the front door. "Can I play with the puppies?" The sweet voice faded as her eyes rolled back and her lashes settled over her high cheekbones.

"Mother?" he grumbled, "now I'm a mother . . . !" But then he stopped dead, dropping to the steps with Honey in his lap. "Honey? Can you hear me? Where are you with your mother? Where are the puppies? Honey!" He tossed a glance at Jillian, who watched in frustration, then turned his full attention on Honey. His right hand gripped her face.

"What!?" she answered testily after he'd shaken her again.

"Where are you? Where are the puppies?" He searched her face.

"I am wherever you have brought me!" she snapped, "and I haven't any puppies!" She pulled herself from his hold. "And I'll thank you not to shake me like that again!" She pressed a hand to her forehead as if to ward off a pain before straightening her bonnet, then jumped from his lap. Raising her skirts, she ran up to where Jillian waited at the door.

"Honey, you have never spoken so strongly before!" Jillian lectured lightly.

"Oh, he makes me so very angry sometimes!"

"And one would almost think he liked it." Jillian looked down at Christopher, still sitting on the steps. "Are you tired, my dear?" she asked Honey.

"No, the nap was just enough to refresh me." Honey attempted to shake the cobwebs from her mind. The self-assuredness she felt only seconds ago had passed, leaving an unsettled feeling.

"Hastings, the small trunk to Miss Honey's room; the rest to mine, if you please."

"Yes, madam. Dinner awaits you in the dining hall. Will there be anything else?" The servant inclined his head as he spoke.

"No, thank you, Hastings. We'll have a bit to eat then we'll be for bed. Honey, is there anything you require?"

"No, ma'am," she said, following Jillian's sweeping steps through the main room, each woman plucking at her gloves as they moved through the foyer to the dining hall.

Jillian waved away the servants as she entered the wide hall.

"So much space," Honey said, working to ignore the growing throb at her temple.

"Country parties," admitted Jillian. "There is a hearth outside near the back gardens. George loved to have his food torched out there, and covered in some sort of spiced honeyed sauce he'd discovered in Italy. He thought, of course, that because he loved the concoction that everyone would, so he had huge garden parties and everyone would bring their plates outside to eat—except when it rained. Then they would all bring their plates inside." Jillian laughed. "George had an uncanny knack for planning his outdoor parties on rainy days." She fell silent for a moment, as if in memory of the dear departed, then looked at Honey. "Chris tells me they eat much the same way in the colonies! Imagine, cooking over open fires. Perhaps we shall have to see if Chris recalls how that was done."

"He does." Chris dropped into a chair at the foot of the table. "But I venture Hastings recalls as well, since I won't be staying for supper."

"You can't mean that you plan to turn back tonight, Chris," she protested. "That's nonsense!"

"No, Jilli, I do not plan to go back tonight, but by noon tomorrow you two will be well into that conversation you have to finish, and won't even realize that I have gone."

Honey cast a glance at Chris, feeling her ire rise,

but she followed Jillian's example and turned back to the food trays placed at the sideboard. She selected fowl and seated herself near the head of the table, taking pains not to look at Chris or admit that she felt frightened that he planned to go on a trip that would take him far from here—far from her.

"I should think it is time for Honey and I to speak of her experiences on the island as well," he said, lifting a brow. "We have not spoken of the island at all, and what you have told Geoffrey means nothing."

"He is a mind reader." Jillian laughed at Honey's astonished expression as she sat down with her plate at the head of the table. "We spoke of that very thing on the road, which reminds me, what have you done with the package you retrieved?"

Chris reached into the pocket of his coat and withdrew a small foil box. He offered the box first to his aunt, who waved it away, so he placed the box beside Honey's plate instead.

"What is this?" she asked.

"A gift from Jillian, I assume," he replied with a raised brow. He moved over to the sideboard and helped himself to food and drink.

Honey's fingers moved gingerly over the cover of the small package before pulling the top off. Nestled in a swath of lace lay the earbob-turned-brooch. The wing-shaped filigree wires had been polished to a high luster, while the sapphires and diamonds twinkled in the candle-lit room.

She gasped in the silence. "Jillian, I don't know what to say. I would never have imagined this could be so beautiful . . . Ahh!"

Suddenly pain seared through her temple, blinding her, and the overwhelming sensation of falling filled her mind.

"Honey, what's wrong!?" She heard the words through the roaring wind in her head, but she could not say whose voice it was. Nor could she answer.

"Air, Christopher! Get her outside!" Jillian pulled Honey's chair away from the table and Chris scooped her up as she fell toward the stone floor. He maneuvered around Hastings and rushed through the kitchen and out the back door to the other side of the garden hedge. The cool wind doused them as he dropped to his knees, cradling Honey across his lap as if she were a child. He tried to pry her hands from either side of her head as he watched for some clue as to what was happening to her, some sign of what he might do to help her.

"Mother," she whispered, "come back. Don't leave me here. *Mother!*" Honey spun in the blackness, crying, clawing at the storm in her mind. It spun her on an endless journey through nowhere. Then very slowly the blackness receded, the pain began to ebb. The cool wind caressed her hot cheeks, and she realized without opening her eyes that strong warm arms held her. The tension that had knotted her body eased away, leaving a dull thud in her temples.

"What was it?" he asked, feeling her body relax. His voice was gentle, his hushed tones were deep and warm. "Tell me what you saw," he pleaded quietly.

"I saw nothing. I never do. It was black and," she shivered, "I was falling down a dark pit."

"And your mother was there?" he urged, waving Jillian back to the house.

"I didn't see her, but we seem to have been parted in the dark. I couldn't find her."

"Or did she leave you? You said, 'Don't leave me here.' Honey, were you abandoned?" His question betrayed his worst fear.

"Oh, no, . . . I don't think so. I seem to know that my mother is there, and I call and call for her and she never answers, and I'm so scared. I just don't know." Tears of frustration overwhelmed her. Burying her face in his shirt, she sobbed. "Will I never know who I am?"

"I didn't think it mattered so much to you," he said, caressing the back of her head, breaking the rhythm only long enough to dash a tear from his own eye.

"I've only just realized that it does," she admitted, pulling her head up and jerking the handkerchief from the sleeve of her dress. She dabbed her eyes.

"You were dreaming when you arrived in the carriage," he reminded her. "You said, 'Are we there yet, Mother? Can I play with the puppies?' Where were you? Do you remember the dream?"

"My dreams are all like that. But I can never remember any of them, only glimpses of people as I wake. For a moment they are there with me, then they're gone, not even a memory." She opened her eyes for the first time. The house glowed yellow behind them. In front of them, over the blackened hills and fields, the night sky salted with twinkling stars made this perch seem like the very edge of her universe.

"It was that pin. It must have belonged to my mother," she whispered.

"Probably," he agreed. "Let's get you inside before you catch your death."

"No . . . not yet. This place is so comforting, like the island. I can almost smell the sea . . ."

"You *can* smell the sea. We are not far inland and there is a port nearby."

"What is out there?" She pointed to the blackness before them as she eased herself carefully from his hold.

"Hills, fields, The rest of England."

She looked so innocent and helpless as she gazed at the vast blackness. He took a strengthening breath, "Come on, you have all summer to sit out here and dream of whatever it is you dream of. We'll talk in the morning." Chris pulled her to her feet, his warm arm encircling her waist in case she hadn't recovered from her spell. Taking his hand, Honey moved to stand but suddenly plunged headfirst into his chest. There was a sound of shredding fabric.

"My dress!" she cried as he danced clumsily from one foot to the other in an effort to free her pinned skirt. Supporting her with one arm, he tried to move free of her, but every step caused more damage. Finally he stood her upright and groped through the darkness for the shreds of her dress.

Honey was unable to stop the low rumble of a giggle that started deep in her throat and tumbled out in the form of outrageous laughter. The rake had stumbled in her presence, proving that the unsinkable Captain Ames was human.

"I should think we are even now, Mr. Ames," she laughed, pulling him upright as she recovered the shredded fabric from his hands. "I'll get that."

"Even?" He dropped the fabric he had managed to find into her hands. He was startled by her mirth, but after a moment he too began to laugh.

"I think not! You owe me at least two more shirts."

Jillian watched from the window of the house, worried for Honey. She wrung her hands, for she could see nothing but darkness from where she stood. But her worries eased when she heard laughter drifting through the garden. She smiled to herself. Chris was laughing out loud—how long had it been since she had heard him laugh? She couldn't even guess.

"Thank you, Lord," she whispered before going up to bed. "Thank you."

Chapter Fifteen

Barley Boe . . . the name rolled round Chris's mind for the third time. Barley Boe . . . there was something vaguely familiar about it, like many of the colorful names sailors chose. Barley could refer to malt ale. It could be a first or last name, or the man could have been named by his shipmates in reference to his attitude. In this case, ugly or bitter. But the presence of the man on the island explained a few things, such as her ability to harvest her own food, her habit of watching over the north bluff for ships, and the man's ring that had been found among her possessions. He might be able to find something out by passing the name around, but Barley Boe . . . He felt foolish just thinking the name.

He dragged a hand through his hair. He would concentrate on Barley Boe later. Right now his concern was for settling the past. He had to know once and for all what had happened to the *Crystal Wing*, and to Jacob Wingfield. That was the sole purpose of this voyage, for he'd learned that he could have no future without his past. He braced himself against the window frame of his own large second-floor room. Below, near the back edge of the sprawling gardens, the subject of his thoughts stood, barefoot and hatless, looking out over the rolling hills. During the gloom of this day the hat surely wasn't necessary, but he wondered if they would ever convince her to wear shoes. Another parallel to little Crystal, who had also hated shoes. He'd often caught her without them and threatened to tattle. Actually, he never really wanted the things he had extorted from her in this way, with the exception of one black puppy, but it did give him the power he longed to have over her. As a girl child she was strong willed, and her defiance often caused him to feel as if she were his equal. Man was supposed to be the leader, woman the follower—meek, mild, and gentle—but as often as he admired those qualities in Crystal, he found them tiresome, even unattractive, in other girls. "How fickle is man," he thought. The memory was strangely pleasant. Something in his belly fluttered. He had never experienced a pleasant memory before and he wondered what it meant.

"May I come in?" Jillian spoke from behind him. "There is a message from the *Wing Master*."

"Yes?" He turned from his daydreams to his aunt.

"Geoffrey is sailing round to meet you at Cardiff." The older woman smiled as she relayed the message, but something in her smile betrayed her feelings.

"That will save me some time, won't it? When does he expect to arrive?"

"Tomorrow."

"Tomorrow," he confirmed. "I see."

Jillian smiled; he looked as though the thought of spending too much time with Honey scared him to death. "You know, Chris, she is the very essence of what you missed most in your early life. You've been granted a second chance to see her grow up. Enjoy her now, for when you return from the sea she'll be a woman. Completely."

He glanced back to the window as Jillian crossed the room to join him. Their ward was playing tug-o-war with the stable dog and a scrap of rope. Already she was no longer the waif who had tried to hold the dancing flame of a bonfire in her hand. If such progress were possible in just two and a half short months . . . but it did not seem possible that she could ever be a woman completely.

"It must be this country air, Jilli," he teased, "but I am inclined to believe part of what you say."

"There is something else. I'd like to find a companion for her, a young lady, perhaps the daughter of a governess."

"Is that necessary?" Chris turned his attention from the yard to his aunt.

"It would give her a model, some idea of how a young lady behaves in public and around young men."

"You're not thinking of entertaining, I hope?" His eyes narrowed at the thought.

"Not right away, of course, but we cannot keep her locked up out here forever, you know. At the very least, we must return to London by mid-winter, before the roads become impassable. And since it sounds as though you don't plan to return before then, I must make plans."

"What you say is true. I had not thought of winter or of her need for a woman her own age. Do you have someone in mind?" The couple moved through the door to Chris's private rooms. Deep burgundies canopied the bed and covered the spread as well as the windows. He had been both surprised and relieved that these rooms had not sparked in him sad memories about his father and mother. On the contrary, he felt closer to them, as though his father had clapped him on the back and said, *"Welcome home, son."* That made him regret not having come home sooner.

"I thought Geoffrey's betrothed might have time to spare, since he is sailing with you," she suggested.

"Ariel, isn't it? If she is agreeable I see no problems with that." He paused, then asked, "Does Honey own a pair of sturdy shoes?"

"Why, of course. She has plenty of shoes." Jillian fought to suppress a smile.

"Well then, why don't you find me a pair and I'll take them to her." He surprised her with a gallant smile. "Perhaps I'll show Honey the horses. They are still here, aren't they?"

"I believe they are. Though I understand Molly died last winter, and she was the last of the original stock. You'll have to find names for the rest, I'm sure." She went to Honey's room and returned with the shoes. "Here you are."

"Thank you." He escorted his aunt down the stairs. Jillian kissed his cheek before moving off to the parlor to finish her sewing while Chris continued out the back door.

Honey growled back playfully at the large black dog whose lively jerks pulled her back along the narrow path behind the budding gardens of Amesly. She laughed as he growled again.

"You are a tough one, aren't you? Just like your master," she teased.

"I'm not sure I appreciate that remark." Chris's voice startled her, and she dropped her end of the rope. The black dog charged between them as Honey whirled to face the man she had just insulted.

The dog bared his teeth at Chris as he protected his

new playmate.

"Hush, Wheelock!" She dragged a hand over the dog's thick black head as she spoke, yet her eyes never left Chris's face. Something from last night's crisis and a conversation she had had with him this morning stayed with her—something warm and easy—yet she knew no name for it.

"Wheelock! Wherever did that name come from!" Chris halted, his brow knitting in a frown. His sudden change of attitude gave her pause.

"I . . . uh, the stableboy said that is his name. Is it not so?" Her gaze turned wary as he paled as if in pain. Then just as suddenly, color returned to his face.

"Must be named after his daddy, or granddaddy, by the looks of him." Chris laughed, allowing the mutt to sniff his upturned palm before scratching his ear with brisk strokes. "Wheelock was the name of my dog many years ago. He was left behind the last time we were here. Looks as though he kept himself busy."

"Oh." The meaning of his jest was completely lost on her. But that was something she was growing accustomed to.

"I've brought you something." He revealed the shoes he had been hiding behind his back. "I thought we would go through the stables, and you could choose a horse for yourself."

He was speaking to her as he had this morning—with less authority and more understanding. Rather than telling her to go and get her shoes, he had brought them to her—quite out of character.

"You'll see why you need them when we get to the stable." He smiled at her confusion.

Chris took her arm and led her to the bench just inside the garden gate, then he turned to admire the newly budding plants. Honey watched him as she hiked up her skirts to brush the earth from her feet. She felt awkward struggling into the stiff, ungiving shoes, awkward too because there was no common ground for conversation, no reason for his sudden interest in her choosing a horse.

"I thought you said you would be leaving today," she blurted out before thinking.

"Disappointed by my attention?" He dared a glance to be certain it was safe to turn back to her.

"Oh, no, that isn't what I meant at all," she stammered, glancing away from his face and willing her heart to slow its pace. The deep sound of his chuckle caused her to stare at him, wondering what could have possibly happened in the last day and a half to cause this change? Usually he could tolerate no more than several minutes in her presence, and except when addressing his aunt, a smile on his darkly tanned face was a rare thing indeed. Yet in less than thirty-six hours she had seen no fewer than three smiles and received a chuckle as well as a favor.

"I know what you mean." The dark look she was accustomed to came back to his face and she relaxed a bit. At least when his mood was bad she knew what to expect.

"Since you love the sea so much," she said, accepting his offered arm, "I thought you had already gone."

Chris brought her back through the gate and they strolled toward a long, two-story stable; to its left an oval whitewashed fence formed a training ring.

"As a matter of fact, I was about to do just that, but Geoff has decided to pick me up near Cardiff. The crew gets nervous should we stay in port too long. Too many fathers of soiled daughters, and too many bad-tempered wives, I suppose."

Soiled daughters? The phrase shook her. "I can not imagine them playing mean tricks on children!" Honey turned to look at Chris as she defended Geoff and his shipmates.

"Mean tricks?" Chris's brows knit together as he considered her statement. Her upturned face looked positively irate.

"I mean, to soil a child . . . What do they do? Push them into the street?"

"Oh . . . !" Chris's laughter rang out without warning. He wrapped one arm around his middle while he slapped his knee with the other, and tears actually slipped from beneath his closed lids. "I suppose that is something your companion will be able to explain." He wiped his eyes and caught his breath before resuming their stroll toward the stable.

Despite all her newly acquired education, when it came to dealing with this man she felt like a fool. His laughter stabbed at her, and for no reason at all she felt the prickle of tears. She fought to hold them back. "Companion?" she whispered, still wondering what was amusing him so. "What companion?"

"Ariel Blackmoore, Geoffrey's betrothed. If it pleases you, she will be coming for a visit. That is, after Master Stockwell has finished with you," he said, clearing his throat at his mirth. "Is that agreeable?"

"Yes." She looked at the ground ahead of them but she knew he was looking at her. Then he stopped, lifting her chin in a fatherly fashion.

"What is wrong?"

"Nothing . . . but . . . Perhaps she won't want to come here and live with a savage."

"One thing about Ariel is that she loves everyone. It doesn't matter who."

The words didn't comfort her.

"What else . . ." He started to speak then faltered, startled by the intensity of her gaze.

"Nothing really." She pulled from his grip and began to walk again. They crossed the expansive lawns and finally gained the stables.

Michael Flynn dashed off his cap as his master entered the stables, unwittingly forming the buffer Honey needed between her and Chris. She needed to breathe again.

"Mister Ames, welcome 'ome!" The Irishman clapped the son of his longtime friend on the back. "I regret the passing of Molly. She was a good un', but I'm proud to present ye with the children born of the matches made between Stonewings and Amesly horseflesh."

"What? How can that be?" Chris scratched his head. "Humphrey gave permission?"

"No, sir, before all the blastin' started, soom time ago, yer father left word to start the breedin', as agreed with Jacob. His four best sires were left here, the colts to be a comin' home present for Jacob himself, but as ye know . . . So the sires were never returned, ahem!" Michael cleared his throat while examining the tops of his shoes. "The fact being, sir, that is, what with all the thievin' that takes place about the country side now, well, you see, it just seemed a shade better if all the 'orses were to be protected together, since Stonewings had no overseer . . . 'Twas a matter taken oop with me own self, sir."

"Oh, is that a fact?" Christopher's eyes took on a new light. "Were any of the offspring or otherwise property of Stonewings ever returned to the new owner?" Christopher worked hard to bury his mirth, but his eyes shone in merriment.

"Well now, I would have to be sayin' yes to that

un', ahem, excepten' for that black beast. We thought there for a while that he had been stole. But funny thing, soon as Humphrey packed oop and headed fer town, that blasted critter showed back oop. Ya kinna think we dinna try to return 'im, boot by then it was too late, and since . . . well, sir, the subject just never came oop again." Michael told his story as sincerely as would anyone truly sorry for a wrongdoing, but like Chris, the smile never left his face.

"Well, you tried." Chris laughed. "By the way, he didn't happen to have . . ."

"Right you be, sir, right this way," he winked, bidding his master to follow.

Chris bestowed a smile on Honey, who had been completely lost in the Irish roll. She had to work so hard to grasp the words that she lost the context of the conversation.

"Have you learned of Ireland? 'Tis north of here, another whole new world," he said.

"Do you mean like France or Spain?" she asked.

"Indeed, have you been to France or Spain?"

"No, I don't think so," she said, glancing to her left in time to see a horse lift his tail. Her nose wrinkled in disgust.

Chris laughed, finally stopping at the largest stall, at the very center of the massive building.

"Oh, Michael," Chris breathed. His eyes turned liquid as he gazed at the large black horse who stomped in displeasure. "How is he?"

"A bit skittish, this one. Grandson of the beast and the Molly, but a summer of work and he'll be as fine a racer as you've ever seen." He slid his cap back over his forehead.

"Do it, Michael," Chris said. "Make him ready for the Autumn Fair."

"You'll be wantin' to race him yerself?" Michael

asked with a musical lilt to his tenor voice.

"Aye, but in case I don't return in time, mark your name on the slate." He spoke without looking at the groom's beaming face.

Honey knew he wouldn't be back in time to race; somehow she thought Michael knew it too.

"Thank ye, sir," he beamed. "If'n you'll be excusin' me now . . ." Michael tipped his hat to Honey, who returned his gesture with the dip of her head. Chris merely waved, still not tearing his eyes from the horse that mirrored the mount his father had favored for the Autumn Fair races, the last social event of the county season. In his childhood Christopher never missed the Autumn Fair, at least while his parents were alive.

"The Autumn Fair." Honey tested the words aloud.

"Sound familiar?" Chris's eyes followed the Irishman's retreat, then he looked back at the horse.

"Not really," she said, but the term seemed to pull at her, wanting to take her back into the dark regions of her mind. She fought it, afraid of the pain it might bring, afraid that she would pass out and awaken only to find Chris had gone. There was always time later to dwell on such phrases.

"Shall we get to the horses? I thought I saw a butterscotch mare here." He scanned the rows of stalls. "Oh yes, over there." He pointed to a stall across the stable. He took her arm as he glanced once more at the black stallion.

Even dressed as he was in his tight black breeches and billowing shirt, he would look just as comfortable sitting on top of that horse, Honey thought. They would fit together as though they were part of a connecting mold. Following his lead, she crossed the stone floor, the damp musty smells invading her senses.

"There now, I'd say someone had you in mind when this foal was birthed." He smiled as he tossed a lead rope over the mare's head. Then he backed her out of the stall to see her new mistress.

"She looks like sand," Honey breathed, petting the animal's silky coat.

"By the time you're ready to learn how to ride, she ought to be saddle broke," he said, inspecting a hoof. "I have a hunch you'll like to ride. It's much like being at sea."

Her smile was wan. The sea was the one thing they had in common. They both loved it as if it were a living creature to be caressed and cherished and respected.

"I miss it too," she said softly, glancing up to meet his gaze. Several heartbeats passed before he broke the spell that bound them. He dropped the horse's hoof, then led the mare back into the stall.

"You're going to be gone a very long time, aren't you?" she asked quietly. "You won't be back to race at all."

"Come," he said, stepping out of the stone-framed stall. "I might find what I'm looking for in just a day."

"If a fleet hunted for months and found nothing, what do you hope to find alone?" she exploded, surprising them both.

"It's none of your business." His face was close to hers as he grasped her elbow to pull her along. But she held firm.

"It *is* my business." Her words were as grim as the look on her face.

"And who is it that has taught you what is and isn't your business, Jason, perhaps?" He glared down at her.

"The nerve! First you accuse Jason of whatever it was you called it, then you treat me like a child! And now you run off to sea." She balled her fists and rested them on her slender hips. "For as much as you think of me as a child, Jason had thought of me otherwise. He had spoken of marriage . . ."

"Is that what you want?" His brows gathered. "Marriage to a penniless teacher?"

"It doesn't appear that I'll receive a better offer, but still, that is not the point."

"What is the point?" His face had grown dark as he stepped yet closer to her. But she vowed not to turn away.

The point, she suddenly realized, was her fear that he would go to sea and never return to her. The point was that she was confused by his sudden attention and by her own strange feelings, and worst of all, the point was she could not say any of those things to Chris's face. "It's just that . . ." she started, working hard not to show her sudden weakness.

"Well?"

"The point is none of your business, either!" She turned to flee the awkward situation. Her face flushed as she realized she had talked herself into a corner.

"Oh, no, you don't!" His hand snaked out and grabbed her wrist before she had gone a step. He jerked her around to face him. "It seems to me you've been harboring a stronger will than is permitted a woman behind your childish frocks. You started this argument, now finish it!" he invited mockingly. "Or perhaps you'd like to think about your answer while I am gone."

"Perhaps I shall marry while you are gone, and move away!" she countered, her lips compressed in a stubborn line.

"You can't. The only way you can marry is with my permission, and I can't very well give it while I'm gone, can I?" He spit out the harsh words, but he had learned enough from her to know that marriage was not what was on her mind.

"What if you never return?" Her eyes widened as she suddenly realized what she had just said. She quit trying to pull away from him.

"Then I don't . . ." he said, suddenly as solemn as she. He had not considered not returning. It was something he had thought about before every other voyage—hence the arrangements for Jillian to own her own home and keep her own accounts. Yet now for the first time he feared his own folly, the folly of leaving this precious girl and never returning.

Spellbound, she watched the blue of his eyes fade to smoke; his head dipped towards hers. Instinctively she pulled back. His hesitation was brief before he pulled her to him, savoring the gentle swell of her hips against his thigh, the soft lift of her breasts against his chest. Her heart thumped against his ribs as his mouth melted into hers. The slender wrist he still held pulsed rapidly against his fingers, while his free hand slid around the small of her back, holding her close.

She felt him tremble, from his gentle kiss to the hand that pressed her from behind, urging her closer to his firm chest. Her left hand molded the bulge of his bicep as her body stretched to fit her mouth more perfectly against his. A faint sigh purred from her throat. Even the strange heat from his thigh filtering through her gown was wonderfully thrilling. She pressed her hips into his, then suddenly he jerked back, leaving her off balance. His look of shock scalded her already flushed cheeks, as though she were not the person he thought she'd been. It was the old Chris looking upon her in disgust. She had committed the final sin. She stepped back, shaking her head in denial, his image distorted through the tears that flooded her eyes. Gasping, she turned toward the nearest door and fled.

Chapter Sixteen

The canvas whipped furiously in the stiff breeze, lashing at Chris's face. Moments later it calmed enough for his deft fingers to push the needle through the coarse fabric. Luckily the tear was small, and if the wind held off for a few more minutes, the repairs would be finished and forgotten. Repairing canvas was not an easy task on the decks, but from forty-some feet above the decks of the *Wing Master* in a gusting wind, the task took balance, skill, and patience. And it was patience he was shortest on.

The heat of the afternoon sun toasted his back. The ship rolled with the natural surge of the sea and threatened to unseat him at every dip. He really should have taken the canvas down, for the narrow beam on which he sat swayed like the pendulum of a clock. The work went slowly, but then that was the whole point of the exercise. It was mind-occupying work.

France, Spain, and Portugal all lay behind them—each with a dozen ports. The crew had spent several days at each, drinking with the natives, losing a few shillings to games of chance, and finally asking the questions they had come to ask. But each weathered face shook his head no or shrugged a shoulder or laughed at the time span in question. They went door to door along the coastal homes and voiced their questions again, but no one wanted to answer. And Chris knew why. These people lived on the salvage of downed ships. Proud of their work or not, they clubbed to death the survivors of sea-wrecked ships in order to claim valuable cargo. No one was willing to say anything about it. Many even refused to name the ships whose treasures they'd laid claim to. There was no Ida in these sleepy little port towns to save anyone who might have lived. And no salvager had recorded a recovery from a ship called the *Crystal Wing*. But that didn't surprise him either; the booty would have far outweighed the reward for saving it.

The towns and cities were beginning to blend together, becoming indistinguishable from one another. So too were the faces, the languages, and the taverns. And still the coastline of Africa lay before them . . .

Chris sighed as he stuck the needle through the canvas again. So much time had passed, but the memory had faded little.

"You won't be back . . ." her voice echoed in his mind. And he could still see those eyes, soft with tears. Eyes so overwhelmingly green, lips so overwhelmingly rosy. Whatever had possessed him to kiss her? Why had he pulled her so close, why had his hand followed the smooth shape of her back to her tiny waist? He could feel, even now, where each curve would fit against him should he ever hold her again. Her fingers had burned against his bicep, but her mouth reaching for his, molding so perfectly against his lips, sent a charge through him.

It baffled him that she so obviously knew how to manipulate him—where to press, when to sigh, and how to command his attention. When had she learned such things? From Jason? She claimed she didn't love him and didn't know what a kiss was. Jillian verified that. According to her, he'd demonstrated a growing affection for his pupil, but had been nothing less than a gentleman at all times. Could she have *guessed* at how to react?

He knew only enough about virgins to want to avoid them at all costs. If Honey hadn't fled when she did, he wasn't sure what would have happened next. He had always been able to walk away from a woman who wanted to give more than he wanted to take, even the sultry Jennifer, who practiced seduction as an art form. But this time he could not honestly be certain. He had wanted to taste those lips from the first time he'd seen her standing on the cliffs . . . In the last two days at Amesly his worst fears had been confirmed; they had more in common than just the love of the sea. Their lives seemed to have run parallel. Then too, she had that don't-tread-on-me spunk that one only expected to find in the colonies. That morning in his study she had told him truthfully about the time she'd spent on the island. She had even shared the story of her first encounter with a sand crab. He had delighted in watching her tell her tale, delighted in being alone with her and actually having a conversation.

What she had said was true—she very well might not be waiting for him when he returned. Already Jason had proposed marriage; who was to say that couldn't happen again? And what if he never returned home?

Suddenly the ship lurched, jerking Chris from his thoughts. His arm shot out to grab the safety line, but the wind blew the line away from him, and his fingers closed on air. His body rolled backward and pitched out over the deck. For several heartbeats he seemed suspended in midair. The deck rushed up to meet him, and somewhere in his mind he knew no one had ever survived this fall. But just then Fate herself brought the ship rolling back, and a beam swung across his path. His left arm shot out, clawing for the safety line that whipped back with the ship. Somehow he managed to get it into his hand, and he jerked on the line until he came to an abrupt halt. He felt his muscles rip, his tendons pull, his bones stretch. His face twisted as the pain shot through his fingers, numbing them.

But he was alive. All he could do for the moment was hang there with his eyes closed, sending his thanks heavenward.

Below him several crew members had stopped in their tracks. One darted from the very spot where Chris would have hit the deck. Their faces pinched in horror as their captain hung suspended by one frail rope at a fatal height over the decks. Through the pain he managed a weak smile and saluted those who gawked.

"Show's over, mates," he called through clenched teeth. He swung his free hand up and over the beam while the wind tugged at his legs. The canvas cracked close to his face as if laughing at his foolishness. *That will surely teach me to think of something other than the sea,* he berated himself, dragging his body over the dried, splintery wood. His heart beat hard against his ribs as he hung for a few moments haphazardly draped over the beam. Her voice echo'd softly in his mind, "What if you never come back?" A smile cracked his lips then faded as he pulled himself painfully the rest of the way up. Finding a wooden cross seat he leaned back against the mast, cradling his injured arm. It had not yet begun to hurt, but it would, he knew, as soon as the circulation came back. It would hurt like the devil and be useless until then.

"Ho there!"

Chris looked down at the voice. It was Geoff. His face was grim.

"I'm fine. Most of the mend is in place. We'll finish her at next port," he called down.

Geoff nodded. "First port of Africa, Morocco, by nightfall."

Chris looked over the sea in the direction Geoff pointed. Land was always in sight on this trip, but ahead he could already see the black spot against the shoreline that marked the dark wood of ships in a harbor. The only difference he would find here, he knew, would be the brand of drink.

Rabat was little more than a trader's market, yet its port was filled with merchants of every description. Woolens, clay pots, rich fabrics, rugs, and pipes were only a few of the items presented for sale. Dark-skinned, black-haired men of various sizes called out prices from beneath the thatched huts that provided the only shade. The women, scant few that there were, were heavily robed and veiled, going silently about their business, though more than one set of almond-shaped eyes glanced in Christopher's direction as he and his party roamed the streets.

It was dusk, yet the dusty streets were still crowded with buyers. Everywhere, strange animals snorted and honked. Voices raised in disagreement joined in the confusion.

"Have you ever been here before?" Geoff asked, matching his long strides to his captain's.

"No, have you?"

"No, but it reminds of the story of Aladdin."

Chris smiled. He had read a few tales about Aladdin himself, but somehow he had not pictured it quite this way.

"Ah, an Eeengleeshmun." An almost toothless man with a weathered face grinned as he bobbed his head up and down in praise. "You buy?"

"No . . . Yes. I buy a speaker." Chris held a gold coin out to the man. The man's black eyes danced as the gold glittered before him.

"Speak," he grinned greedily, his head still moving up and down while his hands seemed to writhe about each other beneath his cloak.

"I want to find out if any of your people have seen a ship . . . or a shipwreck . . ." Chris told his story again as he followed the old man around the marketplace. But the end result was the same as it had been in every other port. Dark face after dark face either grinned meaninglessly or turned away. Many were not even interested enough to listen.

"We'll head back to the ship tonight. Tomorrow we'll try again, but double the watch tonight." Chris glanced at the turban-crowned giants who dragged huge deadly scimitars at their hips. The sooner they left Rabat, the better he'd feel.

Chapter Seventeen

Honey looked out at the raging sea; her mare danced beneath her. The wind whipped unmercifully at her hair and face, but she refused to look away. Somewhere in the midst of all that commotion was Chris. She couldn't help but wonder if he was safe, if he had found a safe port to wait out the storm, if he ever thought of her . . .

The breakers pounded the beach below her with a ferocity that had once terrified her. The sky overhead had blackened and rumbled disconcertingly. She reined her horse inland, and the wind beat at her back as the pair raced across the field, *Please, God,* she prayed silently, *keep him safe.* Then she spurred the sand-colored horse toward Amesly and the first social gathering of the Autumn Fair.

She arrived at the stables as if the very devil were at her heels. Her long dark hair had fallen from its pins and lay twisted in a thick mass of snarls. Her face was flushed and full of color from her breathless ride.

"Miss Honey, they been oot here twice now lookin' fer ya," Michael scolded, but his smile was indulgent. He loved people who loved his horses, and Honey loved hers. And as Chris had predicted, she loved to ride.

"I'm sure," she rolled her eyes as she slid from the saddle. "Has anyone arrived yet?"

"Only Mrs. Humphrey from up the road."

"Oh, good." Her eyes twinkled as she smiled. "She has a manner that keeps Jillian from scolding too long."

Michael laughed. "Aye, but there must be a little Irish in a lass to go oot ina gale like this with not a care but for the scoldin' you'll be gettin'." He chuckled as she tossed him a quick salute, then raced out of the stable for the back door of the house.

"Katie, could you prepare a bath?" she called out as she flew past the kitchens.

"Miss Ariel has one waitin'." The reply floated up behind her as she mounted the stairs. Of course Ariel would have one waiting. She shook her head as she ran down the hall and through her own door.

"How was your ride?" Ariel's soft voice drifted from the armoire.

"It's a bit windy out there today," Honey said as she plopped down on the pink coverlet to unlace her shoes.

"You went down to the coast, didn't you?" Ariel's smile was mildly stern.

"I shan't answer if I'm to be scolded for it." Honey smiled back as Brea came through the door. "You know I did. You know I always do." Dutifully Honey turned her back so that her split riding skirt could be unhooked. Turning back only when it had dropped to the floor, she began to discard the rest of her rumpled clothing.

"I wish I knew how they are too, but going down there is not going to help. Besides, you shouldn't be riding unchaperoned that far from home, and certainly not in this weather."

Ariel's hair was almost black against her porcelain white skin. Her cheekbones were classically high and faintly flushed a bright pink all the time, just like her lips. Yet her eyes were a blue that paled next to Chris's. From the moment they met, Honey had thought Ariel the most beautiful girl that ever lived, as well as the sweetest, most even tempered, and kindest. She held that opinion of her even though Ariel hated horses and almost anything that had to do with being outside. Their one common interest, besides the *Wing Master*, was rose gardening.

Ariel had been at Amesly almost from the moment Chris had departed.

Honey suffered an involuntary shudder as she looked at the tub, and she reflected on the time of her first bath, to that halting moment when her wet, naked flesh had been pressed against the rough skirt covering Chris's chest. She remembered the demon look in his eye and the empty feeling he'd left inside her when he stormed away.

Then six months ago in the stables, Chris had kissed her, drawing her to him and causing a powerful sensation that took her breath away. But what was it? Why had Chris looked so terror stricken? That look on his face had been so beastly . . . as if she had said or done something awful . . . and she just didn't know what. She had breached some unspoken code between men and women, she was sure, but what?

Shortly after Chris had gone, Ariel had come along and escorted her through Franklin Stockwell's chamber of education. And slowly, very slowly, a relationship began to build, but it was difficult for Honey to overcome the intimidation she felt beside Ariel's grace and beauty. Franklin Stockwell had helped there, too. He had said, "Everyone needs an edge, whether it's a name or an ability, and until you find yours, Honey, your brains will be your ally." And it worked! By the time Franklin had completed her training, the awkward part of her personality was gone. She felt less clumsy and graceless. Ariel, too, was grateful for the change, for she so wanted them to be friends. She turned to Ariel, smiling as she spoke.

"It isn't that far. Besides, I like the smell of the ocean. I miss it." Honey turned a wistful eye to the water waiting for her in the tub before she slipped in.

"Don't you like it here?" Ariel stepped back from the wardrobe holding a blue gown out before her. "You are more suited to rich colors. I wonder why Jillian keeps you in pastels?"

"I don't think she knows what to do with me now that my hair has darkened. And yes, I like it here just fine. I've loved the markets and the fairs and watching Michael work the horses. I love riding, and hopefully after tonight I'll be able to say I like the people." She braced a leg against the edge of the tub and began to scrub. "And Jillian keeps me in pastels because 'all young girls love pastels.'"

Ariel laughed at Honey's imitation of Jillian. "Another year and you'll be uncontrollable."

"At least that's something," she sighed as she began to scrub the other leg.

Ariel sank to the bed. Her gaze took in the decor in one sweeping glance. Childish pink ruffles and white furniture filled the room. She couldn't imagine not knowing who she was or forgetting things such as family and friends, or never having been presented at her own ball or attending those of her friends. Honey would never have her season. Just by the looks of her, she was already too old. And while Honey was probably older than Ariel, Honey's life consisted of Jillian, Ariel, Christopher, and whatever servants happened to be employed. One could not learn the ways of life in such limited surroundings.

"Maybe we should tell everyone that you are my cousin from Plymouth. No one ever goes there."

"Jillian has already told someone that I am the daughter of a close friend, taken from home because my sickly mother hasn't the strength to raise me."

"Who did she tell that to?"

"Jason Montgomery." Honey dropped her head forward to wet her hair, then sat upright again to lather the newly darkened strands. A lone chemist had seen her hair as she and Jillian and Ariel wandered the booths of the carnival show. The man had been so fascinated by the naturally bleached hair that he offered her a rinse matched as closely as possible to her naturally darker shade in exchange for a few strands of the sunbleached hair. Both Jillian and Ariel had been thrilled at the prospect of seeing Honey's hair all the same shade, and the two of them had agreed before Honey had even understood what was transpiring. The man disappeared into his tent for a long time, but when he returned he brought a vial of a thick syrup with him. The trio hurried home, not stopping to see the rest of the show. It was the only time Jillian had been grateful that Honey was not wearing a hat.

The change was shocking to everyone, especially Honey. With her tan fading and her hair darkened, she had lost that tropical look that she had grown accustomed to seeing in the mirror every morning. Her skin had lightened to a warm tawny rose, thereby darkening the color of her eyes. Her eyebrows had darkened too, and her lashes, when tinted with kohl, were of a startling length and thickness. There was a new person looking back at her in the mirror every morning, and Honey was not sure that she liked her.

But the real question that plagued her was, would Chris?

"Jason, oh yes, the teacher." Ariel tried to hide her smile at the thought of a man such as Chris defending Honey's honor. "Wherever did he end up?"

"I don't know. I wish I had known what he was up to, though. I miss the fellow."

"No!" Ariel's sharp intake of breath caused Honey to gasp. She peered out from beneath the white froth of suds. "What do you mean, no?"

"It would never do to go about with a man who has no morals."

"He had morals. He just didn't know the truth," Honey grimaced, rinsing her hair. "Besides," she sputtered, "he might have been the most logical way out for Chris." The words were said more to herself than to the other girl.

"You're not still worrying about that? In our social class there are not enough women to go around. Backgrounds are often overlooked."

Honey laughed. "It's having one to overlook that is more the point, don't you think? The worst part is that the smarter I get, the more I realize how important a background is here."

She stood up in the tub as Brea jumped quickly forward to pat her mistress's body dry. The tan lines had all faded to one warm shade of womanly flesh that Ariel secretly envied. She studied the floor, hoping Honey couldn't see her envy, "Mr. Stockwell taught you far more than a woman is due. In fact, he has never before agreed to tutor a female. Many women will resent that; that is why we should concentrate on social graces. After all, you cannot catch a man if you don't know how to talk to him."

"I believe that is *your* job. Ariel, how old would

you say I am?"

"Maybe nineteen, perhaps twenty." Ariel watched as her friend dressed. Her sister was twenty, and she thought there was a similarity in size and manner.

"An old maid. That's why Franklin taught me as he did Chris—because he knew my age . . ." A wave of sudden sadness washed over her. "I am too old to marry."

Ariel sat back thoughtfully. She wanted to have hope, but Honey's words were true. Her only hopes of marriage were old men who had lost their wives or London rakes who had never married and could not be counted on to be faithful or even discreet. As far as Ariel was concerned, Chris fell perfectly into that unfaithful and indiscreet category.

"There might be a few who—"

"Ariel, do you never tire of seeing the world so rosy? There will be no valiant male to rescue me from a life of books and embroidery. Men my age who haven't married don't want to. I'm not permitted to attend any parties until Chris's return, and even then, I'm not certain I would want to."

"Well," Ariel smiled, "you'll have company. I cannot attend certain functions without Geoffrey, either. It would appear as though I had rejected him. So we'll winter together. Maybe we can press Jillian into a small gathering of some of my unmarried friends, informally."

"You mean meet other women?" Honey looked horrified as she sat on the divan and rolled up her stockings then stepped into her shift.

"Of course." The pretty woman laughed at her friend. "Frankly, they are the real test. It is sad to say, but meeting them is not getting to know them. Very few people become friends like we are. Mostly it is a game to see who wears the nicer dresses and who can be more complimentary . . . or who is seeing whom."

"I don't understand." Honey stopped dressing to watch her friend as she spoke.

"This isn't easy to explain, but here is a good example. I have heard through friends that my betrothal is being openly ridiculed by some people. People have said that Geoff is always eager to go to sea so that he can avoid our wedding. But to my face these same people smile and agree with whatever I say."

"Why?"

"Politeness requires that they do so. But if they were real friends they would understand and say nothing. Gossip fills the lives of most people around here, and in London, too. It is just part of life."

"That's awful. Why don't you tell them what they are saying is wrong?"

"It's not worth it. If I say anything, either Geoff or my father will have to champion me in a duel. Not to do so would be to or admit that everything that has been said is true. And because I know it's not true, that is enough for me. Geoff loves me. When he returns with Chris this time he has promised a wedding. Maybe next fall."

"Have you and Geoff ever . . . I mean, has he ever kissed you?" Honey's green eyes gazed into her friend's.

"Well, of course he has. But don't tell anyone." Ariel laughed again.

Honey smiled, "Do you kiss him back?"

"Certainly. He likes that. Why? Has someone tried to kiss you?" The dreamy look left Ariel's eyes as she considered her friend closely.

"No." Honey grabbed the underskirt from the silent Brea and quickly stepped into it. "I mean, not since Jason tried, but maybe someday . . . then I'll not know what to do."

"You slap his face is what you do!" Ariel's wide blue eyes flashed. "It's not right for a man you're not betrothed to to take liberties with your person. Unless you want him to. And then you'd best be discreet yourself, for if a man kisses you and doesn't ask for your hand in marriage, you'll be labeled a . . . a lightskirt!"

"No!" Honey looked back in shock. Was that it? Had she been expected to slap Chris when he kissed her? *Oh my God,* she moaned to herself. No wonder he looked so sickened. She let him ruin her and then fled before he even had the chance to offer . . . But would he have?

"Turn, please." Brea moved her mistress to the bed, where Honey automatically held onto the post while Brea laced her stays into place. In her vexation she hardly noticed as the corset cinched her waist tightly.

"What if . . . what if the girl is so overcome at the time that she runs away from him? Is she still ruined?"

"I suppose only if he brags about it. Then, if it isn't true, her father or suitor challenges the braggart to a duel. Whoever wins is deemed right. Though often an innocent women loses her champion in a duel and is destined to live her life as a recluse."

"That's terrible!" Honey blurted out the words before she realized how harsh they sounded.

"Are you sure nothing has happened? Why all these questions?"

"Really, no, it's just that . . ." Honey sighed as Brea held her dress out before her. "Ariel, I'm scared. I feel like sixteen going on thirty. My life consists of needlepoint and tea with Jillian. Even the thought of my first carnival had me awake most of the night. And now . . . and now I haven't even a family name to carry through the season. I feel like a newborn colt trying hard to stand up, but always falling on my face. I don't want to fall on my face in public."

"You'll be fine. It just takes time to learn about people. The best thing to do the first time or two out is to listen more than talk. If someone asks you a personal question turn it around by gushing over a gown or the food or something. Besides, all your neighbors out here are from different places—maybe one or two are from London—so you won't run into any of them after this is over."

Brea finished hooking up Honey's pale blue gown. The color did little to flatter her features, but she didn't mind. She felt painfully pastel next to Ariel's dramatic color anyway.

Chapter Eighteen

William Humphrey poured yet another glass of brandy for his favorite hostess, Jennifer Bates, the former lady of Brentwood.

He met her today, as he had all summer long, behind the closed curtains of her richly decorated townhouse, only a few short blocks west of Hyde Park.

Jennifer turned a dark eye to her companion. She was glad that the summer would soon end and that her lover's wife and children would return from the country. William was becoming a bore. For a man who had so many contacts and heard so many tales, he didn't gossip a bit. Most of the tantalizing pieces of dirt the man was privy to simply streamed in one ear and out the other. Jennifer could have screamed with the boredom. At least Marcus Long had always partaken of gossip, dandy that he was. He often had the juiciest tales to tell about who had been seen with whom and where, and—best of all—where they went afterward. But Marcus had not been around all summer either. Nor had Christopher, which was the real reason she had spent so much time entertaining William, Christopher's business partner. She had heard, though, that the partners practically hated each other. Still, William was not a bad lover. His thick blond hair had faded to gray, but he hadn't gone to fat the way most men his age had. His belly was soft but trim, and though his fleshy arms were not powerful they were warm. He was truly not bad to look at, but he was neither Marcus nor Christopher.

"Tell me something exciting," she whispered in a throaty voice as he crossed the room to sit beside her on the love seat.

"Like what?" His eyes grazed her ample bosom while a hand strayed to her thigh.

"Surely you have heard some juicy tidbits about someone this summer. Indeed, if summer does not end soon, I shall go mad for all this city quiet. There has been no one to call on and Hyde Park is a graveyard."

"Mmm, so 'tis gossip you want? You have heard, of course, that Christopher has gone and imported a bride?" The news evoked the desired effect, and he watched the woman beside him change from pale white to blush pink before quickly recovering.

"A what? A bride, you say?" Jennifer rose and made her way to the sideboard, where she poured herself another brandy and took a healthy swallow before returning to her guest. Her rich fuchsia dressing gown swished as she walked. Her red lips seemed to pout, but her dark eyes looked dangerous. "None of our ladies is good enough for the boy?" Her laugh died in her throat.

William laughed out loud too. Jennifer was a poor actress. "There is some tutor going about the city in a drunken rage, spouting his sorrowful tale to anyone who'll listen."

"Oh?" Jennifer sipped from her glass again. "Christopher hasn't been around much this summer, has he?"

"No, gone on some fool errand that he refused to talk about. Took only those crew members who have sailed with him exclusively for the past five years. Maybe he is off collecting his in-laws." William slapped his thigh as he chuckled at his own humor. His eyes crinkled as he thought of Christopher, socially ruined for taking a savage bride.

"Who is the lucky girl? An American Indian, perhaps? I've heard stories of their exotic color and beauty." A vision of a shapely red-skinned woman flashed through her mind. Jealousy scalded her veins as she envisioned the woman receiving the body that was meant for her!

"Seems she's an island native from the South Seas. There was a tribe about two hundred years ago, my grandfather told me, that inhabited the West Indies . . . Caribs, or some such name. Many were brought here to serve the Crown. The people were weak, too weak to stand the drizzle. They all died, leaving the islands to the savages, who feasted on many an English voyager."

"A cannibal?" Jennifer's eyes flashed wide in horror as she turned her full attention to her guest.

William laughed at her terror-stricken face.

"Sounds more like some waif taken from a tropical island. Who knows? She could have been a castaway. I heard that young tutor say that Chris had flown into a rage when he walked in on him teaching the girl to dance. Someone else mentioned having heard that Chris has taken her guardianship. Hard to tell which story might be true . . ." He chuckled, taking the last gulp from the glass he had intended for Jennifer. Then he smiled broadly at her. Whatever she might think, she had no secrets from him.

Jennifer smiled back, sweetly, but her mind was

filled with the memory of the last visit she had received from Christopher. Now his mood made sense; he had someone else on his mind that night. He had gazed over the city almost all night long, and when she had awakened near dawn, he was gone.

"What a charming tale," she said at last. Setting her glass down, she turned her back to the settee. "Surely something so fantastic has little truth to it."

"Difficult to follow, that's for sure. Like the story Jasper's doorman told my livery driver about some young girl sitting every morning in the open window of Jillian Ames's house. Then just before this troubadour tutor shows up in town, Jillian and her entire household set off for the country without a word to anyone. Seems to me that her last trip to the country was better than nine years ago. Christopher likewise heads for sea—six months before the tobacco crops are due to ripen. He hauls little else, you know." William's finger drummed against his leg as he thought about all the places Christopher would have to travel through the dangerous winter months. What the devil was so important that it would keep him from the Virginia tobacco harvest? Unless he were looking for someone, something? "The problem is that we don't know which way he went." He spoke more to himself than to Jennifer.

Jennifer silently agreed. "William, dear, I feel a headache coming on. Forgive me, please, but . . ." She pressed a dainty palm to her brow as she turned to leave the lavishly furnished parlor.

William stood. "You have gotten what you wanted, now I shall have what is mine." He jerked her back, crushing her to him. His mouth punished hers. His hands were cruel, bruising her flesh and tearing at her gown. He didn't know how she felt about this savagery; in truth, he didn't care. But she didn't fight him, and the thought crossed his mind somewhere in the midst of his frenzied passion that she was responding as furiously as he.

Lawrence Grant had soft, blond hair and tender blue eyes, and his manner made Honey feel like a shabby chair in a room filled with beautiful furniture. She watched him cross the room to the punch bowl. He even walked with more grace than Ariel, which in itself was a magnificent feat.

"Well?" Ariel sneaked up behind her friend.

"Well, nothing. Look at him! He's perfect. Prettier and more graceful than any girl here. His manners are impeccable, his style irreproachable, and his taste in women superb. He has been asking about you all night." Honey laughed, looking back at her friend.

"Don't be silly. He has been talking to you. In fact, people are beginning to notice how long you have been together."

A clap of thunder sounded outside. As it had threatened to do all day, the weather had finally turned stormy—a sure sign of autumn.

"I almost wish I *were* being silly, but it is you he has been asking about. Although Katherine Hansley has hovered over him all afternoon."

Ariel glanced at the girl Honey had mentioned. "It is a shame she is in the country this season. Rarely does she come out anymore. I wonder why she has decided to make an appearance now?"

"Could be a crush . . ." Honey's eyes filled with mischief. "'T'isn't often I hear that Amesly entertains."

"Too true." Ariel dropped her conspiratorial air as Lawrence crossed back to where the ladies stood. She smiled sweetly as Lawrence offered her the glass of punch he had retrieved for himself.

"Ladies. Might I introduce Clifton Cain, of late from the colonies, now home on family business, I am told." Clifton nodded first to Honey and then to Ariel, then returned his gaze to Honey. He wore buff-colored breeches with a white shirt and a buff waistcoat with a black coat. His dark blond hair was pulled neatly back in a tail that brushed his collar. In contrast, Lawrence was dressed in perfect coordination of silver on baby blue. His long blond locks were loose and wavy. Lawrence appeared almost feminine standing next to Clifton. Honey noticed his lack of lace adornment, and found she preferred the simplest version of male dress.

"How long have you been home, Mr. Cain?" Ariel asked, drawing the man's eyes from Honey to herself.

"A fortnight thus far, and I can say now I look forward to another with eagerness." The man with dark brown eyes smiled at Honey, sending a thrill down her spine. His smile brightened when a flush painted her cheeks.

"I understand the colonies have spread out this past year, Mr. Cain." Honey was shocked to hear herself conversing as though she had been born to it.

"That they are, Miss James, but I fear we have lost an entire settlement somewhere between Virginia and Carolina."

"Indians?" Her eyes widened in speculation.

"We fear that, yes," Clifton nodded. Amusement played in his eyes and a small smile formed on his lips. It was refreshing to find a woman who knew something about the colonies. "The tribes have been violent before."

"Is there nothing you can do about them?" she asked, taking on a slightly insecure look that she had seen Ariel practice a time or two in conversation.

"Though I imagine that it is difficult to send word back and forth when the people have separated themselves so."

"Indeed, that is true."

"And do you wear animal skins for clothing?" Lawrence's voice was cool, but it couldn't break the spell that Clifton's brown eyes held over Honey's.

"I have heard that too," Ariel answered, nudging her friend's arm.

"Tanning is a trade learned by the trappers from the northern Indians, isn't it?" Honey's eyes shifted from Clifton to Ariel then back to Lawrence. "The skin is soaked in water for several days, then the hair is removed with a sharpened bone. Later the skin is softened, dyed, and fashioned into clothing. For warmer clothes, the fur is treated so it can't fall off the leather. I'd hardly call that wearing skins, Mr. Grant. After all, I believe a few of our ancestors dressed much the same way," Honey chided.

Lawrence at least had the good grace to look embarrassed for his cutting remark. But it was the particular look on Clifton's face that brought the flames to Honey's cheeks as she realized she had spoken out of turn. She had been told that women were not permitted to be as well educated as she was, and many men didn't like it. She couldn't tell whether Clifton thought her vulgar or not.

"You seem to know more about my new home than I do. How is it possible that a London socialite knows so much about the dreaded colonies?"

"It is part of history, Mr. Cain. Someday we shall all have relatives living there. It is a part of England. And besides, I am not a socialite, just a bookworm. I fear my new tutor has difficulty finding new lessons for me."

"If we had a few women like you in the colonies,

we could tame the wilds much more quickly."

"Why, thank you." She glanced to the floor then back. "But you have yet to tell us what your part in taming the colonies is."

"I own a tobacco field in Virginia, and in the winter months I do some trapping near the French territory in the north. Beaver mostly, but some mink and raccoon. The Indians like the porcupines, so in order to do a little trading I like to take one now and then."

"Whatever is a porcu . . . what?" Ariel bent forward as she asked her question.

"There is no such thing. He is teasing you." Lawrence said, tossing a wink to Ariel.

"No, really." Clifton looked at Honey. The amusement left his face. "They are . . . they look like fat-headed . . . no . . . like a mole with long quills all over his body, quills he can shoot at his enemies."

"He is teasing all right." Honey turned her gaze to Ariel; disappointment flooded her. She had wanted Clifton to be someone she could talk with without having to play these endless games of *politesse*. Someone she could talk to without feeling as if she had breached some secret pact men had with women.

"Truly, I'm not teasing," he insisted. His warm hand touched her shoulder to get her attention again.

She flinched, unaccustomed to being touched, but she brought her gaze back to him and smiled.

"I happen to have brought some quills back with me. Perhaps tomorrow we could go for a ride and I'll show them to you."

"I'd like that." Her voice was soft. "We'll need chaperones, though." She smiled at Ariel, then endearingly at Lawrence.

"Oh, I detest riding." Ariel wrinkled her nose. "But if Mr. Grant will join us, I can be persuaded."

"Indeed, if the weather relents, why not?" A smirk curled one pale lip, but Clifton ignored the man's petulance, as did Honey.

"Since that is settled, perhaps I should say good night." Clifton looked at Honey with regret. "I have quite a ride ahead of me and the weather is fouling fast." He didn't appear eager to leave, but his rugged features brightened when Honey offered to walk him to the door.

Only Honey saw the quick kiss blown in her direction as he sauntered past the front stair. It was almost her first kiss. But not quite.

Chapter Nineteen

"Lawrence seemed very upset that you gave all your smiles to his friend," Ariel scolded as they helped Brea and Mrs. Mingleson clean up after the last guest had gone. As if to punctuate Ariel's sentence, thunder shook the rafters.

"I think he was more upset that you were betrothed," Honey spoke absently, her mind on the man who had transformed a boring evening into a pleasant one. "Besides, I don't think I have the patience for these things. That party almost put me to sleep. I have never seen so many people talk so much and say so little. And to people they don't even like! Then to have the gall to thank you for such a *lovely time.*"

Ariel laughed. "I'm afraid then you'll have to be happy spending all winter at home, because except for dancing, all they do is talk about each other."

"I like dancing!" Honey exclaimed.

"You two get up to bed," Jillian said. She disapproved of helping servants do what they were paid to do. "You may as well sleep late tomorrow.

This storm looks as though it will last at least the week."

Jillian came very close to being accurate in her prediction, for the following day the rain pelted the ground as steadily as it had the day before. The rhythmic thrum of rain was interrupted only by violent flashes of lightning and earth-shaking crashes of thunder. Tapers had been lighted and burned throughout both days to ward off the gloom. Ariel and Honey filled their time with needlework and reading and practiced pouring tea. Honey found she loved to read—everything from poetry to science to novels. Jillian was certain the novels would lead to the end of Honey's virtue, but Honey thought they offered an insight into life. Some explained what Jillian and Ariel often found difficult to explain—personal questions about men and women. There was one book she'd found hidden in the very back of the bookcase, written by a woman who told of her personal experiences with her many lovers. The woman was shameless in her description of probing tongues and male organs! The descriptions seemed hideous to Honey, yet they stirred the same thrilling sensations Chris had evoked. Twice. The memories woke the butterflies in her stomach and made her breasts swell ever so slightly. After reading this book she often closed her eyes and tried to imagine what would have happened had she not run away. But without Chris, she was left frustrated. Then she worked to keep all thoughts of him from her mind. But that too proved to be futile.

The third day marked the end of the thunderstorm, but the roads were impassable, even for an errand of importance. Finally, two days later, a messenger appeared with an invitation from Clifton Cain. Ariel accepted for them both, for as much as she disliked riding horseback, she also disliked being cooped up so long in the house. Winter, she decided, was going to be tiresome indeed.

The sand-colored horse cantered prettily beside the dark red roan Clifton rode. In front of them, Lawrence rode quietly beside Ariel. Their gentle mares stepped well together, leaving them little to do but watch the countryside.

"Over the next hill," Honey called to the leaders, "there is a pond and a small grove of trees. If you like, we can stop there."

Ariel's mount moved further ahead, with Lawrence's close behind.

"It's perfect," she called back, then asked her companion, "What do you think, sir?"

Lawrence reined his horse to a halt beside Ariel's.

"It will do," he said, with his usual lack of enthusiasm.

"How is it you happen to know of this place?" Clifton looked at Honey, secretly relishing the sight.

"Because, sir," Ariel spoke up, "this young lady often rides farther than she should, unescorted and often without a hat or even . . ."

"And often without a side saddle," Honey mimicked under her breath.

"I'd say you'd be pretty safe here, as long as there hasn't been trouble before." Clifton smiled as the foursome reined their horses into the small grove. He slipped from his horse and tied him to a branch before lifting Honey carefully from the saddle. He was slow to take his hands from her small waist, but his intense gaze finally turned into a smile as he willed his thoughts into safer waters.

Honey tried to smile back, but a self-conscious flush stained her cheeks.

At last Clifton stepped back, allowing her to move away from the horse.

"At home, we use leather saddlebags to carry our goods," he said, lifting the wicker baskets from his horse. "And the men have taken to wearing a new kind of boot. It's short and wide, coming only as high as a snake can leap." He lifted his booted foot for her inspection.

"Lovely," she giggled. "And what do you call your shirt and . . . um, whatever they are."

"Homespun pants. The north country gets mighty cold. A man has to protect himself from frostbite."

"Oh, yes. That is when the flesh freezes solid. A Norman doctor has written about the precautions one needs to take against it." Her gaze followed the ground as they walked to the pond where Ariel and Lawrence waited. She thought that he liked her, but still she couldn't shake the feeling of being out of place with him.

The breeze sent glittering ripples over the gray-green water as the sun warmed the day. This would be one of the last nice days of summer, she was told. Only an occasional fluff of cloud blotted out the warming rays of the sun. They ate and laughed and joked with one another, and Clifton told them stories about life in the colonies. Honey wondered what life was like there. It sounded as if everyone had a job to do and enjoyed doing it. As if one could be occupied with real things rather than this constant idle existence. No one there seemed to care what you were before you got there; background and family blood meant little.

"Except for those who stayed in New York, the first settlement," Clifton added. "They consider themselves the elite."

"It sounds like there is a *new* everything," Honey sighed dreamily, lying on her back and watching a cloud float by. The wind carried the smell of the sea as it always did, and her mind's eye flashed back to the island. What would he say if he knew who she really was? She couldn't guess. She glanced at Clifton and caught him looking back.

"You look like you have a secret," he teased.

"Oh, lots of them, sir," she laughed. "Would you like to hear one?"

"Indeed, I would. I'd like to hear all of them."

"I hate shoes! If we were here alone," her eyes danced, "I'd have taken them off. Then we'd both get a terrible reputation."

"Perhaps," he grinned. "Perhaps I shall have to test that admission."

"Have you that much time?" she asked lazily.

"No, most likely not. I have to leave on the last ship in October. Winter sailing isn't the safest." He picked up a stone and skipped it across the surface of the pond.

"That's less than a month." She sat up to scan the shore for their companions. They had strolled to the other side of the small pond, and Ariel was reading to Lawrence.

"Directly after the Autumn Fair," he said. "Do you plan to attend?"

"Amesly is running a horse at the fair, a big black beast. It is tradition to go when your own house is sponsoring a horse, so I believe we will be there."

"But Amesly isn't really your house."

"No," she admitted, "Christopher Ames is my guardian. I don't have a house."

"That doesn't matter, you know. I haven't one either. Just the shack I use during the winter and a cabin on my farm in the summer."

"It does here."

"Not to me," he answered. His eyes forced hers to look at him.

"Are you asking to escort me to the fair?" she smiled, flushing under his scrutiny.

"Yes."

"Thank you. Jillian and I and Ariel will love to."

"But I didn't ask them, I asked you. And I'll expect you to wear my colors." His voice was firm.

"What do you mean?" Her smile faded to a shy grin, and her eyes were questioning. She had already guessed that an acceptance on her part would mean something more than an escort to the fair.

"Why, my colors for the race—on your hat and your arm." His smile broadened.

"I will do that, Mr. Cain," she hedged, "if you'll explain what it means."

"You can't say that you don't know. But you don't, do you?" His voice faded as he looked at her as if for the first time.

Honey turned away, color flooding her face again. How could one man make her feel so stupid? Her eyes flooded with tears, but she swallowed her shame.

"I'm sure I don't know what you mean," she gulped, striding off toward her horse.

"Honey, ah, Miss James, pray forgive me. We know so little of each other. Why, I just assumed that you were native to England. Apparently that assumption was wrong. May I explain?"

Honey stopped. Why hadn't she paid closer attention to that last novel?

"England is very new to me," she said, turning to face him. "I'm afraid that the customs confuse me and often I'm afraid to ask for explanations. I shouldn't have walked away. I am sorry, too."

Cliff smiled as he reached for her hand. "No need. It is because you are so different from London girls that I like you so much." He pulled her back to the blanket to fully explain the colors at the Autumn Fair.

"You *what!?*" Ariel stood stock-still, her eyes bulging in disbelief.

"You're wearing Geoff's colors, aren't you? What's the difference?"

"The difference is I'm promised to Geoff. If you do this you'll be pledging yourself to Clifton."

"No, I won't. You know that it's all in fun!" Honey dismissed Ariel's beliefs. "Besides, who is to say I don't want to be with Clifton? People in the colonies won't care where I'm from."

"People will always care where you're from," Ariel cried.

"What is all this noise?" Jillian poked her head in the door to find her charges standing back-to-back.

"I told Clifton Cain that I'd wear his colors Saturday." Honey turned to Jillian as if she were a child confessing her sins. "Ariel thinks it is a mistake."

"Oh, dear." Jillian moved into the room and closed the door. "It depends on the spirit in which the offer was made. These races used to be taken very seriously. A young woman often wore the color of the man she hoped to marry—a scarf on her hat, usually. The hats were hung on posts and whoever won the hat won the lady for the day. If a man took a hat not showing his colors, then he was expected to provide proof of his intentions for her. Sometimes this turned into a very messy business . . ." Jillian smiled at each girl. "One time a young lady wanted to be with a young man whose color was burgundy, but another young man wanted her to wear *his* color, so he changed his color to burgundy, claiming later that he had no idea that another man had already chosen the same color. Well, someone else got wind of the scheme and fixed it so that *everyone* at the race had burgundy. And since then the race has meant very little."

Jillian finished her story with tears in her eyes. She hadn't mentioned that it was her brother, George, who had fixed the race, nor that burgundy was the color of her one-time beau.

"Don't worry about it, child." She patted Honey's hand. "Wear whatever colors you wish, but be certain of what you are getting yourself into. What color did he pick?"

"Royal blue."

"Oh?" Jillian laughed again, "Amesly has always been royal blue, the color of the sea and of Regina's eyes. See how things work out?"

Jillian left the room where the girls sat in silence.

"I'm sorry." Ariel was the first to speak.

"For what? You are just trying to protect me. There is nothing wrong with that."

"Oh yes, there is . . ." Ariel turned to her friend. "Suddenly it seemed as if you were going to wear Clifton's colors and then his ring. If you marry him you'll move to the colonies and then . . ." Ariel wiped away a tear. "We haven't been friends long, but . . . I should miss you awfully if you leave me."

"I can't say the thought hasn't crossed my mind, and I can't say it won't happen, but I do know what you mean. I feel the same way about you."

"You do?" Ariel lifted her head, her eyes gleaming with unspent tears.

"Yes, I just don't know what you call it," she sniffed, walking into her friend's hug.

"Friendship," Ariel whispered back. "It's called friendship."

Chapter Twenty

The Autumn Fair began on a Monday with the horse traders showing their breeds to anyone who was interested in purchasing stock. Tents and tables of booksellers and storytellers, medicine wagons, and exotic dancers filled the spaces in between. Large rocks were stacked in the shape of a well. Grates covered the well, and fires beneath them provided both warmth and a place for fairgoers to cook their food.

"George Ames brought this idea back from somewhere," someone said. "Wasn't it George who . . . ?"

"Lord, I haven't thought of that scandal for years," someone else gasped. "I didn't think anyone around here remembered that." Honey heard them and knew she was the reason George Ames was on everyone's mind.

The moment Amesly had been reopened, speculation spread like wildfire across the countryside, and everyone craned their necks to get a look at "the girl" as she strolled by.

By mid-week Honey had become the topic of the season. Who was she? Where had she come from and what was she doing at Amesly? By race time on Saturday it was clear that Honey occupied a special place at Amesly. Not only did she attend the races in the Amesly carriage, she also wore the Amesly colors. But if one were to watch her closely one would note that she encouraged a man who was clearly not from Amesly . . . but who also wore royal blue on his sleeve.

Honey rubbed the spot that Ariel had just elbowed a sixth time. "A lady holds herself reserved!" she repeated. The words no longer meant much, but Honey turned back to the race in time to see Clifton lean into her pole and lift her hat neatly from the peg.

"He got it, Ariel! Did you see him?" Honey's eyes shone with pride as she clutched at her friend's sleeve. She could not suppress her excitement no matter how she tried. She wondered if this was love, the kind of love Ariel felt for Geoff.

"Everyone saw, and by now tongues are wagging," Ariel fairly snapped. "Oh, look! Michael has captured Jillian's bonnet."

"He is a gentleman, that Michael," Honey agreed, but her eyes followed Clifton, still mounted, as he pranced back to the landau where Ariel and Honey sat. Michael pranced beside him carrying Jillian's bonnet. Jillian sat in the next landau with an old friend.

"My lady," Clifton stood in his stirrups, making an elaborate bow as he presented her with his trophy.

"My lord," she echoed regally, "thou art too kind."

"You two will excuse me!" The door slammed open and Ariel stepped down in a flurry of billowing skirts.

"What was that about?"

"She misses her betrothed, I'm certain." Honey watched her friend stride off toward a group of women who chatted among themselves. Then she placed her straw hat back on her head and tied the ribbons beneath her chin. "They should have married this month, but . . ."

"But Chris dragged him off to sea?"

"Something like that," Honey nodded, "and it looks like they shan't return until next . . ." Honey glanced at the huge black animal that Michael rode; he was beginning to dismount. Suddenly there was a dark-haired boy working his way up the horse's side. The word *NO!* echoed through the stillness in a child's voice. The child's blue eyes turned toward her and he laughed. "Chicken . . . Licken Chicken . . ." he sang back as the horse snorted and pawed the ground. Suddenly the beast tossed his head wildly and the boy slipped from the stirrup. He fell underneath the animal just as it reared.

"No!" Honey screamed, jumping from her seat, reaching as if to catch the child before the horse dropped to the ground on top of the child. Her heart thudded in her ears and pain surged through her temples. Then suddenly there was no child, just Michael sending her a bewildered look as he held the horse steady beside him.

"Answer me! What's wrong!" Clifton's hand was on her shoulder, staying her from what would certainly have been a painful fall to the ground over the side of the conveyance.

She looked into his brown eyes. The wild look he had seen in her green eyes subsided.

"Nothing." The word sounded flat, drained of emotion. But her pale flesh told another story.

"I . . . it was nothing. Forgive me, please." Her weak smile failed to reassure him.

"Sit down then." His eyes never left her as he dismounted and moved to stand beside the landau. His horse wandered off toward greener grass, then stopped to graze.

"Why don't you tell me what's wrong?" Clifton leaned against the black leather. He glanced at Michael, who was talking to Jillian as he brushed down his horse.

"I don't know. I looked over by Michael and I thought I saw a child trying to climb onto a horse. It scared me. But of course that couldn't be." She shook her head at her own folly and pulled her cloak tightly around herself as if to ward off the sudden chill. But it wasn't a chilly day. It was the blood in her veins that had turned cold.

"What can't be?" Clifton looked at Michael and looked around for small children. There were a few, but all of them were in their parents' protective care.

"Please forgive my outburst. It was nothing, really." She tried to smile, but she glanced several times at the groom who brushed down the nameless black beast and shivered in spite of herself.

"You are quite sure?" He studied her face closely.

"Quite sure, thank you." She tilted her head and smiled.

"Perhaps some dinner would be in order?" He opened the half door of the landau to hand her down.

"I believe you are right," she nodded. Pulling the basket from the seat beside her, she took his hand and stepped to the ground. They walked silently to where Jillian and Ariel had spread their cloth beneath a large oak. Despite the warmth, Honey pulled her cloak a little closer around her, still trying to shake the haunted feeling that clung to her.

The lawn cloth was a thick fabric resembling homespun. It provided a clean, dry spot to sit, as well as a firm pallet to keep dishes from toppling. The food brought from Amesly and Clifton's estate, Creekwood, was delicious beyond words. Yet Honey hadn't much taste for the foods she consumed. She was conscious of Clifton watching her and knew he must be thinking she was tainted with fool's blood. She couldn't help but wonder herself. She was experiencing many visions of late, and she had to admit that she cared what he thought of her. Was it time to confide in him? Was Ariel right? Yes. Clifton's attentions represented more than just friendship, or his concern wouldn't be affecting her now.

Ariel watched the pair closely. Something was wrong between them, and she had a hunch that it had something to do with the outburst that had come from their carriage earlier. Thankfully, no one knew Honey or Clifton well enough to speculate on a specific subject, but that didn't prohibit curiosity seekers from strolling past nonetheless. By tomorrow, she decided, someone will have written an item for that new scandal sheet that now titillated London on a daily basis.

But now Ariel wondered if Clifton mightn't be the right man for her friend after all. They shared the same likes and dislikes, and he seemed truly to care for her. They shared as close a relationship as could be expected between a man and a woman under the circumstances. Not that she didn't love her husband-to-be, but not everyone could expect to be as lucky as she and Geoff. After all, not everyone fell in love.

"Déjà vu," Ariel whispered later as they rested under a large shade tree.

"That's French. What does it mean?"

"Shhhh," Jillian turned from the lady she was chatting with to glare at the two girls, then she returned to her conversation.

"It means 'already seen,' the feeling that you have done something before," Ariel explained softly.

"Really? That's a relief. I get that feeling a lot."

They fell silent. Honey's thoughts wandered to the gnarled tree that bordered the Amesly/Wingfield boundaries. As she had walked that way one sunny afternoon she had been drawn to that tree. There was something nagging about the shape, the way the twisted branches wound around each other, seemingly clawing their way to the sky. Breathlessness had overtaken her then, as if she had been running, and visions of animal teeth assailed her. The vision passed quickly—just as the one this morning had—leaving her chilled and emotionally exhausted. She truly worried for her sanity, for in the last few days she had suffered more nightmares. The falling-down-dark-passages dreams recurred nightly now, but somehow she never hit the bottom. It was just such a dream that claimed her now, lying there under the tree with Ariel. And as always, she woke with a start.

It was three o'clock before the young ladies were allowed their freedom again—one hour before the next race was to begin. Honey spent part of that hour perched on the Amesly carriage beneath a parasol. She watched Michael brush down the horse she knew only as *the black beast.* Suddenly Michael's form faded out, but this time Chris appeared in his place, lovingly brushing the muscled animal, slapping his shiny hindquarter before trotting him off to the starting pit.

"Someone might get the impression that it's the Irishman you're interested in instead of me," Clifton's voice was soft in her ear.

"What nonsense!" she answered softly, flashing him a smile. "'Tis the horse I'm interested in, not the man."

"In that case, this is for you." He slipped a wide blue band around her arm and tied it in a gigantic bow with fancy fanning edges. "Sisters," he explained before she could ask. "I had three of them. Nurse counted on me to help on a daily basis. She brushed, I tied."

"You? I wouldn't have thought . . ." She smiled down at him, happy that his mood had changed.

"If I win, this will be exchanged for a ring," he said, looking up from his task. "That is how the game is played."

"I have heard that." She glanced at Ariel, who was strolling her way with a friend.

"But?"

"But I won't hold you to it," she added playfully, hoping he'd know what she meant.

"We shall see." He gave her a small salute then strolled back to the pit where Michael held his mount for him.

Ariel arrived just as the gamesmaster climbed to the top of his platform. Raising a cone to his mouth he shouted, "Gentlemen, mount your horses."

Almost in unison the men standing in the center of the long oval ring mounted. Some of the horses snorted and pawed at the dirt, others danced sideways, bumping into each other. One particularly foul-tempered animal reared up to paw at the air.

"Gentlemen, greet your ladies!"

The riders rode forward as one to the crescent-shaped split-rail fence where the carriages were parked. The men tipped their hats or blew kisses to the ladies who wore their colors.

Clifton rode toward the Amesly carriage, but rather than an outrageous display of affection, he simply inclined his head. The message he sent with his eyes was powerful nonetheless. There was no doubt that if Clifton won the race, he would expect Honey to be his bride. She felt it so strongly that she feared he might stand on his horse and shout the news before the race had even been run.

"Gentlemen, take your positions!" the burly man shouted again. Clifton's horse danced sideways to the starting line, but Clifton refused to take his gaze from Honey until the shot sounded from the starting pistol. At once, a dozen horses lunged forward, their hooves pounding the soft earth, kicking up clots of grass and soil. In seconds they sped past the spectators, racing over a hill and out of sight.

"They race around the Edmond property then back up here," Ariel explained. "It takes about a quarter of an hour."

"Really?" Honey focused on the gamesmaster. That strange sensation began to plant itself in the pit of her stomach again. As much as she cared for Clifton, at this moment she was unsure of herself. She looked back at the field. The riders had reappeared; indeed, they had covered so much ground they had already crested the next hill and were slipping out of sight again.

"Where do they finish?" Honey asked.

"I just told you," Ariel scolded. "Are you all right?"

"I think I'm tired," she answered.

"I don't wonder. These Autumn Fair days do get long. They finish there." Ariel pointed to the starting point.

"Same place?"

"Yes. Then whoever wins climbs the platform to get his cup, and the lady who wears his colors must present the prize along with a kiss."

"No!"

"Yes. Sometimes you can get away with a kiss on the cheek, but anything more than that and you're as good as married."

Honey was silent. She deliberated on the rule about slapping a man if he tried to kiss her and decided that it must not apply in this case. Social life was so confusing! Marriage, however, would solve that problem. Clifton would be a kind and faithful husband—there was no doubt of that. He would help her to understand what a wife should and should not do. Moreover, judging from his character, he'd make a wonderful father. Then she could stop worrying about her past . . . *and* her future.

The thundering of hooves drew her attention to the track. Three riders had the lead. Michael and Clifton were among them. The crowd around her began to cheer. Shouts of encouragement echoed through the ranks. Women jumped to their feet clutching folded parasols.

The shiny coats of sweat-soaked horses rippled in the sunlight. Their nostrils flared as the beasts, pushed to their limits, thundered across the finish line. It was almost too close to call.

"One moment," the gamesmaster announced over the shouts and cheers of the onlookers. He rushed down the platform steps and talked to several other men as the last six contestants crossed the finish line. The exhausted panting of the horses and riders added to the anticipation of the crowd.

"We saw Orly cross the line first!" someone called out.

"No! It was Flynn."

"Yer daft, man! 'Twas that new kid who crossed first. I seen 'im with me own eyes," another shouted from the sidelines.

Honey tossed a nervous glance at Ariel. Her heart thudded deep in her chest. She had not really considered that Clifton might win, but here they were, three of them tied for first place, the cup . . . and the kiss. She looked out over the field to where the riders were walking their horses to cool them, but no one had dismounted. Only Clifton was smiling broadly. Michael had already conceded the race to him, and Orly had clearly come in third.

The gamesmaster heaved himself back up the steps of his platform and placed his cone to his mouth again, quieting the restless crowd.

"Gentlemen," he called. "Your winner is Clifton Cain, grandson of the late earl of Dragstone."

The crowd heaved a collected gasp. Had the gamesmaster not reported parentage, the outcome might have been challenged. Now all challenges were dropped and cheers rang out for the man who was to take the place of one of the most beloved earls in the county.

Honey sat numbed by the announcement. Her eyes

flashed up to meet his. Still mounted, he cantered across the field to Honey's carriage.

"My lady," he said, touching his hand to his brow. "Will you be so kind?" He leaned over the horse's neck to unlatch the door of her landau. Accepting his hand, she stepped down from the conveyance. He dismounted, and together they walked like royalty to the platform. Gasps and whispers of surprise had already begun, for it had been widely believed that Honey was somehow tied to Christopher Ames. She lived in his house under the supervision of his aunt and even wore his colors, which happened to be the same as Lord Dragstone's. Perhaps the friendship owed a favor. Perhaps Lord Dragstone was acting on behalf of the guardian.

The crowd hushed as the couple ascended the steps to the platform, each looking straight ahead. But he smiled while she did not . . .

"Clifton, son of Kent, grandson of Carlton. And the lady—Miss Honey James of . . . where?" The gamesmaster leaned close to her to receive her answer.

"The lady, Miss Honey James of Amesly." He handed Honey the gold cup resting on a golden bed of pineboughs and pine cones.

Honey lifted the solid gold cup. "My lord," she said with a curtsy, but this time it wasn't in jest. Betrayal stung her as she worked to hold her tears in place, and she refused to look up at him.

"My lady," he returned, covering her hands with his own until she flushed and was forced to look up at him. He pried one hand from the cup and brought it to his lips, savoring the feel of her soft skin. He was giving her a rare show of public respect. It answered only one question, and that was that he clearly cared.

Below, the crowd exploded in rounds of applause. Shouts of tribute to the new earl sounded along with cheers for his lady of choice. Had the new earl not been in mourning, he would have been expected to appear at the ball given by the gamesmaster and his wife.

"Might I escort you home?" Clifton asked as they reached the bottom of the platform.

"I don't think so," she said, still avoiding his eyes. "You have already been far too kind."

"Kind?" His brows gathered, "The story told is not the fact."

"You are not the grandson of the dead earl?"

"The younger one, yes," he continued, "but I will not be here to claim the title. The king has already been advised of my abdication. He will locate the next heir; it is out of my hands."

"You could have told me," she said as her own deceit echoed through her mind. "But I guess it doesn't matter anymore."

"It matters to me," he said simply.

The crowd around them began to disperse, but those standing close strained to hear the conversation between the mystery lady and the new earl. Clifton looked past them. "We cannot talk here. But we do need to talk. I want you to . . ."

"Don't say any more, please. I . . . I need time, we have known each other for such a short time and there is so much you should know, too."

"Then when? How much time do you need?" he demanded, aware of the milling crowd pressing closer to them than was necessary.

"I don't know. Tomorrow afternoon at the pond?" Her eyes grazed his as she began to pull away from him.

"That's a long time to wait," he said, handing her

back into her landau, "for such an important conversation."

"Please," she sighed.

"All right," Wisely, he didn't repeat the plan in front of Ariel. Instead he nodded to both Ariel's and Jillian's congratulations and went on his way.

Chapter Twenty-One

Honey heeled the sand-colored horse into a gallop. The wind was cool and it felt good against her hot cheeks.

Last night had been the worst she had ever lived through. The dreams she had suffered whirled her through a past she couldn't remember, then woke her in the middle of the night. When she finally did go back to sleep, she dreamed of Chris. It was a new dream, but that was no comfort. One moment she would be dancing with Jason, then Clifton, and then she would look up to find angry, piercing blue eyes glowering down to her accusingly. "You can't marry until I give permission," he said almost mockingly, and then he'd kiss her over and over again, and somewhere through the nightmare she would mercifully awaken. Refusing to be subjected to any more torture, she tossed and turned for hours before prowling about her room the rest of the night. Then, at the very first hint of sunrise, she slipped into her riding skirt and left the house. But now, a full hour later, the feelings still clung closely to her.

She was so lost in thought she didn't hear a second rider approach until he yelled, "I said, hold up! Are you trying to kill yourself?"

Honey's head snapped up as a man's hand reached over to grab for her reins. Her first instinct had been to slap at the hand, but she found herself staring at Clifton Cain.

"Clifton!" She pulled back on the reins, slowing the horse's pace until they came to a stop.

"By the looks of you and that horse, you've been out a while," he said.

Honey looked down at her winded mount; she had never considered his well-being. Her shame-filled blush was hidden by her windburned cheeks. Her long hair lay in a thick mass of knots along her back, and the top buttons on her habit had pulled free, exposing her creamy throat and bosom.

He had never seen a more vitally alive woman.

"What are you doing here at this hour?" she blurted out, suddenly aware of her less-than-ladylike appearance.

"Same thing you are. Trying to sort it out."

Honey smiled. "I can't think that there would be that much for you to worry about." She moistened her pink lips as the horse danced beneath her.

"You are wrong," he said quietly. Taking her reins, he led her to the grove of trees. He dismounted, then moved around her horse to lift her from the saddle. "You ride astride, eh?" he chuckled. He'd thought that Ariel had been joking about that.

Honey flushed both from his observation and from the feel of his hands circling her waist. He set her on the ground in front of him, then smoothed a wisp of hair from her forehead.

"You are the kind of woman I need in the colonies. You have the strength and the passion to survive, but I can't help thinking of how selfish I am wanting to take you from your home." He looked down into her eyes. "I am most certainly in love with you, and I've come to think that you might be safer there."

"Clifton, you can't believe that! Besides, you have to stay here, don't you?" Her hands rested on his arms.

"No, I've told you I've given up the lands. They are not really mine anyway; they belong to my older brother. He'll get the message that he is the new earl sooner or later." He searched her face tenderly. "I have only come to make my family's claim, nothing more."

"But at the . . ."

"A mistake, that's all. Whoever thought he recognized me mistook me for Kent. We have been gone from England since childhood; the mistake is only natural." His fingers flexed gently into her waist. "Besides, even if the lands were mine, I couldn't stay. I love my new home, my new life. There is something about living in the colonies that makes life worth something. Here a man lives high in his earldom, he gets fat and his wife grows lazy and soon . . . he's out and she's down."

Honey laughed. "Those very thoughts were just going through my mind. But there is more to me than that—or perhaps less." She paused, willing her heart to slow its pace. She had never confessed before and she was afraid of his reaction. "Clifton, I don't come from the country. I have no family, as far as anyone knows." She turned away, feeling shame for her past.

Clifton looked for a moment at the spot in front of him, then he followed her to the brook that gurgled through the small woods. Dried twigs and fallen leaves crunched underfoot.

"The truth is that Christopher Ames found me on an island in the tropics, the West Indies." She rubbed the throbbing spot at her temple. "I have no memory of who I am or where I came from or how I even got to be on the island. Only that I had been there from a very young age. Here I have lived a lie. My education is thanks to Chris and his aunt. I have nothing, own nothing, not even a name."

"Can this be true?" His jaw fell as he listened to her fantastic story.

"Chris told me that they called me Honey because I recognized the word when they found me last spring. I couldn't remember how to talk or even reason. I didn't even know enough to be afraid of them." She looked up at him as they strolled. The morning sun glinted on her hair, and he tried not to look at it.

"You can't want to marry a girl who has no name."

"That is the least of it," he said quietly.

"And Chris has refused permission for me to marry until he returns home from his voyage. *If* he returns from his voyage." There, she had said it! She dropped her fidgeting hands and looked at Clifton.

"Who is to say he has the right?" he challenged.

"The king has said so; I am Christopher's ward."

"But you must be too old for . . ." Clifton flushed at his own thoughtlessness.

"I know. I must be twenty at least, but since there is no proof, what can be done?"

"You know that is no excuse at all," he said, grabbing her arm. He swung her around to meet him. "I could, with very little trouble, take you with me this moment." His eyes bore into hers and slowly his mouth moved over hers, tenderly nudging her lips open.

Honey felt his warm lips against hers. He was pleasant to kiss, but that was all. There were no stirrings deep inside and her heart never altered a beat. Something was missing. Something she couldn't name.

"But I don't want you that way," he said. "I want you to *want* to come with me, but the fact that you're not jumping into my arms tells me that you don't feel the same."

"I need time to find out who I am. How could I take your name without knowing my own?" The words came from her heart. "Maybe there will be some answers when he returns." She met his gaze sadly; she knew she had just torn out his heart. She felt his pain.

Clifton smiled. "I think I can understand that. I went to the colonies for the same reasons, or similar ones, I should say. Maybe some day you'll give up this search or . . ."

"Or I'll just show up, knocking on your door."

"And if I'm off trapping?" he joked, but his eyes were suddenly shiny with tears.

"Then I'll find you! I'll ask the Indians where the porcupines live and I'll sit myself down right there and wait for you." She smiled, but tears glistened in her eyes, too.

"Do you love me, Honey?" he finally asked breathlessly.

"For the little I know of love, I think I do," she said looking quickly away.

Clifton touched her shoulder, and she turned into his arms to lay her head on his chest. Like a brother, she really did love him. And like a friend. She was going to miss him terribly. Somehow she thought he knew that she would never show up at his door.

Chapter Twenty-Two

Honey refolded the leather dress decorated with porcupine quills.

"Imagine," Ariel gasped, "wearing only that with nothing beneath."

Honey laughed. On the island she had worn far less. "Porcupines, humm. There really *are* such things."

"What else did the letter say?" the younger woman asked.

They were stationed in the library, curled up in front of a roaring fire. Christmas was less than a month away. Honey examined the seam of the elaborate chair covers she was sewing for Jillian.

Clifton's letter lay beside them.

"He wishes us well and say's he is relieved we are not with him." She pulled at a loose stitch. "The Indians have gone on the warpath."

"Oh, no! Has anyone been killed?"

"He said a whole village was burned and only one small child survived . . ." Her throat tightened as she pictured the chaos Clifton had described in his letter. He had gone on to tell her of the cold, lonely nights of late autumn in a place called Canada, and of a treacherous trip through the forests separated only by rivers and lakes near a place the Indians called Minn-a-so'-ta.

"Are you all right?"

"I guess. But I feel dreadful." She smoothed the cover of the box that held the dress.

"You only did what you had to do."

"I know." Honey wandered back to her sewing.

"Honey, is it the letter that has you so . . . ?"

"Sad? No, I don't know what is wrong with me. Maybe it is Christmas. Thinking of Clifton out there in the cold. Maybe there are feelings left over from before I got lost." Her delicate hand rubbed at her forehead, working to ease the headache that was fast becoming her constant companion. "Jillian's stories about her childhood Christmases sound so familiar."

And I miss Chris. The last sentence was left unspoken. She didn't understand it, even hated the idea of missing him! But she did. Rarely were thoughts of him very far from her mind.

As the snow piled up outside the windows and Christmas came and went and the New Years galas were danced away, he was on her mind more often than not—particularly on New Year's Eve, when the ladies of the Ames household attended a small dinner dance given by the former lady of Brentwood.

Though no one could fathom why the lady had decided on an informal dinner party rather than a grand ball to celebrate the coming of the new year, neither did anyone turn away an invitation to spend the evening with London's most celebrated widow.

Ariel had chosen Honey's gown of forest green and instructed Brea in what fashion her friend's hair should be dressed. The transformation was miraculous.

Honey stood back from the dressing table to face

the oblong silver plate polished to reflect her image. She had never dreamed of looking so pretty. She was fascinated by the hoops that made her gown stand out around her in graceful wide sweeps, and she had grown to appreciate the layers of fabric that formed her full skirts and hid her true figure, but that also kept the chill of winter from biting her flesh. She was transformed to someone new, someone she was a little afraid to meet. The last detail of her toilet was the sapphire and diamond filigree pin that she fixed to the green lace bodice of her gown. The pin was all that remained of the Honey James she remembered.

"Oh no, no!" Ariel was smiling as she came into her friend's room. She removed the sapphire pin from the green lace. "This." She produced a palm full of pearls. There was one tiny strand to pin into her coiffure to hold a twist of thick brown hair in place and one matronly brooch with a golden rose draped in three strands of pearls. "There. You look lovely!" Ariel stepped back, admiring Honey's untarnished youth, "Your first big party."

"Stay by me," Honey smiled nervously.

"Have you ever met Jennifer Bates?"

"No." Honey turned to get a look at her velvet skirts from behind.

"Neither have I. Jillian said that she met her once but . . . It's strange that she would invite us to her party when really we don't know the same people. Unless . . ." Ariel chewed at the tender flesh inside her lip. "I've heard that Christopher and she have . . . stepped out once or twice together." She flushed, knowing that she could never explain to Honey what she meant by *stepping out*.

"Really?" Honey took her eyes from the mirror to her friend. "Then why are we going?"

Ariel shrugged. "My mother will have a fit when

she finds out."

"That doesn't answer my question." Honey turned to face her friend.

"Because I talked Jillian into it," Ariel blurted out triumphantly. "This is the first party we have been allowed all season. Likely there will be only one or two more afternoon teas, and maybe someone will call on us. But we both need to get out, and if it happens that it is out to Lady Bates . . ." A wicked smile crossed her lips and she shrugged.

"None of this makes any sense." Honey turned back to the mirror, deflated by the thought of spending an evening with a woman who was on intimate terms with Chris. But Ariel was right, she was beginning to get restless too. It would do them both good to get out—even if it was to the home of a questionable woman.

The warning sounded inside Honey the moment they mounted the stairs to Jennifer's townhouse. The warning almost never failed her: without even entering the house, she knew she was completely outclassed. But she entered anyway, following Jillian's lead.

No sooner had introductions been made than Honey's night turned into a nightmare. Jennifer grilled her about Clifton and Chris from the time they arrived until the dancing started. With a wicked smile on her face, she forced Honey to confess her summer experiences. Somehow the woman had managed to learn about the events at the Autumn Fair, even the color she had worn on her arm. Summing up the strong points of each man, Jennifer encouraged Honey to choose one before the night was out.

If that were not bad enough, she felt like a country bumpkin compared with the London elite present that evening. Honey's modest gown covered her from chin to heel, while this dark-haired, black-eyed cat was bare to the tips of her breasts. Her velvet gown was scarlet, trimmed in black satin piping. Her wide velvet skirts parted to reveal an elaborately embroidered underskirt. Rubies winked from her ears, her fingers, and her throat. Everything about the woman's demeanor, from the tone of her perfect voice to the style of her perfect hair, was a warning to Honey. It was Jennifer's perfect mouth that smiled in self-admiration when Jillian Ames made their apologies and took her girls home long before midnight. Honey, it seemed, had developed a fierce headache . . .

The first few days of the new year were colder than usual, yet that didn't stop the steady stream of callers at Jillian Ames's home. Everyone wanted to meet Christopher Ames's ward, the one rumored to be his intended bride, the one who had reportedly been honored by the earl of Dragstone, who wore Christopher's colors as a favor. The *Tatler* had reported that she was a native princess, given to Christopher as reward for some heroic act on some obscure island in the West Indies. That rumor, however, was belied simply by looking at her honey-shaded skin and brown hair. Then who was she really? Where was she from? And why had Christopher deserted her after a scant week? Everyone was asking the same questions. It was the most important topic at every social function of the season. Moreover, speculation made her out to be everything from a reformed street waif to foreign royalty escaping an evil monarch.

By mid-February callers were being turned away at the Ameses' door; by mid-March Zachary Lane had become a popular passage for those wishing to catch a glimpse of the mystery girl. Ariel knew that her parents' extended trip abroad was the only reason she remained in the Amesly household, but long before Easter, after a secret trip to the dressmakers, Jillian, Ariel, and Honey slipped out of London and back to the country estate of Amesly. Tempers were growing short and so was time. Nearly a full year had passed since the *Wing Master* had gone to sea, and they all doubted now that it would return.

Chapter Twenty-Three

A month before the *Wing Master* was to return to London, word came to the ship of some to-do over the earl of Dragstone and a girl who was attached to Amesly. Christopher had no need to guess at who that girl might be. He couldn't account for the tightening around his heart when he overheard the sailors of another London merchant ship talk with his crew in a pub in Cape Verde, one of the last stops on his failed mission. Portugal's Cape Verde and the Canary Islands were the only two places left to inquire of the *Crystal Wing*. This stop alone, though, would take up more than a fortnight, with fourteen islands to cover and with many villages dotting each island. No one would be allowed to go unquestioned here, for anyone might have seen something that could be a clue. As for Honey's past, Chris had learned that the only ship lost at sea and last seen in the vicinity of her island was a prison ship carrying women and their children as well as men.

Even the infamous Bloodwell had joined in the search, only to come up empty. No pirates had sailed with children on board. Of course, her combs and earbob could have been stolen booty, but somehow he knew that she was not a refugee from a prison ship.

"Sounds like our little girl is a doing well for herself," Geoff chuckled as he pulled out a chair and sat down.

Chris grimaced and swallowed from his mug of wine.

"The notices are up—Albon and Hux are going from door to door now. We have about three hours before they get back."

Chris rubbed the shoulder that had met the sharp edge of a scimitar almost twelve months ago in Morocco.

"Does it look like trouble out there?" He glanced over the room to see if anyone was watching them too closely. His intuition had proved itself in Rabat, the capital city of Morocco. The giant man in the woven turban had been a market pirate. He and his band of thieves hung around the markets until they found a ship filled with cargo. After the captain and his mate made inquiries about selling it, the pirates would swim out to the ship and slit the throats of the crew. Having looted the ship, they then set fire to it and set it adrift. Only Geoff's keen intuition had saved them from a similar fate.

Jacob himself could have fallen to that fate, but he had no reason to port there. And Chris recalled that they had planned no stops at all. Nonetheless, he extended his search through Gambia, Sierra Leone, Malabo, Luanda, Lüderitz, Cape Town, Durban, Madagascar, around Somalia, past Arabia, to Persia. The smaller ports they reserved for the trip back. Most of these seaports were isolated and thinly populated; the rest were native villages where the reef was too dangerous to cross or the natives hostile enough to make landing ill-advised.

Now that a year had passed, he had no more answers than when he started.

This talk of the new earl of Dragstone didn't help his mood. Kent was the boy's name; no, there were two of them. The older had a fondness for travel, the younger, Chris had heard, had gone off to the colonies. As a second son, he would have no interest in the earldom, unless his older brother died without issue. But what did that matter now? If it were Kent who had come home and won Honey's heart, his lordship would have the power to refute Chris's guardianship. They could very well do as they pleased. If it had been Clinton or Clifton or whatever his name was, he could easily have swept Honey off to the colonies, where British rule was often overlooked.

Chris tipped his head back and tossed down another mug of wine.

"Chris!" Geoff burst from his chair. Chris hadn't even noticed the crewman who had entered the saloon and reported to his first mate, "They found someone who has seen the *Crystal Wing*!"

Honey sat on her knees at the edge of the garden. Her sun hat lay forgotten beside her. Behind her, Ariel and Jillian laughed together as they uncovered the new spring garden. The stock was of a new variety Jillian had obtained by bribing the royal gardener. Together they had planted their secret stock at Amesly, knowing full well that this was another desperate attempt to forget the gossips of London.

It was actually Ariel that both Honey and Jillian worried about. A stained reputation could eliminate her name from all the social lists for the winter season—should she continue to associate with a woman who had called so much attention to herself. But Ariel did not seem to mind, and she permitted herself no embarrassment over their friendship.

"Everything is all right, I trust?" Jillian sent a worried look to her younger charge, who read a letter from Clifton.

"Yes, he insists he is fine." Honey dashed the tear from her eye as she turned back to her friends. "He says that his winter trek will soon be over and he will return to Virginia to check his crops. He has taken a record number of pelts, which he says will make him a fortune."

"That is good news." Ariel smiled as she dug a hole for her seedling.

"What else did he say?" Jillian pressed her plant into place, then moved to the next space to make a hole.

"That's all, except that the Indians are killing people again, but this time they are moving farther out—the colonists, that is." Honey didn't mention the heart-wrenching pleas for her to follow him, to take the very next ship and meet him at his front door. He pleaded that she return his love, no matter in what small amount. She folded the parchment and shoved it into her pocket. Pulling on the thick gloves, she rejoined the gardening, but she wondered how much the fare to the colonies would be.

Chapter Twenty-Four

Captain Christopher Ames strode confidently into the harbormaster's office. "Seth." He grinned wider than Seth had ever seen him smile before.

"You found the woman's family." Seth stood, offering his hand to his favorite captain.

"Better." Chris handed his friend the sworn statement he had obtained in Cape Verde more than a month before. "Pirates, Seth, the *Crystal Wing* went down to pirates. The cargo, the crew—both lost at sea."

Seth dropped back into his chair as he read the English translation of the Portuguese written statement. Indeed, the *Crystal Wing* and her master were never criminals at all. "My friend, would you like to present this at court or shall I?"

"Let us go together. There's a statesman there I'd like to meet."

The harbormaster grabbed his coat and turned over the painted "Gone for the Day" sign that covered his window. "And who is the fellow you are hoping to meet?" Seth followed Chris out the door and down the stairs.

"The new earl of Dragstone." Chris held the door

of the waiting carriage.

"Oh, the Cain boy? He's never shown up. The younger one was here last fall to claim the land in his brother's name, but he's gone back to the colonies. Left late last fall. Heard tell it was some sort of favor to you that he stayed as long as he did."

"Me? I've yet to meet the fellow. How could he have done me a favor?"

Seth laughed. "It's those women, don't you know? My wife has said she heard your young lady is being groomed to be your bride. The Cain boy was to have been her guardian while you were away. Your ward even wore your colors at the Autumn Fair races. Now my daughters tell a different story. Something about a courtship that fell apart the day of the Autumn Fair races. They said they heard her jump up and shout "No" at him. They claim it was a rejection of marriage. But Salis has been delivering letters to your aunt's house on almost a monthly basis—all from the colonies . . . So I'm afraid only your young lady will have your answers for you."

"You mean, she did not go to the colonies with him? She didn't marry the . . . ?"

"The Cain boy abdicated. He had rights by birth since his brother never came to claim the land, but he decided he didn't even want to stand-in until his brother returns. He handed the whole business over to the courts, boarded a ship, and went back to the colonies."

Chris dropped his head back against the seat as the coach jumped forward. He tried to digest all that Seth had told him, but the stories were so conflicting he hadn't a clue about which to believe.

"Hold up!" a voice called from outside the moving vehicle.

Both men looked out the window to see who was

forcing their carriage to stop.

"Chris, they're gone!" Geoff reined his mount in close to the window. "Ariel, Honey, and Jillian, too! The house is deserted."

"Oh, yes, they've moved on to Amesly," Seth supplied. "They had a difficult time in the city here."

"They went to Amesly," Chris repeated out the window. "Go ahead, I'll be along later."

Geoff grinned—as if he'd wait another moment to see his betrothed! He wheeled his horse toward the north road, spurred the animal's sides, and was gone.

"There will be a wedding soon," Seth winked. "Maybe two?"

"No, Seth, that woman is not intended for me. My chance died long ago. But at least I can clear her father's good name."

"That won't bring her back." The older man shook his head. "Haven't you punished yourself enough?"

Chris smiled sadly at the papers folded in his hands. "I know. I have heard the same from Stockwell about the guilt I harbor because they died and I didn't. Maybe so. But you of all people should know what it would be like married to a salt. We eat, sleep, and live for the sea, for the rolling deck and the swabs. I'm losing my first mate to the offices because he traded his love of water for that of a woman. No, thank you! Even a mistress is more than I care to handle. But you say things were difficult for them here?"

Seth laughed, but he didn't miss the concern in Chris's voice. "They've been bored here, Chris. And I can't help but think it was a jealous woman that stirred all the commotion. For some time after the new year started, Hyde Park was less traveled than Zachary Lane. Everyone wanted to gawk at the native savage you brought back from the West Indies. Word was she was hiding from an evil ruler, but that was another story. At the first breath of spring Jillian packed up and returned to Amesly. She sent a messenger by my office the day before they left. She knew you'd stop here before going home."

A groan escaped Christopher as the carriage stopped. What had he done? What *could* he have done? He could have left her on that island, as indeed had been his first thought. He could have married her and saved her from this embarrassment. He could have married her off to Jason. Why he didn't do that he'd never know.

"Seth, how long has it been since you've taken a holiday?" The carriage was waved through the gates at the palace and rumbled to a stop at the wide, ornate stairs.

"Been a while," he nodded, stepping to the ground.

"Yes, I think I have just solved my problem." Chris slammed the carriage door. "I believe a week in the country is just what you and the missus need."

Honey looked out from her bedroom window. Ariel had seen the rider coming and knew instantly who it was. She flung herself out the bedroom door, down the stairs, and out the front door before Honey could even speak.

She watched Geoff jump from his lathered horse and run the last several steps to his beloved. They met head-on and flung themselves into each's arms. Honey heard Ariel's cry of joy as Geoff lifted and swung her around before tenderly kissing her. Then he wiped the tears from her face.

Tears stung at her own eyes as she watched, happy

for her two closest friends. At last she let the curtains fall. Smoothing her gown and wiping her eyes she went down to greet Geoff.

"Honey?" Geoff looked up from the front door as Honey descended the stairs. She almost laughed at the bewildered look on his face, then she touched her hair, which was her own natural color now and had grown back down to her waist.

"What do you think?" She patted a fallen lock.

"I'm shocked!" He smiled, dislodging himself from his betrothed, and moved to the bottom of the stair. He hadn't changed much in the last year, Honey thought. Maybe a little broader through the shoulders, certainly more tan. A little taller.

"You look wonderful," he said at last.

"Thank you, sir." She dipped her head. "You are also looking quite fit. I trust the voyage went well?"

"So well, you see . . ."

"Let's go into the library, shall we?" Ariel pulled Geoff from the stair. "I'll find Jillian. She'll want to know all about this too!"

"Yes!" Honey agreed. "I'll get Brea to bring some refreshments." Ariel rushed off to the back gardens and Honey turned to find the kitchens, but Geoff stopped her.

"Aren't you even going to ask about him?" Geoff searched Honey's downcast eyes.

"Why ever should I do that?" was all she could manage.

"He has been like a caged bear for the last month. Word of you and some earl found us in Cape Verde. What happened?"

"Who is asking, you or Chris?" Honey brought her eyes defiantly up to Geoff's.

"I cannot speak for him, but . . ."

"But he has said nothing. His concern was for his betrothed's father. I hope the news is good," she said, pulling gently from his grasp. But before she moved away she said, "'Tis strange that word of my short relationship with an earl might reach his ears, but not my humiliation at the hands of his lover."

Honey stood for several moments outside the doors to the kitchens. She waited for her heart to stop hurting. She had understood for many months now why they had been invited to Jennifer's dinner party. Too late had Ariel realized what had happened, for she had never left Honey's side. The devious Jennifer had also invited a few elderly men, who converged on Jillian and kept her from Honey's defense. The sport Jennifer had made of her still ate away at her self-esteem. Sometimes she would stand before her polished silver plate and study her body, but she could see little difference between herself and Lady Bates—except for the way the other woman held herself. Perhaps if she held her head a little higher, her shoulders back a little further . . . Of course, that wouldn't make up for her lack of experience. Unfortunately, she was limited to two kisses and a library of books, ranging from novels that Jillian would prefer she not read to works that explored the human body and mind. None were very helpful in finding a cure for her ailment, for being made a laughingstock wasn't a curable malady—but then again, neither was it fatal. And now Christopher was back. It thrilled her and scared her half to death. To compound her anxiety, he was going to take his own sweet time coming home to face her. She felt like a child awaiting her first spanking, both dreading the pain and eager to get the punishment over with.

She took a deep breath before moving through the

kitchen to leave orders for luncheon before joining the rest of her adopted family on the veranda.

Several days before Chris's arrival, word came that there was to be a celebration, a double celebration—one in honor of the heroic Jacob Wingfield, who died at sea without giving quarter to the enemy, the other to celebrate the forthcoming wedding of his first mate to Miss Ariel Blackmoore.

The message from Chris arrived with a dozen new servants and a wagon filled with delicacies that Honey had only read about. A pack of hounds were delivered as well, and an adorable little animal with a sharp nose and pointed ears. He looked so sad and frightened Honey was tempted to release him without even knowing why he had been delivered.

A pair of gardeners descended on the half-finished garden, and three extra stable hands scrubbed and polished the stables from top to bottom. No one was happier about that than Michael Flynn himself, who eagerly joined in the scrubbing.

Nothing in the house was left in its original place. Rooms were redecorated and carpets replaced. Jillian, who had a love of cleaning, was in her glory, commanding a garrison of servants armed with dust cloths, mops, brooms, and brushes.

Everyone had a job, and Ariel's job was Honey. The two women were granted the use of a carriage with Geoff as chaperon. They journeyed to Cardiff in search of a dressmaker.

Honey was accustomed to the ritual by now, and long used to all the trappings and ties and contraptions that women were forced to wear in the name of fashion.

She ordered a new habit, again in palm green

velvet, with shortened sleeves and a matching jacket with wide cuffs. She chose a ball gown, though she had one that she had never even tried on, several day gowns, and a few morning gowns. All pastels, all fitted for a young woman. However, as Ariel took her turn in the fitting room, Honey scanned the pages of the fashion books from London and France and changed her order completely without telling anyone. With a secret smile pasted to her lips, she relaxed and enjoyed the ride back to Amesly.

Chapter Twenty-Five

The sun had set more than an hour ago, yet teal blue still streaked the sky and a dull red orange tinted the horizon.

The small family lounged before a fire in the library after dinner had been finished and cleared. A quiet camaraderie drew them together as Honey stitched, Jillian crocheted, and Ariel read aloud to them from a book of proverbs. This was their last family night alone together. Tomorrow thirty invited guests would descend upon Amesly for the weekend celebrations.

Somewhere on the road to Amesly, Chris mulled over the real reasons for his guest list: to feed the scandal mongers, the gossip seekers, the malicious curiosity of the fashionably elite. Although they were his own class, he had learned to see them from the other side of life thanks to Ida, who showed him the hard life lived by the wretched poor—subjected daily to the high and mighty attitudes of the wealthy, who passed out unjust sentences for petty, self-righteous reasons. Now a member of his household was under attack by these same people.

He'd discovered that stories about Honey had

filled every club in London. Even in court he was congratulated on his forthcoming marriage. Jennifer's name had also been mentioned, and the essence of *that* story left him dumbstruck. He didn't want to believe Jennifer capable of such a thing, though he knew well what a manipulating woman she was. And he knew well how to handle her. After this weekend she'd be one lover short.

Yes, this celebration was the best course of action. Ariel and Geoff would protect Honey from those who pried too deeply, and then when they had all had a chance to meet her, he would grant her permission to go to the colonies to marry her earl. He felt certain that the letter he had been entrusted to carry from the mate of the *Spin Drift* to Miss Honey James was a summons from her lord, Clifton of Dragstone. That would be best, he reasoned, a life in lovely Virginia, where tobacco planters were already making a name for themselves. Huge houses of wood were being built and fashions from London dressed the ladies, who had begun their own winter seasons. Clifton, he had learned, was one of the more preeminent tobacco growers in the New World. Oddly enough, the shipment Chris had lost in last year's storm had been from Creekwood plantation, owned by none other than Clifton Cain. Creekwood had been his last stop before the storms tossed them to the south, to Honey's little island. Oh, the irony of it all! But even the irony couldn't make him smile.

Several hours later, in the shadows of the setting sun, Christopher stood over Christine Wingfield's grave. The stone had aged since the last time he'd stopped here, and a blanket of green covered the grave beside her. The name on that stone was Crystal's. In a few days the stone he had ordered would be delivered, and the three of them could rest together at last. Tears rushed to his eyes, but he bit them back as he placed the parchment on Christine's grave. It was Jacob's Decree of Pardon. He used the knife strapped to his hip to pin the paper in place. On the next grave he placed a single black-eyed Susan. Still carefully reining in his emotions, he turned to leave. But he took the long way home.

The boxes were delivered just before luncheon on the opening day of the celebrations. Both Ariel and Honey rushed to their adjoining rooms and began ripping open their packages. Gown after gown was assessed and closeted.

"Perfect!" Honey breathed, tossing one day dress aside for the next. Rich colors splashed against a wealth of fabrics, and each one was as well cut as the next. Some had short sleeves with button-down fitted waists or scooped necks with puffed off-the-shoulder lace drapes; others had frothy white chemises of the finest lace, with petticoats so stiff she wondered if she would be able to sit down in them.

They were gowns made for a woman, not a girl. Her depression lifted at last. When Jennifer Bates arrived Honey would meet her rival head-on. Dressed in her gown of royal blue, Honey smiled at the woman she saw looking back at her in the mirror. The gown was made of a lightweight fabric that seemed to float around her as she moved. The fitted bodice had a square-cut neckline trimmed with tiny fans of lace. The sleeves, too, were fitted to the elbow, where wide angel sleeves dripped with matching lace. The pinched waist flared out to a full skirt that was captured and held back by two white lace bows to show a simple pale blue petticoat. The only flaw she could see was the warm rose texture of her skin. But there was nothing she could do about that.

The final touch was the twist she had learned to put to her rich chestnut brown hair. She tucked the long ends into a small crown at the top of her head with one small curl dangling from the top, lending a careless look to her coiffure.

"Well? What do you think?" She whirled through the door that joined the girls' rooms.

"Oh! Honey . . . It's a bit daring, don't you think?" Ariel gasped, but her eyes betrayed the envy she had for her friend's taste.

"You know, I feel wonderful! I've hated fitted sleeves and high necks from the start. At last I feel like me. Me! Whoever that is." Honey smiled as she brought her billowing skirts to rest in a puff on Ariel's feather tick.

"You're right. The color and the style suit you well." Ariel stood in front of her own mirror and yanked the high-buttoned jacket from her gown to reveal short puffed sleeves and a fitted bodice. "The jackets suit me better," she shrugged.

"Maybe if you wore a lace neckline instead of a jacket . . ." Honey suggested. "It would look open but not revealing."

"Yes, that would suit me." She hooked a plain white kerchief over the scoop neck of the gown. "Let's go down and give Jillian a chance to rest."

Honey preceded Ariel out the door and held her skirts aside so that her friend might join her.

"Do you think Lawrence will come?" Honey dropped her skirts and took her friend's arm.

"I don't know," Ariel giggled. "You were right about him. He might just want to get a look at Geoff. And he will most likely turn to you for consolation now that Clifton is gone."

Honey laughed out loud as they reached the stairs.

"Oh, no! My first new rule of spring is that no young man prettier than I . . . shall . . ." Her voice trailed off as she saw a man dressed in black knee breeches and a billowing white shirt. He smiled warmly up at the women.

Clutching the railing, Honey willed herself to breathe. He was somehow bigger than she recalled, and he sported a new scar just beside his left eye. His tan was rich and healthy and his hair needed to be cut, but she couldn't tear her eyes from him. He took a step forward, then stopped, smiling at Ariel. But his smile faded when his gaze came to rest on Honey. She could tell he didn't know who she was, yet she said nothing.

"Christopher!" Ariel broke the silence as she swept around Honey to offer him her hands. "We were wondering if you had decided not to attend your own party." She laughed, noting the look that passed between this man and the woman behind her on the stairs. "I'll bet you scarcely recognized Honey. A year changes one, does it not?"

"Welcome home," Honey almost whispered while her blood throbbed through her temples. She had not expected this. She had hoped for warning before they met again, one more chance to rethink what had happened between them, one more moment to overcome the growing anxiety she felt about his homecoming.

"Thank you. You are well, I trust?" His voice was softer than she recalled. His blue eyes locked on hers as he considered the dramatic change in her. The richness of her chestnut hair—worn up now—conflicted with his memory of her, and her tanned flesh had lightened to a pleasing warm rose. She seemed more poised, more refined, somehow more womanly. Only the green of those velvet eyes remained the same. Were it not for the eyes he'd not have known her at all.

"I've been well, thank you," she answered, ignoring the tightness in her dry throat.

"You will excuse us, sir," Ariel smiled to her host. "Jillian is expecting us to relieve her that she might be ready to greet her guests, and I'm sure you'd like to freshen up. Shall we send up a tub?"

"Yes, do." Christopher barely glanced at Ariel as she passed him, but when Honey tried to pass, he captured her wrist, bringing her back to face him.

"I'll want to talk with you later."

Her eyes flashed up at him and she remembered their last encounter as if it had been yesterday. She looked pointedly at his hand then back at his face. "As you say, sir." She spoke too sweetly to be sweet. She twisted her wrist from his grasp while their eyes locked. She needed to escape before she acted on the impulse to throw her arms around him and welcome him home properly. "Pray, excuse me." She whirled away and down the stairs without looking back.

Several moments passed before Chris recovered enough to move from the landing. Unfortunately, the tantalizing scent of her perfume followed him to his chambers, prohibiting rational thought.

By mid-afternoon most of the guests had already arrived. Amesly was alive as it had not been in thirteen years. Honey watched from her window as Jennifer Bates strolled across the green lawn toward the gardens that lined the massive back veranda. Many couples strolled in the gardens, whiling away the time before the simple supper that had been planned. After that, Geoff and Ariel would take the middle landing of the central staircase and make their announcement.

"Honey, my parents have just arrived! Come down. I cannot wait for you to meet them!" Ariel rushed into the room to find Honey staring wistfully out her window. "Don't let *her* bother you!" She pulled Honey away from the window as she scolded.

"What makes you think she bothers me?" Honey laughed weakly.

"That laugh does. Besides, I saw the way Chris looked at you this morning. I think there's more going on here than you've been letting on." Ariel touched Honey's chest just over her heart. "Isn't there?"

"I don't know what you mean," Honey sniffed. "But if you're trying to tell me that I might be interested in him . . ."

"Maybe you're not, but I'd say you owe him something for that New Year's dinner at Jennifer's." Ariel smiled to herself. Not interested, indeed! "Well, just in case you really want to set his teeth on edge, ignore him."

"What?" Honey eyed her friend suspiciously.

"Yes, ignore him. Talk to everyone but him. If he starts coming toward you, pretend you don't see him and walk the other way. If he tries to flag your attention, ask whoever is beside you a question. Spend the whole weekend out of his reach. Sit at other tables. If he catches you alone, plead a headache or pretend you've forgotten to attend to some errand. You know, he has always been the charmer. Geoff boasts that no woman has ever refused him, and no charming rake can stand to be ignored by the opposite sex."

"This deceit from you?" Honey's brows drew together as she tried to understand.

"How do you think I caught Geoff?" A self-satisfied smile curled Ariel's lips. "And how my mother caught my father?"

"I thought yours was a love simple and true."

"Well, dear," Ariel laughed, "sometimes a man doesn't realize what's good for him. They need a little shove in the right direction. If it's right, there will be more love than you'll know what to do with."

"This from you . . . I'm surprised." Honey returned the wicked little grin.

"It isn't often that the demon in me comes out, but when he is needed . . ."

"Does Geoff know of this demon of yours?"

"Not yet." This time Ariel laughed out loud, her dark eyes dancing merrily.

"Not till after the wedding?"

"Maybe. Who knows? The demon might never be needed again."

"Until you have a daughter to marry off?"

"Something like that, I am sure. But my parents are waiting."

Honey followed Ariel to the library, where she met Ariel's parents. They were a pleasant couple, as quiet and correct as Ariel. She enjoyed their company for the short time that remained before dinner. Then much to her own surprise, Ariel draped Honey's arm over that of a young man who had cut through the library from the veranda.

"Charles Atkinson, Miss Honey James." Ariel smiled that wicked smile. "Miss James, meet a longtime friend, Mr. Atkinson." Then Ariel whisked her parents out of the room.

"Well, I do believe we have been introduced," Honey said, still watching the empty hall into which Ariel had disappeared.

"I should say so." The man smiled down at the pretty woman who had suddenly appeared on his arm. "It would be my pleasure to escort you to dinner, Miss James."

His eyes were an indefinable shade of brown that faded to gold. His smooth complexion and well-cut waistcoat and satin coat bespoke his wealth. His face was softly oval and kind, if a bit shy.

"Thank you, sir," she answered.

"So you are the mystery woman I've been reading about?"

"Reading about?" Honey's brow rose.

"In the *Tatler*, of course. It's a new publication. Comes on a weekly basis, you know."

"Really? I didn't know, but you say they have written about me?" Honey watched Chris out of the corner of her eye. He was across the room holding a chair for Jennifer. She wondered why he tried to look around the room while pretending not to, then she looked about for Ariel and Geoff. "What have they said?"

"They have made several uncomplimentary speculations on your background. However, it now seems that instead of the country pauper you were originally thought to be, you are a tribal princess from a tropical land in search of a worthy husband."

Honey turned her full attention to Charles, now sitting beside her. Appearances were deceiving, she thought. He wasn't the least bit shy. She laughed delightfully. "A tropical princess? Whose silly idea was that?"

"Not true, eh?" Her escort reached for his dinner wine. "Too bad, I was hoping to toss my glove at your feet."

"Your glove at my feet?" Honey followed Charles's lead and sipped from her dinner wine. The fruity flavor exploded in her mouth as she experienced her first taste of spirits. She liked it. Behind her, a parade of servants filed around the tables, offering each guest a selection of dishes.

"Ah, now we are getting somewhere. Any true Londoner would know the term. It means I had hoped to compete, to be considered worthy to rule a tropical land."

"I see. Then I fear you must be disappointed, for I am neither a princess nor in search of a husband."

"Ah, you have already made your choice. That was the other story I read. So who is the lucky chap? Christopher? Or the Cain boy?"

Honey caught her breath, then laughed, hoping he was just trying to bait her.

"Again I fear you'll be disappointed. I really am not looking for a husband." She smiled, hoping she was doing this right. "I think I am too headstrong to be as submissive as marriage demands."

"No, you don't look like the type, at that," he agreed, with a brow raised charmingly.

The meal of fish and vegetable greens was served with light sauces created by a French cook. The succulent feast was larger than the light dinner that had been promised, but no one complained.

"Shall I take that as an insult?" Honey inquired innocently.

"Indeed, no! I'm not much for marriage myself," he winked back at her.

Honey laughed indulgently, but the wink sent a warning through her. She searched out Ariel and found her sitting several places down at the same table. The younger woman looked sheepish as she realized that her spontaneous gesture had matched Honey with London's most notorious rake. Honey was trapped for the duration, for on the other side of the table sat Mrs. Gates and her husband, who had eyes only for each other. Next to them, Muriel

Stetland pursed Puritan lips at the strange woman who fraternized with the rake so well, and over whom so much had been written in the *Tatler.* No help there. And on her own side of the table the Pepperding girls were pointedly ignoring the newcomer who commanded far too much attention from one man.

Unwittingly, though, it was Chris who aided her in her clever conversation. Seated at the head of the table, with Jillian on his left and Jennifer on his right, he would often crane his neck to look her way. To her surprise, he grimaced every time she laughed, frowned every time Charles laughed, and turned a tad red whenever they laughed together. He paid neither Jennifer nor Jillian much attention. Jennifer watched Chris watch Honey. And Honey glanced up to find more than one scathing look coming from Jennifer, to which she responded with sweet flutter of her lashes or a sweet country-girl smile.

The bell signaling the end of dinner permitted the ladies to stand and move to the library, while the men stayed to smoke tobacco, take snuff, or puff on a cigar while enjoying a brandy. Meanwhile, the ladies sipped sherry and talked of the summer events. Honey wasn't sure if she was avoiding Jennifer or if Jennifer was avoiding her, but either way was fine for Honey. She accepted a sherry and sipped, rather enjoying the hot trail it left from her throat to her stomach. The warmth sent a beautiful flush to her face, and she suddenly felt lightheaded. Had the room not been so crowded she might have danced with herself, enjoying this carefree sense of weightlessness. With a little smile she watched and listened to the buzz of conversation until the ladies were summoned to meet the men in the central hall at the front of the house. She found a spot near the railing, tipping her head back to see Christopher, who stood with Geoff and Ariel on the first landing.

"Hello," a voice whispered in her ear. Honey turned to find Lawrence grinning at her.

"We wondered if you were going to join us," Honey whispered as Chris cleared his throat and called for attention. Behind him, Ariel had slipped her arm through Geoff's. They looked so happy that her heart ached with their joy.

"Friends," Chris began, "this week we are celebrating first the betrothal of my first mate, Geoffrey Grey, to the lovely Ariel Blackmoore." The crowd below them applauded and glasses raised were in tribute to the couple. All except Lawrence's . . .

Honey moved to stand beside him. He looked so dejected she had to quell the urge to hug him in consolation. Instead she slipped her arm through his and gave him a smile. "There are other women as special as Ariel," she whispered.

He smiled down at her. "Perhaps, but she is the one I could have cherished."

"I don't know, Lawrence. She has a little demon in her, that one does."

"There isn't an indecent thread in her gown," he said stoutly.

"You'd be surprised," she murmured, looking up to find Chris's eyes on her. She trembled as his gaze flicked over Lawrence before returning to his speech.

"The second reason for this celebration," he continued, "also explains the diversity of our guest list. This is a Decree of Pardon, signed five days ago by William." He read: "I, William, who doth rule with my beloved Mary beside parliament, and with their blessings, do on this day, having heard the testimony and read for myself the eyewitness account of the sinking of the *Crystal Wing* by pirates on September 12, 1689 A.D., grant full pardon for the loss of a consignment of the crown jewels destined for Persia in that same year and do posthumously grant knighthood to Jacob J. Wingfield, for refusing to give quarter at the seat of battle against the enemy of the Crown. Signed, William, sovereign of England, this day, May 16, 1701."

The words whirled through Honey's mind. A stabbing pain pierced her temple. The *Crystal Wing*—what an odd name for a ship. She brought a hand to her head. Wingfield, *Jacob Wingfield.* She had heard that name before . . . oh yes, in the carriage last year Jillian had told her a story about the woman and the little girl. But something nagged her about the story. *Fight it,* she thought, clenching her teeth to fight off the pain. *Fight the pain. Perhaps my parents had known them. That little girl and I would have been close to the same age. Perhaps my family lived around here? No, then I would have known Chris, too.* Crystal Wing, *it was that fan of water at the bow of a ship—spindrift, someone had called it. Like crystal clear wings* . . . the pain increased and her breath labored until she released the thoughts of the ship. Her mind flashed back to the island and the first sight of Chris's ship. Why couldn't that Wingfield child have lived? She would know. She would remember if they had met before. Crystal could have told her what these memories meant. Tears welled in Honey's eyes as the buzz faded from her ears and she returned to the foyer. The group had just finished their applause for the restoration of the Wingfield name. Elizabeth, Jacob's sister, accepted the sword of knighthood Chris presented her. Then in turn, she honored Chris by giving it back. She kissed him on each cheek as she wiped the tears from her eyes and thanked him again for discovering the truth.

Honey was touched by the look on Chris's face; tears spilled down her cheeks. She felt drained, as if she had suffered a spell. Suddenly distressed, she excused herself from Lawrence and fled to the sanctuary of the dark, black night.

Chapter Twenty-Six

Chris scanned the hall to find Lawrence standing alone. Beside him, Elizabeth was beginning her third speech of gratitude, but Chris smiled down at her, kissed her cheek, and sent her after her husband, who had been flirting with someone else's wife.

Determined not to let her sudden disappearance bother him, he looked at Geoff. "Geoff, old boy, have you set your date?"

"Thirty days from today, sir," Ariel answered, while her betrothed grinned indulgently.

God, she was already taking over, Chris thought as he scanned the room again. His real concern was for Honey. She'd looked pale the last time he'd seen her, and he worried that she'd suffered another spell.

But he also wanted to give her the letter and grant her the permission he was sure she desired—to marry Clifton. And he had to do it before he another chance to think about it. He hadn't been prepared for her standing at the top of the stairs earlier, and he was surprised to see her carrying on conversations with well-known rakes and fops alike. Where had all *this* education come from? How long had she known Charles? Or, perhaps a better question, how *well* did she know him?

"Chris?" Geoff's voice filtered through his thoughts. Chris looked up expectantly. "You will be my second, won't you?"

Chris laughed, "I've already planned on that." He took the steps down to the main floor and followed the group to the library, where the Pepperding sisters were about to play their harps.

Much later, the table had been laid with desserts and sweets, but most of the guests were more interested in finding their sleeping chambers for the night. Some, however, slipped away to walk in the moonlit garden. Others strolled the stables, admiring the thoroughbreds brought for the hunt.

Honey had gone outside long before the gardens were converged upon by hopeful lovers. She walked past the lights of the house and surrounding structures to where complete blackness would swallow her. She wandered past the hill that separated civilization from utter darkness and wished that she could somehow be magically transported to her island.

The envy that Ariel had tried to explain to her the day of the races had found its way into her heart. In thirty days Ariel would be married to Geoff. Next week she would be leaving Amesly to prepare for her wedding, leaving Honey alone. Honey had grown to depend on Ariel much more than she realized. Her skirts billowed as she sat down. Stretching her legs out in front of her, she kicked off her shoes and wiggled her toes. It felt good to be free of the silken slippers. She wished desperately that she could remove the petticoats, corsets, and stockings. She started with the stockings . . . rolling them down her legs and off her feet. The cool breeze skimmed over her bare legs, reminding her of the island again. It was the smell of the sea, she reasoned. The island had not crossed her mind in weeks, almost months. Perhaps it was because she was about to lose her best friend. That was likely too. That and Chris and this party. And Jennifer . . . She had never longed for her little island more than now.

Slowly she realized how much time had passed since she left the party. She gathered her things to walk back to Amesly. At the top of the hill, she looked out over the fields to see only a faint glow of light from the windows of the house. It must be later than she thought. If the lights were extinguished before she could get back, she would get lost. She would wander in the dark all night before finding her way home . . .

To make matters worse, the sky had become overcast. The faint rumble of thunder whispered in the distance. Hiking her skirts up, Honey began to run toward the light, praying that it was the custom to leave a light on all night for the comfort of the guests. The dry grass was stiff beneath her tender feet, but when it turned soft she knew she had crossed onto Amesly lawns. Breathless, she reached the side stair to the veranda. Her bare feet slapped softly on the marble of the deck. The French doors were open, the sheer silk curtains fluttered invitingly in the growing breeze, and she smiled. Hastings must have known she was out. How often had that man protected her secret walks? She couldn't even venture to guess. Someday she would do something nice for him, she thought, pulling the door closed behind her.

"Don't. I like the air."

Honey jumped, her head snapped upright, and she turned to find Christopher leaning casually against the bookcase. He swirled his brandy around the goblet that he held. The dim light gave him a dashing air. He was so handsome, so tall, and so much a man and that it frightened her.

"How did you know?" she asked, bewildered by his presence.

"I didn't. I thought, as had everyone else, that you had gone to bed long ago."

"I . . . went for a walk." A roll of thunder echoed in the distance and the wind picked up.

"Do you realize how foolish that was?" He dropped the casual tone of voice and pushed himself away from the cabinet to refill his glass. "What if I had extinguished the lamps and locked the door before you returned. You could have stumbled into a camp of thieves!" A sudden flash of lightning punctuated his statement; an angry crack of thunder followed.

Honey turned as the gusting winds suddenly hit her from behind. Her hair had already slipped from its pins as she fought the stiff wind to close the violently banging doors. It was a losing battle; the wind refused to release the doors until Chris's strong arms came to her aid. She felt the heat of his body against her back, surrounding her like a blanket, yet she dare not turn to face him. Her heart pounded in her ears as she longed to recapture the kiss that had haunted her since last spring. But she was too afraid, afraid of what it meant. Chris, she had learned from Ariel and Jennifer, was not a man to make a commitment to any woman. He had buried thoughts of marriage with his beloved Crystal, and his innocent love with Ida. If she turned now would he try to kiss her? Would she let him? Honey lifted her head a little higher, turning to look at him. Slowly her shoulders followed. She would turn and fold her arms around him and . . .

"I was asked to deliver this from the *Morning Star*," he said abruptly, pulling the parchment envelope from the inner pocket of his jacket and handing it to her. "From the colonies." He didn't miss the slight brightening of her face as he handed the letter to her. "Talk is, he asked to marry you."

They were within arm's reach, as close as they had ever been, yet farther apart than ever.

"Thank you." Her voice sounded quiet even to her own ears. She confirmed the author by glancing at the writing. It was indeed from Clifton. "He . . . hasn't really asked . . ."

Chris turned, moving a safer distance from her. He refilled his glass. "I see. In the event that he does bring himself to confront you, be assured permission will be granted. Passage can be arranged within the week, if necessary." His gaze centered on his glass, his shoulder hunched slightly, and his dark head tipped forward as if the conversation bored him.

"I don't understand."

"Don't you? It is what you want, isn't it? All of London has told the story of the new earl and the lady from Amesly. Clearly that must be you, for I see Jillian has a new interest and Ariel is as steadfast as they come. You are the only unattached female left in the house."

Honey turned away from his scowling face. Hurt mixed with humiliation and stained her cheeks as she clutched her letter to her chest. He made it so easy to leave. So easy.

"I guess you're right. It is what I would want. If he asks, you can be sure I will consent." The words whispered from her throat. "Good night then." She rushed off, shoes and stockings in hand. He moved as if to reach for her as she fled, but then thought better of it. Outside, the night brewed as violent a storm as he had ever seen, and the howling winds, flashes of light, and raging thunder mirrored his inner torment. She had been right, he thought, remembering the first time she had seen herself in a mirror: she did have dark hair.

Honey leaned against the door of her room. Sobs caught in her throat as the tears rolled unchecked over her cheeks. Pain . . . pain that only he could give her jabbed at her heart. It was like what she felt earlier knowing that Ariel soon would be gone from her. But this was so much stronger. Could it be that she loved Chris as Ariel loved Geoff? As Jillian had often spoken of her beloved? Could fate be cruel enough to set her heart for a man who would never love her in return? Had it not already been cruel to that very man? A new surge of pain invaded her. Perhaps the best thing would be to say yes to Clifton. He was kind and he cared naught for her background. He would teach her everything she needed to know about love. He would be honest about how he felt. Still sniffing, she broke the seal on the envelope and read the carefully lined pages. She dropped the letter, staring into the fire for several moments before rereading the last paragraph.

Forgive me, Honey, but I have come to realize that your heart belongs elsewhere or you would have been here by now. Unhappily, I can wait no longer for a wife. Sarah is kind and gentle, and I know you would love her as I have come to love her. By the time this letter reaches you she will already have become my wife. At least please write me one last time and tell me who has so completely taken your heart that you would stay somewhere where you are so truly unhappy. My guess is that his colors are the same as mine were in the autumn races.

Loving you always,
Clifton Cain

She was strangely comforted that he had married—happy that he would be loved as he deserved to be. He was a good man.

But for Chris . . . Honey reclined against the feather pillows of her bed. Perhaps if she tried not to care so much for him, in time the pain would stop. But that didn't seem too likely. Now she hadn't even America to go to, though she could possibly find her way as an indentured servant.

Honey had heard of people who exchanged services for the cost of passage, but she'd read that seven years of labor were usually required. That appeared to be her only option next to marriage. Neither sounded very favorable. She had also heard how the holders of such contracts often treated their servants . . . but then, she had learned that marriage to some "gentlemen" in London could lead to the same cruelty. These thoughts whirled through her tired mind as, fully dressed, she drifted off to sleep. Clifton's letter drifted to the floor while the lightning and thunder passed overhead, leaving Amesly in the mist of the gently pelting rain.

Chapter Twenty-Seven

He could still see her standing against the frame of the door, her loosened hair framing her face, shoulders, and hips. He had smelled that haunting perfume when he had helped her close the doors, and he had felt her stiffen at his touch. Her refusal to turn in his arms told him that she had indeed settled for Clifton Cain. What would he have done with her, anyway? A virgin. He had never tried one, but for some silly reason that mattered now. It mattered that Clifton had been honorable with her while he had been away. It made it easier to let her go. Let her go? Get rid of her, was more like it. At least she had not spilled anything on him in the short time that they had been together. Much to his relief, she had sat at the other end of the table. But that relief soon fled when he glimpsed her seated beside Atkinson. That man would use any device to bed a woman—young or old, tested or not. He had ruined one young woman of good standing and refused to admit his deed, so that the child had to be married off to an old count, who'd been more than grateful to have an heir already seeded. Still, all of London knew who had sired the child. And old counts in need of heirs were few and far between.

Christopher's blood heated when he thought of another man tasting her sweet lips, touching her warm flesh. The thrust of her breasts beneath the fanning lace of her bodice had trapped his attention more than once in the course of the day. He hadn't failed to notice the mature cut of her gown. Indeed, she was as Jillian had predicted—a woman. In every sense of the word. He sighed as he poured the last of the brandy into his glass and swallowed it down. Getting drunk was a privilege he could not afford to take while he had guests in the house, so he extinguished the lamps before finding his room, and his bed, cold and empty.

He didn't see the shadow that blended into the doorway further along the corridor, but the shadow had seen Honey come up minutes earlier, carrying her shoes and silk stockings, her hair loose and sensual, swirling about her flushed face. The shadow also noticed the hesitation in Chris's step as he passed Honey's door before silently slipping through his own.

The rain had stopped long before dawn, and the early morning sun worked overtime to dry up the puddles that soaked the vast lawns. Already, ladies in fine morning gowns were choosing partners for lawn games. And talk over breakfast was that Chris and some of the other gentlemen would be showing their prize horses. A few, in fact, had already gone to the stables to see to the grooming of the animals.

Honey listened to the buzz around her and wondered listlessly what the day would bring.

Normally Jillian would have seen to her schedule, but Jillian had, as Chris suggested, met a gentleman whose interest had already gone beyond the old acquaintance stage. Honey was happy for her. It had been forty years since her betrothed's death, and Jillian, with all of her love and kindness, deserved to have them returned. Ariel too would have seen to Honey except that she was occupied with her man. Ariel and Geoff were the essence of young love itself as they strolled the gardens, making their plans and smiling into each other's eyes.

Honey, along with several other guests, was served her breakfast on the veranda. As always, conversation stopped as she stepped to where the tables had been placed. It seemed that few of the guests believed that she was just an old family acquaintance from a small northern town. But no one dared inquire further, precisely as Chris had planned. Honey glanced at the door through which she had entered the library the night before. Black creases dented the white frame where the wind had slammed it into the hard cornerstone of the house. Would things have been different had she returned sooner? Probably not, but the question would haunt her forever. She picked at the cold food on her plate. To her left she could see the stable yard and the people milling about as the horses marched around in grand fashion. There was no missing the largest animal of all as he paraded by with Christopher on his back. As usual, Chris's hair was unpowdered, simply tied back with a black ribbon, and his coat was of the blue-black fabric that he favored above all others.

Honey dropped her fork onto her plate. In love with him! How could that ever have happened? True, he had always commanded her attention, even from the first moment she saw him standing over her at the tide pools. But love . . . when did that start? The only time they had ever really gotten along was the day she had been ordered to tell him about her time on the island. He had laughed at her stories and felt her sadness when she told him of Barley Boe's passing. Even the next day had been pleasant until they had walked through the stables. It just made no sense at all.

"Lovely morning, isn't it?" The woman slid into a chair and was served immediately, though she didn't touch her food either.

"Good morning, Mrs. Bates," Honey's reply was polite, but as she looked into Jennifer's narrowed eyes she knew that the lovely part of the morning was over. "It's so pleasant to have you here at Amesly," she finished cattily. Politeness didn't matter any more, and neither did this vicious woman.

"I'm sure you mean that," Jennifer cooed.

Honey took a deep breath. She wasn't interested in a sparring contest this morning. "As you say." She smiled.

"And your retreat last night was successful, I trust?" Jennifer's smile stiffened, her over-made face distorted with emotion.

"Retreat?" Honey's brows rose innocently. Her eyes questioned Jennifer's intent.

"Oh come, dear." Jennifer lifted her fork delicately to her mouth. "A little bird saw you creep up the stairs last night. Shall we say, still flushed from your little tryst? That same bird noticed your lover not far behind you."

"You must be mistaken, Mrs. Bates." Honey smiled at the other woman's irritation, but Jennifer's remarks began to make sense. Honey *had* been quite windblown, and she had forgotten about the shoes . . . and Chris had been the only other person not in his rooms.

"Hardly that, dear." Jennifer's nose wrinkled.

"The same bird saw your lover creep up into his room as well. Foolish of you to be seen, even more foolish if you're seen again." The older woman's eyes narrowed with meaning.

Honey tucked her fears away. She would never have Chris so she had nothing to lose. "I am quite sure you don't mean to threaten me, Jennifer. However, if you're foolish enough to think you can, think again. You might have chosen a more powerful enemy than you are willing to face." Honey stood, dusting the crumbs from her butter yellow gown, and smiled her most congenial smile. "Do have a lovely day, dear," she added before sweeping back into the house.

"My, my, my . . ." Charles Atkinson whispered into Honey's ear later when he found her engrossed in a lawn game between Geoff and Ariel and the Gateses. "Whatever did you say to rile the ex-lady of Brentwood?"

She jumped at the sound of his gentle voice, then smiled over her shoulder at him. "Nothing she didn't need to hear."

"A bit spoiled, isn't she?" he grinned, tossing his glance at the veranda where Jennifer stood glowering at them.

"Just a bit," she laughed, refusing the other woman the satisfaction of looking up. "You must know her as well as—"

"Oh, no! Mustn't mention names. Quite impolite, you know," he grinned again, giving a tug to his waistcoat. "Actually, the lady has had it out for my hide for some time now. You see, she has thought me to be quite below her standard, and I, being the man that I am, could not let that go unchallenged."

Honey faced him, a wicked smile creasing her lips. "What did you do?"

"Why, nothing, of course. But I hear tell that a fellow who managed to sit behind her at the theatre one eve spilled a bit of Spanish flower in her drink. Its seeds make one amorous, you know. Then some time later her escort became mysteriously ill and had to return home immediately." He smiled devilishly while he played with his lovelock.

"And then?"

"And then I took full advantage of the lady's intense need to please a man and found my way into her bed." He chuckled. "She has never seen clear to forgive me, even though it was she who did the inviting."

He looked so pleased with himself that Honey had to laugh, though she understood very little of the story.

"There, see?" he said in softer tone. "You are lovely when you smile."

She looked up at the well-dressed man, her eyes sparkling before turning coyly away. She had been warned to keep her distance from this one, but his charm was undeniable and she needed a friend.

"Have you played this game?"

"Ah, yes, some time ago. And you?"

"No, never," she answered, looking back to the match. Mr. and Mrs. Gates were in the lead.

"We'll take the winners," Charles called to Gates, who was poised for the hit. He nodded without looking up.

"How long have those two been married?"

"Long time. They have two children, grown and married, and some outrageous number of grandchildren."

"That must be real love they share." Honey looked

longingly at the woman, who kissed her man as he sank his shot.

"I've yet to see any greater," he admitted, following her look. "He was a sailor on an explorer. As the story goes, his ship was lost at sea. The navigator and the captain and the mate died of some scourge. The crew of six remained, but none of them were any good at navigation. They apparently wandered the oceans, half starved, until they were taken by Spanish pirates. The Spaniards strung them up and tortured them. Somehow two of them got away and found their way home. That was fifteen years after they had set sail. Gates had already married her, and the woman and their two children were waiting for him. After he returned they were embarrassing to be around, always kissing and cooing to each other. Then nine months later she almost died of the fever. He stayed beside her, praying for God to spare her life and offering his own soul early should the Lord take his love away. God didn't want either of them. Here they are, making the rest of us wish that he had."

"What a wonderful story! They are so lucky to have found each other. Don't you wish . . ."

"Pishposh." He glanced back at the stables. "That kind of thing comes round once every hundred years or so, and then only to reward the punished few. But I wonder . . ." He leaned boldly her way, one arm still resting on the stone wall that supported the veranda. The twinkle in his eyes told her that this was his game, that she was to be his next conquest. To her shame and surprise she wondered if his kiss was anything like Chris's, but she placed a staying hand on his chest.

"Game time," Mr. Gates called, shaking hands with Geoff and kissing Ariel's hand before boldly kissing his wife.

From the look of it, Honey had thought that the game was more difficult than it actually was—though she could see why concentration was so necessary when your partner was a notorious flirt. She smiled as she smacked her ball toward the first hole, then smiled again triumphantly as the ball dropped through the hole in the ground. Feeling rather smart, she picked up her ball and moved away for the next player. Charles stood on the sidelines, his club tucked under one arm as he delicately applauded her move. She gave him a token curtsy before sweeping an open hand across the playing field, indicating that it was Mrs. Gates's turn to play.

"You know these two rarely lose," he grinned. "'Twould positively make my weekend should we goose them."

"Well, sir, here is your chance." She watched Mrs. Gates hit her ball, sending it past the hole. Mrs. Gates frowned as she took several more swings before sinking the shot.

Charles strolled out on the green circle and played his in two swings. Retrieving his ball from the hole, he grinned to the older man and kissed his own game ball.

"'Tis a bit of a mean streak you have, sir," Honey commented as he joined her and Mr. Gates moved out to play.

"'Twas only in fun," he defended impishly.

Honey gave him a snicker as she poised herself for her swing. This time her luck had run out. The morning breeze carried her ball into a small grove of bushes, and she not only spent several swings trying to play it out, she practically ruined her gown.

The next hole went very well for both Honey and Charles; however, Mr. Gates was beginning to look a bit annoyed that someone might actually beat him at his favorite game.

Charles's skill developed quite nicely, as did Honey's, but at the last hole Honey missed the hole on her second swing, and Charles positively fell apart, leaving the Gateses with the only advantage they had had all day.

Mr. Gates was never one to miss an advantage, so he spent a great deal of time concentrating on his ball and judging the distance to the hole. Finally he sank his putt, winning the game. "There may be a noble streak in you after all," Honey teased as they strolled over the lawn to watch the raising of the maypole.

"Shhh, if that gets out I'll lose my notorious reputation."

"I should think you'd want that, too," Honey replied, nodding at another couple strolling past them. Her small hand rested in the crook of Charles's arm.

"Hark, no!" he gasped. "Then every well-intentioned mother would have her daughter at my front door in time for a June wedding. My lot is not to wed. Why, there is only myself, our gallant host, and one Sir Marcus Long left. To lose one of the ranks would mean devastation for the other two," he laughed, his eyes twinkling merrily. "We are too old and too set in our ways to withstand the nagging of a wife or the squalling of children. And our fortunes will long outlast us unless we handle the spending properly. That would never do."

"I can understand that," she answered thoughtfully.

"I see you can. I mean," Charles realized his *faux pas* too late.

"'Tis all right, Mr. Atkinson. I am well aware that

I am an old maid, and really, I don't mind. Last season at the Autumn Fair those same well-meaning mothers made it clear that I stood in their daughters' bridal paths."

"I didn't mean to imply . . ."

"I know you didn't." She stopped to look at him, unaware that they were very near the stables. "Believe me, I am quite content being an old maid."

Charles smiled then. "In that case, I shall be happy for you, and perhaps it wouldn't be too unseemly to be seen together? Perhaps at the theatre or a jaunt around Hyde Park back in London?"

"I believe that could be managed, Mr. Atkinson. That is, if you promise to behave yourself in the most gentlemanly fashion," she teased.

"That—"

"That would be impossible for Charles," Christopher said, strolling up behind them, "for he is no gentleman, nor will he ever be."

"One has heard similar stories of you, sir," Honey stated sweetly, batting her lashes. She was captured by that cryptic look in his blue eyes, but she forced herself to look away. He *was* just like Charles, she reminded herself, and deserved the same treatment as he handed out.

"And you, m'lady?" he countered with a bow.

"'Tis scarcely the same," she quipped, dropping Charles's arm. "I shall bid you both a good afternoon, gentlemen." She dipped her head slightly then swept off toward the house. It was 11:30, time to rest before the midday meal.

"Honey, wait!" Ariel called, forcing her thoughts from the handsome rogue who haunted her.

"Ariel, I haven't seen you all day," she said absently.

"You certainly have, you goose. Less than an hour

ago on the lawn." She eyed her friend suspiciously.

"Oh, yes. I remember," Honey answered without looking at her friend. "It's nap time, isn't it?"

"Yes, it is." Ariel fell silent, wondering if Honey's mood had been brought about by her brief conversation with Christopher just now or by the letter she'd found on Honey's dressing table. Yes, she had read it, certain that it contained a new proposal of marriage from Clifton. Her heart had failed her when she read the last part. She had heard her friend's tears the night before as well, though she had no way of knowing what they were caused by.

"Honey, is there something you want to talk about?" Ariel approached the subject with caution.

Honey looked at her friend. "Should there be?"

"Well, no, I . . ."

"Wait! Who is that man?" Honey gasped urgently. She stopped to look at the blond man who was crossing the lawn toward Charles and Chris. The blood drained from her face and her hands turned cold.

"Honey, are you going to faint?" Ariel became alarmed.

"Shhhh!" She grabbed her friend's wrist in her cold hand. Her thudding heart felt like fear itself racing through her. "Don't let him see us!" she begged quickly, ducking behind a giant bush in the garden before the man looked in their direction.

"Why, what's wrong?" Concern etched her face as she looked from Honey to the man on the lawn, "That's Chris's partner, Elizabeth's husband, William Humphrey. He took over Jacob's part of the business after . . . Honey, you're trembling. My God, what's wrong?"

"Nothing . . . I mean, I don't know. I've never seen him before but . . . Look at me! I am drenched in sweat. I have no reason to fear him, do I?"

"I should hope not. He has become a most respectable merchant."

Slowly Honey's racing heart calmed itself, and warmth returned to her extremities. But she could not shake her fear of that man . . .

Chapter Twenty-Eight

The custom was that the ladies rested again during the late afternoon, rising just in time to dress for dinner. That ritual often took two hours.

For Jillian's sake, Honey followed the rules with just a few variations. First, she helped Brea and Katie by keeping her water pitcher full enough to cloth bathe. In this way there was then no need to call for a tub in the middle of the day. Second, she stashed a cache of good books beneath her bed, for she found the limited activity of civilized life failed to tire her out to the point where she needed to nap.

Honey turned in front of the mirror. The forest green gown suited her well. Beneath the velvet fichu collar, the fitted silk midriff skimmed her waist to where the three-tiered skirt had been stitched. The overskirt of forest green velvet had been split and pulled apart like draperies to show the next skirt, which was also split and pulled back to show yet another skirt, but this was of a lighter shade of silk and was beautifully embroidered with vines and flowers in the same shades as the two overskirts. Velvet ribbons woven through her coiffure put the finishing touch to her toilette. She felt beautiful, and perhaps older, and she couldn't decide if that was good or bad. But she nearly danced herself down to dinner.

"Miss Honey!" Lawrence Grant caught her hand as she entered the dining room.

"Mr. Grant," she smiled. "You have enjoyed your day, I trust?"

"Yes, thank you," he smiled in return. It was the first smile she had ever seen from him. "And you?"

"Yes, quite. Mr. Atkinson has taught me to play golf, though I understand we played a short version of the game, and we have discussed going to the theatre in the fall."

"May I escort you to dinner?"

"Please," she smiled, wondering why Lawrence was acting so considerate.

Dinner couldn't have been more delightful. Charles sat on the other side of her and struggled to keep her attention from Lawrence; on his part, Lawrence struggled to keep her entertained. She couldn't tell if he was using her as a distraction from his obsession with Ariel or if he wanted to be with her, though really his intentions didn't matter.

At the other end of the long table Chris was having the devil's own time trying to keep an eye on her. He had seen his ward enter sometime earlier and was struck by her poise, by her beauty. He had denied the truth long enough. She had become the woman he had always dreamed of—and feared . . . He had no close relationships with a woman other than with Ida, who had helped him over the loss of his mother. Suddenly he realized his own fear of loving, of being loved. Of loving a woman out of bed as well as in. Of being the first and only man to possess one woman . . . God, where did these realizations come from? His musings continued into the night, until the musicians played the first minuet.

While Honey danced her first dance with Charles, her guardian struggled to watch that they not hold each other too close. His throat tightened when he recalled the first time he had seen her dance. It needled him that she found Charles so amusing that she didn't look his way once all night.

Honey looked at her escort as Charles brought her around the room again; she was impressed by his command of the dance.

"See, he is just there, watching us," he said, glancing back at Chris.

"He is angry, no doubt. He has warned me that you are a rake," she teased, "and he insists that no women's virtue is safe in your hands."

"In your case, I must admit that he is right." Charles licked his lips as a wolf before a lamb. "You are too difficult to figure out. Either you are a very good actress and not true in your innocent ways, or truly from the darkest country imaginable."

Honey laughed as the music came to an end. "Not so dark."

"Again she says nothing. When will she learn to trust me?" He looked wounded.

"As I've told you, sir, I have been warned."

Honey danced next with Geoff, and then with Lawrence. Toward evening's end she wandered round the room, catching sight of the couples that slipped out through the veranda to steal kisses beneath the moon.

But the evening ended early. Except for those engaged in secret rendezvous, the rest wanted an early start for the hunt the following day. After the final dance with Charles, Honey bid both Charles and Lawrence good night.

* * *

As dawn streaked the sky, the servants knocked on chamber doors, softly calling out hunt times. Honey, already awake, stood at her window watching a couple so unwilling to part. The woman stretched up to meet the man as they kissed their farewells and parted. She wondered if Chris was parting from Jennifer in much the same way this morning. Her stomach knotted as she thought of the two together, clinging like the pair she had just witnessed.

It was too painful to consider. Dropping the curtain, she prayed to make it through the day. Perhaps if Charles were free again he would keep her company. She liked Charles and felt comfortable with him. At least she knew where she stood with Charles. But that might be too much to expect of him. He had other things on his mind, one of them being to relieve her of her virtue. How he could joke about it and not make it seem sinful she didn't understand. Had she not been warned of him, it well could have been Charles kissing her under the morning sky. He had confessed while dancing that his interests were only fervent until a woman succumbed. After that the challenge no longer existed, nor did the pursuit.

What little she knew of romance she'd read in Shakespeare and Congreve and other writers who penned the emotions of love so well that she yearned for the experience. Would she have to settle for taking lovers to experience this wonder? Or would she fatten up pleasantly like Jillian, waiting until her golden years before being taken from her shelf and tested?

Leaving was the only answer. Charming Charles, even sweet Clifton, had not stirred in her the emotions that Chris had. She sighed. Knowing Chris didn't love her she just couldn't stay here any longer. Yes, perhaps when the guests left on Tuesday there would be enough confusion that she could take her horse and perhaps a small parcel and go to the coast, where she could indenture herself or take a contract as a groom. She had heard of several old maids doing just that. After all, she was grown, and could even go before the king for her release from Christopher's hold. Her plan made, she dressed in her new riding habit and made her way to breakfast.

The hunt was both exhilarating and horrid. First the equestrians mounted and paraded before the guests who'd decided not to hunt, who applauded their friends. Then the horn sounded and hounds, chained six to a leash, hurled themselves in front of the horses, stuck their noses to the ground and their tails in the air, and started off. Hastings unhooked the leashes, sending the pack of salivating hounds forward with the hunters right behind. Next to Honey, Charles lurched forward with his mount, but managed to stay behind the rest.

"What's wrong?" Honey called to her friend over the thundering hooves.

"Eh? No stomach for this, you know."

"No, I don't know. I haven't the faintest idea of what we are hunting for." She cantered up beside him.

"Surely you have hunted before?" he snickered.

"No," she shook her head frankly, "this is quite new to me."

"Indeed! The first thing this morning Hastings brought out a cage with a little red fox in it. He opened the door and scared the wits out of the critter so that he would run and hide . . ."

"Oh dear, I have read about this. They'll kill it, won't they?" She turned back in the saddle and spurred her mount on, working hard to catch the group who rode on ahead.

Frantically Honey fought her way through the throng of riders. Sandy danced easily round the clumps of earth and mud kicked up by the horses as they followed their leader through thickets, over hills, and across ravines and creeks.

At one point Honey's smartly veiled hat caught in the low-hanging tree branches and was left dangling behind her, but she refused to slow her pace until she caught up with the leader of the hunting party. Working her way through horses and riders until she was lost among them, her eyes searched for the one who could stop this nonsense. There, far ahead, rode Chris, with Jennifer not far behind him, thrilling to the chase.

"No!" Honey gasped from her dry throat as she watched Chris get off a shot. The wind brought tears to her eyes as she worried for the defenseless fox. She spurred her horse around the last of the riders and brought herself up even with Chris.

"No!" she pleaded over the chaos of the barking dogs and nickering horses. "Please, you can't kill so small a thing without reason."

His look was incredulous as he turned to see the tear-streaked face of his ward. She was breathing hard as she strained to keep up.

"'Tis the game," he said stupidly, his body turning in the saddle. "If you have not taste for the sport you should have stayed home."

Beyond him Jennifer scowled a look of warning, but Honey ignored her. Tearfully she turned out of the group. The hard look he'd given her burned in her mind's eye. How could he be so cruel?

Blindly she rode off, crossed the ravine, and rode for her favorite place: the grove of trees beside the creek where she'd said goodbye to Clifton several months ago. She should have gone with him, she realized. Clifton was an honest man and he'd have cherished her whether she fell in love with him or not. He'd have helped her learn what she needed to know to live in the New World. But in her heart she knew that wouldn't have been fair to him. He'd have met Sarah and they'd have fallen in love and Clifton wouldn't have been free to marry her. She sighed, knowing it would have been all wrong for both of them.

The leaves that were crisp last autumn were now soggy and damp underfoot, and the little creek gurgled with new vitality. The trees had lost that tired autumn look and fresh buds had burst into tiny leaves. Tears gathered behind her lids as she squeezed them shut.

How could she love a man who was capable of such cruelty as to hunt down a defenseless animal? The tears slipped out and she opened her eyes. The creek bed was a blur as she stumbled toward it. The wind rushed the trees and she swiped at the hair that fluttered into her eyes. Had she known what the hunt was, she'd have let the fox go the day it had arrived. What would her guardian have said about that?

Behind her a twig snapped and she turned to see Chris looking down at her, tall in the saddle, his eyes bluer than they had ever been. He looked angry, but she wasn't sure. He said nothing as he walked his horse toward her. Ducking under the low branches, he dropped a cloth bag into her arms, then turned to rejoin the hunting party that had passed just beyond the hill out of sight.

Something in the bag moved. Whatever was inside was wrestling to get free. Tears flooded her eyes and she dropped to her knees as she broke the string and the little fox popped out. Fearlessly he grabbed the bag and shook it for all he was worth—punishment for holding him captive. She laughed as he rolled off-balance, taking himself and the bag into the creek. She laughed until she cried as the creature stood, shaking himself furiously. He eyed the stranger, then with a yip he scampered into the woods.

Honey watched the space where the little fox had disappeared for a long time. A sense of wonder filled her. Chris had done this for her. Despite Jennifer, despite any number of guests who would look upon this act as a weakness of character. . . . Hope filled her heart. Tonight, the last night of the weekend . . . what might it bring?

Chapter Twenty-Nine

"I can't believe it," she breathed to herself. Honey turned once more in front of the mirror. She didn't trust the image in royal blue velvet that looked back. The shoulder-to-shoulder collar was draped in blue velvet and trimmed with white needlepoint lace. Beneath the collar the fitted gown clung to her before gathering itself at the waist to flow to the floor in a wide sweeping skirt, cleverly drawn back to expose the blue and white striped silk underskirt beneath. It was so simple, so beautiful, and so soft. She moved away from the image, then back again.

Brea rummaged through a drawer, looking for the blue velvet fans that would adorn the French coiffure the maid had spent the last hour fashioning.

Downstairs that music began to play. Carefully Honey lifted the puff of white powder and began to pat the russet sculpture.

The quiet of the room served only to enhance what she was feeling inside. She trembled as if she was to be the only woman at the ball. She set the puff aside and looked at herself once again. Blue and white . . . simple and elegant.

"Ah . . ." Brea gasped as she turned to look at her

mistress. She placed the fans like butterflies on the left side of the powdered hair and pinned the filigree pin just over Honey's breast.

The door opened and Ariel attempted to sweep through, but her wide skirts held her back. The cream silk of her gown was lavishly beautiful but did little to enhance the color of her skin. Ariel glowed nonetheless. She had seen two seasons without a ball, and at last it was her turn to shine.

"Honey, the gown is so lovely but . . ."

"But I should be in white? Virginal and such?"

Ariel flushed and looked down. The dilemma was one they had often discussed and never agreed upon.

"You know I don't mean to . . ."

"I know," Honey replied honestly, "but this will be my first and last formal ball, and I intend to make the most of it. Come what may!"

"Oh, no it won't!" Ariel grabbed up her wide skirts and forced her way through the door. "You are to second me at my wedding! There will be a feast and a ball. It's going to be so grand!"

Honey caught her friend as she popped through the door. "That is a job for your best friend. Not some waif found from the sea." She laughed as her arms came around Ariel.

"You *are* my best friend. No one could have taken as good care of me while Geoff was away. And surely no one would have kept the secrets you have. I mean, I couldn't love you more if you were my sister."

"Truly?" Honey squeaked as she threw herself into Ariel's arms and they embraced over the bells of their gowns. "I'm going to miss you so."

"Just look at you two . . ." Jillian smiled from behind the slightly open door. "Stop now or you'll end up wearing each other's gowns! Here, Honey."

Jillian opened the door the rest of the way. A pearl rope dangled from her fingers. The teardrop sapphire framed in silver hung from the center of the necklace. "I've permission to lend this to you. But once you are seen with it in public it might well become a gift," she confided as she hooked the jewel around Honey's throat.

"Such a lovely thing . . ." She fingered the cool, heavy stone as it found its place just below her breastbone. Matching bobs completed the loan. "I don't know what to say," she whispered, looking at the glitter of her jewels.

"Just say thank you to the right person." Jillian gave her a motherly smile. "I want to tell you," Jillian beamed, "Gregory has proposed and I have accepted."

Honey rushed to her guardian with Ariel. The three hugged until Jillian shook them off. "'Twill be announced tonight, though we'll wed quietly next week. Honey, dear, Gregory and I want you with us. Our fortunes will join, and because we have no heirs between us, nor shall have, we would like to appoint you as our heiress. Gregory wishes that you would consider taking his name . . ." Jillian let the words slide as she watched Honey's reaction to the request. "Even should you decide to wed Mr. Cain, the fortunes would become yours and your children's. And should you refuse him, the house on Zachary Lane would welcome you, since Gregory and I will be living at his estates."

"Of course, there is that," Honey agreed quietly. "Please tell Mr. Bentley I shall consider his offer and that I am honored that he would think so highly of me."

"We can discuss this later." Jillian's eyes twinkled

with happiness, "Looking at you tonight, we shall be lucky to fend off the hopefuls." She squeezed the younger girl's hand, then left the room.

"Don't think of it just now," Ariel said, slipping an arm around her friend.

"Think of what?" Honey sniffed, forcing a smile.

"Don't think of Clifton, Honey. I read the letter. It was lying on the floor when I peeked in the other morning."

"I was going to tell you about it. I guess I forgot."

"Forgot?" Ariel sniffed. "I doubt that, but we have a ball to go to. As Jillian said, you may well have to fight off the hopefuls."

Ariel pulled her friend through the door toward the main stair.

"Oh no," Honey protested, "I thought we could go down the back, and . . ."

"Not on your life! This night you make an entrance." Ariel pulled her to the top stair and shoved her gently down the first two steps. The sudden movement was enough to command the attention of those below.

Honey gasped at the faces staring up at her, then looked back to Ariel for support. Ariel drew herself erect, bracing her shoulders and holding her head high in example. Honey swallowed her fear and took a deep breath before descending the stairs—refusing to look down to see if Chris was watching.

The words Chris was about to say died in his throat as he looked up the staircase to see what the sudden hush was all about.

An image filled his memory: the image of the woman after whom he'd been named, now floating down the staircase before his very eyes. Suddenly the woman on the stairs resembled the mother instead of the daughter. He shook off the memory; he didn't want those old chains around his neck—not tonight. Honey was more beautiful than yesterday, even more beautiful than this morning, when he had tossed her the bagged fox.

Charles waited for her at the base of the stair. As he drew her away the chatter resumed, but with a new urgency.

"'Tis no wonder you were so interested in the lady's past," Seth hummed in Chris's ear after Charles and Honey disappeared near the refreshment table.

Chris lifted the glass to his lips, but his eyes followed the blue gown. He wondered who told her to pick that shade. He wondered if she knew its secrets.

"She is my ward, Seth," he answered simply.

"And no man has ever married his ward, has he?" the harbormaster commented, watching his friend closely.

Chris smiled. "No one with any morals, you mean."

"It's morals that make a man marry one, rather than just bed one."

When the music started he wasn't surprised to see Honey transported across the floor in Charles's arms. Several other couples soon closed in around them, but Chris had no trouble spotting the blue fans she wore. Chris watched as they whirled in and out of the crowd, back across the veranda, then across the room and out again, but never into the shadows of the night.

A short time later Gregory Bentley commanded a

dance, followed by Lawrence. And Chris's anxiety mounted as if it were his own first ball.

"You can dance with her, you know. Fact, I'd say 'twould almost be expected." Seth grabbed another glass of champagne from a passing servant, then scouted the room for his wife. "At least that." Chris turned to scowl at him, but Seth had already joined his wife.

Chris turned back to the dance floor and watched as the dance ended and Lawrence escorted Honey to where Charles waited for them with glasses of chilled champagne. Chris smiled; at least he needn't worry about Charles. The warning he'd issued his friend had been well taken. Yet despite the agreement, Charles remained her constant companion. Chris wasn't sure if he was worried about that or not. Just then the music started again, and the "Golden Rake," as Chris had been fond of calling his longtime friend, swept Honey back out onto the floor.

It was 11:30 before Gregory Bentley made his way up to the platform. He waited until the servants had passed out glasses of champagne to make the unexpected toast.

"Friends," he began in his soft voice, "I have today done the one thing I have never done before. I have asked Miss Jillian Ames to be my bride."

The crowd cheered at the unexpected news. Gregory offered his arm to Jillian, who joined her betrothed on the platform.

"What did she say?" someone called out, and everyone laughed.

"The wonderful event will be private, but once we are settled in at home there will be a ball. To my bride!" Gregory raised his glass to salute Jillian, who blushed as furiously as any virgin bride.

"Try this." Charles handed Honey his kerchief.

"Thank you." She sniffed and dabbed at her tears. "She so deserves to be happy. You know she was betrothed once before. Her fiancé was killed in a hunting accident. She has sworn to marry only for love."

Charles nudged her chin with a knuckle. A smile of indulgence touched his lips. "I'll get us some punch," he said. "'Twould seem champagne makes you weepy."

Chris set his glass aside and tried to quell his flutters. Since she was promised to another, he had nothing to fear from her.

Honey looked up to see Chris boldly striding her way. Her heart stopped, then pounded at her ribs, and her breath caught in her throat. She glanced around for an escape, but he reached her before she could move away.

"You look lovely tonight," he whispered as his arms closed around her. "Dance?" The thrill shot through her and settled like butterflies in her stomach.

"I . . . thank you for the loan of the jewelry. 'Tis more beautiful than I have ever seen." She glanced over his shoulder, then looked back to find him devouring her with his eyes.

"They were a gift from Christine to my mother."

"They . . . must have been great friends," she whispered, wishing she could look away from him.

He only nodded as he turned her out onto the veranda then back in again.

"I let the fox go," she whispered suddenly. His

arms tightened carefully around her, and she felt his heart tripping into hers, his breath shallow on her cheek.

Abruptly he stopped. She hadn't been aware they had left the room, nor was she aware of the darkened marble walls that surrounded them.

"I've never killed one," he admitted, leaning slowly toward her. He was going to kiss her, she knew, and she was ready. Her eyes faded shut and her breath was tight in her lungs. But he pulled back at the sound of a shoe scraping the marble floor just behind them. Flushed dancers slipped back into the light of the ballroom, embarrassed that they had stumbled into someone else's private moment. But the magic, the moment was gone.

Flushed and breathless, Chris escorted her back into the room. His tight-lipped expression suggested that she had angered him. Without a word he left her in Charles's company. He crossed the room as if to leave, but he was waylaid by Jennifer.

Honey bit back the humiliation that grew in her heart.

"Sink me! You've in love with the cad!" The words fell from Charles's mouth as if he'd been a fool.

"Don't be silly," she snapped. "We don't even like each other!"

"You don't love him? Then I shall kill him for toying with you."

"You wouldn't!" she gasped, her eyes wide in horror.

"You just said you didn't care for him," Charles smiled wickedly. Setting aside their glasses he whirled her back to the dance floor.

"I said we don't like each other. But if you killed him, where would I go?"

"I'd marry you," he said gallantly, his golden eyes looking deeply into hers as their arms arched over their heads. At the last second she averted her eyes.

"Adore you as I do, Charles, why would I marry you when you'd have every lady in London sharing our bed."

He laughed then, and they stepped apart. He bowed, she curtsied. "Perhaps you don't know me as well as you think. Perhaps you are my destiny. As your tutor of love, think of the pleasures we could bring each other."

Honey blushed at his candor. "Pleasure is a major pastime here, isn't it? Is there nothing better for people to do but play 'Bed, bed, who's in my bed?' "

He threw back his head and laughed. "Gad, you are an innocent! Of course, as I have told you before, when one has money enough to last two lifetimes and no skill for labor, what else is there?"

"You will end up like Gregory—alone. And there may not be a Jillian to comfort you that late in life."

"There will always be Jillians," he returned confidently.

"Maybe, but I'll wager that you'd disappear the second I said yes to you." She smiled at him sadly. She had come to know him well in a short space of time.

"Beg pardon, sir." The voice came from behind Honey, sending little prickles of fear along her neck.

"Oh, if I must." Charles whirled her neatly into another man's arms, and Honey lifted her lashes to find William Humphrey looking at her.

He was acutely aware of the tremor of fear that shot through her. "You know me, don't you?" It was a statement, not a question.

"No, sir." She forced herself not to tremble in his

arms. "I mean, I have been told that you are partners with Christopher, but . . ." She stiffened against the convulsive shiver.

"Then why are you afraid of me?" His brows dipped over his nose; suspicion laced his voice.

"I have no reason to fear you, sir." She looked away from him, afraid he'd see her lie. "Perhaps there is someone from my past whom you resemble, 'tis all."

"Your past? From an island? Perhaps your shyness is truly desire. Could that be? 'Tis said a wench fears the man she desires because he can read her thoughts, can know her pleasures better than anyone."

"No! I . . . 'Tis nothing, sir, I assure you. Please!" She broke from his hold the moment they passed beyond the veranda doors. Breathless, she stumbled past the library and down the stairs into the garden. Afraid that he might follow her, she slipped behind a trellis at the corner of the house and waited, trembling in a cold fear. Tears welled in her eyes. Who was this man? How could he command her fear as he had? He did not look dangerous, except when he leered, and he was married to the most gentle woman that Honey had ever met. It was wrong that a woman who attracted Honey as maternally as did Elizabeth would be married to a man who instilled such overwhelming fear.

A light suddenly glowed from the window next to her. Silhouettes moved along the curtains. She swallowed a sob so as not to be caught in such a compromising position.

"Don't lie to me!" the woman raged. Snatching a vase from a table, she sent it crashing across the room.

"That is enough of that!" The man's voice was Christopher's.

"You are right—enough of that! Have you

brought me here to make a fool out of me?"

"'Tis you who cause your own grief. The girl is nothing to me. A drowned rat to make good my seamanship. Was I to leave her to die alone there? Or perhaps to the mercy of pirates? What do you suppose Bloodwell would do with her?" His voice was calm, almost mocking.

"I want her out of here!" Jennifer hissed. "Ship her off with Jillian or pack her off to that mock earl of hers in the colonies." Christopher's chuckle slipped through the window, ripping at Honey's heart. "Do you think I want her around any more than you do? She'll be gone one way or another soon enough. Go enjoy the party before the sea waif begins to pick on another of your lovers." His voice was hard.

"You have bedded her, haven't you?"

"I don't bed children."

Jennifer gasped, and the sound of a glass being slammed to the table reached Honey, but she couldn't see what was happening.

"I've told you, she is nothing to me. Now stop this foolishness!"

Honey heard another gasp, then laboring breath, then a long silence.

"Not here!" Jennifer barely protested.

The implication of the hungry words hit her. A fresh spring of tears trickled down her face as the betrayal bit into her heart. Slipping from her spot behind the trellis, she stumbled past the garden and lawns into the English night, heedless of her direction, uncaring of the passage of time.

"She's breathing." The voice seemed distant to Honey's ears. The accent was different from any she had heard before. Her mind wandered through black tunnels that wound ever closer to daylight until finally she opened her eyes.

She gasped at the dark-skinned faces that bent over her.

"Let me see her." The voice was mysteriously deep and without inflection. A face appeared: a wrinkled woman of dark skin and tired blue eyes. The blue eyes were in startling contrast to those of her black-eyed companions. A hot, fleshy hand covered her arm. "She will live," the same voice hummed, but now Honey heard a strange accent.

"Who are you, child?"

Honey's gaze flicked from face to face, five in all standing over her. Black-eyed, black-haired people, so startlingly beautiful.

"I . . . my name is Honey. I mean, that is what they call me. I don't really know my name." She struggled to sit up from the damp ground where she must have lain all night.

"Go! All of you." The woman suddenly turned to the small group and they backed away, returning to the brightly painted wagons that waited several yards away.

"Who are you?" Honey looked at the woman dressed in a billowing orange peasant blouse tucked into a full black skirt. A red belt splashed across the orange at her blouse. She had draped scarves of green and blue over her short gray curls, her cheeks and lips were rouged pink, and her wrinkled eyelids were painted light blue.

"We are the family Bouquet. We are gyspies, child, destined to wander. Come, we will take you home."

Home! The word frightened her. How could she go back now? No one there wanted her. Hadn't she planned to leave this very day anyway? If she went back now her chance would be missed.

"I don't have a home," she said, looking about for some familiar landmark. Her swollen eyes ached as she scanned the hills. But nothing looked familiar.

"I must have walked all night," she said more to herself than to the woman. "Do you know where we are?"

"Bristol is to the south. That is where we have been. Come, we will rest here until you have recovered yourself." The old woman helped Honey to her feet. "Rollio!" she called. "Break the horses. We will rest here."

"So you will have something to show your grand-

Chapter Thirty

Honey smiled at the big man who lifted the pot from the open fire. She was cooking stew for her new gypsy family, and despite bitter memories of the overheard conversation several days before, she was happy.

She had traded her fine gown for a plain white top that skimmed her bare midriff, and a colorful calico skirt. She had washed the powder from her hair with a concoction made by the old woman, Leonie, and had left the long strands flowing free of the ribbons and binders Jillian had forced her to wear. No more stays, no more petticoats, and no more stockings. The freedom was heaven-sent, and so was the family who'd accepted her. It mattered not to them that she had learned to speak English at the age of nineteen or twenty, or that she was a "gorgio," a non-gypsy.

"Thank you, Leroy," she said, stirring the stew with a wooden spoon before touching the mixture to her lips. "Mmm, 'tis perfect."

"I'll spread the word," he grinned, showing her his blackened teeth. The seven-foot man ambled toward Leonie's wagon while she began to set out stacks of plates and spoons. Jugs of homemade wine wrapped in straw to protect the glass sat at either end of the table. It didn't take long for the family to begin drifting over from their wagons—Rollio along with his wife, Ali, and their daughter, Lotus; Angelic, the exotic almond-eyed, raven-haired beauty with her beautiful sister, Germaine; Karein, Marie, Ithal, Westphal, Otto . . . There were twenty-five people with this caravan.

"Isn't there bread?" Eugene demanded, grabbing a plate for himself. He was tall and darkly handsome. Like the rest of his family, he wore his shirts with his sleeves rolled up past his elbows, as if always prepared for a fight. When he looked at a woman his eye seemed to miss nothing.

"Under the cloth," she answered in her usual calm voice. She had learned to avoid Eugene when his mood was foul. And it would seem that it took only the smallest offense to set him off. But in his good moods he could be very nice.

Leroy found his way back to the table. Taking a plate for himself, he slopped it full of stew and ripped apart a large bun of bread. "*Puri dai.* Leonie wants to see you," he said, finding his favorite spot beside the low fire to eat his supper.

"Thank you." Wiping her hands on her apron, Honey cut across the grassy meadow to the yellow wagon. Stars and planets, human hands cupped to hold water, and pictures of crystal balls were painted in vivid detail on both sides of the old woman's home.

The wooden stairs had softened with age and were in need of painting, but Honey was beyond noticing such things. There was little enough money to provide food and clothing, let alone repair something that still worked. She knocked on the back frame before pushing the curtain aside to let herself in.

"Come in, child." Leonie's voice was as toneless as it had been the day they met. If it fluctuated at all it was only to get deeper. Honey believed the voice to be a trick of the trade. Fortune-telling, however accurate it could be, did take a bit of theatrics to be convincing.

"Leonie."

"Sit down, please. There is something on your mind. It has been there since the day we found you. Ask. Do not be afraid." The old woman's blue eyes seemed to see everything and nothing, her gnarled hands worked the cloth over her crystal ball until it gleamed. The wagon was dark, with shimmering black and silver curtains lining the walls. Leonie's personal items could not be seen.

They sat at a table covered by a beige cloth with the letters Ouija embroidered on it. The letters of the alphabet had been embroidered in the shape of a giant eye across the cloth. The letters A through M formed the upper lid, N through Z formed the lower. In the center of the eye were the words *Yes* and *No,* skillfully placed to look like a pupil. Overhead, an oil lamp, black from long hours of use, flickered.

"There is nothing, Leonie. I am happy here. I love your family . . . There is nothing more to want." Honey looked at her hands folded in her lap.

"Come, child, you have few secrets from me. What is the question you wish most to ask?"

Honey looked up, ashamed of her lie, and smiled meekly. "'Tis something a friend told me once."

"On a day that was sad for you."

"Yes. On a ship a long time ago. He said, 'Be of

good cheer. Perhaps some day we will run across a band of gypsies, and find the truth about your past.'"

"And still you have no memory," Leonie supplied.

"None. All of the clues might be there, but the answer is not."

The old woman lifted the crystal ball from the table and nestled it in the crook of her arm. Her ringed fingers petted the globe as if it were a favored pet. She peered into the crystal depths then closed her eyes as if drifting off to sleep. Then she opened them again and stared at Honey without seeing her.

"The future is your past," she murmured in a deepened voice. "You will fulfill the desires of your youth. But your destiny will not find you, you must find it."

"How will I find it?" Honey stared at the old woman in awe.

"When you look for the mate, you will know." Leonie suddenly sat erect in her chair.

"That makes little sense, Leonie. What does it mean?"

"You will know when the time is right," she said, setting the ball back on its stand.

"How can I? My future is my past, but I have no future so how can it be my past? And if I cannot remember my youth, how will I know what I desire? Unless . . . unless I return to the island?"

Leonie smiled weakly. "You will know. If you must question it, it cannot be so. I will have my dinner here. You may serve me."

"Of course." Honey stumbled from the wagon, Leonie's voice coursing through her mind. The cryptic message continued to repeat itself until well after the dinner plates had been washed and stored and the sunset glowed orange in the distance. Still, her only conclusion was that she cherished this new freedom. Nothing compared to the barefoot joy of living under the sun.

"Come on, Honey," Germaine called from the bonfire. "We're going to dance."

"My future is my past." Honey glanced and nodded to the other girl. "The past must then be my future. But is it the island? Or is it . . . Amesly? But I shall never go back there," she muttered.

"What?"

Honey shook her head and yanked off her apron, then joined Germaine at the fire.

Stepping next to Marie, Germaine on her other side, the three girls began to move to the sounds of an ancient lute. At first they moved together with their arms interlocked until the lute player teased one long cord and the innocent song became more sensual. Then the girls broke from one another, spinning off in a series of high kicks and spins. The thrill of the tempo caught Honey, and she whipped her hair around, letting the mass slide from her face as she tilted her head. Her movement became provocative now, and she dreamed of Chris standing beside the fire's edge watching her, wanting her—as she knew she wanted him. She was aware of herself as she had never been before. She was a woman much like Jennifer, and her own sensual awareness surged through her at the prompting of the music. She answered the call with a passion she never knew she possessed. The eerie chord of the lute penetrated her fantasy and she collapsed to the ground beside Germaine and Marie, as if flung there by some impatient lover. The group that had gathered near the fire cheered as the three pulled themselves from the ground. The girls smiled as they caught their breath, then they backed into the human ring as Angelic sauntered through the crowd, her hands resting in indignation on her hips. The lute joined forces with a guitar and the lead dancer posed briefly before she began to dance. Her dance skirted the boundaries of decency. Set against the flaming fire, her body assumed the red glow of the firelight. Honey watched, still breathless from her dance, and she took a lesson from Angelic—a lesson she could implement in her own dance.

In the next town they would perform their dance and hope that the people would throw coins to them. Half would go to the common fund, the rest the three would divide evenly among themselves. It was the way of the gypsies.

Honey loved working with the girls and the rest of the family. She felt like something more than just an ornament of the house, for the first time she felt needed. Cooking was not her only function. In the afternoon she and the other girls would dance for the early patrons, leaving Angelic for the men who visited under the cover of night. At night she collected the coins rendered for palm and tarot card readings, while Germaine handled the line that always formed beside Leonie's wagon. Leroy entertained with feats of strength and also served as camp protector should anyone get out of line. Rollio breathed fire and swallowed swords.

But it was Angelic who drew the largest crowd—the men who envisioned the sultry gypsy in their beds. While the men fantasized over the gypsy girl their wives slipped into the wagons to hear predictions of love—from a devout husband or a mysterious lover, it didn't matter.

This night, as always, Angelic's dance ended with

all the splendor and heartbreak of a love story. The group applauded and cheered as the music came to a sad end—all except Eugene, who sulked at the edge of the circle, nearer the shadows than the fire. At the end he turned away and was not seen for the rest of the night.

Rollio performed next, but his tenor voice cracked as the smoke from the fire drifted his way. Just before the moon began its path to the west, the group broke up and moved to their own wagons.

Germaine held the flap to their wagon aside as Karein and Honey climbed in. It had been Karein who invited her to join them, and Germaine who suggested Honey dance in place of Karein after she had twisted an ankle.

It was cozy on this chilly night as the three of them heated up the wagon with talk and laughter. Honey took the floor between the bunks that were built into the walls on either side of the wagon. The room reminded her of the *Wing Master*, and her first real bed. But with summer approaching, Honey realized it would soon get too hot for the three of them to sleep in the same wagon. She planned to save the money she earned to buy her own wagon eventually, but she knew that having enough money for that would take her a long time. So for now she made her bed between Karein and Germaine and dreamed as always of dark blue eyes that watched her dance, strong arms she longed to hold her, and the fiery kisses that had awakened the woman in her.

Two days later the band of colorful gypsy wagons rumbled into Reading. Leonie parted the curtains and looked out at the shops as the caravan moved slowly down the main road. It was Leonie's word that would make them stay or go.

"The town can afford us," she proclaimed when they reached the edge of the village. A clearing was chosen and the wagons were positioned for business. The wagons for palm reading, Tarot cards, and fortune-telling formed a half circle around the fire. The other wagons, used for eating and sleeping, were tucked back in a grove of trees. The children played there, and workers rested there, out of sight of the townspeople.

At noon Rollio brought out his banjo and Wig his bandor, and Honey began to dance with her friends. Slowly a crowd began to gather and she felt the excitement of performing. Little boys giggled at the shameless display of pretty legs, women were silently awed, and the men looked as though they might be interested in what was under the colorful skirts. At the end, coins showered the ground and the three girls fell instantly to their knees to retrieve them.

At sunset the small camp took on a carnivallike atmosphere. The ill searched for miracle cures while the lonely and depressed joined the lines behind Leonie's wagon. By midnight Angelic was dancing around the fire, and by one the camp had settled in for the night.

The second day proved to be just as profitable, but on the third day rumors of a gypsy woman caught stealing frm a young man whom she had bedded caused them to pack up and leave town before nightfall.

Exhausted by the past few days, Leonie called for a respite. The little caravan found a large pond to camp by and took three days rest. Honey began hers by washing the dust from her skin. Wading into the pond with her skirt hiked up and tucked into her waistband, she rinsed her arms and legs before cooking the afternoon meal. It was after dark when she slipped down to the pond and shed her clothes. The water was cool on her bare flesh. She lathered her body, then her hair, and rinsed. The pond reminded her of her own ponds, one on Amesly where she had gone to swim once, the other her island pond where she would swim every day. "Stay in the forest during the hot parts of the day, girl. In the heat of summer, swim often. The fresh water is good for the constitution." That was Barley Boe's advice. She recalled his ruddy face and the raspy voice she still heard in her mind. With a smile she drifted toward shore, but at the sound of footsteps she stopped. Her heartbeat quickened in fear that the footsteps might belong to someone not of her new family.

"It happens every time." Leroy's voice filtered through the shrubs. "She's whoring and we both know it. Leonie knows it, but no one is . . ."

"'Tis not our concern," Rollio's voice answered.

"And I say it is. She is giving us all a bad name. We are not well accepted now, how will it be if we are not accepted at all? Then what? Where will we go to feed our families then?"

"The talk is we'll be headed west soon anyway. To the colonies," Rollio said thoughtfully. The sound of snapping branches followed.

"That doesn't matter. We'll be unwanted there, too. Eugene should take hold of himself and show that woman what's right!"

"Hush, man. Time handles all." Rollio snapped another branch. "Let's get these back now."

"Won't Honey be surprised come morning?" Leroy answered, following his companion from the woods.

Honey smiled. She should have known that it was

the pair of them supplying her kindling for morning cooking. But their conversation remained as cryptic as Leonie's prediction for her future. Angelic and Eugene? It couldn't be. She treated him like dirt. Nonetheless, their remarks made some sense, considering the way he had shied away from the midnight dancing. But why would he be expected to take her in hand? They were not related, as far as she knew. Though each caravan was considered its own family, most of these folks were no closer than sixth or seventh cousins, if there were any blood relations at all.

She pulled herself from the pool. Grabbing up a towel, she patted the water from her body, enjoying the brisk cold of the country air. Overhead the sky winked with thousands of stars, and a full moon was rising. An eerie orange glow erupted from the center of the camp. Long black shadows imitated Angelic as she danced.

Rubbing her head with her towel, Honey watched from the edge of the pond. The shadows snaked over the ground in three directions, arching and kicking as sensuously as the dancer herself. Her agility was hypnotic, and Honey found it hard to look away as she dressed and crossed the field to the edge of the wagons.

"Do you envy her?" Eugene startled her as he emerged from the shadows behind her.

"I believe I am supposed to." She smiled at the shadow.

"It is because you don't that she dislikes you." His honesty surprised her.

"Then I would say she will dislike me for a long time to come."

His hard features broke into a smile. "Tell me why

you stay so kind to me when I have treated you no better than she has."

"You haven't been unkind to me," Honey pointed out. "Sometimes you are angry. I wish I knew why, but I have had a friend who is angry like you sometimes. I guess I have become accustomed to it."

"I hate her, you know." He stepped from the shadow. "The way she treats people, the things she does for . . ."

Honey was shocked by his words, but even more shocked by what they meant. "I don't believe you hate her at all," she whispered, straining to see his twisted expression. "You are in love with her!"

"Maybe once," he frowned. "We have Leonie's promise. We have been committed for marriage, yet she resists. Time has gone by and still she is chasing other men."

"Is there nothing you can do?"

"Until the words are spoken she is free to run. Her papa, he warned me that she was a hard one to break. Caa, I should have listened. Yesterday was just one more time. Another man's bed . . . I could wrap my hands around her throat and . . ." His voice hardened and eyes blazed in passionate anger; she watched his hands ball into fists.

"Maybe just a good spanking." She laughed nervously, patting his flexed arm, praying the effect would calm him. Then suddenly he relaxed. His eyes lightened with humor and he smiled again.

"Good night, Eugene." She touched his shoulder and turned into camp just as Angelic came around the corner of the wagon.

The gypsy's eyes narrowed and she slammed her shoulder into Honey's as she passed. "Stay away from my man!" she growled.

Honey almost laughed out loud. Jennifer was surely more of a threat than this. "Take care of your man, or he might not be your man much longer." Honey tossed her hair back and crossed the camp. But the burn she felt in the middle of her back could only be Angelic's killing glare.

Chapter Thirty-One

A gentle rain subdued the camp the following two days. The occupants of each wagon ate whatever foodstuffs they had on hand, relieving Honey of having to cook in the rain.

The bleak days blended together, making Honey wish for the first time that she was at Amesly. She thought of sitting in her favorite chair before the wide fireplace with a book in her lap and a hot chocolate beside her. She longed for a book about the sea and ships. Lying on her straw pallet, she traced the lines of wood grains on the planked floor next to her pillow as she half listened to Karein's story about Angelic and the problems she had caused. Germaine, sitting cross-legged on her bunk, told a romantic story of her own. Then the pair begged for Honey to tell them of life in a grand manor. They yearned for stories of freedom to do as one pleased without having to do chores.

Homesickness slowly wound its way around Honey's heart as she described the gardens of Amesly, her horse and pond, and the fashions that the ladies wore at balls. As she talked she realized that Jillian must be worried sick for her. Ariel was probably frantic. Perhaps she should send a letter from the next town, but she decided she would tell them only that she was happy and in good health, and she would make it clear that while she loved them and would miss them, she would never be returning to Amesly. Loving Christopher so much and knowing how he felt about her was too painful to live with. And Charles, kind as his offer had been, would never be a faithful husband. Honey knew that she could tolerate nothing less.

Night fell and storytime ended with Honey dripping tears silently into her pillow until sleep overtook her.

Sometime near dawn a scuffle started outside the circle of the wagons. A man's voice shouted and a woman's voice retorted in a language Honey didn't understand. Then silence hung over the camp until dawn.

"What happened last night?" she asked when her companions awoke. Germaine stretched and yawned.

"Sounded like Cleo yelling."

"Wonder what that demon is up to now?" Honey mumbled. "I swear, you people have the hottest blood I've ever seen." She added the last as a picture of Chris flashed through her mind. "Well, very close to it . . ."

Probably someone went for a walk and startled someone else, she reasoned. Pulling on her clothes, Honey tossed a shawl over her shoulders to ward off the dismal morning chill.

"Honey?" Germaine looked at the oldest of the three girls, who was going to prepare the morning meal. "Don't you miss it? The splendor, the fashions . . ."

"The rich men," Karein added.

A smile curved Honey's lips. "That is another story," she said, dropping the curtain behind her. Only Leonie had been trusted with her past, and it was better that way.

Breakfast was tense. Cleo, whose family was relatively new to the caravan, sat at a makeshift table with his back to the fire while his wife gathered food enough for her family and went back to their wagon. The children were not seen at all.

A few more sleepy drifters appeared, followed by Angelic, who threw Cleo an unreadable look as she helped herself to stewed oats and a slab of ham. Yet with her arrival the tension became a more tangible thing, like the calm before a storm. Angelic shook out her long hair and pulled a stool up beside Cleo's. She was barefoot and her skirts draped around the stump. Cleo, who was usually content just to work his show and manage his family, looked horror-stricken and jumped to his feet, but not before Eugene stalked around his wagon with a look of pure rage in his eyes.

"This is enough! And that too much!!" he thundered, red faced. "It is not enough for you on the outside, that you must bring your poison home?"

Angelic looked smug for a brief moment, but her eyes widened with every measured step Eugene took toward her. Cleo vanished beneath the table and crawled to a place of safety, from which he too watched with deep fascination at the man Eugene had become.

"It's none of your concern," she cried, taking a step back from her betrothed.

"It was always my concern," he growled back, grasping her wrist and jerking her forward. "Come!"

he snarled.

"No! I will not go with you!" She raised herself up and tried to glare at him.

"Then suffer your punishment here, before your family." He dropped into the nearest chair and pulled Angelic across his lap, fanny up. Then with sweeping blows he spanked her, hard and long, until she wept for mercy.

Honey stared with guilty eyes. True, this had been her suggestion—preferable to murder, certainly. But a public spanking? The humiliation . . . She watched the play of emotions cross the faces of the family members who watched. Lotus wept into her mother's bosom, and Karein hid behind Germaine. Cleo's wife couldn't hide her smile as she peeked from behind a wagon. Leroy and his constant companion, Rollio, snickered. For most who gathered to watch, the punishment seemed long overdue. Honey glanced at the edge of the circle. The yellow wagon's tent flap was lifted, and the old woman looked out, her pale blue eyes seeming to twinkle merrily. Her chin dipped ever so slightly toward Honey before she smiled. Then the curtain dropped.

"Now you will come with me," Eugene ordered as he shoved Angelic from his lap to the ground. Grabbing her upper arm, he dragged her to the wagon furthest from camp. An eruption of applause followed them.

"'Twas much less than she deserved," Ali confided over the breakfast dishes later. Her husband sat at the long table filling his pipe. Honey stacked the plates near the end of the table, where they would be ready for the next meal. The ground was still cool and damp beneath her bare feet. The sky remained a bleak shade of gray, and Honey wondered if she would ever see the sun again.

"Too true," Rollio answered, taking a drag from his pipe. On the pipe's bowl there was a carving of a man's face and hand holding a pipe, and on *that* little pipe was a tiny face with a tiny hand smoking a pipe. Honey stared at the pipe, leaning closer and closer, trying to count the tiny men.

Honey waved at the smoke Rollio exhaled in order to get a better look.

"Any closer and you'll singe your nose," he said quietly.

She flushed and pulled back in time to see Ali smiling her famous motherly smile. "It happens with that pipe. He made it just for that reason, I think."

"You made it?" Honey asked. "How?"

Rollio pulled a blade from his boot. It wasn't a knife, exactly. "A whittle blade."

"You used that huge thing to carve that tiny little man?" Her eyes widened in disbelief.

"No, I have several sizes, depending on what I am working on."

"Do you sell your craft in the towns we visit?"

"Sometimes. But mostly it's just for fun," he said. "Well, I had best see if we'll be moving tonight." He heaved himself from his stool, planted a kiss on his wife's mouth, and gave a tug on Honey's hair.

"I'll bet we stay," Ali said. "It might be days before Eugene returns from his honeymoon. He should have spanked that girl years ago." Ali was a full-bodied woman. Her hips were wide, her waist small, and her bust full. Too full to dance. Her chores varied with the needs of the camp. Sometimes she sewed, other times she cooked, more often she watched the children while everyone else did what they needed to do. "Come to think of it, her father should have."

"She has no mother?"

"Eh? Who can tell? In autumn we band together in groups of a hundred or more and migrate to wherever is chosen. Sometimes we get a few mixed up. Brothers and sisters come and go. The stories about Angelic's parentage are varied. But a man, perhaps her father, Edgar, raised her—doted on her, spoiled her terribly. We live a free life, yes, but common courtesies should never be overlooked. With children, love does little without the guidance of a firm hand."

Honey smiled. She had never thought of children before. Suddenly she noticed that these travelers took care of their own children. It wasn't like that in London, she knew, where day nurses, night nurses, wet nurses, and nannies raised the children. In some homes the parents scarcely saw their children until the day they came of age.

By dinnertime the misty rain had stopped. Rollio and Leroy disappeared into the woods, and nothing was heard from Eugene, who had packed up his wagon and his wife and rumbled off to parts unknown. But the matriarch told Rollio that the caravan would wait for their return. She gave them one week. In the meantime, the group was to relax and enjoy, because from here on life could only get better.

Rollio set the spark to the pyramid of sticks and fanned the embers until a flame licked at the wood. Patiently he fed the fire until it grew to be a good size. The family members who gathered there seemed to glow from the hot flames.

Leonie joined the group for a change, taking the chair that was placed near the fire for her. "Ali, it has been a long time since you have given us a story." Her old voice cracked.

"Aye, how 'bout it, Ali?" someone said, and others agreed. Ali moved forward.

She took a spot beside the fire and pulled her shawl over her long dark hair. The firelight played on her face, casting long shadows beneath her eyebrows and along her nose. Her voice became hypnotic as she spun a tale of lost gypsies and haunted forests, of spirits of the dead, unable to rest until their bodies were properly buried and marked.

Cleo told the next story, a chilling tale of a murderous wife, which more than a few hoped had no bearing on this morning's events. Leonie finished with a tragic story of a young man who wandered through the spirits of his dead, searching for a way home.

"To this day he searches. He calls to the god of his people, begging for a clue to what he seeks." Her pale blue eyes focused on Honey, giving her a meaningful look that was not lost on Honey. But neither did it offer much hope.

The story stayed with Honey for several days. Images of a bone-weary Chris, sagging heavily over his saddle while images of female ghosts whirled around his drooping head, filled her mind. She longed to reach out and hold that image, to comfort him. But she wasn't the one he was searching for, or he would never have treated her as he did.

Leonie offered Honey the use of Angelic's wagon. "Should you stay," the old woman said, "it will be yours. Angelic will live with her husband."

"Of course I plan to stay." Honey watched the

woman carefully. "That is, if you'll have me."

"The group shall decide, but you have a decision to make. We will vote the night after Eugene returns. The night after that you must decide your future." The conversation ended abruptly.

Eugene returned with his doting bride just two days later. He grinned broadly as he pulled his wagon into the same spot as before. Beside him, Angelic wore a sweet smile of contentment. At last she fit her name, for she indeed looked positively angelic, flushed from her retreat with her man and not in the least bit embarrassed by their hasty departure or the scarf that now covered her head, signifying her marriage. She jumped down from the wagon the moment it stopped, guiding the team of horses in, as the other wives did for their husbands, and tossed the log beneath the wheel to keep the wagon from rolling back as the team was unhitched.

It was as though Eugene had traded the old Angelic in for a new one. The change was beyond what anyone could have imagined. She helped Honey with the cooking, served her husband his dinner at the table, jumping whenever he needed something, and even played with the children.

That night, after the cooking fire had been stoked to a bonfire, Angelic sat on the ground next to her husband, her arm resting idly on her husband's knee as she watched Karein, Germaine, and Honey dance.

Two of the younger men danced after that. Angelic's song came next, and all faces turned expectantly toward her, but she only looked up at her husband. "Angelic dances no more," he said simply. His words were taken as law. Angelic smiled complacently at her husband's decree.

"We need a new dancer," Cleo's voice called from

the back of the ring.

"Karein is well, let her take the lead," someone said.

"How about Germaine?" came another voice.

"Let Honey do it. She dances well," Germaine said from beside her friend.

Marie chimed in her agreement.

"I cannot dance so well. Karein should be your choice. And she is beautiful, besides. I would not bring the same coin that she would."

"'Tis not true," Karein said back. "Your beauty rivals mine. And your dance is perfect."

"Karein!" Honey rolled her eyes at her friend. "You are so lovely and dark, my pale flesh pales even more in comparison. Please, I could not dance at night anyway. The townsmen want to see gypsy flesh, not 'gorgio.'"

"Dance together!" The suggestion came from a woman.

"Yes, do." Angelic's smile was strained. Tamed for the moment she might be, but no doubt she was riled to see her former position bartered for.

Karein smiled and pulled Honey to her feet. They faced each other across the fire and listened as the teasing strings of the violin mingled with Wig's lute. The beautiful melody sent each girl surging into the dance. Honey closed her eyes as she always did, letting the rhythms vibrate through her as she thought of Chris. She kicked out, throwing her head back, and circled the fire, her skirt flaring around her bare legs, She stepped to her toes, arching her back at her imagined audience of one, and as the music wound down she wilted to the ground, her head falling forward dramatically.

Panting hard but more than secretly thrilled with her creation, Honey heard the ominous silence that engulfed the group. Were they awed or offended at her brazen display? Lifting her head, she smiled, but the group looked to a point behind her, and she turned.

His image flared as if he'd sprouted from the hot flames of the fire. He stood not six steps away from her, hands on hips. An amused smile touched his mouth, but her heart stilled and her eyes consumed him. He appeared like Satan over her, and in her fear she remained frozen to the ground until he came forward and pulled her to her feet. His trembling hand gently pushed her wild hair from her face. He glanced once behind her as the gypsies followed Rollio's lead and left the pair alone.

"I can't believe I found you." His voice shook with emotion. "I can't believe you're alive." His tears shone in the firelight. Suddenly he pulled her to him and his mouth descended upon hers, capturing her in a kiss that shook the depths of her soul. She sighed as she pressed herself against him, her curves fitting into his muscular valleys as if the two of them had been molded at birth. His body burned through his clothes. His tears were hot as they fell to her face and mingled with her own. He pulled her more closely to him, wrapping her protectively in his arms and showering her face with a frenzy of kisses.

"I've come to take you home," he murmured in her ear.

Chapter Thirty-Two

The ache began inside her chest then shuddered down through her, stealing her breath as it moved to a secret place in her belly, then lower.

They stood in her wagon; a lamp burned dimly in the corner. Chris trembled as he stepped back from her. He watched her as she watched him. He would undress her, as the men in the books had undressed the women they desired. The anticipation was almost too much for her to bear. His fingers managed the tiny hooks of her blouse with ease, and the blouse fell apart under the weight of her breasts.

He looked at the open edges of the blouse before pulling it aside, his breath catching in his throat. He allowed one callused finger to trace a line over the tip of one pink nipple, and as he did, a jolt shot through her belly to her thighs, igniting her need for him. She gasped as her nipple hardened and stood out for him, as if asking to be touched again. Instead he removed his own shirt, then slid his fingers over her shoulders, pushing the blouse to the floor. The skirt billowed to the floor on top of the blouse as he eased her back onto the bed. She shivered as he shed his trousers. His body was hard and tan and his manhood jutted out, commanding her attention. He smiled when he saw where she looked, then he slid onto the bunk beside her. He took his time looking at her, his eyes drinking in what he had thought was lost to him forever. At last he cupped her breast. Fire shot through her again. She gasped, closing her eyes.

"What are you doing to me?" she whispered sweetly.

"I am loving you," he answered, lowering his mouth to suckle at her breast. His teeth rolled the excited nipple back and forth as she arched up to him, willing that he take more as his hand slid down her thigh. Fingers spread, he tested the crease between her inner thigh and her soft mound. She gasped again as his fingers sought the warm milky flesh beween her nether lips. His mouth moved to her other breast, and she sucked her breath in in pleasure. Then suddenly his finger slid into her swollen womanhood. There was wonder in the sensation, a feeling that no name suited.

She opened her eyes to find him looking at her. The look was hard, yet not angry.

"Trust me," he said, covering her mouth with his own as he rolled to cover her body. His hips moved rhythmically against hers until she began to move against him. The heightening sensations left her mindless of anything but pleasure. Suddenly she felt a searing pain. His mouth kept her cry from being heard, then carefully—as the pain ebbed—he stroked her quivering body, bringing the sweet sensations back.

This was what she had desired most, to fill her arms with this man and kiss away his hurts. She had wanted this enough to abandon everything when she thought it had been denied her.

A sigh escaped her as she rubbed herself against

him. He quivered and groaned as she danced on his shaft, tempting his seed to come to her. Their mouths met as the tempest catapulted them over the top of the storm. In racking shudders they clutched each other close. Their hearts raced, beating together; their breaths mingled as the kiss was slow to part. With eyes closed they lay wrapped together, moist with perspiration, unwilling to separate.

What a lovely dream, Honey thought. She had dreamed this dream for almost three weeks now. He would be there, magically there, wanting her so badly that there was no time for words, no time for explanations that could be misunderstood. There were only the moments of their passion and their love. She smiled and snuggled closer to the man in the dream. But the soft warm flesh was real and it snuggled back. His breath was warm against her shoulder; his long body curled against her from behind. She could feel the mellow rise and fall of his chest. This was not a dream. The faint throb between her thighs told her that it was real . . .

She rolled slowly in his arms to face him. He was naked against her. She flushed at the delicious sensation of flesh against flesh. Her eyes roamed over his sleeping face, a mere inch or so away from hers. Asleep, his face was more passive than she had ever seen it. The scowl that he so often wore was replaced by features so calm and soft she had trouble believing this was Chris.

She'd never seen him look so handsome, so young. He might be very close to her own age, she thought, now that she could see him without that constant scowl on his face.

A smile crossed her lips. She knew now what the

poets and playwrights based so much of their writings on. There was nothing to compare with physical love. The sensations, the thrills, that last climactic moment!

But how had he known where she'd be? And why did he bother looking at all? Why did he kiss her the way he did?

He didn't bed children . . . She was nothing to him. The words stung as she remembered them, remembered the night she left Amesly behind. Life in the caravan had been so simple. The clothes, the food, the attitude and morals of the gypsies were beyond compare. Tears welled briefly, then faded as she worked herself out from under his arm to slip from the bed. But his arm snaked out, capturing her wrist, pulling her back down beside him.

Their eyes clashed for a long moment.

"You ran away, didn't you?" Disbelief marred his features. He stared at her, waiting for an explanation.

Honey looked away, swallowing her shame.

"It is no longer your concern!" she said, rolling away, only to be jerked back.

"By God, it *is* my concern!" His growling voice was low. "Have you no care for the people you left behind to worry about you?" His arms tightened around her.

"I am sorry for that. I was going to send a note from the next town."

"A *note?*" He shook his head. "Jillian has all but withered with worry. Ariel has taken to her bed, afraid for the worst. I have searched for better than a fortnight for you, only to find you dancing before a fire like a . . ." The vision in his mind halted him. The sight of her dancing, bathed in firelight and dressed as a gypsy, sent his pulse racing again. There were no words to describe the effect she had on him.

His concerns for her had turned into a hunger he could no longer deny.

"How dare you call me a whore!" she growled, jumping from his grasp. She whipped the blanket from the bed and pulled it around herself, but not before he saw her fully naked in the golden glow of the lamplight.

"Whore was not the word I had in mind," he retorted. "But you are lucky you haven't been ravished, throwing yourself about the countryside like that!"

"Oh? Then what is it you call this?'"'

"I call this long overdue," he grimaced, sitting upright, unashamed of his own nakedness.

"Well, I certainly understand that statement!" she snapped.

"About as much as I understand why you left in the first place!" he shot back.

"What do you care? Isn't your life full enough without me? You have your ghosts to make love to and when they aren't enough, there is always Jennifer!" She cried the words without yelling them. "I'm sick of being compared to a ghost! And sick of your constant irritation at everything I do. God! Why didn't you just leave me be!" She stamped a bare foot on the wooden floor.

"For the same reasons you make me so damned angry. But it's not you, it's me. I am angry with myself for feeling the things I feel when I look at you."

"Wha . . ."

"I can't explain it," he said, wrapping the sheet around his waist and staring at the floor. Raking a hand through his hair, he sighed, at a loss for the right words.

"From the moment I saw you standing on the cliff,

from the second you crossed the deck of the ship stark naked, from the time of your first bath—you've stirred something in me. Something I hadn't felt since . . . since the loss of Crystal. Of course I cared deeply for Crystal. We were to spend our lives together. We grew up together . . . It's not just that you remind me of her. It's that you're the person I had hoped she'd grow up to be. But if I were married to her right now, what kind of husband would I be? And how can I think of you and not think of that?"

He pulled her down to sit beside him, to capture her eyes with his. "It is so much easier going through life surrounded by women whose barbs and attitudes can't hurt you. If Jenny died today I'd feel a passing grief, but nothing like I felt when I noticed you were missing. It tore at my gut. All I could think was, *God! Not again!* And no one knew if you had run away or been taken or fallen somewhere in the dark or on one of your blasted midnight walks. You don't understand that, do you?" He watched her confused face.

"I understand that you were busy in the library about the time I left. How long past midnight was it before you noticed I wasn't there?" she answered back.

He at least had the grace to look sheepish—too well did he recall what he had said that night. "Jennifer, as you well know, can be quite the bitch."

"Yes, I've heard that."

"I was wrong, Honey. Wrong to try to push you out of my life. Wrong to punish you because you made me feel so alive. Wrong to punish myself because I had lost my self-control and kissed you. Wrong to tell Jennifer that you meant nothing to me." His eyes met hers; his voice became a whisper. "Wrong to think about letting you go to the colonies."

Honey was looking up at him, listening to every word as if entranced. Her eyes closed automatically as he laid her carefully back on the bed. "Jillian was right," he rasped as he pulled the blanket from her and pushed her to the bed. "You are every inch a woman.

Chapter Thirty-Three

Wiping away her tears, Honey hugged Germaine and Karein goodbye.

"I shall never forget you, any of you. When you're near Amesly you must stop and stay for a few days," she sniffed.

Angelic was next, followed by Eugene.

"If ever you run away again you'll know our route. You can come home." Eugene hugged her.

"If she ever does that again I'll wring her neck for her." Chris laughed as he shook Eugene's hand.

"Well, maybe just a good spanking will do." Eugene winked at Honey then slid an arm around his blushing wife. Honey laughed as she hugged Leroy, leaving a kiss on his big stubbly cheek.

"Now would be a good time to thank you and Rollio for all the kindling," she whispered to Leroy, delighted by the startled look on his face.

"What?" Rollio looked over at her as she hugged him. Then he grinned. "You just can't keep a secret from a woman, can you!" he said. But he grinned again and presented her with a tiny figure carved from wood. It was a woman dancing gypsy style.

"So you will have something to show your grandchildren."

"Oh, Rollio, she's beautiful! And look! She looks like me! Thank you, Rollio. Ali, you have been so good to me."

Leonie presented her hands to Honey. She was the last one to say goodbye to. "It is as it should be." Leonie smiled a rare smile then patted the younger woman's hands. "Perhaps it will help to know that you will find the truth sooner than even you think is possible."

"I pray you are right," Honey smiled. "Thank you. Thank you all so much." Then she turned to Chris, who had brought their horse around.

"We ride double," he grinned. "It will take longer to get home that way," he whispered as he mounted, then pulled her up behind him.

Chris turned the horse onto the road that led home, and Honey waved to the troupe who had become her family for a short time. They would remain in her heart always.

"How far from Amesly are we?" Honey sat chewing a piece of bread packed for them by Ali. Beside her, Chris had stretched himself out in the grassy meadow, while his horse munched the sweet grass not too far away.

"Another two days," he said. "Are you tired of living on the road already?"

"Never. I love the road life." She bent down and kissed him. Her thick, loose hair floated on the breeze. "The sun overhead and the smell of sweet grass on the wind. Better than dirty old London any day."

He laughed as he stole a bite of her bread before

pulling her down to kiss him. "You should never have run from me that day in the stables," he whispered between kisses. "You'd have had me then and maybe we'd—"

"Had you? You should have seen the look on your face," she giggled. "It was as if I were some viper erupted from hell."

"It's the passion in you. I'd guessed it might be there, judging from that temper of yours."

"Mine? Shall we compare tempers?"

"I've got a better idea," he said, pressing his hips into hers. She pressed back.

"Under the sun," she murmured, kissing him full on the mouth. Her hips nested into his. It didn't take long for him to pull her blouse from her shoulders. His lips moved from her mouth to her breasts, where he alternately nibbled and kneaded her pink nipples until they jutted out, begging for more.

The sun was warm on her bare chest, though not as hot as her lover's mouth. He seared her wind-cooled body with kisses while his fingers popped the hooks on her skirt and whisked it off. His mouth continued past her belly, past her hips to her mound, where his tongue parted her woman's lips and burned the center of her. She gasped, arching her back. He smiled, thrilled with his new sense of power. Few women had ever refused him, and he had always prided himself on the fact that none would go unsatisfied, but with Honey there was something else, something more than just pleasing a lover. It was loving a woman who had never loved any other man. A woman who never would love any other man. He brought his mouth back to hers as he shed his breeches. Then he pressed against her.

She gasped as he entered her and panted as he stroked her side, kissing her fully on the mouth then nibbling her lip. Her every sound heightened his pleasure in a way he never thought possible. She clung to him as they soared together in the sweet meadow.

"It must always be like this," she sighed. It never crossed her mind to wonder how she came to be on top of him.

"Only with the right people." His arms tightened around her.

"You mean it is different with everyone?" Her eyes became wide and her brows knitted as she asked the question.

"Of course. It's the main reason many husbands stray from home. A good marriage match isn't always good in bed, I guess."

"Would you?" she asked shyly, glancing away from those piercing eyes to the waves of meadow grasses.

"Stray from home? Only if there are more of you around." He grinned, pulling her chin back to face him. "I have had more than my share of the ladies."

Honey's heart raced as she absorbed his confession. She didn't want to know who, or how many. She pushed her hair back from her face and rolled away from him. Grabbing her skirt, she stepped into it, then pulled her blouse over her shoulders. "I don't think I want . . ."

"Well, you shall hear it! Perhaps this has been too much for you, but these are the facts. And they are facts you'll end up living with—just as I've seen how many men would have you if they could. Shall I name a few of them?"

She flushed, her gaze lowered. "There is no need to explain anything, but . . ."

"But what?" he urged, nudging her arm playfully.

"But," she swallowed hard, afraid of the answer

she might receive. "There was one woman you truly cared about. When you were a boy, Ida, wasn't it?"

"How did you know about Ida?" he asked.

"Jillian was worried about you the first time you passed through Dunn. She broke down and told me what happened. She believes that you still miss her . . ."

"I do, and I loved Ida." He looked thoughtfully across the land, then back at Honey. The wind blew at his hair. Lazy clouds floated overhead, so similar to the summer days spent at Dunn. "I felt love and respect for a woman who could fight the odds like she did. Her life was hell but she never complained about it. The men she worked for abused her in ways no woman should endure. I stayed because they seemed to leave her alone whenever I was near. I almost killed one man who . . . well, be that as it may, she seemed to need me. And I needed to be needed." He paused and laughed sadly. "Listen to me, trying to tell you what it's like to be left alone in the world."

"Yet, I never knew." She smiled at him. "I didn't know it until I saw . . ." A jabbing pain shattered her temple, throwing her head forward.

Chris was instantly over her, pushing the mass of auburn hair away. "What is it?" he cried, trying to lift her face. "Honey!"

The pain eased slowly. Only seconds had passed, but she could hear him calling to her. She pulled her hand from beneath his grasp. Covering his with her own, she squeezed gently. Three seconds later she panted with relief.

"This has happened before!" he snapped in frustration. "In the cove on the island and again at Amesly. Is it memories? Is it dreams? What is it? Is it a memory of a ship?"

She blinked back a tear. "Please, could we just go

home?" Honey rolled into his embrace, resting her head against his shoulder. She felt safe there. Nothing could harm her when his arms were around her.

"Aye, we'll go home." He petted her hair until her heartbeat slowed.

"Do you have all of your things?" he asked, helping her to stand.

She glanced around the spot where they had rested while he repacked their small sack of food. "I must have; there is nothing here." But she felt something missing. "I guess my memory is worse than I thought. There seems to be something." A stiff gust of wind blew her skirt against her legs, then whipped it up and over her knees.

Chris laughed at the way her eyes suddenly popped open wide. Quickly her hand moved to her fanny, as if she were feeling through the fabric. Her pants were gone. "I guess I *am* missing something," she muttered. Her brows knit together as she looked at Chris.

His eyes met hers, then glanced behind her to the clump of high bushes and small trees quaking in the wind as if laughing at their new ornament.

Honey saw her gypsy pants waving in the breeze at the top of the thicket like the Union Jack itself.

"How'd they . . . Never mind." She flushed at the stupidity of her own question. "Would you mind?" She gestured delicately in the direction of the tree.

"How am I supposed to get up there?" He snickered as he stuffed the pouch into the rolled blanket strapped to the small saddle.

"Who put them there?" She cocked her head in mock exasperation.

He laughed. "Leave em. I'll buy you a new pair."

"Oh, that's fine. Except that you cannot buy them;

they are from the gypsies. I had thought you'd know that Englishwomen don't wear such things." She paused for effect. "But how do you suppose my bottom is going to feel tonight after all day on a saddle with nothing between me and it? That is, unless you don't care that I will be too sore to . . ."

He crossed the clearing in three strides. Another two steps had him in the tree retrieving the pants. Honey laughed at his gentlemanly expression as he handed the garment over.

"Thank you, sir," she dipped in short tribute.

Chris grinned, turning his back while she stepped into her undergarment. "I always wondered what gypsies wore under those skirts," he teased.

"Next time, don't throw them so far," she suggested.

"Next time, leave them home." He ducked as her hand came around to smack him, but before she could recoil he had her off her feet and on the horse. Swinging his leg over the horse's neck, he too mounted.

It was dusk before they stopped again. Chris built a small fire while Honey prepared the stew she had made for her gypsy friends.

"You make a fair gypsy," he commented as he pulled the wooden bowls from the food sack.

"So would you," she smiled back. "Would you always have made a good gypsy?"

"A sea gypsy, maybe." He handed the bowls over to her and she filled them with steaming thick stew. "Why?"

"You have changed so much. I wonder if this is you or if . . ."

"Two weeks alone on the road is a nasty way to get

to know yourself. I didn't want to think you had run away, but I could see why you would. But if you had been kidnapped and were dead, I don't know what I'd have done." He gazed at her tenderly. "I regretted not kissing you that first night at Amesly. I regretted not enjoying the sight of you running barefoot all the time."

A low flush kissed her cheeks, and her heart erupted in love as he spoke. "It's learning what Jillian tried to tell me all along, something I should have realized long ago. Nothing is forever."

Honey said nothing; there was nothing to say. They ate in silence, then sat wrapped in each other's arms and watched the fire. They gazed at the stars and slowly explored each other's bodies. Tasting and touching, licking, caressing, and loving with an endless passion.

Chapter Thirty-Four

Michael spotted the riders about a mile from home. He raced back to the main house shouting the news. *"Mr. Ames has found her! Honey's come home!"*

By the time Chris and Honey ambled into the yard every servant and friend who had anxiously waited out the three weeks had gathered in front of the house. Honey was amazed that she could have been missed so much.

Tears trailed over Jillian's cheeks as she bounced impatiently, her arms stretched to embrace Honey, who was still mounted. Geoff, who had stayed behind to care for the women, held Ariel's hand as she ran to greet her friend.

Honey cried, embracing one after another and accepting her scoldings with a broad smile. Charles had returned to the country house the moment he had learned of her disappearance, but he arrived too late to help aid in the search.

Over the noise and confusion, Jillian called to Brea to prepare a bath, but just as the group moved toward the house another rider raced into the yard, his horse lathered and breathing hard from the long ride. Everyone turned in silence to see what the emergency was all about.

"Captain Ames! It's the *Night Wing*, sir. She's been stole!" The seaman shouted his words.

"When?"

"Last eve. The guards were found on the shore. Dead, sir, both of them."

"Michael! Two fresh horses!" he called as he trotted across the yard. "Do you know who? Or see which way they went?"

"Nay, sir. We canvased the quay. No one was there."

Michael came around the house pulling the black beast and the chestnut behind him. The sailor grabbed the reins and remounted. Chris did the same, but then he turned back to face the group of curious faces, searching out the one he wanted most to see.

"Don't worry, I'll be back," he promised before starting off behind his sailmate. Geoff followed, having retrieved his own horse from the stable, leaving the women alone again and worried.

Elizabeth sat on Honey's bed as she watched Brea place the finishing touches to Honey's elaborate coiffure. Ariel curled up in the chair next to the fireplace and played with a silver comb.

"'Tis brave you were to dance like that!" Elizabeth shook her head at Honey's story.

"I believe Honey has nerve for almost anything," Ariel said with a smile.

"But what made you go?" Elizabeth asked.

Honey looked at the woman who sat on her bed. *That woman's husband scared her to death!* He was the reason she ended up outside that library window, but how could she say so?

She picked up the comb Ariel had just finished inspecting and pretended to study it. "I never intended to run away," she lied. "I just walked farther than I should have and got lost. The gypsies were so very kind to me. Their way of life is so simple that I just decided not to come back."

Maybe that was closer to the truth than she thought.

"Well, we are glad to have you back. You have no idea what Jillian's been through. She loves you like her own, you know."

Honey smiled sheepishly. "I know."

"Where's your brush?" Ariel asked. She moved to the dressing table to look at herself in the mirror.

"I don't have one." Honey handed the comb back to her friend. "I had combs on the island. It never occurred to me to use a brush."

Ariel laughed, teasing her short bangs with the silver comb. "That is so like you."

"I've got some extra brushes back at Stonewings. You may have one if you'd like." Elizabeth giggled at Honey's attitude. She wished her own was more relaxed. "I wish I had your outlook on life."

"Why? Nothing is wrong with yours." Honey laughed with the slightly older woman. "You really should visit more often."

"I'd like that too, but I never know when William will come home. He keeps no schedule, so should I wish to see him I must wait at home. But that should not stop you from coming to visit me." She stood up from the bed, smoothing her simple gown. "Come to think, he did say he would be home tonight. He does have a thoughtful moment, you know. I must be off then. Perhaps tomorrow you'll come for tea?" She smiled.

Honey glanced at Ariel and back at Elizabeth.

"We'll be there. Jillian too."

"Oh, yes! Do bring Jillian! You know, Jillian and I should have been related by now. Had Crystal, my niece, lived, she'd be married to her nephew. But then you know that, don't you?"

Both girls laughed and nodded.

"Until tomorrow, then." Elizabeth swept from the room with a smile on her face.

"I think she is sorry that she can't call Jillian auntie, don't you?" Honey turned to Ariel. She tried not to tug at her corset as it dug into her breasts.

"Yes, she often looks so sad." Ariel looked up from the silver comb.

"I don't think kindly of that husband of hers. You know, Charles said that he saw William coming from Jennifer's apartments in the wee hours of the morning, just before sunrise." The image of William caused a cold chill to descend over Honey. She almost tasted fear, but she tried to shake it off. She would have to mention this fear to Chris when he returned; perhaps he would understand it.

"Somehow I'm not surprised. That Jennifer is as light-skirted as a tavern wench." Ariel scowled in uncharacteristic anger. "Elli doesn't deserve such treatment."

"But now, tell me everything that happened in the gypsy camp."

Suddenly Honey felt much older than Ariel. "It's a whole different world, but there are guests downstairs, you know."

"Oh yes, Charles is still here. And so are Gregory and the Pepperding girls."

"Let's go down early; we can talk tonight," Honey suggested. She wasn't quite ready to share any secrets yet.

* * *

Dinner was lively as Honey related the stories about the gypsies—those suitable for mixed company, that is. It was late when her voice finally turned hoarse from all the questions. Honey was grateful for her soft bed as she eased her aching body down for the night. She smiled and sighed as she thought of all the things she didn't say at dinner, all of the feelings she wasn't ready to share. Suddenly it didn't seem real. The last few weeks seemed like a lifetime away already.

Knowing that he loved her made all her life worthwhile. He must love her or he'd not have confessed his feelings of guilt, even though he had not actually said, "I love you." She wondered whether or not to tell Jillian or Ariel about her love for Chris. Because of the sudden emergency upon their return, there had been no chance to tell anyone about them, though just what they would have said she wasn't sure. He had not asked for her hand. And there was no guarantee that he would.

A string of doubt wound its way around her heart. If he didn't marry her, she would be left a deflowered old maid. Women like that turned into Jennifer Bateses to survive. She closed her eyes and sighed. She could be ruined for life. Not that she would want anyone else now. Still, Chris had never committed himself to marriage; he had barely admitted love. She wondered if she were merely being set up to take Jennifer's place. She fell asleep on that sour note and dreamed, as always, of loving Chris.

It was midmorning when the women of Amesly arrived at Stonewings. For as many times as they had visited over the last two years, Honey never failed to be awestruck by the vastness of the properties and the beauty of the stone facade. Gossamer curtains fluttered in the breeze from wide-hinged windows, lending a welcoming air to the three-story stone manor. The stones were a matched beige while the window ledges were wide, flat stones of burnt red. The outer framing of the house was edged with the same stones.

Huge trees opened like umbrellas, standing almost even with the rafters, some even taller. A broad pond surrounded by a wild garden ornamented one side of the manor. In the back, an expansive garden wound its way around another stately maple. A whitewashed bench circled the tree like a choker of pearls. Matched gazebos and arching trellises decorated the corners of the garden. Unlike the gardens at Amesly, the flowers here had been allowed to grow naturally, their vines and shoots unconfined by stakes and lashes. Neither were the hedges sculpted in the shapes of exotic animals, as was the custom at most manors; Elizabeth's were merely rounded or ovaled. It was a relaxing place, and Honey always felt peaceful when she was here, as if it were her own home.

"I know how you love the garden," Elizabeth was saying. "So luncheon will be served there."

"How thoughtful of you," Jillian responded, smiling at both Honey and Elizabeth. Ariel pretended not to notice the edge in Jillian's voice, but she knew how Elizabeth's gardens drove neat and tidy Jillian to distraction.

"Martin, we shall take tea in the garden," Elizabeth said, leading her guests through the house and out the French doors in the parlor.

The terrace was cool. Honey tugged at the ribbon that held her hat in place and pulled her straw hat off. Jillian watched and said nothing. Ariel smiled; Honey always removed her hat when visiting Stonewings though it certainly wouldn't be proper anywhere else.

"Honey, shall we go up and see if we can find that brush?" Elizabeth asked before the conversation turned to gossip.

"Why don't you send Martin, dear?" Jillian smiled at her hostess, amused that Elizabeth never asked a servant to do what she thought she could do herself.

"You know, we could, but I fear he'd not find it." She laughed. "Martin might be faithful, but he is none too bright."

Ariel giggled, setting her cup aside. "I think, then, that Miss Jillian and I shall have to tour these beautiful gardens while you are gone."

"Splendid idea," Jillian said, looking pointedly at Ariel.

"We won't be long," Honey offered as she followed Elizabeth to the back of the house and up three flights of stairs.

"The servants have some of these rooms, but back here is where we've stored . . ." Elizabeth looked sad, "the things that were left behind." Her voice faltered as she spoke.

"You still miss them, don't you?" Honey said as they reached the top.

"I can't help it. I was coming to stay while Jacob was away, just a month after . . . the murders. It is so hard to believe anyone can be that brutal. And it's worse to know that whoever it was is still out there. William insists that some of these rooms are haunted. He never comes up here anymore. He said he tried once and his path was barred by something he couldn't see." Ellie laughed. "I watched what he was drinking for several days after that."

"I hadn't thought of that." Honey remembered the story Ali told at the Gypsy camp several days ago: *the dead had roamed the forest until their bodies had been properly buried and marked.* "You know you're always welcome at Amesly," she said. "I mean, if William spends great amounts of time away and you become nervous."

"Thank you, Honey. It is comforting to know that you are close by, but the children and I have a pact—there is always to be at least one servant in the house at all times." Elli stopped to unlock the door at the end of the hall.

"Isn't that expected?"

"Normally it is, but you see, on the night of the murders one of the house servants was getting married. Of course, everyone was invited, but Christine stayed behind because her child was ill. She was such a doting mother, you know. The slightest sneeze and that babe was put to bed." Elizabeth swiped at a cobweb and led the way through the dim room.

Daylight filtered through the dense tangle of tree branches to the neglected windows and into the dusty room.

"There, I think it's that trunk." She pointed to the matched trucks stationed along a wall. "Or this one."

"I'll take one if you take the other?" Honey dropped to her knees, her silks billowing around her as she flipped the lid open.

"Mrs. Humphrey." Martin's voice startled both women as he appeared in the door.

"Yes, Martin?"

"Mrs. Perry and Mrs. Appel to see you, ma'am."

Elli gave Honey an amused look, as if to say, *see what I mean?*

"Please, go ahead, I'll find it and be right down." Honey smiled back.

"I can't leave you up here." Elizabeth turned to the butler. "Martin, have you shown them to the garden?"

"No, ma'am." He issued a guilty cough.

"Go. I'll be fine," Honey insisted as she turned back to the trunk and looked in.

"I'll be back as soon as I get my guests introduced downstairs." Elli squeezed Honey's shoulder as she passed her, then left the room with Martin on her heels.

Honey laughed to herself as she watched the pair retreat. Elizabeth certainly had her hands full with that one.

Honey jumped when a tree branch scratched at the window. She turned startled eyes at the window, then smiled at her own silliness. Goose bumps rose on her arms as a sudden coolness assaulted her flesh. *Like being hugged by a ghost,* she thought humorlessly. Shaking off the uneasy feeling, she glanced quickly around the room. It was filled wall to wall with outdated items of every variety; she knew at once that this was Crystal's past. Portraits covered with oilcloths, beds and rockers, a crib and several chests filled the curtainless room. Pieces of the past.

She turned back to her trunk and shuffled through the contents. "Not this one," she said out loud.

A sudden swirl of dust danced in a thin sunbeam near the window. Honey whipped her head around to see what was there. She laughed again at her folly, but the hair on the back of her head suddenly stood on end. Dropping the lid of the trunk she moved to the trunk Elizabeth was to have looked into and shoved the lid back. The trunk was filled with little girls' things. Miniature dresses, now grayed with age, wilted laces and curled slippers—they all seemed to whisper the name of the dead. A rag doll smothered in small ruffled petticoats and night rails in soft brushed fabrics adorned with wide ribbons lay over yet more layers of clothing. Beneath the night rails Honey found the brush. The silver had tarnished like her own, and as Elizabeth had said, the pattern was startlingly close to the one on her comb. Carelessly she reached for the trunk's lid from where it had nestled into a cloth-covered portrait, but her hand slipped, bringing the cloth down with it, and Honey looked up to find the haunting face of a beautiful young woman suddenly looking back at her. The bright blue eyes seemed to look lovingly at her. A gentle smile played about her slender lips—as if she were about to tell a secret. Gooseflesh erupted across her body and her heart fluttered beneath her ribs as her gaze moved slowly over the painting. The familiar dull roar began in her skull. When she touched the royal blue gown the roar became a hurricane as she recognized the blue sapphire and diamond filigree earbobs. Suddenly she was a small child, hiding behind a curtain . . .

"What do you want?" Her mother's beautiful eyes were wide with fear. "I've told you, I love my husband. There can never be anything between us!"

The man gave an evil laugh, "Then you lose, my dear, for you love a dead man. The Crystal Wing *went down over a fortnight ago off the Canary Islands."*

"What have you done!" Christine's hand curled tightly over the fireplace prod. Rage mixed with fear played across her lovely face. "If you've hurt him, I'll kill you." She whispered the words.

"No, you won't. I have much better plans for us." The blond man crossed the room. His hand reached out to caress her smooth cheek.

She knocked his hand away. "You have wasted your life chasing a woman who will never love you. Dead or alive, no man will ever replace Jacob."

"Then you are a fool! He is dead. Gone forever!" Hate filled his eyes. "And I will replace him."

"No!" The woman turned to run but he grabbed her arm and swung her back. She was ready for him. Her hand rose and the prod came down, ready to crush his skull. He blocked the attack with a thrusting blow of his forearm that sent Christine reeling into the mantel. The dull thud of her head striking the stone fireplace caused terror to rise in the child's throat.

"No! Mama!" She rushed out from behind the curtain to her mother's side—too late. She flung herself to the floor grabbing on to her body and holding on for dear life.

"No! Mama!" The voice came from Honey kneeling beside the portrait of her dead mother as she fingered the brooch pinned to her breast. "Mama," she wept as her fingers traced the lines of the lips that once kissed her forehead at bedtime. She touched the painted earbobs and the lines of those blue eyes as a lifetime of grief spilled from her eyes. Then she stopped. Looking back at the portrait, she suddenly realized, "I'm Crystal Wingfield. Oh, God! I remember! Mama, I remember!" she cried.

"These are my things; this is my house. I lived here." Cold embraced her once more as she stood.

"William . . ."

She couldn't tell if the sound issued from her own throat or someone else's.

"Dear God, William! I must leave here! Surely he knows!"

She whirled to the door, rushing down the hall and

down the stairs. Chris! She'd find Chris and tell him. He'd know what to do. Her heart raced as she took the second set of stairs. Her skirts billowed around her as she turned on the last landing. The pins fell from her hair in her haste.

The front door was at last within reach. Throwing it open wide, she rushed right into the waiting arms of William Humphrey. Her eyes went wide with paralyzing fear. The color drained from her face and a fresh flood of tears filled her eyes.

"Now you know me." He grinned wide. "I must say, you've grown up quite nicely."

Honey gasped as his hand wound its way through her fallen hair. "We have business to discuss, do we not?" he snarled as he half dragged her to his carriage still parked in the drive. "No!" she jerked back, opening her mouth to scream. But the hand that pulled hard on her hair suddenly thrust her forward, sending her headlong down the stair and into the side of the carriage.

"Quickly, Hanson," she heard him call out. "We must get this child to a doctor."

Chapter Thirty-Five

Chris shoved the drunken man back to the chair. "I thought you told me he was sobered up."

"He had a keg o' ale in 'im, sir. We've been workin' on him nigh on six hours," the sailor replied.

"Well, he isn't much good now, is he?" Chris turned away from the drunk to face the seaman. "What's his name?"

"Heathen somethin' or other."

"Heathen?" Chris shook his head—exactly the kind of name he'd expect to find in a filthy harbor pub.

"Heathen Barley." The man in the chair hiccuped and gave a soggy salute. "But yer can call me Heath." He grinned stupidly as his head wobbled loosely on his shoulders.

A lion's head ring on the man's finger winked as Heath dropped his hand back to his lap.

"Where'd you get that ring?" Chris asked, eyeing the brass piece a little closer.

"'Tis mine," the drunk said defensively as he pulled the hand back, shielding it with the other. "Me father gave it to me. One for me brother, too."

"Yer . . ." Chris cleared his throat, embarrassed

that he'd spoken slang. "Your brother? What is his name?" A knot formed between Chris's eyes. *Barley* . . . Could this be connected with Barley Boe, perhaps?

"'Twon't do ye no good. He won't give ya his, neither. That is, if ya kin find him . . ." Heath thought about what he had just said a moment ago, then looked at Chris for the first time. "Yah," he nodded, agreeing with himself.

"I don't give a . . . I don't want his ring. I want his name and I want it now!" the captain growled, moving very close to the drunk's face. He pulled back, almost gagging on Heath's putrid breath.

"Well, he ain't been around for years. Pro'bly dead by now."

"His name!" Chris pulled the man up by his collar and shook him until his teeth rattled in his cheeks.

"Like me. Barley. Burly Joe Barley!" Heath's eyes grew wide at the sight of Chris's expression. He was sobering rather quickly now. His sodden wits worked to overcome the fear of the man who threatened him. "Yer Ames, ain'tcha?"

"That's right!" Chris glowered. "What happened to your brother, do you know?"

"He set off with one yer crews some ten years ago, maybe fifteen. Ain't seen him since."

"Which ship? Do you know? Was it the *Crystal Wing*?"

"Let me see, it was a wing something. Not Crystal, but . . ." The man rubbed at his stubbled jaw for several moments. "'Twas the *Sea Wing*, yah. He kept sayin' I should come along. A ship with as pretty a name as that. That's it!" He grinned, proud of his sudden recollection.

"What is wrong with that?" He asked the question to himself, but he looked at the sailor who'd been guarding the door of the pub.

"Ho, the *Sea Wing* was stole about then," the sailor who'd been silent all this time said. "What yer tryin' to pull?"

"Aye, that's right." Heath sat up straighter. "Joe said that he had something to put to right. He said . . . uh . . . what was that about playin' pirate. . . 'Tis been a long time since I've wondered of Joe."

"Do you know anyone else who was aboard that ship at the same time?" Chris asked.

"Not any more." The sailor thought, then his eyes lit up. "Aye, Captain. Kinden, old Cap'n Kinden. He's old now, but I'll bet he remembers what happened then."

"Where can we find him?"

"Over at Greenwich Hospital."

"Let's go."

Captain Kinden was beyond old. He was on his way out of this life when Chris, Scotts, and one other sailor rushed through the hospital doors and found his room. Beside the withered old man another man, presumably his grandson, sat vigil.

The smell of iodine and death filled the air. Even the seamen balked at the stench.

"I don't think he has the strength to answer your questions now," the younger man said. "He's lived a tragic life, filled with fear, for God's sake! Let him die in peace."

"Let him die in peace?" Chris gagged on the words. "Lives have been lost. Lives can be saved. I must know what happened when that ship disappeared, and why it suddenly returned."

"It's time, Jamie." The whisper came from the

flesh-covered skeleton on the bed. His sunken eyes were a blind, colorless dinge that was once blue. "It was a man named Humphrey stole the *Sea Wing*." He paused for air.

"He near kilt me takin' her, but he won out. Clubbed me, he did, then threatened to kill my wife and child."

"William Humphrey?"

"Aye, that be him. We caught and sank the *Crystal Wing* under the flag of the pirate." The old man wheezed, trying to cough. "So they told me, I was near dead in the hold when the cannons sounded." He paused again, his strength ebbing fast. "He be a mean one. I heard him laughin' that someday the ships and the woman would all be his. They told me he laughed like the devil himself as she sank." His head rolled in despair and tears oozed from his sightless eyes.

"I couldn't tell ya, couldn't tell no one. He would kill my family." His toothless mouth seemed to spasm. "He would, too!"

"I understand," Chris whispered. Sadness filled his heart for this old man who had lived with murder and fear his entire life—a very long life.

"'Twas the same with the child."

"What child?" he asked as he considered what to do next.

"The Wingfield babe. I begged him not to toss her over the side, but it done no good." The old man writhed in pain as the tears rolled down his cheeks. "The ma was already dead, but the babe . . . 'Tis never a night goes by that I don't hear that child's screams."

"What are you saying, Captain Kinden!" Chris bent over the man, his face a mask of disbelief. 'He threw Crystal overboard? When? When could he have done that?"

"In the fall of the year. Eight months after the *Crystal Wing* went down. He took out by himself from Cardiff. We done the deed, then he dumped me off on an explorer. 'Twas another six years before I found my home and my grandson. By then it was too late to tell anyone what happened. They was all dead." The withered old man rolled from side to side again, clutching his belly and crying, "I'd have stopped it if I could. I tried and he crippled me. I'm sorry! Oh, God! I'm so sorry."

Chris looked at the grandson. "Is this all true?" he asked. "He's not out of his head?"

Jamie shook his head sadly. "It's all he has been able to talk about this last year. I wanted to come to you but Grandfather forbade it. He thought you might kill me for making up lies." The young man dashed at his own tears as he watched his grandfather writhe on his deathbed.

"What else can you tell me? Is there anything he left out this time?" Chris asked softly.

"Only that another man disappeared on that night. I don't know his name. But Grandfather said he suspected the man was an old sailor name of Barney. Or Barley. That's all I know."

she went down with it.

Chapter Thirty-Six

Crystal Regina Wingfield stood beside the carriage at the waterfront, still dazed from her fall. William barked instructions to the barrel-chested man who eyed her. He was dressed as a clerk but displayed the manner of a seaman. Yes, she recalled all too well what seamen looked like now—how they smelled and how they talked. After all, she'd been raised on it. Recalled too Uncle George and beautiful Aunt Regina, with eyes as blue as Chris's, and Chris . . . Chris who challenged her temper constantly. It was Chris who used to pull her up into the tree that edged the two properties, where they read stories together of knights and princesses and evil wizards. The comfort of the place was still there, she had often been drawn to the same tree when she was troubled.

It was Regina who had planted the garden outside Amesly and placed the trellis beside the library window where she had hidden the night of the ball. Regina who had planted each rock, side by side, framing the whole garden. Both Crystal and Christopher had helped . . . She recalled suddenly that she was named Crystal to match Christopher, and Christopher was named for her mother, Christine.

Then she thought of her father, Jacob. There had never been time to mourn for either of them. Like now, everything happened too fast. She started to feel the rage that Chris had lived with for so many years. William had murdered her family . . .

And Chris, he was nothing like she'd have imagined him to be. Where was the devil-may-care boy who lorded over her day and night? She would have been his wife by now. They'd have had children and built a house somewhere on the line between the two properties of Amesly and Stonewings.

The hot tears stung at her eyes but she forced them back. William had made it clear that he cared not whether she lived or died, and tears might decide the issue for her. She couldn't do that to Chris. She wouldn't make him mourn her death twice, even if this time he didn't know for whom he mourned.

"Get that thing off her." William indicated the buggy whip. "If she screams, you know what to do." He turned away and ambled off toward the little ramshackle town.

"What's that?" she asked in almost a whisper. Her eyes grew wide as she watched the big man fumble with the lash that bound her wrists together.

"This?"

"No, if I scream . . ."

He showed her a toothless grin. "I get ta' hit ya." He chuckled eagerly.

"Oh." She considered her predicament. It was literally hopeless. This dilapidated village housed only the lawless. Filth was strewn everywhere; the odorous waste filled the sea air. The few people who wandered about out of doors were dressed in filthy rags.

There would be no help here. Her gaze moved out

to sea as her guard shoved her toward the long hanging pier built for both high and low tide.

The shallows were too rocky to survive a jump from the high pier. But farther out . . . could she swim in these skirts? Would they drag her down by tangling her legs? Could she push her guard over the edge and run without getting caught? The carriage was only a short distance behind. Yes, that she could do. Maybe. Anything was worth a try. She couldn't leave the life she'd just found! Not so soon. Not now!

The water surged and sprayed around the rocky shore below them. Her breath caught tight in her chest as she watched for the right moment. Six more steps . . . one, two, three, four, five . . . six! She halted, firm in her track, watching as the man turned in mild surprise. His grip loosened just for a second, but that was all she needed. She shoved at him with her body, knocking him back over the edge of the wooden pier. It was like hitting a stone wall. The blow knocked the wind from her lungs and she gasped to recover before turning toward the carriage at the other end of the pier. But it was much further away than she recalled. Her tears burned and her heart pounded against her ribs, sending a stabbing pain through her chest. Before she could take even a few steps something grabbed her ankle. She shrieked as she looked down to find the man she'd just tried to kill hanging by one hand from the edge of the dock, his other meaty hand closed like a vise around her ankle. Fury mixed with eager revenge etched his ugly mouth. She kicked at him, at his hand, at his face, and he jerked her foot out from under her. She slammed into the deck and cried out in pain. Her skirts splayed over and around her, showing her shift and tangling her legs, but exposure was the least of her worries.

"No! Please," she rasped, kicking still at the man's head as he pulled himself over the edge, coming at her like a wounded animal.

Crystal had scrambled to her feet, sheer terror filling her, when one soft slipper caught at the hem of her gown. Somehow she dislodged it and dodged his grasping hands, running mindlessly in the wrong direction. Turning to look for her tormentor, she stumbled forward blindly into nothing but empty space. She plunged sideways down forty feet of air into the ocean, landing dangerously close to where the surf crashed brutally into the rocks.

The cold suddenly surrounded her; the salt water stung her eyes as she watched the surface overhead. The light of day became just a hazy shadow in the distance as she plunged deeper and deeper. The sudden silence surprised her. The roaring sound of the surf had disappeared. Only the lazy gurgle of air escaping her clothing could be heard. Everything was suddenly calm. Despite the burning in her lungs, there seemed to be no reason to stop the gradual descent. The gentle swell from the surf carried her first in then out. Her hair floated in a ghostly fashion around her upturned face, and her gown billowed around her as if it had come to life and was relishing its newfound weightlessness.

"First thing is, don't panic," came the voice. It was Barley Boe. *"And don't suck water. The sea will keep you calm as long as you don't suck water."*

"Then what?" her mind answered. She was a child again, learning how to swim in the surging waves of a tropical island.

"Kick hard once and you'll go forward. Then wait. Your skirts will billow out like a sail. Then kick

again and the surf will bring you ashore. Long as you don't try to fight it."

"Oooh." The child's voice played through her mind and she smiled. Looking up again, she noticed that the light overhead seemed closer, the cloudy surface began to take shape again.

That's right, kick, she said to herself in the aquatic silence. *With the surge.* Her natural buoyancy propelled her up. With the movement, her lungs began to burn for relief, her eyes stung, and the sense of calm began to fade. The light became blinding as she broke the surface, as if shot from the bottom from a cannon. Her breath exploded from her lungs and she drew a fresh lungful, but her chest throbbed with stabbing pain. She knew she had been under much longer than she realized.

A movement overhead drew her attention.

"There! Down there. She's alive!" a voice shouted from the dock as Crystal bobbed in the surf below. Panic hit her. Her escape had failed badly and she was trapped between the treacherous shore and big blue sea. Hot tears burned her cold eyes and the chill of the water began to hurt her joints. She worked to stay afloat, then relaxed and just floated as if someone had just reminded her again not to panic.

On the cliff above, William stood barking orders. Several men scrambled over the cliffs to scale their way down to her. It mattered little to him whether she lived or died, and where she chose to die didn't matter either.

The next wave carried her close to the rocks. Using a side kick she positioned herself between two boulders. The backwash took her out with it, then the next wave carried her in again. *Ride it out. It might take time, but relax and ride—you can make it.*

The words were as comforting as the fact that danced in her mind. Barley Boe had saved her life. Again.

On the next swell a man appeared between the same two rocks and plucked her effortlessly from the water. His long arm snaked around her waist; he moved with ease back the way he had come, never speaking or even looking at her, like she was a thing, not a person. At the shoreline, he tossed her over his shoulder and scaled the cliff, seemingly mindless to the torrents of water that dripped cold against his heated flesh. Someone grabbed her from behind and hauled her over the edge of the cliff before setting her on her feet, still dripping, next to William.

His expression was slightly amused. "Death preferable to me? Or did you think you could swim off into the sunset with no one the wiser? Well, you're not Christine, but I think I'd have noticed you were gone," he snapped.

The cool wind cut through her wet gown. It hung limp around her hips and molded her breasts. Her hair had lost its shape and was molded to the oval of her head. Water dripped from her chin and nose, and the puddle at her feet was spreading.

He shook his head in disgust as he grabbed her arm himself and started for the dock once more.

"She took me by surprise . . ." Her original guard almost whimpered behind them.

"I don't care to hear it!" The blond man bit off the words. "Get over to that leech and get my package! Try not to lose it on the way back!"

Crystal heard his sigh of relief as the big man turned away from them and trotted toward town.

"What is this place?" she asked between chattering teeth.

"This is noplace. It has no name, but places like

this litter the coast. It's where the riffraff disappeared to now that Mary has ordered her king to clean up the docks in London. They didn't really think they could stop us, they just didn't want to have to look at us," he supplied, shoving her toward the dock once more. "Like Treavor there, who carried you up the side. He's from a slaver."

"What's that?" The wind bit at her cheeks as they waited for the dock to be lowered. William nudged her forward as she marveled at the new invention: the dock could be hoisted up or down as the tides dictated, via block and tackle.

"Come, my dear. You have not been so protected that . . . Then again, perhaps you have." He leered at her. "A slaver takes young brides like yourself to other parts of the world, such as the colonies, Constantinople, or China. Places where the dark-skinned men have a taste for delicate white flesh." He paused at the landing to observe her honey-colored hand. "I imagine there is a market for your color as well." He chuckled, thinking of the tan lines he had heard the servants discussing one afternoon last year. "Maybe I shouldn't soil such a prize." He dragged a finger over her breast.

Crystal shrank from him in horror. Hands grabbed her from behind and pushed her onto the seat in the center of the boat. William dropped down beside her.

The oarsmen pulled on their oars, pushing the boat through the cold gray waves to the ship that waited in the bay.

Her cut was different from that of the *Crystal Wing* or even the *Wing Master*, but the design was, without a doubt, a Sea Wings original. The name *Night Wing* had been burned into the side like the others in the fleet. The wispy letters looked as though they were birds' wings, the feathers bent to spell the words gracefully.

Like the *Wing Master*, the nets tossed over the side formed the ladder up, and again Crystal was tossed over a shoulder to be hauled up over the side of the ship.

"Many of those brides were not so eager to meet their grooms, either," William called up to her, looking at her humiliated face as she bobbed over the man's shoulder. Contempt filled her eyes, contempt that caused him to chuckle deep in his chest.

"Oh, yes, you'll be a fighter." He licked his lips at the thought of the thrill he'd receive while trying to bed this one. No doubt she would fight more then Jenny ever had. He might even have to resort to tying her to the bed. Even then she would thrash beneath him. He never doubted her virtue, and he knew that virgins always fought more. His urges stirred as he boarded the ship and led her along the narrow gangway to the cabin at the far end.

"We shall have fun, you and I." He cupped her breast suggestively. "I'll be back," he scoffed.

Crystal said nothing. Her eyes narrowed, as he laughed in eagerness and pulled the door closed behind him. The lock rattled and clicked into place and she glared at the spot where he had just been. Twelve years of rage came together and seared her being.

She glowered at the door. He was right. No one had seen them leave Stonewings. No one knew who she really was, though if they checked the attic they would guess. But still, who could have predicted this? Chris would search the countryside thinking she had run away again. He would never think that she had been taken by the same man who murdered her mother. He'd never look to the sea for her, just as no one had before. And if he did, he'd think only the worst of her. That was his nature.

Slowly she removed her clothes. Wringing the sea from them, she wrapped herself in a blanket.

"Whatever it takes, William, I'll live. And I'll see you die. Whatever it takes . . ."

Chapter Thirty-Seven

The lathered horse labored to breathe beneath the rider. Chris knew his mount could go on like this no more, even if he was only halfway to Amesly. He had done a foolish thing riding so hard when he knew the horse needed to be paced in order to make another ride back so soon, but his mind hadn't been on the horse. It had been on the stunning realization that the old man lying near death in the hospital room behind him had spoken the truth. The captain had no more reason to keep silent. Lies weren't going to save his wretched life now.

Christopher felt more ill with every mile he passed, sensing that he would be too late, that she was already gone.

The horse's hooves drummed against the hard-packed road. How could it be? How could it *not* be? The ship that disappeared a few days after Jake sailed, the skull and crossbones . . . To sink an unsuspecting ship not equipped for war was no difficult thing. It was all too smooth; it worked out all too well.

And there could not be two Burly Joe Barleys, unless Barley Boe meant something completely different . . . But then there was the ring. Their father had the rings made—Heath had said so. Then why this nagging doubt that it was all too far-fetched to be true?

Because he wished it so badly? Suddenly it was the only thing that mattered! Not just Honey being Crystal, but Honey having a name, a real name given to her by real parents. And having a background and knowing from where she came. And then that nagging doubt: What if she didn't want him? Now that she had all that belonged to her, what if she didn't need him anymore?

The black horse wheezed and his knees began to buckle; he stumbled painfully. Chris leaped to the ground. "There, boy." He coaxed the frothing beast back to his feet. His mane shook and his glossy sides heaved in anguished breaths. The horse complained and threw his head back as if saying, *Don't touch me again, you brute.*

"I know, boy." The man stood back, his mouth compressed in a thin white line. Now what? Dunn was behind him, Amesly several miles ahead. But his ears perked as a distant drumming warned him of an approaching rider, riding hard and fast, just as he had done.

Chris grabbed for his reins and pushed his mount back to the very edge of the road to avoid a collision. The other rider blurred past him, his coat flaring out behind him. He turned to look at Chris, then pulled up on his reins so hard that the mare reared, forcing the rider to hold onto the horse's neck with both arms until she came down hard on all fours again.

"'Ere now!" Michael slid to the ground and raced back to Chris, who watched in disbelief. "Glory be! What good luck to catch you so soon. We was afraid you'd be off after that ship!"

"Michael? What the devil . . ."

"It's Miss Honey. She's gone. Sometime this mornin'. She went up to Stonewings with Miss Jillian and Miss Ariel. They said she was in the storeroom lookin' for something. Then, *poof!* she was gone."

"What do you mean, gone!" Chris leaped forward, grabbing his groom by the collar.

"Gone. She was left alone for a few minutes and then disappeared. Mrs. Humphrey is hysterical. Says she's the dead girl from Stonewings! That butler of hers, Martin, found the mistress in the storeroom looking at a painting of Miss Christine and blubberin' something about ghosts. And then the young lady were nowhere to be found. We searched the grounds, the groom and me, and some of the tenants helped. We searched most of the day but we can't find a thing! Not a track on the place."

"No one saw her leave?" Chris glared hard at the man, who didn't so much as blink under his glare.

"Nary a one."

"What about William? Is he still—"

"He hasn't been around all day. The maid's oldest boy said he saw the carriage pull up, but it left again before the boy could call for the livery hand."

"And he saw nothing?" The words came between clamped teeth.

"Only heard someone callin' for a doctor; something about a child needing a doctor." Michael rubbed his neck where Chris had grabbed his collar.

"What could have happened?" The sea captain raked both hands through his hair as he turned away from Michael. "Think! If you stole a ship from London and a woman from Cardiff . . ."

"The hole!" Michael jumped at his employer. "It's as damned, dirty, ugly place as you'll find, but the thievin' from London and Cardiff built up their own little hovel there after the king started ruling the harbors."

"Where is it?" Chris whirled on Michael.

"In a cove north of Pembrook."

"Where exactly?" Chris's face came close to Michael's again.

"Just follow the shore north around the bend and hold up near the woods. You'll see it marked by their long pier. They've built a pier rigged to rise and fall with the tide. Some genius pirate built it."

"How is it *you* happen to know of this place?" Chris wondered out loud as he headed for Michael's fresher mount.

"No secrets now, but . . ." Michael's voice grew soft as he tilted his head up to look at his friend. "Is it possible? Is she . . . she really . . . her? I mean, is she Crystal?"

"Did they say whether or not she saw that painting?"

"Miss Jillian said there was no way she coulda' missed it."

"Then I expect that she is, Michael," he said sincerely. His gaze shifted from his friend to the jittery horse beneath him. "Get back to Amesly. Send a rider to the *Wing Master*; have Mr. Grey bring her around to Cardiff. Tell him I'll meet him there. And keep 'em calm at home, Michael. I'll do what I can."

Michael watched Chris gallop off for several moments. The ghosts at Amesly were at last destined to make peace with their maker. "And it's about time, too." His thick burr gave the words life. But he'd miss that wispy figure who prowled the storeroom late at night. He and the Stonewings stableman often watched for her after their card games were over and their Irish whiskey gone. Then he turned to the horse, who eyed him suspiciously. "Coom oon, laddy. Let us get ya 'ome."

Crystal heard the rush of activity on board. Hard voices hollered "Hoist it up there, boys!" and "Get the boom outta the way! No, up, I said; raise em up!"

The ship creaked around her, complaining, it seemed, of such use. Outside, the wind worked its magic, rolling the ship from side to side.

William had returned just once to pour a bit of powder into a wooden mug and swallow it down with a dipper of his private stock of water.

Indeed, he had thought of everything. His cabin housed a good deal of clothing and most of his own foods, as well as his private supply of fresh water.

"Heard tell of men gone mad out here," he answered her unasked questions. "Fouling the water supply, dumping the food over the side. Well, not on this trip. Rations will be installed right off, so no one's fighting over who gets what."

Her gaze fixed on the cup in his hand.

"Special stuff from the leech. I am quite sure Chris has boasted of my ah . . . affliction." William watched her closely.

She shook her head. "He has said nothing to me."

"This," he held the cup up for her to admire, "will put an end to that, anyway. A powder to keep the sickness from spoiling our trip. It averts the sickness. Seasickness."

Crystal shrugged but watched as he stashed the small fabric packets into a drawer. He turned back to her with another grin on his face. "It's too bad I'm needed on deck just now." His eyes flicked up and down her blanket-wrapped body. "I want you ready, but not too ready. You couldn't be that, though, could you? Brave little face that you show. Don't worry, your first taste of a man will not disappoint you." He chuckled. The thought of deflowering a virgin brought mist to his eyes and an eager stirring to his crotch. His time on deck would be aptly spent anticipating the moment he would take her. His hand strayed to his swollen member as it bulged through his fitted breeches. He rubbed it while watching her eyes grow in horror at his lewd movement, then he smiled. *Yes, just the way he wanted her.*

"The tides take us out within the next hour," he said through his smile. "I'll be back some time after that." Then he was gone.

But his timing was wrong. Less than fifteen minutes later she felt the flow of water. They were moving out to sea from the small bay through St. George's Channel, past Bristol and Cardiff. But the open sea would not greet them until some time late tomorrow. As swift as the ships of Sea Wings Enterprises were, she knew it might take as many as three months to cross the ocean to New Providence. Then a smile lit her lips. It was the first thing that Chris had taught her. "Under normal conditions this trip might take three months to complete," he'd said, gazing out to sea. "But these winds are strong, and pushing us from behind so well that we could likely make the trip in as little as six weeks." The vision of him standing on deck, his crisp white shirt plastered to his full broad chest and his hair ruffling beneath the sun tugged at her heart. Often he'd have a long glass pushed to his eye as he scanned the waters around them. Occasionally, word of a ship sighting came from the crow's nest. The sailor would call out his find in a singsong voice, pointing in the direction of the ship. The flag, if not already flying over the mainmast, would be hoisted up to wave in friendship. That was only eighteen months ago, but it seemed much longer now. All the bickering and fighting was over. She thought of the time she had spent wondering where he was and what he might be thinking, what she should do next and what he might expect of her . . . and what she expected of herself whenever he was near.

In that respect he had changed hardly at all. He was demanding even as a child. A typical male, secure in his status as heir not only to his family's fortune but to hers as well. The smile became a soft laugh as she recalled his jibes. "When we marry you won't have but what I give you." He'd push his little chest out as if to confirm his masculinity. "And unless you're kind to me, I shall give you only bread to eat and water to drink."

And she'd puff out her little chest and say, "Then sleep with one eye open, lad, for I shan't take to that treatment at all." Then she'd march away in search of Aunt Regina, who would pet her and tell her that when she was grown the world would be hers, for a man was only as great as his wife allowed him to be.

Suddenly tears welled up from deep inside of her. Those unfinished days had been stolen from them as surely as lives of those they had loved.

Crystal pulled herself up to the small porthole and watched the shore of England roll past. Her eyes scanned back and forth, as if looking for that final miracle: the rider on the big black horse who had saved her once before. But as the land slipped by, so did her chances of rescue.

"This time, my dear girl, you'll have to save yourself," she whispered, checking her clothes. Returning to the bed, she leaned back against the wall, filling her mind with memories. She could almost smell her mother's perfume as she relived the short time she remembered being with her family. Somewhere in the midst of the reverie she fell asleep.

It was dusk before Chris allowed the horse to slow his breakneck pace. He studied the road as the lane turned toward the sea. Just ahead, a grubby little town rose up from the cliffs.

Chris swung down from the saddle before the mare had even halted and grabbed for the first man he could find. Holding the man by the collar, Chris shook him, his face close enough to get a whiff of the man's fetid breath.

"The *Night Wing*!" he shouted. "Where is she?"

The man pointed to the choppy bay, where only one broken-down ship bobbed in the waves.

"Where?" Chris shook the man again, studying his face. Then he thrust the man away impatiently and ran to the pier. He ran all the way to the end, trying to see out into the channel. But he caught sight of only a very small white dot set against the sunset. A reflection, possibly.

"Was she here, the *Night Wing*?" Chris turned to ask another who passed by. His blood pounded in his ears.

"Aye, that be her." The sailor pointed to the sunset, then went on about his business. Still breathless, Chris returned to the mare and remounted. He was less than twenty minutes from Pembroke, where he could find a fresh mount, then he'd head straight for Cardiff. With any luck at all Geoff would be ready to set sail soon.

Chapter Thirty-Eight

Luck was as long coming as was the *Wing Master*. For a day and a half Chris paced the shore waiting for the sight of the billowing sails of the *Wing Master* to come into view, and when she did, she wasn't seaready, so they missed the next tide. Jillian, Ariel, and Elizabeth came to port that afternoon, each looking as though all hope had died.

"There is no doubt in my mind, Chris." Jillian squeezed her nephew's arm. "When you see that portrait you'll know there is no other explanation."

Chris nodded, subduing his own emotions.

"All this time I thought her fear of William was a lark. Do you think she knew?" Ariel wept. She spoke as if her friend were already dead.

"She might. Then again, the painting might have meant nothing to her. William could have found her there. I don't know." Christopher had already asked himself these questions.

"No, she has to know. Christine wore the filigree earrings to pose for that portrait, the same ones we made into a pin for Honey." Jillian began to sob again. Ariel led her back to the carriage. Elizabeth put her arms around the older woman and gave her a brief hug before Ariel led her away.

"We'll find lodging here." Ellie suddenly took charge of the situation, shrugging off her milksop personality. "She'll be fine, Chris. I've sent for Gregory; he'll be here soon. You just find that blackguard I married, and if there is enough of him left when you're finished with him, I'd like a chance at him myself." Elizabeth's eyes blazed; her voice was firm.

He saluted her, blessing her sudden strength. "After tonight go back to London. We might be a month just trying to catch up to them."

"Chris?" she said more softly, embarrassed by the admiration she read in his eyes. "He talked much about New Providence. How someday life might lead him there."

Chris watched the woman turn away, misty-eyed as she directed the driver into town. She didn't look back as the carriage kicked up dust from the dirt road.

Chris turned back toward the ship and followed the pier to the longboat, where a crew waited to take him out to the *Wing Master*.

Elizabeth was another reason he had such ill-will for William Humphrey. Perhaps she thought that the high-necked and long-sleeved gowns she wore would hide the marks that William had inflicted on her pale skin, but Chris's keen eye had seen them often. What is more, he had walked in on one of those punishment sessions. One late afternoon, Elizabeth had gone to the warehouse to bring her husband his supper and had disturbed his tryst with a strumpet.

Chris had walked in about five minutes later. As Elizabeth's punishment, William had ripped her clothes from her body and had taken her by force on the hard-packed floor. He'd taken malicious pleasure in hurting her, had actually laughed at her cries for mercy and had delighted in her groans. And he had threatened to beat her should she be get with child.

Chris wished he had killed William then. But Elizabeth had begged him to stay out of it. "If William leaves me, I'll have nothing that was once my brother's. He has vowed to take my children, and he will, I know he will." Chris remembered all too well the trembling woman he soothed after William had stormed off. It took him many months at sea to wash away the hatred he felt for William. It was only for Elizabeth's sake that he stayed away from William after that.

Chris shook off the bitter thoughts. His gaze turned seaward as he stood tall in his place behind the wheel of the *Wing Master*.

The first day out offered nothing but blue skies and grey water. On the second day two ships were sighted, both sailing in the wrong direction. The crew seemed as solemn as if a burial at sea was about to take place—and the victim was yet to be named.

Crewmen took turns manning the crow's nest, and Chris rode the forward mast when he wasn't at the wheel. Anyone who wasn't assigned a specific duty was set to watch for sails in the distance.

Crystal woke with a start. Someone was groaning outside the door of the cabin . . .

Her wide eyes peered vainly into the dark as she strained to see who had suddenly thrown the door open. Dim yellow light shrouded the figure, who fell forward to the floor.

"He poisoned me!" William groaned into the deck, holding his gut in both hands. "Help me, damn you!" he growled at the woman who sat motionless on the bunk.

"Who poisoned you?" she whispered as she turned up the lamp and rushed to his side. His head burned with fever, his stomach was hard as rock.

Between the two of them they managed to get him into the bunk.

"That leech! That blasted leech who made up those . . . oh . . . get me a pail," he moaned. He fell forward and hung his head over the edge of the bunk, vomiting the second she slid the chamber pot beneath his face, then he stood back in horror and, finally, belated relief.

His illness was exceedingly convenient, she thought, watching him struggle with another bout.

"Why would the leech poison you?" she mused out loud, her eyes never leaving his crumpled form.

"Maybe that lug did it!" he groaned, still clutching his swollen belly. "Did you see how happy he was I let him run for my powders? I'll kill him. Once this is past, I'll kill the dog."

Crystal removed the pot and crossed to the cabin door, thinking to call out to have it dumped, but then she hesitated. What sailor would stop long enough to answer her request for such a distasteful job? And these were not even real sailors. They were felons and lowlifes, no better than William himself. Setting the pot aside, she moved back to the table where her things hung, still damp, and considered her alternatives. If William were about to die, perhaps she could get the ship turned around and headed back for England. Chris would surely pay whatever sum these thieves demanded for her safe return. Yes. She dropped the blanket to the floor and began to dress, keeping one eye on William still groaning on the bed. Hope tingled in her chest as she fastened the hooks of her gown.

"What are you doing?" he demanded.

"Getting dressed," she snapped. "If I'm to get that pot emptied for you I must certainly be dressed!"

"Get it emptied? You jest! Once that crew finds out I am sick they'll . . ." he gagged, "be all over you!"

Crystal stood stock still; a shudder rippled through her. "What do you mean?"

"I mean," he groaned, "the second I lose command that crew will toss me over the side and tie you in my bunk. And if you're not dead in a week, they'll sell ya to the next ship they cross . . . or kill you."

"That's not so!" she cried. But in her heart she knew it was true. She recalled all the warnings she'd received as a child about the waterfront. It was true. If William died she'd die too, a slow, painful, degrading death.

She sank into a chair, resting a hand on her head for a moment. Her stomach contracted painfully. She had no choice now but to try and save the man she had planned to murder. Now he was her only hope. She would have to keep him alive long enough to get him to New Providence, if for no other reason than to run away and chance the same fate she faced here.

"Well?" The sick moan came again from the bed.

"There doesn't appear to be much choice, does there?" She got to her feet, lifted the chamber pot, and stepped on the bed over her patient. Wrestling the latch on the porthole, she pushed it out far enough to dump the pot through. Then she rinsed the pot and placed it near William's head.

Going to his wardrobe trunk, she pulled out a shirt and shredded it into cloths to bath his feverish head.

"Are you sure this is poison?" she asked softly. "It feels more like a plague."

"How would you know about plague?" he whimpered as his stomach heaved again.

"I read about it in a book at Amesly," she answered, rinsing the cloth she had applied to his head again. "Your fever is so high. I don't know, of course, but . . . It would help to know what kind of stores you've got here."

The man grabbed his belly tighter and rolled to the side. Minutes passed in silence and she wondered if he was dead. But an occasional groan reassured her that he lived.

Stepping from his side, she checked his barrels of food, finding salted meats and cheeses and a few pieces of fruit that she didn't think would last long. She chose those foods that wouldn't keep for her first meal on the *Night Wing*. Then she decided that she'd approach the morning crew with an offer of a trade: fruit for more sustaining foods—perhaps something cooked fresh, rather than oversalted meats.

It didn't come to that, though. In the morning two breakfast trays were left at the door. Biscuits and porridge, much like the gypsies cooked. After trying to get a couple of mouthfuls into William, she ate as much of both breakfasts as she could, fearing that someone might notice a full tray coming out of the room and suspect something.

The next day the smell in the room turned sour. William's vitals seemed not to work at all, and by the end of the second day his flesh had turned a chalky white. And the groaning stopped . . .

Crystal didn't panic, but the idea of being locked in a room with a dead man for better than seventy more days filled her with dread. The day faded to night and the moon cast the ocean and sky in the same eerie blue-black glow that had haunted all of her nights on her island. The hues were strangely comforting. She didn't need to see the silver ripple over the ink-black ocean to know how it glittered. It was etched in her mind as fresh as if it had been yesterday.

After a few moments she moved to sit beside William. Her forefingers searched for the weak pulse in his wrist before she tried to drip a few more drops of water down his throat. Water was the only thing she knew for sure he required to live. If in fact he had been poisoned, there was little she could for him besides drip water down his throat. Even so, she often dribbled a few sips of porridge or stew.

Midway through this water ritual Crystal jumped as a low rap came at the door.

"Cap'n! Cap'n!" the raspy voice called through the door.

Crystal held her breath, wondering if he'd go away if he thought they were sleeping. But the rap came louder and the voice became more insistent.

Her heart drummed in her throat. Terrified that she'd be discovered, she jumped to her feet and hissed through the door, "I thought you were told not to disturb us!"

"Yes'm," the voice answered, "but we got us some company out here. A ship comin' in fast from the south."

"The south?" she asked stupidly. The brief hope that it could be Chris coming to save her was dashed.

"Yes'm. Ain't flyin' a flag, neither. Looks like Bloodwell!"

"Bloodwell the pirate?" she asked fearfully, her blood chilling as she recalled the atrocities Bloodwell had committed.

"We need the cap'n, ma'am," he said through the door, sounding more like a lost little boy than a hard-core criminal.

"The captain says to follow standard procedures.

If they don't work, run." She improvised the instruction, not knowing what "standard procedures" were.

"But we don't have a flag to fly but the skull n' bones, and it's suicide to run that up so soon." He sounded curious now. She heard the board creak under his shifting weight. "If she's Spanish we're damned."

Crystal held her silence for a moment, hoping he'd think she was conferring with William, before saying, "Lose them," she reasoned. "The captain says if that doesn't work, pull the group together and use your wits. Now, we are busy!" Crystal placed a palm to her head trying to ward off the flush and fever that suddenly flashed through her.

"Yes, ma'am," he said, but she practically heard him shaking his head in confusion.

Moments later the ship heeled hard to the right. The timbers creaked in complaint, but the fine old vessel straightened some minutes later and set off on her new course.

Crystal stepped up on the bunk, mindless of the unconscious man at her feet, to get a look at the other ship. She was sleek, sporting four masts and a jib boom fully rigged for a chase.

She was still quite a distance away but easily seen as she glowed blue-white beneath the moon. The ship turned in silent pursuit. So she was to be giving chase? That meant a crewman would be back soon to report the results of their defensive move. He would expect to find a captain who cared enough about his own ship to crawl out of bed and lead them. Her immediate future had been less than rosy yesterday, but tonight it looked as bleak as imaginable. What could she do? Should she confess to the crew and demand to be turned around and sailed home? As if anyone would take orders from her . . . As if there was a possibility that they could outrun the other ship . . . Her choice was this crew of cutthroats or that crew of pirates. Though it had not yet been determined who crewed the other ship, the fact that they flew no flag at all almost certainly meant they were pirates.

Her delicate hand sailed through her long loose hair. She was miserable, dirty, tired, and scared. Yes, scared to death. She didn't want to die! She didn't want to be misused, and she wanted no man other than Chris to claim her body. It wasn't fair that she finally discovered who she really was only to be taken away again, unable to share the news with those she loved and with little hope of ever seeing them again. Would Chris ever recover from losing another woman? Or would he miss her at all?

She jumped at the sound of heavy fists pounding on the door. Her heart shot to her throat.

"What is it?" she called, one hand touching her throat as if to will her pulse to slow its pace.

"They're givin' chase, Cap'n. They ought ta have us by sunrise." Thankfully, it was the same voice as before.

"That's fine. If they get within firing range, you know what to do." She spoke with as much authority as she could muster.

"See what I told ya?" the voice whispered none too quietly outside the door.

Crystal's eyes narrowed as she strained to hear what they were saying, then suddenly another fist pounded on the door.

"Open up! We're comin' in," a deeper voice called.

"Don't you dare!" She panicked as the words flew from her lips. "I'm not dressed!"

"Open up!" She barely heard him bellow over the

din of pummeling hands on the other side of the wooden door.

"No! Don't! You don't understand," she called back. Tears gathered in her eyes and throat as she backed away from the door. Her glance flew to the bed, willing a miracle, but none was there. *"No!"* She rushed the door and pressed against it, her tears spilling free. "It's the pox!" Her words carried clearly through the door.

The pounding stopped and she took a breath. Her hands shook as she continued. "If you come in you'll all be exposed. You'll expose the ship. Please, don't risk it!"

The silence was unnerving. The crew murmured among themselves as they decided whether or not she spoke the truth.

"You lie!" The words were followed by more pounding and soon she could tell that others had joined in.

"No, 'tis not a lie, 'tis true. But risk it if you dare!" she called back. "Your captain is near dead and I have been exposed to him. I care not if you die with me." Her own wit startled her, and she waited in silence as the men outside the door reconsidered her story.

"Well, I ain't goin' in there," a voice muttered. "I seen the pox afore. Ain't no way."

"She ain't worth the pox," said another voice.

"If it be the pox, what'll we do?"

"Leave 'em die! They can't pass it once they're dead."

"Sure can!" someone else rebutted. "Gotta burn 'em! Gotta burn the room and all; 'at's the only way to kill the pox."

"Yeah," another voice chimed in, then several more agreed. "Let 'em die, then we'll set fire to the ship and join up with whoever's on the schooner."

"Oh, you think they'll take us on after they find out we be hauling the pox around?"

"Tell 'em the fire was an accident," a voice called from beyond the group.

The rest of the crew agreed with the suggestion and began to file away from the door.

The next several hours were like living in a madhouse. The stores were thrown open and the rum someone had smuggled onboard was tapped and the singing and brawls began.

"If we ain't gonna live past tomorrow, then let's have some fun tonight!" someone cried. The verses were made up as they sang drunkenly, and from the stomping overhead Crystal knew they were kicking up their heels and having a devil of a good time.

Crystal wasn't comforted by the noise as she listened from her foul-smelling cabin. This was her last night, too, but she had no one but a half-dead murderer to share it with. Tears welled in her eyes and she shuddered as they rolled down her fevered cheeks and spattered onto her soiled gown. She could have been with them up there, passed around like a jug of rum, but she chose instead to be burned alive.

The night passed slowly. Crystal had taken up vigil at her open porthole, watching the shimmering black night turn to pastel dawn. The other ship had gained on them considerably but was nowhere near ready to fire on them. She sensed the hushed crew standing along the rail somewhere above gauging the time before they would be called to quarter.

William's shallow breaths had deepened and his color was somewhat better than it had been. It was the first hope she'd had for his life in twenty-four hours.

Suddenly someone started hammering on her

door, while someone else seemed to be piling in the gangway.

So they've decided to take no chances, she thought. Her death warrant had been signed and delivered.

"Here, look here!" A sudden shout from the deck brought her head snapping around to the window.

"Blimey, another ship!"

"'E's too far off, that one is."

"But look, the sails be comin' straight! Fly 'em, mates! Hoist up the death flag. One of 'em's gotta to be with us!"

The new round of activity broke the hush that had followed the all-night celebration. Crystal strained against the hole to hear what they were saying, but they had moved away from the rail and not so much as a whisper floated her way. There was only the sound of more wood being piled near her door.

Close to two hours passed before she heard the sound of cannon fire. The ball whistled through the air and splashed well short of the *Night Wing*'s decks. Seconds later, the smell of smoke seeped into the cabin.

It had begun.

Chapter Thirty-Nine

Christopher lowered the glass from his eye.

"That's the *Night Wing* all right." But his eyes darkened as he watched the flag being run up the line. The skull and crossbones seemed to snicker in his direction.

"What's the other?" Geoff asked.

"I don't know, she looks Spanish." The pair fell silent, neither daring to voice his fear. The Spanish had no mercy when they dealt with pirates. Often, in their perverse sense of duty to the high seas, they sank anything not Spanish and killed anyone who offended them—which was anyone who was not Spanish. Judging from the scene ahead, it was the Spanish who'd get there first, and there was nothing anyone could do about it.

They watched in horror as the ball sailed through the air and landed several feet from the ship. Moments later the sound reached them. Chris looked at his fully rigged canvas, which was already giving its all, before looking back at the ship that had served in his fleet for so many years. He knew that this day he would watch it sink, and that very possibly he would even hear the screams of the woman he loved as she went down with it.

Another ball volleyed and fell short, followed by another, but the *Night Wing* sailed on as if having no care for them. She didn't even fire back.

"Chris?"

"I see that." Chris set the glass to his eye again and realized for the first time that the crew had lined the upper decks of the ship, watching as the other two ships gave chase. Even more startling was the fact that the upper deck was vacant. There was no Crystal, no William, and no captain.

"Look to the center." Chris swung his glass back to see the sails gradually being lowered. He saw a wisp of smoke spiral up from the main companionway.

"Looks like smoke."

"Yes, it does." Chris brought the glass down again and checked the distance. "We're better than thirty minutes from her, too."

"Lord, they've gotta see it! Why hasn't the alarm been sounded? They'll sink before the galleon reaches her side."

"Unless they started it." The two men looked at each other, each thinking the same thing; it couldn't be . . . Even a thief wouldn't sink his own booty in the middle of the sea. But they both looked on in suspicion as the wisp grew larger and no one on board paid it even the slightest heed.

Crystal clung to the porthole for air. Outside the sturdy door she could hear the crackling flames eating up the wood. Thankfully, the designers of the *Night Wing* took time and expense with her fittings, so her doors all fit well into their frames. Unfortunately, that might also be the fact that caused her death.

She heard repeated volleys fired from the chase ship. They were under attack and surely the crew knew it, but still they returned no fire or apparently even bothered to raise a white flag. And what of the other ship? There seemed to be little commotion coming from that direction.

The next second brought a thundering boom reverberating across the deck. The ship shuddered violently, tossing Crystal to the bunk, where she sprawled over William's cold body before rapping her head on the metal frame of the bunk. Stars danced before her eyes as she fought to recover, but a nauseating dizziness captured her senses.

The deck overhead exploded and splintered wood rained to the floorboards as the sounds of a man's agonized screamed faded. Suddenly men were moving, screaming, calling, shouting, and jumping overboard. Crystal struggled to stand; she watched in horror as frantic seamen flung themselves into the sea.

The longboats were lowered just outside her porthole. They were filled to capacity until they hit the water below, where more men threatened to overturn them as they scrambled for a place. She watched as the men in the longboats beat each other over the head with scraps of planking from the main deck, rowing oars, and even shoes to keep the others from overloading the small boats. Men who couldn't swim leaped to their deaths, floundering barely long enough to call for help. She saw their faces twist in agony as they sank beneath the waves.

Another thundering crash exploded just outside the door, and sparks shot under the door into the cabin. The long groan began above her again and carried over the sounds of the other pained and panicked sailors. From the screams and ear-splitting crash she knew the mainmast had toppled, crushing whoever stood in its path.

Crystal looked at the door then rushed to beat the flaming sparks out with a blanket. Behind her William groaned and rolled her way, but she ignored the movement, intent on staying alive as long as possible. Perhaps the second ship held hope. Even another pirate ship might be better than drowning like a rat in a cage or choking to death on wood smoke.

Terror seized her as the next volley hit the bow. The entire ship lurched forward and pitched down, throwing her like a rag doll to the floor. Instantly she knew they'd suffered the fatal blow. The holds below were taking on water fast; it rushed in to hasten her death.

Frantically she raced to the door, pounding and crying and working the knob, only to find that it wouldn't budge and that there was no one left on board to hear her screams.

Crystal raced back to the porthole. Launching herself from the bed she tried to throw herself out, but only her head and shoulders made it through the small opening. She waved furiously to the other ship, praying they were near enough to see her. But even if someone saw her, would it really matter? In her filthy gown and knotted hair she looked no different than a deckhand. It seemed she was doomed . . .

Giving up on the window, Crystal turned to try the door again, but she now found the cabin filled with smoke. It slithered in under the door and through the panels. The edges had turned black, and glowing embers sizzled through the scorched cracks in the door and flared in giant tongues of orange flame. They arched up at odd angles to the handle of the door as the front of the ship continued to dip and her world tilted at a crazy angle.

William began to slide from the bed. Unintelligible mumblings trickled from his lips. He shuddered, then fell silent again. She looked at him in contempt, wishing it were she who would die in deep sleep and that he were the one looking for some small means of escape.

Another volley smashed into the deck overhead. Timbers cracked and fell to the deck, and the ship groaned as if crying in pain . . . or as if in despair for her graceless death.

"You're right, ol' girl," she whispered. "Old ships *should* die with honor." Crystal patted the wall as though it were a pet. The ship groaned again and the floor tilted further.

In one last fleeting attempt to live, she grabbed a heavy chair from its place at the table and hurled it with unaccustomed strength at the fire-weakened door. Her heart leaped as the wood began to give way. She grabbed another chair and tried again, but the smoke was becoming too thick and the effort too great. Her strength was slipping away. She fell to the floor gasping for air not laced with smoke, then she pushed herself up to grab another chair and try once more. This time, the chair shattered the door, knocking a small hole through it. Flames filled the companionway and licked greedily at the dried wood, but there was still hope . . .

She rushed forward, grabbing at her skirts as she kicked at the charred wood. To her surprise, the door fell loose and she was free! Suddenly the ship plunged forward and her feet slid along the decking.

Her wrenching cry filled the room. She wept bitter tears of frustration. With her skirts held in one hand, she crawled on her hands and knees along the floor that now tilted upward at a dangerous angle. The door frame burned as she placed her hands on the fiery coals and pulled herself over.

Her progress was slow, slower, it seemed, than the sinking of the ship. Fire scorched her from every direction and her clothes itched and burned as she edged around the hole where the fire had been started. As the ship tilted farther, the remaining logs rolled to the stair and threatened her escape again. She reached the stairs just as the charred logs began to flame, but she stumbled over them nonetheless, heedless of the flames that scorched her skirt. Crystal held her breath. She was almost free! But when she looked up she found the stairs set at a useless angle and nearly cried. But she fell upon them anyway and began dragging her tired body up. Her muscles ached and her head throbbed as her lungs burned from the smoke. But still she had hope. When she was but three steps from the deck, the sinking ship slipped lower into the sea. Water gushed in, filling her mouth and lungs and dousing the flames and washing her back down the companionway.

The steam hissed and smoked and stank of the sea. It burned her throat as she gasped for air, but she struggled to her feet and stumbled on, hanging on to anything she could reach, burning or not, and continued to fight for her life. Fatigue was claiming her. The fight was all but lost as she finally pulled herself forward.

"Don't let me die this way. God, please!" she cried. She had made the stairs again. The water gushed in faster and she pulled harder until she was near the top.

Suddenly sunlight filled her eyes! Sunlight and blue sky and Chris!

Chris! Chris! Chris! She cried his name over and over, but her scorched throat let no sound pass. He stood like the Colossus of Rhodes until his warm, strong arms came around her, and then he was hushing her and crying and telling her that she was safe and that no one would hurt her ever again.

He pulled her from the stair, tied a rope to her waist, and called to someone somewhere. She was ripped from his arms as his crew hauled on the rope. Suddenly she was hanging over the ship. Chris too swung upward on the rope, dangling only inches below her.

Beneath them the *Night Wing* boiled angrily and slipped under the sea, leaving frothing, hissing swells in its wake—taking William along with it.

It was over. At very long last it was over . . .

Chapter Forty

Chris stood with his back to her. He didn't want her to see the agony that twisted his face.

"I have a friend who can recover the money from New Providence," he said without emotion.

"It's like losing them all over again, isn't it?" Her voice was raspy and sounded sore. But she was peaceful as she caressed the blue velvet coverlet that had once been her own. For some reason she was not surprised to find it covering the bunk in Chris's cabin.

"It is," he agreed, still not turning to face her.

Her hands were salved and wrapped in strips of cloth. Tendrils of hair curled around her face and shoulders where the first mate had trimmed off her singed locks. A large purple lump bulged from her temples, a memento of the attack from the Spanish ship *Vengador*, "Avenger." Its mission had been to rid the sea of pirates and pirates only. In fact, the captain had been horrified to find a woman on board. He pledged restitution in a full report submitted to his king. Chris accepted the honor on her behalf, since she was in no condition to do anything at the time of the offering.

There was just one thing left to resolve, hopefully before London came into view. But neither Chris nor Crystal ventured to speak of it. Each was unwilling to face the other's reaction to the news. It was thus in silence that Chris left the cabin, closing the door firmly behind him, while Crystal made a closer examination of the blue velvet coverlet.

She pulled the fabric close, nestling her face into the soft folds and inhaling the smell of him—filling her mind and lungs and heart with him. He must know, she thought. He must know the truth. Probably he resents the fact that he has another new partner. A woman partner. What else could it be? The thought stung her. There had to be more between them than just ships and oceans.

Or perhaps he didn't know who she was. Perhaps he thought that William had . . . or that she let him . . . Crystal sighed, blinking at a tear. If he believed that then surely there'd been nothing between them but lies.

She dropped back against the pillow and looked out through the broad windows at the back of the ship, watching the sky tease the clouds that drifted along behind them. It was suddenly strange to think that these ships were half hers, along with the company and the estates and farms. At last she had the means to pay Chris back for all he had done for her.

And Elizabeth was her aunt! And Jillian should have been her aunt by marriage. Her eyes overflowed at the last thought. Yes, Jillian should have really been her aunt. She would know where the contract was that her father had signed with George, sealing the bargain to marry. At least she would have that, if not the man himself. She stared sadly out the window. He'd wanted Crystal all along, and now that she was here, she no longer mattered.

Chris moved along the upper decks. The black night shrouded them. The stars flashed silver overhead. In his mind he saw the flames that engulfed the *Night Wing*. The masts fell in his mind's eye just as they had the day before, the riggings trailing behind like the ribbons on a woman's bonnet.

He would never forget the way the sinking ship moved beneath his feet, nor the soot-smudged, tangled mess that had been Honey clawing her way to freedom. Crystal had always had that much determination too. They were the same woman. They had to be. He should be overjoyed that Honey was his Crystal but he was at a loss to understand. His prayers had been answered, and now they frightened him.

If she knew who she was, why had she said nothing? If he told her who she was how would she take the news? She would scoff; she would spit in his eye and say, "Is that how you get whatever you desire? Just wish it and it becomes so?" Or, "Would you have treated me the same, Chris? Had you known from the start, would you have behaved the same toward me?" He knew he would have treated her much differently. He'd already gone too far without telling her how he felt. And now she owned half the company, half of the very ship on which they sailed. She couldn't have realized it yet, for surely she'd have recognized that the coverlet that now warmed her shoulders was from her own bed at Stonewings.

Crystal stretched and yawned, slowly coming

awake at the soft rap at the door.

"Good morning, sleepyhead." Geoff peeked around the door.

"Good morning." She smiled, feeling safe and warm.

"Brought you some breakfast," he said, slipping inside the cabin.

"Mmm, porridge, my favorite." Her lip curled in mock distaste. "Do you not serve real food on this voyage?" She laughed as much as her sore throat would allow. "Isn't this trip a little longer than the trip out?"

Geoff frowned then shoved the door closed. Jerking a thumb upward, he said, "I don't know what's wrong with him. He has everything he ever wanted and he acts like he doesn't deserve it now. I just don't know!"

Crystal looked away quickly. "I know the feeling. It's overwhelming—ending twelve years of wondering. Knowing that you're orphaned. Remembering all the things you've forgotten for so long."

Geoff's eyes narrowed as she slipped from the bed, dressed in only a white shirt that covered her to the knees. She tossed her hair back over her shoulder before taking a chair. "You should have brought yours, too; then we could eat together like we used to."

"You or him?" Geoff asked stupidly.

"Me or him what?" She lifted her lashes to meet her friends.

"I think you know what I mean. You saw that portrait and you know, don't you?" he demanded, but his eyes twinkled.

"Yes, I know." She set her spoon aside. "I'll bet Chris knows too, doesn't he? That's why he's avoiding me."

"He knows, all right." His voice was quiet as he watched her silently struggle with her tears. "But to tell you the truth, I think he's thinking of all that self-pity he's wallowed in for so many years."

"Philosophy now, eh?" She tried to smile at her own jest.

Geoff laughed out loud, taking a chair at the table. "Maybe so, but I do know that man needs a good shaking up, and if you're not the one to give it to him, then you're not the Crystal Wingfield I've heard so much about."

"We've had our days." She stirred her porridge as a tear rolled down her cheek.

Geoff touched her face. "Come, we've been sailing next to a bunch of whales. Do you want to see them?"

Crystal nodded and jumped into a pair of sailors' loose-fitting pants and cinch that tied the waist. Forever the gentleman, Geoff waited outside the door until she came out, her hair bound behind like a sailor. The cool sea wind caressed her scalded face and hands. She closed her eyes and relished the moist ocean air. Except for the bandages on her hands, this might have been her first voyage on the *Wing Master*.

From the main stair, Geoff steered her to the rail, where a whale almost twice the size of the ship cruised alongside them. An occasional froth of water mixed with air spouted from his back.

"He's been with us for two days now," Geoff said.

"An escort home," Crystal smiled back.

"Just what do you think you're doing on deck dressed like that?"

Crystal jumped at the unexpected voice from behind.

"I'm looking at the whales," she answered without looking at him.

"Well, I won't have you prancing around this ship

dressed like that for all the world to see! Now get back below and stay there until we reach port!" He turned to walk away.

"No!" She didn't even bother to turn to face him as she spoke.

Geoff's eyes grew round, and he fought the urge to back away from the pair. From the corner of his eye he saw Chris halt in mid-step. He turned slowly to face this outright defiance.

"What?"

"Clearly you heard me," she said again without looking his way.

"I must have been mistaken," he growled softly, eyeing her sideways. "I thought you said . . ."

"No," she finished for him. "You were not mistaken. I said no. And I said it clearly." She looked at him out of the corner of her eye before she too turned to look his way. She met his glare squarely, her chin set, her lips pursed.

"I said get below, and I mean it." His face darkened and his teeth clenched. "Or would you rather I carry you there?"

"I wouldn't if I were you," she answered as steadily as he.

Around them crew members stood frozen in disbelief as the woman matched her will to their captain's. The hush grew so that only the sounds of the creaking of the ship and the gush of the whale could be heard.

Chris reached for her arm, but she stepped aside, her eyes never leaving his.

"Think you're smart, don't you?" He half smiled. "Don't think I won't toss you over my shoulder and haul you down there myself."

"Not if you want to marry me you won't!"

"Marry you? A half-baked sand crab from a lump

himself. "And I think we'll finish this trip right here," he moaned as he pulled her to him. And she willingly agreed.

The sails of a ship hovered in the hazy place between the sea and sky. A man standing on the bluff watched it for several moments, then smiled to his wife who stepped up beside him.

"It's time to go home," he said, smoothing back a wisp of sun-lightened auburn hair before turning to the scuffle that had started at the tide pool below them.

"George, stop teasing your brother. Jake, you behave too!" their mother scolded.

"So, Mrs. Ames, when are we going to add Christine and Regina to this troop?" he asked, steering her to the harbor, where a ship portraying a trace of Spanish design swayed on the gentle sea. The name *Crystal Wing II* was burned into its side.

"Sooner than you think, Mr. Ames." She smiled up at him. "Much sooner than you think . . ."